**Praise for Kurt R. A. Giambastiani's
alternate histories**

"The Fallen Cloud Saga certainly comprise two of my favorite books in recent years. I can hardly wait for *Shadow of the Storm*. . . . [The] adventures of Custers Junior and Senior shows just what alternate history should be!"   —Robert Metzger, author of *Picoverse*

The Year the Cloud Fell

"An entertaining alternate historical tale. . . . The story line is fast-paced and will gain author Kurt R. A. Giambastiani much praise. Fans of alternate history novels know they have a new hero in Mr. Giambastiani."
—*Midwest Book Review*

"An impressive first novel . . . an intriguing mix of historical speculation and downright invention that is entertaining and skillfully plotted."   —*Science Fiction Chronicle*

"Here is a book where the journey is the primary pleasure . . . skillfully done."   —*Talebones*

"Combines Custer, Jules Verne, and dinosaurs to make a great page-turner. Alternate history fans will love this book."   —*KLIATT*

"An exceptional work of speculative history."
—*Strange Horizons*

continued . . .

The Spirit of Thunder

"[An] informed, reverent extrapolation on Cheyenne culture."
—*Booklist*

"The clashes between the increasingly well-matched enemies are intense, brutal, and upsetting. . . . The exquisite detail and respect shown in his portrayal of Cheyenne society is enormously compelling."
—*Locus*

"An extremely entertaining alternative history work that readers will thoroughly enjoy . . . a work that [fans] will consider a classic."
—BookBrowser

"Novels such as this one resonate with special intensity."
—*The Davis Enterprise*

SHADOW OF THE STORM

Kurt R. A. Giambastiani

A ROC BOOK

ROC
Published by New American Library, a division of
Penguin Putnam Inc., 375 Hudson Street,
New York, New York 10014, U.S.A.
Penguin Books Ltd, 80 Strand,
London WC2R 0RL, England
Penguin Books Australia Ltd, 250 Camberwell Road,
Camberwell, Victoria 3124, Australia
Penguin Books Canada Ltd, 10 Alcorn Avenue,
Toronto, Ontario, Canada M4V 3B2
Penguin Books (N.Z.) Ltd, Cnr Rosedale and Airborne Roads,
Albany, Auckland 1310, New Zealand

Penguin Books Ltd, Registered Offices:
Harmondsworth, Middlesex, England

First published by Roc, an imprint of New American Library,
a division of Penguin Putnam Inc.

First Printing, March 2003
10 9 8 7 6 5 4 3 2 1

For three women:
Celeste, Sara, & Ilene.
Without you, I would not be who I am.

ACKNOWLEDGMENTS

I would like to thank the readers I have met and heard from during the past year. Your enthusiasm for these books has been both gratifying and contagious, and I hope to hear from more of you in the future.

I owe a great debt to Ann Jordan and K. A. Corlett, for their helpful comments and critiques. The result of your input is a much better book, which I proffer in partial repayment for your efforts.

And, as always, to my wife, my greatest thanks for her greatest patience. May it all, in the end, prove worthwhile.

A portion of the author's proceeds from these books is donated to the St. Labre organization, a group of schools on the Tongue River in Ashland, Montana, that provides educational opportunities to the Northern Cheyenne and Crow people.

THE WORLD OF THE
FALLEN CLOUD

Imagine a world that began much like our own.

Sixty-five million years ago, North America bade farewell to the islands of Europe from across the newly born Atlantic, Australia stretched to separate itself from Antarctica, and the Indian subcontinent was sailing away from Africa, bound for its collision with the heart of Asia. In every place, life abounded, and dinosaurs—some larger than a house, and others as small as your thumb—ruled the land, the sea, and the air, living out their lives in the forests and swamps that dominated the coastlands along the shallow Cretaceous seas.

Then the world broke open, unleashing a volcanic fury the like of which had not been seen for an aeon. The Deccan Traps gushed molten lava, covering half of India with a million cubic kilometers of basalt. The ranges of Antarctica cracked, spewing iridium-laced ash into darkening skies. For 500,000 years, the planet rang with violence. Mountains were born, seas shrank, and life trembled. Across the globe, resources of food and prey disappeared as the climate shifted from wet to arid. Populations competed, starved, and then collapsed. Over the next million years, half of all species died out, unable to adapt in time as habitats vanished in a geologic heartbeat.[2]

[2] For a more detailed analysis of this nonimpact theory of the end of the Cretaceous period, see *The Great Dinosaur Extinction Controversy*, by Jake Page and Charles B. Officer.

In North America, the continental plate was compressed, thrusting the Rocky Mountains miles into the air. The inland seaway that stretched from the Caribbean to the Arctic began to recede, taking with it the moist marshes and fens upon which the last of the world's dinosaurs depended. The waters ebbed, revealing vast sedimentary plains, retreating for a thousand miles before they came to a halt. The sea that remained was a fraction of its former size; a short arm of warm, shallow water that thrust up from the Caribbean to the Sand Hills of Nebraska.

It was on these placid shores that a few species of those great dinosaurs clung to life. Reduced in size and number, they were given by the gentle sea the time they needed to adapt and survive. Eventually, some species left the sea's humid forests for the broad expanses to the north, finding ecological niches among the mammals that had begun to dominate the prairie.

Life continued. Continents moved. The glacial ices advanced and retreated like a tide. In Africa's Great Rift Valley, a small ape stood and peered over the savannah grass. Humans emerged, migrated into Asia and Europe, and history was born. Events unfolded mostly unchanged, until the European civilization came to the Great Plains of North America.

In the centuries before the first Spaniard brought the first horse to the New World, the Cheyenne had been riding across the Great Plains on lizardlike beasts of unmatched speed and power. In defense against their new white-skinned foe, the Cheyenne allied with other tribes, and when the tide of European colonialism came to the prairie frontier, it crashed against the Alliance, and was denied. For a hundred years, the Alliance matched the Horse Nations move for move, strength for strength, shifting the course of history.

Then, through advances in technology and industry, the Americans, led by an officer named George Armstrong Custer, began to make headway, and the Alliance was pushed back beyond the Mississippi, beyond the Arkansas, all the way to the banks of the Missouri and the Santee. A few years later that same officer—now President Custer—sent his only son on a reconnaissance mission beyond those rivers, only to hear of his capture by the Cheyenne. In the three years since, young George has lived with the Cheyenne, and has sided with them against his own father's forces.

This is the World of the Fallen Cloud.

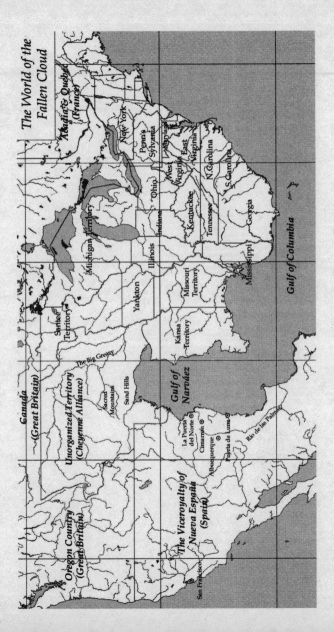

*The World of the
Fallen Cloud*

Acadia & Quebec
(France)

Canada
(Great Britain)

New York

Penn's
Sylvania

Maryland

West
Virginia

East
Virginia

Ohio

Kentuckee

N. Carolina

Indiana

Tennessee

S. Carolina

Michigan Territory

Illinois

Georgia

Mississippi

Yankton

Santee
Territory

Missouri
Territory

Gulf of Columbia

Unorganized Territory
(Cheyenne Alliance)

The Big Greasy

Kansa
Territory

Gulf of Narváez

Sacred
Mountains

Sand Hills

La Puerta
del Norte

Cimarrón

Oregon Country
(Great Britain)

Puerto de Luna

Río de las Palmas

Albuquerque

The Viceroyalty of
Nueva España
(Spain)

San Francisco

CHAPTER 1

George walked through the dappled sunshine of late afternoon and felt no pain. The trees above his head rustled, sending their autumn leaves fluttering down upon him in swirls of somber colors. The forest floor shushed at him as he walked up the leaf-strewn path, and the air was full of the dark, moist smell of home. He hopped over a mushroom-ripe log and marveled at how well he felt, after feeling so poorly for so long.

Walking out of the trees, he found the meadows he had known since his youth. The grass had greened up again with the fall rains, and lay thick like an emerald blanket on the ground. Up ahead, the split-rail fences crosshatched their way through the pastures. The wind shifted, and George smelled manure and woodsmoke in the air. From within the darkness of the trees beyond the fence came a bay horse, dancing out of the shadows, his flanks shiny in the slanting sun. George felt a pang of heartache, but could not help smiling.

"Dandy," he said as he came up to the fence rails. The light-limbed horse tiptoed up to him, nodding in recognition. George held out his hand and Dandy allowed his muzzle to be stroked. "What are you doing out here?" George asked him.

In answer, Dandy whickered and bounded back the way he'd come. George watched him run until he disappeared into the shade of the trees. The wind freshened again, bringing the moist smells of cooking and the sound of a fiddle's spry song. George's smile broadened to a grin. Jesse had come to call from his spread down the road.

He put his hands on the fence rail to hop over but stopped. He stared at his hands, thinking that something was different—not wrong, just different—but he couldn't see his way through to exactly what it might be. He gripped the rail and vaulted the fence, landing on the far side as lightly as a tumbler. He felt fine, and trotted off toward home, the aroma of roasting goose and baking bread leading him by the nose.

Seeing the old homestead brought him to a halt. It always surprised him, how large it was: broad and imposing in its simple lines built tall on a slow rise of land. The deep covered porch wrapped its long arm along the front and around the side of the house. Chamfered pillars supported the porch roof. In winter, the slate-shingled canopy sheltered the double-hung windows from the storms that boiled up from behind the southwestern hills, and on long summer evenings it provided shade in which the family might sit and chat while they enjoyed the polite northeasterly breeze. Above the porch, the house pushed its white clapboard sides up into high, steep gables. The sash windows on the second floor were open and the wind teased the lace-bordered curtains, calling them out to play. The dark green trim at the corners, eaves, and sills contrasted with the paling leaflets of the walnut trees that stood in the yard, turning the view into an artist's rendering in simple hues of green, gray, and bright white.

Dandy stood under one of the walnut trees, pawing the grass, his tail frisking the air. The front door opened and out came two mismatched dogs—one stocky and aged, one lean and agile.

"Tuck! Cardigan!" George shouted as they ran to him. "How are you, boys?" He knelt to receive their greetings of wet noses and joyful tongues, took them by the scruff and wrestled with them, laughing at their exuberance. He patted their sides, enjoying the hollow, ripe-melon sound of their chests, and then stood as the dogs ran back toward the house.

His sisters stood on the porch, Lydia and Maria, looking so grown-up and so pretty with their hair pulled up and their faces framed by artful ringlets. His mother came out, drying her hands with a hand towel, and George saw her smile when she spied him by the fence. Then came his uncles—Boston, Nevin, and even Tom—and then George knew something *was* wrong, and not just different, for Tom had died back in— But the thought was interrupted as his father came out of the house and joined the rest of the family.

Family. George felt the same snare catch in his throat that had tripped when he first caught sight of Dandy. The family waved to him, and he waved back. His hand—the little finger on his left hand—it was whole where it should have been missing two joints. He stared at it as if it belonged to someone else. He flexed his fingers.

"George!" his father shouted. "Come on in, son. We've been waiting."

He looked up and saw them all. His father smiled at him, and he felt his heart leap, felt the ache of a son too long left in the shadows.

The Old Man, smiling at me, he thought as his eyes welled up with tears. I must be dreaming.

And with clarity he knew that he was, but looking at his family, he didn't care.

"George," his mother called. "Supper's ready."

He waved again. "I'm coming, Mother." He ran toward the house. He ran, but it was such a very long way. His limbs grew leaden. The air was thick like honey. He ran, waving, seeing them, seeing them all. Pale-haired Father, hand still raised in welcome. His mother's sweet face and sad eyes. His uncles' grins. Lydia's dark beauty and Maria's dimples. He ran until he got a stitch in his side, until the stitch became an ache, a pain. A sharp pain.

He awoke lying on a bed, covered in the softness of furs and blankets. His side throbbed with pain, as did his arm, as did his head. He thought of his family, and the emotions of the dream swept over him. This time he did not try to keep the tears at bay, but weeping only made his head hurt more. It swam and pounded. Pain sliced his arm at every move. His side . . . his side . . .

Slowly, it came back to him. The battle at Fort Assurance, the sweet dust of gunsmoke, the wild ululation of Cheyenne soldiers riding into heavy fire. The memory of bright sunshine, hard spears of light glinting off the barrels of the cannon, the concussions as he fired shells at the dark walls of the army fort, the marigolds of fire as they hit their marks. And then, nothing; nothing except the pain. Breathing through the pain, talking through it. Riding through it. Riding home to see Mouse Road. Riding to get home.

Home? he wondered. Home?

Thinking of his dream and the family farm up in Michigan Territory, he rolled over on his back and opened his eyes a crack. His vision was still smeared and blurry, but it was good enough to show that he was not back home in Monroe. He was in a lodge, the firelight dim. Up through the smokehole, the sky showed him a deep purple, but gave no clue whether it was dawn or dusk. He heard the tick and snap of coals dying in the firepit. He blinked. It hurt, but it helped to clear his vision, so he blinked again. He saw the walls of the lodge in the dim light, saw a familiar knife hanging from a lodgepole.

My lodge. My home.

He turned his head to look at the fire and was jolted wide-awake. His heart stumbled and thudded in his aching chest and he blinked again in spite of the pain.

Two men sat across the fire from him, their skin so black it swallowed up the light. Blacker than any Negro; George could tell that they were not colored men.

Their hair was straight, shiny black, and hung long and loose down their backs. Their features were those of the People: broad of brow, long of face, with straight noses and almond-shaped eyes. Like enough to be twins, they sat cross-legged on the guest's side of the hearth, silent, staring into the orange light of the fire's dying coals. They wore fringed leggings, beaded moccasins, and decorated breechclouts, but remained bare-chested. On the skin of their chests—so black—were white circles representing hail, and on their arms were the jagged yellow lines of lightning. The right arm of one bore a shiny scar where a lightning bolt should have been.

They were not Negroes. If George's guess was right, they were not even men. He had seen them before, years ago it seemed, and only from a distance. He had described them to Stands Tall in Timber, the People's spiritual leader. As

George stared at his two guests, the holy man's response echoed in his mind.

I think the Thunder Beings have taken an interest in you.

Thunder Beings. Creatures from the Cheyenne spirit world. As he slowly forced himself up into a sitting position, George considered the possibility that the old chief had been right. He considered, too, that he might still be dreaming—which seemed far more likely—but decided that it made no difference. They were here.

"Haaahe," he said in greeting. "Welcome to my home."

They smiled—sudden white teeth in dark faces—and glanced up briefly before looking back to the fire in polite though wordless response. Then, with the sign language common throughout the Alliance, the one on the right— the one with the scar on his arm—asked after his health.

"I am doing better," George said.

Good, the other signed, and then they both stood.

"Wait," George said, holding up a hand. "Is that all you came for? To see how I am feeling?"

Yes, the one signed.

"But . . . why?" George asked. "Why do you care about me?"

The spirit men looked puzzled by the question. They sat down again by the fire. *You Are One Who Flies,* the first one signed. *You rode the cloud-that-fell.*

George remembered his trip in the experimental airship and the storm that caused it to crash. "That 'cloud' fell because you brought it down," he said. "You brought it down, and you've been influencing the course of my life ever since, haven't you?"

Yes. Of course.

George felt an urgency, a pressure of events, and wondered again if this was a dream. "Is it over now?" he asked. "Are you done with me?"

No.

"Why not? What's so important that you keep me from living my own life?"

The dark men conferred with each other in silence. *What do you want that you do not have?* the first one signed.

George thought for a moment, his head swimming with weakness, pain, and the odd dreaminess of the encounter.

The men sat patiently across the fire from him, hands on their knees, waiting for his reply.

What do I want? he asked himself, and as soon as the question was formed, he knew. The images from his dream made it plain.

"I want my family."

Family, signed the other one, and pointed toward the lodgeskin wall and the camp that lay beyond it. *Your family is here.*

"Yes," George said quietly, thinking of his neighbors and friends. He recalled his ride home after the battle, pushing himself to continue regardless of his injuries and his fear of death. He remembered the one thing he wanted to see before he died: Mouse Road's smile. And when he saw it, its sweetness had filled him. "Yes, I have family of a sort here," he said. "But there is another family I left behind. I want to see them. I want to make peace with my father."

Long Hair, the first one signed. *Chief of the Horse Nations.*

"Long Hair," George agreed, embarrassed that even in the spirit world his father's reputation rode before him. "But that is what I want," he said, feeling his resolve solidify. "I have been your instrument for years and now I want something in return."

You have nothing? the other one signed, pointing to the doorflap.

"One Who Flies?" came a voice from outside. The doorflap opened and Mouse Road looked inside. "What are you doing up?" she scolded. She stepped into the lodge, a burden of firewood on her back. Outside, the sky had lightened with the coming dawn, and snow had begun to fall.

George looked at the two dark men as she stepped into the family side of the lodge. He saw them smile as they watched her put her load of firewood near the lodgeskin wall. From the hearthside she took the last of the dry wood and put it on the tired coals.

"I thought I heard you talking," she said as she tended to the fire. "Who were you talking to?"

George looked again at the dark men across the crackling fire. *Family,* the first one signed, and pointed at Mouse Road. He smiled at George.

The two men stood. The first one stepped forward into

the hearthpit. The fire's rising heat caught him like a feather, a leaf, and he rose up through the smokehole. Then the other one smiled. *Family is important,* he signed as he, too, stepped forward to float skyward with the smoke.

"One Who Flies?" Mouse Road asked. "Are you all right?"

George blinked, feeling all his weakness and pain begin to overwhelm him. "Yes," he said. "I am just tired."

"Who were you talking to?"

"No one," he said as he lay back down into his bed of furs. Mouse Road glanced at him, concern overcoming her manners. "Truly," he said and smiled to assuage her fears. "I am well."

She laughed. "You are *not* well," she said. "But I am glad to see you are feeling better. Mother is making skillet-bread. Are you feeling well enough to eat?"

He tried to say that he was, but he felt himself drifting away. Am I dreaming still? he wondered. Mouse Road came over to him, and his vision was filled with the beauty of her face.

"Maybe later," she said as she pulled the covers over him. He felt her hand on his cheek, and then, as warmth filled him once more, he slept.

CHAPTER 2

Thursday, February 28, A.D. 1889
Cherry and Pelham Streets, Seventh Ward
New York City, New York

"**O**! Fortuna!"

Passersby ignored Cesare as he put down his bundle of rags and wiped a sleeve across his sweaty brow. Though evening, the sudden and unseasonable heat wave still lay atop the city like an old woolen coat: musty and thick. He looked up at the cracked windows of the workshop's third floor. Dusty lamplight peeked out through chips in the overpainted glass.

"Fortuna!" he shouted, and went to hammer a fist on the main door. It was locked and the first floor was dark, but that meant nothing to the women left sewing upstairs in the dusty lofts. He could see the hint of light from within, and could hear the chatter of sergers and treadle machines from the street. *"Fortuna!"*

A shadow appeared on one of the whitewashed panes and the sash surged upward half a foot, then a foot more. A woman stuck her head out and looked down. "Cesare Uccido, what a noise you are making!"

"Ah, Giovanna-Patrizia," he said, recognizing one of his sister's coworkers. "I've come to take Fortuna home. It's half past eight already. When will the Beast let you all go?"

"Siete calmo, Cesare," she said with a white-toothed grin and a glance back into the shop. "He will hear you. He made some of us to stay to finish up an order of coats, but he only needed a few of us. Your sister left half an hour ago."

"She walked home alone?"

Giovanna-Patrizia grinned again. "She is a big girl now. The same age as you, Cesare. You can't watch over her forever."

"What are you saying? Is she meeting someone? Who? Who is she meeting?"

"Calmate, calmate. You are so easy to tease. She went straight home, you fool. Go home yourself and you'll see." Another glance behind her. "I must go. Go home, Cesare." The window closed and her shadow shrank down into nothing.

Cesare turned and looked up the alleyway, up from the riverfront and away from the wharves where he had spent his day. Today had been a good day. He had found work: twelve humid hours in a heat more suitable to May than nearly March, hauling garbage onto barges in the shadow of the gigantic plinths of the new bridge between New York City and Brooklyn. He had borne each burden from the shore to the scows, dumped it, and picked through it for rags and salvage. The work was miserable, but he was grateful for it, for now he had forty cents wrapped in a rag in his pocket—his earnings for the day—and a bundle of rags and cast-off cloth that he might sell for a few cents more. It wasn't much to add to the family's coffers; in fact it was only half what a German or an Irishman or a Slav would have received for the same work, but it was all the bosses would pay for an Italian. His family's rent was coming due—they had been going hungry for the past week in order to save up the ten dollars they needed for their shared room—and every penny made a difference. He shouldered his bundle and headed on toward home, thinking once more of Fortuna.

Silly girl, he thought, irritated by his sister's impulsiveness. A sweet-faced *bambina* like her, alone on these streets.

But he had to admit that Giovanna-Patrizia was right: She wasn't a *bambina* anymore. Fortuna, his twin, was eighteen years old, old enough to have a family of her own if she had a mind to begin one. Cesare was glad that she didn't, since that meant she would leave her family for a husband's. He headed up the alleyway, joining the rest of the men walking home from the wharves.

Refuse clung to the low corners of buildings like

sloughed skin. Rats, bold in the darkness, chittered and scurried through the piles. A man ahead of him stopped and Cesare bumped into him.

" 'Ey! Whattaya doin'?" the other demanded.

"Coglioni," Cesare responded without a thought as he continued around the man. "Why don't you—"

A hand shoved him from behind. Hard. Cesare stumbled but kept his feet. He dropped the bundle of rags and whirled, feet apart, fists ready. A circle of space formed around them as others stepped back, waiting to see if there would be a bit of evening entertainment. Cesare faced his opponent, peered into the dim light to seek the measure of the man he faced.

The street lamp was far down the street behind the other man, and all Cesare saw was a hulking shadow in a sweat-soaked shirt, a beaten hat with three waggling feathers, and too-short trousers held up by braces.

Too-short trousers? he thought to himself. He squinted.

"Marco?" he said.

"Cesare?"

The men surrounding them groaned and started off again homeward while Cesare and his upstreet neighbor laughed in the void left by their dissipating belligerence.

"What are you doing here?" Cesare asked.

"Mama is sick. She wants a tonic and does not trust Bellini."

"Ha! Nor should she."

"If you are looking for your sister," Marco offered, "I saw her. Up in the Bend."

"No, you are mistaken. She went straight home. Giovanna-Patrizia told me so."

Marco smiled. *"Paisano,* I mean this with the greatest respect, but when a man sees your sister, he is never mistaken."

Cesare felt his pulse quicken, though not in anger at Marco's words. "You saw her in the Bend?"

Marco nodded and grimaced. "Talking with Bernardo."

"And you did nothing?"

"What should I have done, eh?" He punctuated his question with a tap on Cesare's chest. "She is not *my* sister."

Cesare wasted no more breath on words. Rag bundle forgotten, he ran up the street, thrusting past men and pushcarts as he headed for Mulberry Bend. There was only one reason a man like Bernardo would be talking with Fortuna.

He reached the Bend. It was aswarm with laborers and workers arriving home, and with denizens trying to escape the suffocating closeness of their tenement homes, but quickly he spied three of the Bend's regulars slouching at the street lamp. He did not hesitate. Never otherwise would he have deigned to speak with such men, but tonight it was his sister's reputation in jeopardy. He walked straight toward them, fists clenched and murder pounding in his ears.

"Where is Bernardo?"

"Oooh," one of the toughs sang. "Someone is all agitated." The three shared a laugh at Cesare's expense.

"Where is Bernardo?"

"You want something?" another asked. "A girl?" He smiled at his cohorts. "A boy?"

Cesare reached, caught him by the lapel, and pulled him up to his feet. The other two grabbed Cesare's arms, but Cesare had his father's strength and his mother's passion. He simply held the one man closer, both hands on him now, grinned, and asked again, "Where is Bernardo?"

"*Calmate, calmate,*" the man said, and his fellows held back. "He was talking with a girl. He took her home." Cesare released him and he fell back against the building.

"When?"

"Just a few moments, no more."

Cesare headed toward home, ignoring the taunts they threw at his back. He didn't live far from the Bend, but it was a dark and lonely time of night for his sister to be in the company of a known pimp. Terrible things happened in the cavelike alleys during the night hours, when people were more apt to look away and ignore a woman's muffled cries for help.

As he headed north, the streets held fewer people but became more crowded with the lines of carts and wagons brought home for the night. In some places it was blocked to anything but foot traffic, and Cesare had to wend his way between conveyances that stank of refuse, rags, and produce long past its prime.

Tall "double-decker" tenements stood shoulder to shoulder and seventy feet high. Lantern light flickered in a few windows, but the street lamps were not lit, leaving the narrow, urban canyon in deep darkness. Up ahead, far down the street from his own tenement, past swirls and eddies of neighbors, stood two people—a man and a woman—talking in the street. The woman was leaning up against a pushcart and the man stood in front of her, leaning in close. Cesare trotted toward them.

"Fortuna!"

The woman started. She looked his way and then glanced around as if for a way to escape, but there was no time. Cesare was there and Bernardo turned to greet him.

"Ah, there you are," the slick-talking pimp said with a broad wave of his arm. "We were just talking about you." His smile was obsequious but his manner haughty.

"Fortuna," Cesare said. "Come. I'm taking you home."

"That's not very polite," Bernardo said. "Your sister and I were having a conversation."

"She has nothing to say to you."

"If you say so."

"I do." He reached over to take his sister's arm but she pulled it away, and for the first time Cesare saw her expression.

She glared at him in fierce defiance. He extended his hand again, but she slapped it away and pushed past him. Bernardo grinned at Fortuna's censure of her twin.

Cesare pointed a meaty finger at the pimp. "You leave her alone," he warned.

Bernardo leaned back against the pushcart and snickered. "We were only talking," he said with a shrug.

Cesare turned and walked quickly to catch up with Fortuna. "What did he want with you?" he asked, then shook his head. "No, never mind. I know what he wanted. But why were you talking to him? You should have gone straight home. The Bend was not on your way. What were you doing there? You know what kind of man loafs around there." She stopped and whirled to face him.

She was majestic in the gloom, standing tall and slender, her large, dark eyes glaring, her dark hair pulled back to show her long, straight neck and the silver crucifix at her throat. Cesare was once more stunned by his sister's striking beauty. Apart from their natal day, he and his twin had little in common. Where he was muscular, she was lithe like their mother. Where he was quick-tempered, she was quiet and reflective like their father. Quiet, that is, until she was truly angered. At such times her less tender emotions overcame her control and she was as sharp and uncompromising as Cesare and his mother put together.

Like now, he thought, meeting her icy stare.

"You are such a fool," she said scornfully. "It was *I* who went to find *him*."

Cesare stood stunned as she walked away. "What do you mean?" he asked as he trotted to catch up to her. "Why would you be looking for him?"

"You don't understand."

"I hope I do not! Fortuna!" And here he did take her by the arm to stop her. "Why did you go looking for Bernardo? What do you want with him?"

She turned and her cheeks shone with the wetness of tears.

"Fortuna," he said. "What is it? What were you doing?"

Her stiffness began to crumble, revealing once more the young innocence behind her angry façade. She looked up into the sky. The glow from a hundred dimly lit windows showed the sharp limit of her jaw, the tendons that stood out in her neck. She folded thin arms across her breast and held tight to her own shoulders. She took a hesitant step toward Cesare, another, and then leaned in against his chest. Bewildered, he put his arms around her.

"What will happen to us?" she asked.

"What? Nothing is going to happen to us," he assured her.

She exhaled in a half laugh. "That is what I am afraid of."

"So you go to Bernardo? How will that help us?"

"He will pay me money. A lot of money." Her voice was low but not timid. "Especially for the first time," she said.

Cesare marveled at her. So calmly she talked of such things. "Some things are more precious than money."

She leaned back and glared at him. "You are such a *man*," she said. "Don't you see? Don't you see that we are all trapped in this place? Papa will push his cart until he drops. You and I will work every hour we can. Mama and the babies will do their piecework, just so we can scrape together the coin we need, and *still* we will have to share the flat with Widow Scottolini in order to get by." She stepped out of his embrace and pointed to the dark bulk of their tenement house. "Mama is dying because of this place. And what of Salvatore and the babies? What about them? What kind of life can they hope for?"

Cesare was confused, angry, and frightened all at once. "But *cara*, it takes more than money to live uptown. It takes a whiter skin. It takes a different accent. How is money going to help us with that?"

"Not money," she said, solidly sure of her purpose. "Land, my sweet. *Land.*"

He almost laughed. "Land? How much money do you think Bernardo is going to give you?" He regretted his words at once. "I didn't mean . . . Not that you . . ."

She touched his face and graced him with a small, sad smile. "Thank you," she said, and took his arm. They turned and walked through the milling crowd toward their building. "The government is giving away land, out in the West. I heard about it and asked some of the girls at work. There is so much land out there that they are giving it away. All we have to do is get to the frontier. But we have to get there soon, Cesare, before it is all gone."

He could not think of what to say. It was too much news at one time. His head hurt from frowning at such thoughts.

"You see, don't you?" she went on. "All we need is the train fare and some supplies." She squeezed his arm. "Certainly you think I'm worth that much."

He stopped at their front stoop. "Do not joke about it," he said. "You should be ashamed for even *thinking* about it. To sell yourself? It's a sin, and it would kill Papa. You cannot be serious."

He could not see her expression in the shadows that clung to the sides of their building, so when she said, "Of course not. Of course not," he could not tell what she was denying.

He grabbed her by the shoulders and made her face him. "*Cara*, promise me. Promise me you will not do this."

The building's murk obscured her expression and she stood unresisting in his grasp. "I promise," she said.

Still unsure, he led her inside.

At the corner of Bowery and Canal, Alejandro Miguel Tomás Silveira-Rioja, assistant to the ambassador from New Spain, stepped down from his carriage, adjusted his coat and top hat, and crossed the crowded street, hating every step he took.

It was nine o'clock, and night had settled in on lower Manhattan. A welcome breeze was rising off the East River, but the riverborn zephyr did little to sweep away the day's foul, parboiling heat. The chaotic press of the immigrant poor filled the walkways from storefront to street with the humid heat of their own humanity. Men shouted to one another and to wives in upstairs windows. Toddlers bawled and babies wailed as their guardians— children themselves of only six or seven years—kept them corralled near home. Peddlers wrestled pushcarts from avenues onto tiny streets, and drivers maneuvered mules and horse-drawn wagons through the jammed thoroughfare. The ground rumbled as the elevated train rattled by overhead, its metal-on-metal screams echoing off the dirty faces of storefronts and tenements.

Alejandro pushed past a cluster of locals who had congregated at the curb to argue in the impassioned tones and grand gesticulations of southern Europe the legality of a pushcart's positioning. He stopped at the corner, buffeted by the flow of foot traffic, and turned from the main thoroughfare to follow a smaller river of men into the narrow darkness of Pell Street. Tenements rose tall on either side, blotting out the struggling stars with six stories of dimly lit, poorly ventilated, closely packed apartments. His foot slipped on the slick cobblestones. The humid air—untouched by the breeze in these twisted warrens of poverty—was thick with the pungency of urine and filth.

I have lived too long, he thought to himself, to fall so far. I was once a commander of men, an officer with honor, but now . . .

A group of dark-haired boys plunged out of the darkness, swerving around empty carts and idle men. One boy ran headlong into Alejandro and with a muttered *"Scusi,"* ran on, a smile on his face and the devil in his eyes. Out of reflex, Alejandro checked his billfold and his watch. Both were still there, and he continued on into the ghetto.

The Sixth Ward, sometimes known as New Italy, was a maze of shadowed streets, dark alleys, and empty doorways. It was the dirtiest, poorest, foulest corner of the city, and that was precisely why Alejandro was there. His superior, the ambassador from New Spain, insisted on authenticity in his . . . predilections . . . and to achieve it took discretion. For years now, the ambassador had trusted this errand to no one but Alejandro, safe in the knowledge that his private assistant's sense of dignity and prudence would keep quiet those things that were best left quiet.

Here, farther off the Bowery, away from the barber colleges, fruit stands, and cobbler's dens, Alejandro began to draw more attention; a tall, elderly, well-dressed gentleman in tall hat and topcoat, a pink rose in his lapel, and shod in high-topped shoes was a rare thing in these streets. Stares followed him as he walked down a street that became more of an alley as he progressed. Sullen-faced women halted in conversation on stoops to make moues of mock disbelief. Men with drunken eyes commented rudely in Italian. Alejandro chose not to understand them and walked on, heading down toward Mulberry Bend.

As he approached the intersection of Cross and Mulberry, the brownstones leaned in. Laundry lines fluttered overhead, and the stream of pedestrians was compressed even further. Ahead, a dim, moth-circled street lamp cast a feeble light that served only to deepen the doorway shadows. Young men stood around and sat on stoops, but these were not the idle drunk or the disconsolate unemployed. These men were lean, spare, and wary. Alejandro saw several furtive glances cast his way.

Bien, he thought. Perhaps tonight will prove easier. He walked past them to a building on the corner, where the light from the gas lamp did not reach. He stood, careful not to lean against the grimy bricks, and looked around as if waiting for someone. He reached into his vest pocket and retrieved a coin.

Two men detached themselves from either side of the stoop. The first waved off the second, and a brief argument ensued, after which the loser sat back down and the winner proceeded toward Alejandro. The man was young, perhaps twenty-five, though the years had been cruel to him, leaving lines at the corners of his eyes and a harshness on his mouth that lived on even in his smile.

"Sommathing you want, *signore?* Sommathing I can get for you?"

Alejandro looked down at the shorter man, not caring if he appeared imperious. The man was a worm, trading in all things illegal, and deserving of contempt. Unfortunately, Alejandro needed him.

"Yes, there is something I want," Alejandro said, his accent informing the man of his Creole descent. "But it is not easy to find."

"Very good," the other said with a wink. "I am Bernardo, and I am your servant. Whatever it izza you want, I can get it."

"It is for my master. He would like . . ." Alejandro paused. Though he had done this a dozen times and more, it always disquieted him. "He would like a girl."

"A girl?" Bernardo asked. "A *puttana?* This is an easy thing, *signore.*"

"No," Alejandro told him. "Not a whore. A girl. My master . . . he enjoys the *deflorare. Capite?*" And now came the part that Alejandro despised the most.

"Oh, *sì signore,*" Bernardo said with a lascivious grin. "*Capisco.* He wants a *vergine,* no?"

"*Sì,*" Alejandro said, tasting bile at having consigned one more man's daughter to perdition. "That is exactly what he wants."

Bernardo grew serious. "*La vergine,* she must come at a price, *signore.*"

"We will make it worthwhile," Alejandro said. He turned up his palm. Even from this distance, the lamplight reached greedily to glint from the edges of the Spanish gold coins he held. Just one of these old "doubloons"—as they were still called on the Bowery and in other dark corners throughout New York—would pay this scum's rent for two months. The coins had been outlawed as legal tender for a score of years, but Alejandro knew he wasn't bargaining with a greengrocer over the price of turnips.

Bernardo's face grew satyric at the sight of gold. "*Dio*

Cane! Very fine, *signore*. Very fine! I know just the girl for your *maestro*. Just the girl. When do you . . . *permesso* . . . when does your *maestro* want this girl?"

"Tomorrow at midnight. Bring her to Constanza Oubliette's establishment."

"Tomorrow? Oh, no, *signore*. That is too soon. This girl, she will take some convincing."

"Tomorrow," Alejandro said, flashing the coins again and pointing to the men who ranged by the stoop. "Or I'll ask your friend over there."

"No, no. *Sì, sì, signore*. Tomorrow. Tomorrow it will be, as you say. Very fine. Midnight tomorrow, at Stanzi's. I bring you the girl."

Alejandro sniffed and held out the coins, pulling them back just as Bernardo reached for them. "Upon delivery. For now . . ." He produced two silver pesos of New Spain—each worth a dollar on their own. "Make sure she is clean, Bernardo. And be warned: My master is quite a connoisseur and this will not be the first time he has tasted this particular fruit." He rubbed the coins' milled edges together. "He is a man of position and influence. It will not go well with you if he discovers that he has been . . . cheated . . . of his prize." He dropped the coins into Bernardo's hand.

"Ah, *sì signore*. Very fine. All is good. The *maestro* will not be disappointed. Bernardo will bring her."

Unfortunately, Alejandro was sure that he would.

On his way back through the cobbled maze toward his waiting carriage, he thought of his own daughter. He imagined Isabella, the flower of his family, sitting with her mother on the balcony of their San Francisco villa, looking out over the sunset waters of the Pacific. He imagined her far from this place, and far from the knowledge of things such as he had set in motion tonight. He thanked God above for their ignorance of his activities, and that his own dishonor—a stain that stretched back nearly thirty years to a single battle against a single man—had not brought them anywhere close to the streets like the one he now trod. It had been a long, repugnant journey back from disgrace to the penumbra of power, and he had done many things in which he held no pride, things he had shared with neither man nor confessor.

He walked up to his carriage and the driver opened the door. Alejandro climbed inside. Tomorrow night, he knew, someone else's daughter would sell her virtue for a coin of gold. He prayed, as they crept into the Bowery's slow-moving traffic, that his many sins would only help to keep his own family from such degradation.

CHAPTER 3

Friday, March 1, A.D. 1889
Broome and Mott Streets, Fourteenth Ward
New York City, New York

Again the next night, Fortuna had not waited for Cesare to escort her home from work. It was not until he was a block from home that he caught up with her.

"Why did you leave without me?" he asked, coming up beside her.

She walked with her arms folded, as if protecting something. "I . . . the building was too hot. I had to get out into the air."

"That's no excuse," he told her angrily. "I don't want you on these streets by yourself. It's not safe for you—"

"I'm not a *child,* Cesare." She stopped and met his anger with her own, hands on hips and brow furrowed. She began to say something more but stopped, pointed at him, tried again but failed. She turned then and, arms folded once more, stalked away. "I'm not a child," she said.

They walked in silence to their tenement. Cesare did not know what to make of his sister's mood, and was concerned that she should get angry twice in as many days. It was unlike her to be so irascible. That was supposed to be *his* shortcoming.

They entered the darkness of their building. The narrow hallway was unlit. The building held on to the day's wet heat like a miser with a gutter-found copper. Cesare led the way, moving forward by feel, shoetips reaching ahead to shove refuse to the side. The air was close with the moist scent of humans living in close quarters and ripe with the stench of waste. From under the Colletti family's door came a faint spill of wavering candlelight, and from across the hall Cesare heard Mrs. Bocciacco arguing with her husband about a purchase he had made. It didn't matter what the purchase had been . . . Mrs. Bocciacco complained about anything old Pietro bought.

In the larger space of the central stairwell, the air relaxed and Cesare felt able to breathe. Wails from the three Fiorello babies dripped down from the third floor, and voices from a hundred mouths echoed through the stairwell. Cesare and Fortuna began the climb up to the fourth floor. At each landing, windows looked into the airshafts that pinched the middle of the building into its dumbbell shape. The windows, however, could provide neither air nor light, as a brick wall stood two feet away from the glass and their frames had long ago been nailed shut to discourage residents from tossing their garbage out to accumulate at the bottom of the shaft. As they climbed, raised voices grew louder and more familiar. Cesare recognized Salvatore's adolescent plaint. He heard the Widow Scottolini adding her opinion. One voice, though, a strident alto, he heard above all the rest.

"Mama," he said. "Hurry, something's wrong."

They clambered up the last two switchbacked flights and headed down the corridor. The sound of their mother's temper bounced along the hard plaster from the apartment's open door. Yellow light silhouetted a figure in the doorway, a cloth-wrapped bundle at his feet. It was Salvatore, their younger brother.

"Don't you close that door," their mother warned. "Don't you walk away from this family."

Fortuna went inside, and Cesare came up behind his brother. With a strong hand on his brother's shoulder, he looked inside the tiny ten-by-fifteen-foot apartment.

"Ah, thank the Blessed Virgin you two are home," his mother said.

Francesca Uccido stood near the table, anger welting her brow. On the other side of the table sat Giuseppe, her husband, his head in his hands and the whole of him nearly hidden by the piles of unfinished coats and uncut fabric on the table—piecework the family brought home to earn a few more pennies. Mrs. Scottolini, the widow who shared their flat, stood behind their mother, hands on hips and calamity in her eyes. On the floor at their feet was little Vincenzo, barely six years old but already knowing when to remain silent. Lucia, nearly eight, sat on the floor across the small room, past the cold stove and the rag-stuffed mattresses. She ignored the argument completely, her hands busily stitching a silk lining into the shell of a woolen coat.

"This boy"—Francesca pointed at Salvatore—"he says he is leaving. Leaving his family. Just like the other one. Just like *him*."

"Mama, I'm not *like* Emilio."

She spat at the mention of the name, then swayed and put a hand to her brow, reeling on her feet.

"Sit, Mama." Fortuna brought a chair and she and Mrs. Scottolini helped her to sit. Their mother's weakness was as plain as sunshine in summer. Her arms were like sticks, and the bones of her face were stark beneath sunken eyes. She coughed—an evil, rattly thing—and eased herself into the chair, but her sharp-edged gaze did not leave Salvatore.

Cesare could feel his younger brother tremble. He knew that at fourteen, Salvatore was prone to grand gestures, and hoped that the bundle on the threshold was just such a thing: a gesture, a theatric designed to provoke a response. Even if he did not intend to follow through with his threat to leave, he had definitely succeeded in getting his mother's attention.

With that attention, however, came her temper. "Papa," Salvatore said, unwilling to treat with his mother's anger. "You tell her. You know what it's like." But Giuseppe just held up a blind hand, warding off involvement, saying that he did not care to hear anything his son might say. Francesca, bolstered by her husband's abdication, sat up straighter in the stiff-backed chair. Salvatore looked at the floor, and Cesare knew the argument was over; regardless of what his brother had wanted to say, it would remain unsaid, unheard. He gripped his brother's shoulder, led him outside into the corridor. Once away from the door, he slapped him in the back of the head.

"Aiah!" Salvatore whined, but did not contest his older brother's reproach.

They walked down the narrow darkness, passed by an open doorway guarded by spying neighbors eavesdropping on the argument. Cesare grabbed the knob and yanked the door shut. He led his brother to the stairs.

"Sit," he told him.

Salvatore descended a few steps and sat. Cesare took a place next to him. They were in the heart of the building, and its pulse surrounded them. People, their sounds, their smells—crying, laughter, earnest talk; sweat, filth, simmering soups, drying linens—all were in the air, all wafted through the dark vertical space of the stairwell. Cesare could smell mud left on the steps by a thousand thousand shoes, heard the clink of crockery, sensed the presence of four hundred souls, above and below, all within the sound of his voice. He heard a quiet step on the landing as Fortuna came to join them, seating herself on the step above Salvatore and pulling him to lean back into her embrace. They sat there awhile in mutual silence, a quiet trio listening to the life of the tenement and its inhabitants. Finally, Cesare sighed.

"What did you expect?" It came out like an accusation.

"I don't know," Salvatore muttered sullenly. "They took it all wrong."

"And how were they to take it?" Fortuna asked. "You wanted to leave."

"I wanted to help," he said, turning as best he could to see her in the darkness. "One less mouth to feed. One less cause for worry."

"As if we wouldn't worry anyway," Cesare said.

"I just wanted to do something, something to help." He looked forward again, down into the gloom of the stairwell. "But they took it . . . she took it . . ."

"As an insult," Cesare finished for him.

Salvatore scuffed his foot on the step. "She wouldn't let me explain."

"She was angry," Fortuna said, and Cesare heard the emotion in her voice. "And so am I." She held her younger brother tightly. "We are all we have. We need each other. One less mouth to feed? One less brother to work for us all. One less to worry about? If you weren't with us, we would only worry more, like we did for Emilio."

"I'm not *like* him," Salvatore insisted. "I'm not!"

"Then quit acting like him," Cesare said. He calmed himself and started again in a cooler tone. "We know you're not like him. And Mama knows, too. She's just afraid. She doesn't want to lose you like we lost Emilio."

"It's not my fault that he got himself killed."

"No," Fortuna said. "It was his own fault. But that doesn't keep Mama and Papa from blaming themselves. Or from fearing that you might repeat his mistakes." She rocked him slowly back and forth. "We are a family, Salvatore. And we must stick together. We are stronger together than apart. We lost Emilio, and I don't want to lose anyone else. Not you, not Mama, not Papa, not Cesare or the babies. I want us all to be together." She was weeping now. "Don't you feel the same way?" she asked him. "Don't you want to stay a family?"

Salvatore's breathing grew harsh as he tried to keep his tears inside. "Yes," he said then. "But that's what I was trying to do. Trying to help the family."

"I know," she said. "But you won't help us by breaking us apart."

They sat there, the three of them, staring into the darkness. Then Cesare patted his brother's knee. "You've got to go back in there now."

"No," Salvatore said.

"You have to," he said.

"I won't!" He shook off his sister's embrace.

"Oh, yes, you will!" Cesare reached out and snatched his brother by the collar to keep him from heading down the stairs. He stood and marched Salvatore up to the landing. "Go on," he said, shoving him toward the apartment. "Be a man. Go tell Mama you love her and that you are sorry."

"But I didn't do anything *wrong*."

Fortuna stood and kissed him on the cheek. "Let her be right tonight."

Reluctantly, Salvatore turned. Fortuna sent him on his way. He walked down the hall, and the door to their apartment closed.

"It will be all right," Cesare told her.

"I know," she said. "But for how long?" They sat down again and she snuggled up against him. He put his arm around her.

"What are you afraid of?" he asked her. "He's just a stupid kid. He's bound to make some mistakes."

She shook her head. "It's not that. I just don't know how long we will be able to stay a family in this place. Mama is so sick, and Papa works so hard—we all do. Every month is a struggle, and soon you'll meet some nice girl and want to make a family with her—"

Cesare chuckled. "She would have to be an idiot."

"But you'll love her," she said with a small laugh. "And what will you do with your spinster sister then?"

"And why do you think you won't find a man who you'll love just as much?"

"Who will marry a ragpicker's daughter? Who will court a girl from the ghetto?" She cut off his half-voiced repudiation. "No! Tell me who will, Cesare. Another tenement rat? Like Benutto's son? Like that weasel-faced Grimaldi? You've heard what goes on behind these doors. You hear how these men treat their women. Don't you see? This is all I have before me. This, or living alone, and how can I do that? How can I live alone in this city when our family can barely scrape by with all of us working together?"

He felt her frustration, knowing it to be cut from the same cloth as his own. He knew of only one answer for her. "I will take care of you." Part promise, part declaration; he held her close and whispered it over and over. She cried quietly against his chest for a while, then quieted, and they returned home.

Exhausted by the day's work and the evening's argument, Cesare's mother retired for the night. She took Lucia and Vincenzo into the apartment's only other room, a tiny, windowless chamber with two plank beds and little space between them. She tucked the two youngsters in for the night, and then finally lay down herself. Her muffled cough and the unseasonable heat reminded Cesare of summer nights back in Tuscany, lying in bed with the shutters thrown wide to let in the soft breeze, and with it the sound of a distant dog, barking.

Mrs. Scottolini rose and went to the bed she shared with Fortuna while Fortuna and Salvatore both stayed at the table, leaning close to the lamplight, sewing linings into coats. Cesare, whose fingers were too clumsy for such tasks, and his father, whose fingers were too stiff, both sat and watched the other two sew. They worked with small, strong stitches, affixing panels of gray jacquard to the thick wool. Feeling useless, Cesare went over to the window—the family was fortunate in having an apartment that faced the street. He checked on the two heavy flowerpots that sat on the sill.

In each of the thick terra-cotta pots was a grapevine, still bare from winter's dormancy. Cesare carried them over to the table and inspected them in the light. They were gnarled and twisted with years of encased growth, but had four strong canes apiece, each about two feet tall. On one of them, he spied the pale swellings of springtime growth.

"Look, Papa," he said, bringing one of the pots over to his father. "They're beginning to bud."

"Throw those things out," his father said. "They're no use to anyone. Not in this place."

"Oh, no, Papa. I couldn't."

"I said throw them *out!*" Giuseppe grabbed the pot and threw it. It bounced across the floor and hit the wall. The thick clay cracked, splitting in two, dislodging the vine and spilling soil. Everyone stared at the mess, the empty pot, the vine's broken canes, the exposed roots.

Cesare leapt to salvage the plant. Giuseppe had brought the vines from Italy when the family had immigrated to America. I want to plant them in prosperous soil, he had said, but after a few years in the city, his frustrations bloomed into neglect. Cesare had taken up their guardianship then, warding off whitefly and aphid, bringing them water, and training them for five summers to send their pale tendrils along the bricks outside the open window. They had never bloomed, had never in all that time borne fruit, but they had survived, their rooted feet tight in their own clay tenements. To Cesare, his father's act of rage was an assault on a member of the family, and with quick hands he tried to rescue the vine. The others were silent as he reinterred the roots in dirt and clay, and wound a shank of string around the pot to hold the broken halves together. With tender care, he placed the pot back on the sill next to its twin.

"One never knows," Fortuna said, trying to salve the room's wounded mood with calm words. She concentrated once more on her stitches. "Things might change, Papa."

Cesare glared at her, knowing what she was thinking, afraid of what she was planning, but she did not look up again.

Later, after they had all gone to bed, Cesare drifted between waking and sleeping. Next to him in the bed, Salvatore snored intermittently and kept him from enjoying full unconsciousness. Instead Cesare lay there, banked between his brother's heat and the plastered wall. He stared up at the ceiling, his eyelids heavy but unclosable, and watched the patterns of mildew and water stain swirl and bloat in his nighttime vision. His mother coughed in the other room. One of the youngsters mewed in dreaming. In the chimera of his own somnolent state, he placed himself somewhere he had never been: in solitude. In his tiny Tuscan hometown, crammed into the steerage decks en route to America, and in tenement after tenement during their years in America's greatest city, he had never known the paradise of aloneness. Never once in his entire life had he been out of sight of others; not in a room, not in an alleyway, not even in the hidden play spaces of his younger years. Always there was someone nearby, and usually there were many, bumping into him, breathing down his neck, treading on his feet, or shoving him to one side.

Move aside, you Guinea bastard!

Clear off, Dago!

O, amico! Dove andate?

To be alone, what would that be like? he half dreamed. To hear nothing but the wind and the ringing of my own ears?

He dozed and woke with a start. Rising up on an elbow, he looked across the dark room to where his sister slept. Mrs. Scottolini sprawled across its width. Fortuna was gone.

Gently he pushed off the thin sheet and crawled over his brother's sleeping form.

"What?" Salvatore said through the syrup of sleep.

"Nothing," Cesare told him. "It is nothing." He grabbed his coat from the hook on the wall. Salvatore was sitting up, rubbing his face with his hand.

"Where are you going?" he whispered.

"Out," Cesare said. "Stay here. Do not say anything."

"What's wrong?"

"Nothing," he said. "I hope. Stay here."

He left, closing the door quietly and walking smoothly down the hallway. He looked down the stairs but saw no one, heard nothing but the various snores and mutterings that came from hundreds sleeping in close proximity.

Alone, he thought. Not quite what I had hoped for.

He went down the stairs and out onto the street. Two men wove their way down the street toward him, talking loudly in drunken tones. Cesare avoided them and ran toward the Bend. He didn't know what time it was, but it was late, very late. At the Bend he saw two shadows sitting on a tenement stoop. He headed for them.

Even before he reached them the shadows stood and walked off in opposite directions. He knew Bernardo's form, though, and ran to catch him by the collar.

"Where is she?" he demanded, throwing Bernardo up against a pushcart.

The pimp laughed. "Who?" he asked, and was answered by a quick fist to his ribs. Bernardo was several years older than Cesare, but he was thin and no match for a man who could lift a bale of cotton on his back. The pimp put a hand in his coat and Cesare whirled him around, grabbing his wrist. The wan light of the street lamp glinted off the bared knife. Cesare cracked Bernardo's hand against the corner of the cart, and the knife clattered to the cobbles.

"Where is she?" he asked, feeling fury's gallop in his breast. "Last chance."

"I don't know who you—" He grunted with the blow to his kidney. "Cesare, wait!"

"No! Where is she?"

Another blow. Teeth bared, he demanded again, "Where? Tell me *where!*"

"She's doing it for you," Bernardo said. "For your family! I didn't force her."

It was too much, that this *thing* should know his sister's hidden fears, that he should think it somehow *noble* to ruin her. He grabbed Bernardo by the scruff of his coat and slammed his head down into the cart's iron-bound wheel. Bernardo grunted with the impact. "Tell me where she *is!*"

Bernardo fell like a boneless doll. He spat thick blood onto the slick gutterstones. Cesare kicked him in the side and Bernardo rolled over, a hand raised in surrender. He muttered something Cesare did not understand. "Speak!" he ordered.

"She is . . . at Stanzi's." He wiped at bloody lips and laughed at the irony. "On Maiden Lane."

Another kick and Cesare was running. Eight blocks through nighttime streets. Few were out, but those few stared at the lone man running across the Worth, under the tracks on Park Row, down past Chambers and past the pilings under the Brooklyn Bridge. He headed down Gold Street into a Jewtown eerily deserted in the midnight hour. Suddenly, rather than wanting to be alone, Cesare wanted nothing more than an army at his back, a hundred men to help him save his sister from her own folly. He met Pearl Street, hooked left on Maiden Lane, and headed down toward Pier 18 and the water.

Constanza Oubliette was a well-known whore of mighty proportion and legendary talent. She ran a seamy bordello above the barber college at Maiden Lane and Front Street. It was a neighborhood on the cusp of two worlds, straddling the fashionable and the destitute, the famous and the notorious, and thus attracted a particular kind of clientele: a man of means who wanted to experience the thrill of danger without actually being threatened by it. As Cesare ran the last blocks to her place, he felt his rage at such men build, that they might make sport of his sister's disgrace.

He crossed Water Street and saw their cabriolets and barouche boxes, four of them in a polite line. Their sleek, curried horses gleamed in the warm light from the second-story windows. Servants and drivers in fine black cutaways and riding boots stood beside the carriages' lacquered doors, waiting for their masters' return. Music from a piano clinked and pattered through the stony night, its happy tune inflaming Cesare's heart and fury. He ran up to the door that led into Constanza's parlor and shoved aside the man who watched the entryway.

"Fortuna!"

He burst into a parlor filled with overstuffed chairs, carpets, and sweet perfume. Ringlets and soft flesh squealed in surprise and waistcoats and watchfobs rose in well-practiced indignation. Cesare ignored them.

"Fortuna!"

A well-heeled gent with gray hair came at him with a tumbler of whiskey and a haughty air. Cesare shoved him back onto a velvet-covered divan. A woman appeared from behind a draped doorway. With dark hair piled high and acres of bosom jouncing above yards of silk and lace, it could be none other than Constanza herself.

"Where is she?" Cesare demanded. "Where is my sister?"

"Get out of here," Constanza ordered him in turn, but her eyes betrayed her as she glanced toward an open doorway at the back of the parlor. Others noticed her lapse and stepped in to block his way, but gentlemen and overripe whores could not hope to stop him.

More stairs. "Fortuna!" A long hallway. He opened doors, exposing sex, simple and depraved, in pairs and in trios. "Fortuna!" He heard a scream. Down the hall, on the right. He threw open the door.

The man had her on the bed beneath him, her pale legs and breasts exposed, her teeth bared, her eyes closed in belated refusal. He was naked between her legs, pinning her hands above her head, thrusting up into her, grunting above her screams. Sweat plastered his long gray hair to his neck. His flaccid whiteness flubbered atop her firm beauty like sin itself. Cesare thought no more.

He grabbed the man by his hair and pulled him off. The man roared and elbowed Cesare in the gut, shoving him backward. Cesare fell against a bureau and grabbed onto it for support. The man turned and came at him, a feral rage in his eyes. He slammed into Cesare, knocking him back into the wall. Lath and plaster cracked. Cesare struck back with the first thing the street had taught him: The man grunted as Cesare slammed a foot up into his erection and testicles. He stumbled toward the bed, clutching his injury but snarling still. Fortuna had scrambled backward against the headboard, pulling the sheet up to cover her nakedness. Cesare saw the bruise on her face, the blood on her lip from where the man had struck her.

His sister's rapist came at him again, but this time Cesare was prepared. He sidestepped the attack and, with a hand around the older man's neck, propelled him into the already cracked wall. The man fell to the floor, shaking his head. Cesare picked up the heavy lamp from the bureau and smashed it into the man's face. The glass chimney shattered, and the flame went out. The man grunted, a sound so much like the sounds he had made atop his sister that it deserved to be extinguished. In the fresh darkness, Cesare put the lamp to him once more. The man grunted again, writhing on the floor between Cesare's feet. He put the lamp to him again. And again. The grunting stopped, but Cesare did not. He struck again. And again. He struck, pounding the man's skull until he felt it give way, felt the bones break like the pastry shell on a holiday *cannoli*, cracking to reveal the sought-for custard within. He struck again, a number of times, not knowing how many, until a shout finally penetrated his murderous temper.

"Cesare!"

He stopped. The light from the open doorway filled the room with a dreamy grayness. His sister stood before him, naked, beautiful but painfully thin, every muscle and tendon taut as she screamed.

"Cesare, stop!"

He dropped the lamp. Voices raised in fear and anger could be heard out in the hallway. He looked down at the body between his feet, the blood-spattered torso, the still-engorged penis, the evil darkness of a shattered skull. He smelled lamp oil and stepped backward out of reflex. Fortuna wrapped herself in a sheet and gathered up clothing.

"We must go."

He looked at her dumbly.

"Cesare," she said, pulling him by the arm. "We must go."

She tugged him out into the hallway. Frightened faces saw them, saw him, and retreated. Their fear brought him back to his wits. He put a bloody hand on his sister's shoulder and escorted her down the hallway. Behind him, someone entered the room and screamed. Hands reached out for him but he pushed them back, shoved them, made them respect his strength. When they reached the parlor, it was empty. The stairway to the street was likewise. In moments they were in the street. An elderly man in fine clothes looked out of his carriage window. At the sight of Cesare and Fortuna he stepped out.

"What has happened?" he asked through a thick Spanish accent.

Cesare ignored him. He took his sister up in his arms and whisked her off into the darkness. Behind them, voices began to echo through the streets. Shouts of "Murder!" could be heard above the rattle of departing carriages. Cesare gritted his teeth and bore his sister homeward. Fortuna, so light in his arms, buried her face in the crook of his neck, and shook with silent tears.

He was numb. He tried to think, tried to form a plan, but he could not hold on to anything. Except Fortuna. He held on to her, keeping her close. He suddenly found himself across from City Hall, realized that he had been walking the main streets, saw the gawking faces of the rummies and hopeless staring at him from the darker shadows beyond the light of the square. Looking down at the sheet-swathed woman in his arms, at the bloody hands that held her, he realized the danger. He had to get her home, quickly and quietly; it was a thought his befuddled mind could grab and hold.

He dashed to Spruce Street, ducked down a small side-street, and thence to an alleyway that led up between the backsides of tenements. Lean-tos and shanties had been tacked together in the yards behind the tenements, hovels so much more miserable than Cesare's own home that he could barely conceive of life within them. He hurried along, dodging across the larger streets, keeping to the shadows, until he reached their own street and headed toward home.

"Wait," Fortuna said quietly. "Go around the back."

He backtracked and went around behind the building, tiptoeing past several small, one-man, refuse-roofed shacks where indigents slept in depraved squalor. They reached the back of the house and he set her down.

"We can't let you inside looking like that," she whispered. "Take off your shirt."

She took his shirt and gave him the clothing she had been carrying. Then, still swaddled in her stolen sheet, she dunked the shirt in a half-barrel of stagnant rainwater, squeezing and rubbing out the bloodstains from sleeves and front. Cesare looked at the clothing she'd handed him. There was more there than just her own dress and under-clothes. He felt thick wool and satin, too. He unrolled the bundle.

Coat. Vest. Trousers and braces. The murdered man's clothes.

The hair on his arms rose as if a ghost had breathed across his neck. In reflex he started to throw the clothes away, wanting nothing to do with either that rapist's sin or his own, but something made him stop. The trousers, the clothes themselves were heavier than their fine fabrics would allow. He knelt and inspected them more closely.

In the vest he found an engraved silver matchbox and a pocket watch with a gold chain and fob. From within the trousers he pulled a silver cigar clipper, an ivory comb, a cloisonné snuffbox, and coins of gold and silver. The pockets of the coat produced a fountain pen, a few letters and papers, a billfold crammed with notes, and a coinpurse heavy with money. Cesare laid out the items on the coat's silk lining and stared at them.

It was a grand wealth. More money than the family would see in a year. He heard a plop and then a small gasp. Fortuna stood staring, her hands over her mouth and his half-wrung shirt in a wet pile at her feet.

"Il mio Dio," she said as she crossed herself.

"Who was he?" Cesare asked, but she only stared at the fortune at their feet.

"I don't know."

He grabbed her by the arms. "Who was he?" he rasped in a harsh whisper. "Who have I killed?"

She shook her head. "I don't know," she said through tears. "Bernardo didn't tell me."

Bernardo. Cesare groaned as the reality of his crime bloomed before him. Word was already out, a man murdered in Stanzi's whorehouse. Quickly the police would find Bernardo, and just as quickly Bernardo would lead them to him. He saw that Fortuna had been thinking the same thing.

"You must leave the city," she said.

"And go where?"

"I don't know! Somewhere. *Anywhere.*" She pointed to the treasure on the coat. "You can go anywhere. But you have to go."

He looked at it all. Embossed gold, carved ivory, engraved silver. "We all can," he said.

Her eyes widened as she stared at him.

"We can all go," he said. "Just as you planned."

"We must move quickly," she said, and knelt. "Come. Give me a hand."

Alejandro held the lamp and stared down at the body. He had not seen such carnage since the Battle of El Brazito.

The ambassador was naked, no one bothering to cover either his indignity or the horror that was left of his head. His skull had been crushed, and blood and brains sprayed across the floor. Blood was spattered, too, up the wall, and even on the ceiling, as the killer had hauled back his arm for blow after blow. The dented base of a brass lamp lay nearby, and the sharpness of lamp oil mingled with the earthy, metallic scent of gore.

As Alejandro stared at the corpse, all he could see was the face of the youth who had fled the brothel, taking the girl with him. A lover or brother, come too late to rescue the girl from the ambassador's assault on her maidenhead? The girl that Alejandro had procured? The sin that he had allowed?

"Was it a sin?" he asked the corpse. "Was it a sin for me to let the sinner sin?" But he knew that it had been, for he had done more than simply allow it to happen. He had prepared the way, and had turned a blind eye to its commission. He was as responsible as the cooling carcass at his feet.

He grabbed a blanket from the bedstead and tossed it over the obscenity of lewdness and murder.

"Thanks be to God. That is the last time I'll have to cover over your crimes," he said. Then he went out into the hall, down the stairs, and waited for the constabulary to arrive.

CHAPTER 4

Monday, March 4, A.D. 1889
Inauguration Day
Capitol Building
Washington, District of Columbia

The air was muggy, and Custer pulled at the high, starched collar of his pleated shirt.

"Autie, leave that be," Libbie said under her breath. The offices of outgoing Vice President Hayes were filled: Judges and dignitaries chatted amiably, senators and officers conferred in quiet tones, and aides and pages scurried in and out of every door. But the assemblage thoughtfully provided Custer and his family with a bubble of pretended privacy in which they might make their last-minute preparations for the day's formalities. Libbie fiddled with the velvet collar of her husband's black cutaway and smoothed the fabric across his thin shoulders.

"I don't cut quite the same figure these days, do I, sweet?"

"Nonsense," she said. "You're my Beau Saber, and just as dashing as ever."

Custer smirked. He'd seen himself in the mirror. He knew better. His skin was too taut these days, as pale and tight as an old drumhead. His eyes, while still the same forget-me-not blue as in his youth, were no longer able to conjure the hawklike gaze that had served him so well during his military years. And, of course, the hair—his last vanity—faded and growing sparse despite its old-fashioned length. Even his mustache had more gray than red in it these days. The last few months had been especially hard. Coming to terms with Herron's description of young George's violent death had wracked Custer like a storm, disturbing his days and destroying his nights, leaving him as dry as an old cornstalk.

Of course, he was not the only one affected. Libbie was not immune to the changes wrought by their last few years together. The tiny lines the Frontier had planted at the corners of her eyes had deepened. The round, high apples of her cheeks had lost some luster, and the strong line of her jaw had in it a touch of the jowl. Life as a congressman's wife and as First Lady had left its indelible mark, a mark that their most recent grief had only accentuated.

But still, he thought—looking at her quiet smile and seeing in her face the small-town beauty he had courted so many, many years before—she is stronger for it all, while I . . . He did not finish the thought.

"You really should eat something," his brother Boston said from his seat on the davenport. Standing nearby, Nevin nodded in agreement.

"This heat saps my appetite," he told them. Libbie raised an eyebrow. "I'll grab a bite afterward. Hayes is giving luncheon in here after all the speeches are done."

She finished fussing with his clothing and took a step back. "There," she said with satisfaction. "I must say, you seem remarkably calm."

"Why shouldn't I be?"

"You know why," Boston said, "and don't tell me you don't. There are a quarter million people standing out there in the heat, and half of them would be pleased as punch if you dropped dead on the way to the podium."

"Slightly more than half," Nevin said with a chuckle, "according to the final tally."

"Please, brothers," Libbie said, hushing them. "The girls." She glanced briefly toward her daughters, but Lydia and Maria were busy, heads together, whispering secret opinions on the guests in the crowded offices.

"Don't worry," Custer said. "There's nothing the people can do but shout and complain." He noticed his attaché making his way briskly toward him through the gathering. "They're stuck with us for four more years and there's nothing they can do. Isn't that right, Samuel?"

The elderly Samuel Prendergast bowed briefly to the First Lady, to the brothers, and then turned to his employer. "I hope that you are right, Mr. President. They're turning ugly out there."

"Oh, not you, too?" Custer protested.

"I'm glad to hear that someone outside the family agrees with me," Libbie said.

"Then you'll be glad to know, Mrs. Custer, that there are many of us outside your family who are worried about today's events. Higgins and Campbell are concerned that—"

"Oh, rot," Custer said cheerfully. "Higgins and Campbell are always concerned. It's their job. Now let's change the subject."

Samuel nodded deferentially. "As a matter of fact, sir, there *is* something I need to talk to you about. It's a bit delicate."

Grateful for the distraction, Custer took a relieved breath. "Fine. If you all will please excuse us?"

The president and his attaché navigated through the thickening forest of uniforms, robes, and black cutaways. Samuel ushered his president into a small room off the main office and closed the heavy door after them. Custer found the sudden and relative quiet of the carpeted room oddly disturbing, as if, alone, he were more vulnerable than when surrounded by others. He took a deep breath to dispel the sensation.

"Something wrong, sir?"

He shook his head. "Nothing," he said. "I just want this day to be over. What was it you wanted to discuss?"

"The Ambassador from New Spain will be unable to attend the inaugural ball this evening."

"Oh?" Custer sneered. "Any reason in particular?"

"He's dead. Murdered, actually."

"Good Lord. Murdered? When?"

"Two nights ago, sir. In New York. From all reports he was killed . . ."

Custer urged him on with a nod.

"In a brothel, sir. In one of the worst wards of the city."

Custer shook his head. "Well, now, isn't that a peach? The old miscreant finally got what he deserved but didn't have the decency to do it in his own country." He sighed. "What's our damage in this?"

Samuel shrugged. "Very little, actually. The ambassador was attacked by the brother of the young woman—girl, really—with whom he was . . . occupied."

"Have they found him? The brother, I mean?"

"No, sir. He and his sister disappeared into the ghetto. They may have left the city."

"Tsk. One can hardly blame the young man, I suppose. Well, let's try to keep the details quiet. Send my personal condolences to the ambassador's family, and to that dandy of a viceroy, as well. And invite the viceroy to send a new ambassador to us at his earliest convenience. Let's hope his next choice isn't such a reprobate as the last."

Samuel nodded. "Yes, sir. Very good, sir."

Custer pulled his watch from his pocket. "Almost time, old friend. Are you ready?"

"Are you, Mr. President?"

Custer smiled. "Have I any choice?"

They returned to the main room. Custer was glad to be back in the company of others. He drew a personal energy from their excitement, energy he had not of late been able to provide himself. He walked over to Libbie, gave her a tiny kiss on the cheek, and was rewarded by a blush. Lydia and Maria stepped up on either side.

He regarded his women and the other members of his family, and recognized the first touch of healing on his heart. His dreams of a Custer dynasty might have died on the frontier with his son, but he needed to remember that he was still a father—could still be a grandfather. He put an arm around each of his girls.

"I believe we are ready," he said.

Samuel nodded to the head of the inauguration's executive committee, who nodded to his assistant, who nodded to an aide, who pointed to several of the pages. The office doors opened, letting in the light from the corridor windows and the sound of the throng gathered without the building.

"First guests to the platform," the pages chimed, moving through the offices to gather up their charges. Hayes came up to Custer and the old man extended his hand.

"Good luck, Mr. President," he said.

Custer put a hand on his first vice president's shoulder. "Thank you for your help in the first term, Rutherford."

Hayes nodded, then turned to go out onto the platform. The second wave was called for.

"That'll be you," Custer said to his family. Libbie, Lydia, and Maria—all looking fine in their long, dark dresses and high-piled coiffures—took the arms of Custer's brothers, who escorted them to the door. Custer felt a pang as he watched his daughters glance back with a smile. Lydia, a second-year debutante, had had a difficult coming-out, what with the scandalous difficulties George and the Cheyenne had brought. But soon, he knew, the tide would turn, the social memory would grow dim, and the moment he both hoped for and feared would come; Lydia and Maria would wed and leave him.

As he watched them walk out the door, he thought to himself: My second term is to be one of things lost.

The cheers of the supporting crowds echoed down the halls from the east portico. As they subsided, the chants of those who came to remonstrate and censure his administration grew in primacy. Their rhythmic thunder became like a pulse in Custer's brain, a heartbeat that was not his own.

"Boisterous, are they not?" It was the Vice President–elect, L. P. Morton, the thin-faced banker from New York who had joined the ticket after Hayes's demurral on a second term.

"Boisterous?" Custer remarked. "Is that what they call it in New York?"

Morton's smile was full of narrow teeth. "Until they start throwing things," he said. "Then we call it 'raucous.' "

Custer had to smile at the man's aplomb. "You know, Levi, initially I opposed you as a replacement for Hayes."

"Only initially?"

Custer nodded. "But now I think your peculiar sense of . . . realism, if you will . . . shall be quite an asset to our efforts."

Morton chuckled, but then sobered. "If you would permit me to give you a bit of . . . realistic advice?"

"Of course."

"Be aware of the crowd," he said. "What we have out there is little short of a mob. Keep one eye on the exit, but keep the other on the rabble."

"Is it going to get raucous, Levi?"

Morton looked at him frankly. "Yes," he said.

The committee chairman came over to the two men. "It's time," he said.

The justices, the Vice President–elect, and Custer left the offices and walked down the long hallway to the east portico. The day was bright against the building's marble. An overcast sky multiplied the sun's light rather than diminished it, and clamped a lid on the day's unseasonable heat. The chants grew louder as they approached the foyer.

He caught a glimpse of the reviewing platform where his swearing-in would take place. Expectant faces looked toward his entrance. Beyond them, draperies of red-white-and-blue bunting decorated the rails, and hundreds of flags hung in a valance of patriotic pride, all undulating lethargically in a slothful breeze that moved the air but did not cool.

Custer realized his hands were empty. "My Bible," he said.

"I have it here," said the Chief Justice. He held out the book and Custer recognized the pebbled leather binding of the ancient French volume he had found in the White House library the previous year—the night he had learned of the destruction of the rail bridge spanning the Missouri. Custer had requested that Bible specifically for the inaugural, eschewing others sent to him as "gifts" from hopefuls both political and corporate.

"Thank you," he said, and walked out onto the platform.

The nearby crowd burst into a rallying cry of support, flags waving, hats held high. Beyond them, Custer saw the banners of his detractors. "Union & Labor" some said, and "Don't Tread on the Workers" read others.

He saw Libbie standing out by the railing, hands clasped before her, jaw set, the soggy northwesterly wind tugging at her curls and her dress. Custer walked toward the podium. A chant built from the far reaches of the crowd and swept its way up toward the assembled guests on the reviewing stand.

"Tyrant! Traitor!"

"Boisterous," he said to Morton as he walked past.

"For the moment," the other said.

They reached the front and Custer waved to the crowd, sending his advocates into fresh paroxysms of support.

Then he turned to face the Chief Justice. The old jurist held out the Bible. Custer put his left hand upon it and raised his right.

"I do solemnly swear . . ."

The first bottle sailed in and crashed against the railing. The tone for the rest of the day was set.

CHAPTER 5

Light Snow Moon, Waxing
Fifty-six Years after the Star Fell
Where the Sheep River Meets the Elk River
Alliance Territory

George grimaced as he kept himself mounted with his knees and worked the lever on his rifle. His whistler bugled, a long three-note call that echoed through the forest. In front of them, the flight of deer flashed tails of warning and bounded away through the blue-green boughs of shaggy spruce. He fired a shot into the air, grunted with the recoil, and grabbed the ropes of his saddle as they swerved to follow the fleeing herd.

His recovery from his wounds was incomplete, but there were things that needed to be done, things that wouldn't wait until he was completely well. This was such a thing. He worked the Winchester's lever again, ejecting the spent casing and pulling in another round from the magazine. The deer ahead of him veered left. He toed his mount to move in and cut them off; he fired the rifle again. The deer turned back to the right, heading straight down the forested slope. George followed.

His whistler leapt across a creekbed and George felt a snag in his side. He grunted with the pain, but forced himself onward, goading his mount ahead as the herd broke out of the trees and into a clearing.

The meadow was bright with patches of snow. The deer exhaled billows of frosty breath. Here in the open, the whistler could have her head. George pushed her around the herd's right flank, forcing the deer toward the narrow end of the meadow. They ran for the darkness of the forest.

He fired a third shot, increasing their panic and saw their eyes roll white as they looked back to their pursuers.

From within the gloom of the trees a huge form appeared. On great strong legs she pushed forward into the sunlight, opening a maw that was as deep as a man could reach. She struck the deer in quick silence, grabbing a doe by the neck and snapping it, turning and knocking two others down with her thick tail.

George watched as his walker killed two, then three of the deer before the rest of the herd scattered into the forest. She was magnificent, even after her long winter's fasting. She stood over her kills: ten feet tall, twenty feet long, with two powerful rear legs, a long counterbalancing tail, and an immense, narrow, tooth-filled head. She chuffed twice—a harsh, coughing sound like that of a monstrous bird—and then bellowed her killing call. The hair on George's arms stood up and his whistler mewled and shied from the walker's force. The great beast looked over at her kills.

"Nóxa'e," George said, commanding her to wait. She looked up. Her wattle flushed a splotchy pink and she roared and took a step toward the downed deer. George grabbed his rifle and slid off the whistler's back. A slap on the whistler's rear flank sent the smaller beast running downslope, back toward camp and the safety of her own flock. George turned his attention back to his walker.

She towered over him, the most fearsome beast in the world. "Nóxa'e," he repeated, and again she defied him with a roar. George, wincing with pain at every other step, walked up to her. She cocked her head and peered at him with one eye like a gigantic robin eyeing a worm. Her silky winter hair gleamed like an aura in the sunlight, but her flanks were thin and her ribs were starkly apparent. The smell of blood was thick, even in the cold air. George saw her dilated pupils, her flared nostrils, her gouts of frosted breath. He walked up to her, standing in her shadow next to her kills.

"Nóxa'e," he said in a strong voice, asserting his authority, and then, "Sweet girl. Step back."

She grumbled: a low, fluttering sound that emanated from her keel-like chest rather than her head. She stomped the snow with one of her three-toed feet, ducked her head once, twice, and then, finally, took a step backward.

"Good girl," he said, his tone conciliatory. Taking his knife from the sheath that hung over his shoulder, he set to cutting the haunches from the deer. On a whim, he took one of the tails as well. Then he stepped back.

"Good girl," he told her again. "You can eat now." She looked at him, with both eyes this time, and he saw her uncertainty, her hesitation. Having yielded to his supremacy regarding the kills, she was unsure of taking it back.

He threw the haunches off to one side and stepped away from the rest. "Yes," he said and motioned her forward. "Eat."

She fell to. She planted a foot on one of the carcasses, grabbed a mouthful, and pulled. With small champing motions her teeth sawed through muscle, sinew, and bone, separating huge gobbets, which she then swallowed whole.

While his walker worked on her meal, George finished dressing and tying up the haunches he'd taken. He looked at the tail he'd taken from the deer—brown on one side, white with black stripes on the other. The People considered the tail of the timber-deer-waving to be a symbol of love. George couldn't think of why he had taken it, but then corrected himself. He did know, but did not want to admit his reasons; not to himself, not to anyone.

When she was finished, the walker crouched down in the sharp sunlight of the early-spring afternoon. She curled her neck and picked her teeth with the claws of her short forelegs, cleaning out the bits of flesh and gristle that had caught in the deep interstices. George came up beside her and patted her belly, now distended with the bulk of her hastily eaten meal. Her skin had gone all bumpy and her downy hair stood tall to conserve the warmth she had built up in the exertion of the hunt. Her wattle was blue again, signaling her intent to sleep. George needed her awake for a little while, though.

He threw the tied haunches over her spine and grabbed onto the first rope. The walker's saddle, unlike a whistler's, was more than just a few loops of rope. It had a pad of buffalo hide and wicker backrest to keep the rider from sliding down the ridged length of her backbone. She grumbled as he pulled himself up into the seat. George tapped her flank with his toe.

"Up," he commanded, and after a glance back in his direction, she rose onto her hind legs. "Let's go," he said, and they started off at a long, slow waddle.

As they came down out of the hills, the conifers gave way to bare cottonwoods and sweet gum trees. Through the bony lacework of branches George could see the grass-lands and the river that would lead him back home. They traveled slowly, for her benefit and his, for her belly got in the way of her legs, and George's wounds were far from healed. His arm and head were fine, but the wound caused by the bullet he'd taken to his body still caused problems.

He lifted up his tunic and checked the dressings that wrapped around his torso. The cloth covering the entrance wound under his ribs looked fine. Gently he reached around and touched the dressing over the exit wound. It was wet. His fingers were touched with blood.

"Damnation," he said to his walker, patting her shoulder. "It's a good thing Speaks While Leaving isn't here. She wouldn't let me leave camp for another two moons. Think how hungry you'd be then."

The walker only belched up a bubble of carrion-scented air.

They were approaching the camp when George saw Mouse Road. She was on whistler-back, riding fast, headed his way past the small waterfall and the ice-rimmed pond. She rode head down, letting her whistler find the path.

"Mouse Road!" he called. She reined in her whistler and looked around in surprise. Her cheeks were wet with tears, and she was evidently upset. "What is wrong?" he asked her.

She did not answer. She grabbed the first rope and kicked her whistler's flank. The beast leapt back into motion, carrying her past him and out toward the grasslands. George could not follow her, not on a gorged walker, so he headed up toward his lodge.

George's lodge was just up the hill from the lodge of Mouse Road and her mother, Picking Bones Woman. He stepped off his walker's back, took down the haunches and his rifle, and let his walker settle herself down into her nest.

Her nest was a pile of leaves, bracken, and boughs about six feet high and eight feet long. With her back feet, she scratched it all together, and then she walked into it, nestling into its insulating depth. George heard her rumble, a contented sound this time, and her milk-white inner eyelids nictitated as she quickly fell asleep.

George took the deer haunches and walked down the hill to his neighbor's lodge.

"It is One Who Flies," he said, using his Cheyenne name. "I brought some meat for you."

"Leave it outside," Picking Bones Woman said. Her voice was weak and trembling.

"What is wrong? I saw Mouse Road ride off in a hurry."

"What did she tell you?"

"Nothing. She barely stopped."

"Come in, One Who Flies."

George opened the doorflap and stepped inside. Picking Bones Woman sat before the small fire of sticks and whistler chips. Her cheeks were wet, as her daughter's had been. He hung the haunches of meat on one of the lodgepoles and sat down on the guest side of the fire.

"The two of you were arguing," he said simply.

"Yes." She looked very old and very tired, her high cheekbones prominent and her dark eyes sunken in their orbits. Her hair was almost gray throughout, and she had lost some weight during the winter. As she poked at the coals to liven them, George noticed a slight tremor in her right hand, but he knew Picking Bones Woman could be sly and duplicitous when it suited her needs, and he wondered if she was really unwell or just playing to his sympathy.

"What were you arguing about?" he asked.

"You," she said without looking up from the fire. George waited for her to elaborate, but she did not. He did not want to play this game with her.

"I see," he said, and stood up to go.

"I want to visit my son," the old woman said, still staring into the fire.

George sat down once more. "In a few moons the People will gather for the summer. We will all be together then."

She met his gaze, a rudeness in Cheyenne society. "Look at me," she said. "Look at this hand. It shakes like a leaf and I cannot stop it. My right leg is no longer the stronger of the two. My hip aches with every sunset. My breath rattles in my chest, and I tire with the smallest chore." She looked away finally, returning her attention to the small fire. "I saw these things when my husband sickened and eventually died. My time is coming, and I want to see my son."

George was stunned by her challenge and her bluntness. It was most unlike her usual methods of wheedling and patient negotiation. "Then we go," he said.

"I knew you would agree," Picking Bones Woman said. "So did she."

"Mouse Road? She agreed with you? Then what were the two of you arguing about?"

Picking Bones Woman did not answer him, except to eventually say, "Ask her, One Who Flies. I do not understand her anymore."

George took his leave of her and walked out to search for Mouse Road. He took one of his yearling whistlers, leaving his walker to sleep off her meal. He rode down the path he'd seen her travel, but did not know where she had gone.

"Hó'ésta," he directed his mount, and the beast bugled, a rising yodel that started in its breast and rose up through the hollow bone that crested its skull. George listened as the echoes died and was rewarded by an answer, another call from the grass-clad slopes to the south. *"Nóheto,"* he ordered, and grabbed the first rope as his whistler pushed off.

A whistler's forelegs were not like a walker's. They were long enough to be used in slow locomotion and for digging up roots or snow-covered grasses, but when they ran, they preferred to move as walkers did, on just their powerful rear legs. George's whistler tucked her forelegs in close to her breast as she picked up speed. Patches of snow crunched as she broke through the springtime crust. In moments she reached the place of the other's call, and George called her to a halt. He kept a grip on the first rope, his head swimming with the simple exertion of keeping his seat.

"Mouse Road," George said loudly, wincing as he did so. "Where are you?" He waited, and finally she answered.

"Here," he heard her say. He tapped his whistler's flank and the beast walked forward toward the voice.

Mouse Road's own whistler was bedded down nearby and she herself was perched on the long, low branch of a cottonwood tree. She sniffed and wiped her nose. George rode his whistler up alongside the low branch and put a hand on it to steady himself.

"I spoke with your mother," he said.

"When do we leave?" Her dejection was unmistakable.

He laughed. He could not help it. "What is wrong? Don't you want to see your brother?"

"You don't understand."

"No. I don't." His whistler took another step, unbidden but not unwelcome, as it brought him closer to Mouse Road. "But I might," he said, "if you told me what it is that is bothering you."

She looked up into the branches, off into the distance, down at the ground, everywhere in search of the words she wanted. "You are not well enough," she said.

He chuckled again. "I can ride well enough to keep up with an old woman."

"You bleed every day," she snapped. "I see the dressings."

He ceased in his levity, for she was right. The wound that pierced him front to back seeped blood with his slightest exertion, just as it had today. His rib, shattered by an army bullet, wobbled with every breath, and he was still weaker than he cared to admit to anyone, himself most of all.

"But your mother, she's not well either. This visit, it seems very important to her."

"And what of the things that are important to me?" she said sharply, and for the second time that day George found his gaze met. "What of me? My mother thinks only of my brother—Storm Arriving did this, Storm Arriving said that—and she dreams only of my poor dead sister. There is no room for me in what she sees. There is no room for Mouse Road and the things that *she* cares about."

She realized her breach of etiquette and looked down at her hands. Her skin was flushed beneath the darkness of her skin, and George stared at her beauty, unable to look away.

"What is it that you care about?" he asked.

"Many things," she said, quiet and shy once more. "Family, home, the years ahead." She reached out and timidly put her hand on his. "And you."

George felt his heart race. It was what he had hoped to hear, but not what he was prepared for. "I . . . I am almost ten years older than you," he said.

She did not remove her hand. "My father was fifteen years older than my mother," she said. "And I am nearly eighteen summers; more than old enough. . . ." She took her hand away. "*Eya.* I have said too much. I should get home and help Mother with the household work."

George grabbed her arm before she left the branch, holding her back, wanting anything but for her to leave. Her lashes were wet with fresh tears. She *was* younger than he was, but he didn't want that to matter. He reached out to wipe her tears away and she leaned into his touch.

"One Who Flies," she said, a quaver in her voice.

"Don't go," he said, not knowing what else to say. "It will be all right. I want it to be all right."

CHAPTER 6

Thursday, March 7, A.D. 1889
Chicago & Rock Island Railroad
Outside Chicago, Illinois

Cesare entered the passenger car and came face-to-face with a large woman. She frowned at him from beneath the wide brim of her feathered black hat and wrinkled her nose as if she smelled something bad. Cesare did not take it personally. She was rich and he was poor; she was American and he was Italian. It was the way of things in this country, and as long as he kept his distance there would be no fuss. His difficulty, however, was trying to keep his distance in the narrow aisle of the bumping railcar.

He flattened himself against the window, touched his hat, and swept a hand before her. "Please," he said. "After you."

An unhappy expression still on her pursed lips, she moved forward. Cesare prayed to the Holy Mother that the car did not lurch as she squeezed past him; the last thing he wanted right now was trouble. The heavy fabric that covered her ample hips crunched and swished as it was constrained between Cesare and the far wall. The locomotive whistle blew—a high-pitched shrill. Cesare held his breath, but no lurch, no sudden jolt came, and the woman continued onward with only a backward glance and a "humph" of contempt.

"Grazie," Cesare said to the heavens, and continued on to the end of the car. He could hear Vincenzo crying before he opened the compartment door. Inside, his father, mother, Fortuna, and Salvatore all sat crammed onto the bench seat on the left. Lucia and the petulant Vincenzo

sat on their elder siblings' laps. The family's belongings—bundles of clothes, a crate filled with crockery—were tucked between their legs or stuffed in the rack overhead. Crammed in a corner were the precious grapevines, the one still in its twine-bound pot. On the right-hand side of the compartment a German couple and their reed-necked son sat in studious silence, ignoring the Uccidos one and all, hiding behind their newspapers and dime novels. Had the Germans sat closer together, Cesare could have shared the bench with them, but they made no move to consolidate their holdings. Cesare slid the door closed and sat down on the floor. Vincenzo wriggled and whined.

"Where are we going, eh?" his mother asked in Italian from her seat near the window. She had been in a foul humor ever since the family's hasty departure from New York, liking neither Cesare's sudden fortune nor Fortuna's plan for a new life out West. She waved an arm at the countryside passing outside the window. "We ride these trains for days. We sleep sitting up in train stations and climb up and down from a hundred railroad cars. We must be going in circles. This country cannot be so big!"

Vincenzo renewed his wailing and his father leaned over to smack him on the head. *"Basta!"* he said. Enough!

"Mama," Fortuna said in the quiet voice she used to reason with her mother. "Cesare and I told you, and we all agreed. We're going to the far edge of America, where they are going to give us some of the land they have out there. It's a big country, and it's a long way to travel."

"Pff," she said, and waved a hand. "So you say. So you say. But I say that no one *gives* away land. This is some sort of trick they've played on you; trick the stupid Italians, eh? You, boy." She pointed at Cesare. "You've lived here long enough to know. The American never gives the Italian anything!"

"Francesca," their father said. "Let them be."

"And ask no questions?" she said, but was halted in her tirade by a fit of ragged coughing. Her thin chest heaved with the tearing, ripping paroxysms, gripping her for minutes. When she was through, she could barely hold her head up. She leaned against her husband, her eyelids drooping and her skin sallow. Wisps of hair escaped her bun and waved in the breeze from the half-open window like Medusan threads. But she was not willing to concede the argument.

"Am I so old that I should let myself be carted around?" she continued weakly. "I want to know where we are going. I want to know why we had to leave so quickly. And I want to know where they got the money for all this!"

"Mama, don't!" Cesare said in a tone that brought his mother up short. He glanced over at the Germans and caught the teenage son peeking over his book. The boy saw Cesare and went back into hiding. Little Vincenzo squirmed again and wailed. Cesare's mother stared at her eldest surviving son, wide eyes demanding an explanation for his insolence.

"Mama," Cesare said, by way of an apology. "Let Fortuna and me take the little ones for a treat. They could use some food."

"Food that you'll pay for with what? This money that came from nowhere?"

"Mama." Cesare looked at her sternly. "I beg you. Please, do not ask about the money."

His mother sat back in her seat and folded her arms, her brow a dark-winged shelf above angry eyes. "No good will come of this," she said. "No good at all."

Cesare motioned to Fortuna. "Come. You, too, Salvatore." They rose, taking Lucia and Vincenzo, and left their suspicious parents to the silence of the Germans.

They made their way up the rocking passageway, stumbling through car after car until they got to the diner. Cesare held open the door for his siblings to enter when a large arm blocked their way.

"Where you think you're goin'?" asked a Negro in a white coat and black pants.

"My family," Cesare said. "They are hungry."

"Unh-uh," the waiter said with a shake of his head. "Not in here. Not with them. Sorry, friend."

"But the little ones, they are hungry." Cesare smelled beef and fish and coffee. He could see, farther up in the car, mustached men with pomaded hair chatting with ladies who wore wreaths of lace and chiffon at their necks and wide skirts of shiny cloth. Waiters like the man blocking Cesare's way served food on china and crystal. Cesare looked up at the black man. "Is it money? We have money." He reached into a pocket. The Negro held up a meaty hand.

"You're not comin' in here," he said, but paused when Vincenzo began to whimper. He glanced behind him. "Listen, you stay here. I'll see what I can do."

The door closed.

Cesare turned to face his siblings. Vincenzo cried quietly. Salvatore frowned in humiliated rage. Fortuna shook her head, resigned. Lucia was simply confused.

"Why won't they give us any of their food?" Lucia asked in Italian.

Salvatore rapped her shoulder. "Speak English," he said. "Only stupid dagos speak Italian."

"Leave her alone," Cesare said, but then to his sister said, "Speak in English, *cara*. You want to be an American, don't you?"

Lucia nodded and was about to speak again when the door to the dining car reopened.

The Negro waiter held a collection of small parcels in brown paper. "Samwiches," he said, handing them to Cesare. Then he reached back inside the galley and came back with two small paper cones. He knelt on one knee and handed one each to Lucia and Vincenzo. "Some sweets for the little ones," he said with a smile.

"Many thanks," Cesare said. He handed the sandwiches to Salvatore and reached into his pocket. "How much do I owe?"

"Nothin'," the black man said.

"No," Cesare said. "Thank you, but I want to pay for the food, please."

The waiter made a small sound and nodded at Cesare's insistence. "All right. A man who pays his debts. I can appreciate that. Two bits, then."

Cesare looked through his coins and pulled out one of the Spanish *pesetas*. He held it up. "Will you take this?"

"Perfectly good once we're west of the Mississippi," he said with a grin. He took the coin, winked, and closed the door. Cesare and his siblings headed back to their compartment.

"Where *did* you get all that money?" Salvatore asked.

Fortuna shushed him.

"What?" Salvatore asked. "You think no one else is

going to ask?" They squeezed their way past others coming
in the opposite direction. "Especially all those Spanish
coins you have. And the folding money? You think that no
one at this Land Rush is going to think twice about a bunch
of dirty dagoes with money like that?"

"Basta," Cesare said, switching back to Italian and glancing nervously at the faces around them. "People will hear
you."

Salvatore stopped and faced his brother. "I knew there
was something to worry about," he said, still in English. "I
heard whispers in the halls as we left New York. You better
tell me about it, big brother. I don't want any surprises
when we get to Yankton."

Cesare grabbed Salvatore by the collar. "What are you
thinking of? Huh? How much do you know? I swear, if
you breathe a word—"

"Hush. Both of you." Fortuna glared at the two young
men and moved her head, indicating the people nearby.
"You say too much." Cesare glanced in the nearby compartment. A man with a red beard and a flat-topped hat
met Cesare's gaze for a long moment, and then looked
back down at his newspaper.

"Move," Cesare said. "We'll talk about it later."

"Later," Salvatore said with a sneer. "In Yankton, you
mean."

"Yes, little brother," he said, asserting his authority.
"In Yankton."

Salvatore stared at Cesare for several heartbeats, then
turned and walked on toward their own compartment, back
near the baggage cars. Cesare noticed the bearded man
watching them once again as they headed off.

Back in their compartment, Fortuna took the duty of
parceling out the food. Cesare, standing by the door, saw
the bearded man. He had to be following them, for there
was nothing in the cars beyond but baggage and freight.
Cesare beckoned to Fortuna and stepped to where his parents could not see him. A moment later, Fortuna came out,
closing the door behind her.

The bearded man came up to Cesare and smiled.

"What do you want?" Cesare asked warily. Fortuna was
more kind.

"Can we help you?" she asked.

The man lifted his hat from his head, revealing a bald pate shiny with sweat. The damp curls that fringed his scalp were gray and red like his mustache, and his blue eyes crinkled up as he smiled. "Well, children, I thought I might be able to help you." His voice was a rumble, like thunder from a distant storm, and his smile was full of even white teeth.

Cesare, still taut with suspicion, looked the man up and down. While his clothes were well-to-do and he smelled of perfumed soap, his boots were scuffed and in need of polishing. "How can you help us?"

"With some friendly advice," the man said. "Might I be so bold as to invite you for a cup of tea?"

"Thank you," Fortuna said, "but no, thank you."

"They won't serve us in there," Cesare said.

"What say you let me worry about that?" He beckoned them onward down the railcar.

Cesare looked to Fortuna for her opinion. She wrinkled her brow and shrugged, her way of saying, *Why not?*

"Thank you," Cesare said, and ushered his sister forward. The bearded man followed them.

At the dining car, a quick word and an exchange of coin saw them seated at a small table near the door. Simple cups of plain china were set before them. A platter was settled into a shallow depression into the table's top. On the platter were the makings of a fine tea: a fat ceramic teapot painted with small flowers; a silver creamer, sugar bowl, and tableware; and a three-tiered cut-glass carry-all piled with slivers of cake, puffed almond cookies, chunks of thick chocolate, and sugar-glazed fruits. Cesare smelled the bite of the steeping tea and the sweetness of the cakes, and his mouth began to water. It was some of the finest food he'd ever seen.

"Looks good, doesn't it," the man said. "Allow me to introduce myself. My name is Arnold Blaschke. I'm a businessman from Chicago. I'm heading down to Yankton to meet my partners." He offered up his hand. "And you are . . . ?"

Cesare shook Blaschke's hand and introduced himself and his sister. Fortuna, ever capable, ever calm, reached for the teapot and gracefully began to pour.

"I hope you don't mind," Blaschke said, "but I could

not help overhearing your discussion. I gather that you are also headed to Yankton. And that you hope to partake in the Land Rush on the nineteenth of April?"

Cesare did not answer right away, but eventually saw that it was silly to deny it. He had overheard Salvatore—everyone in the car had—and so he took a piece of cake and a silver fork and said, "Yes, we are. My sister told us about it."

"A lot of people are coming out here for it," Blaschke said, sipping his tea. "Thousands, I'd say. Maybe even tens of thousands."

Cesare did not understand the man's point and so said nothing rather than betray his confusion. The rich cake tasted of honey and flowers and melted in his mouth. He sipped the tea and found its bitterness a cleansing contrast.

"You'll have a lot of competition out there," Blaschke continued. "Do you have a plan?"

"A plan?" Cesare said without thinking.

Blaschke nodded. "Yes. A plan. To get out onto the Frontier before the rest of the hopefuls."

Cesare looked at Fortuna and she looked back at him. Blaschke chuckled.

"As I said, you'll be competing with thousands of others. Everyone will want the best parcels of land: a parcel with a creek or river running through it, for instance, or land that isn't rocky. You'll need a plan in order to get to the best spots."

Again, Cesare was benumbed. Idiot! He berated himself. Why did I think that *any*thing in this country would be done fairly or honestly? Why did I think that we'd be free of the *padroni* instead of simply exchanging one for another? He looked again at Fortuna. She sighed and shook her head in despair.

"Oh, dear," Blaschke said. He offered them both the plate of almond cookies. Fortuna silently refused. Cesare took one and ate without tasting. "Don't be disheartened, my friends. I think I know a way to help."

"Yes?" Cesare asked. "How?"

"Have you heard of 'Sooners'?" Blaschke asked. "No, I can see by your faces that you haven't. Well, a 'Sooner' is what they're calling those squatters who sneak out into the territory before the starting gun on April nineteenth. You could do that. It's not without risk, of course, but it will get you a prime piece of land for you and your family."

"We just sneak across?"

"No, no. That's too dangerous. But I know a man," Blaschke told him, "who, for a modest fee, can get you across the starting line before the gun."

Cesare smelled a trap. "A modest fee," he said. "Which we give to you, and then we never see you again."

Blaschke sat up straight in his chair. "Why, no," he said, affronted. "You won't give me anything. I just thought I might help you and your pretty sister here, but it is obvious that I was mistaken." He motioned to the waiter. "Boy."

Fortuna put a hand on Blaschke's arm. "No," she said quietly. "Wait."

The waiter stepped to their table. "Yes, sir? Can I get you something, sir?"

Blaschke looked at Fortuna for a long moment. "Some hot tea, boy. This has gone cold."

"I'm sorry, sir. I'll get it right away." He took the tea-pot away.

"I apologize for my brother's suspicions, Mr. Blaschke. As you can tell, we are not a rich family. It is unusual for someone like you to be so kind to people like us. Isn't that right, Cesare?"

Cesare winced under her gaze. "Yes," he said. "I apologize."

Blaschke smiled, shrugged, and gave a little laugh. "Of course," he said. "Entirely understandable. After all, you don't know me from Adam, and I'm sure there are those who wouldn't think twice about taking advantage of two innocents such as yourselves." He settled back into his seat and, as the waiter returned with a fresh teapot, helped himself to a rugged chunk of chocolate.

Cesare checked again with his sister. He did not want to trust this man. During his seven years in America, no one but fellow Italians had been of help—and even they had often preyed on their own. But now this dubious American said he wanted to help, fed them fine food, and had nothing to gain from his actions. This did not seem to worry Fortuna, but it worried Cesare. It worried him plenty.

"Mr. Blaschke," he said. "We are grateful for the help you are offering us. Our family can use some help right now, but I am still curious. What is it that you get out of this?"

Blaschke nodded. "Now that question I understand. You see, I was once an immigrant's son, myself. Cheated at every turn, treated like dirt. I spent most of my youth with either a blackened eye or a bloodied nose. What do I get out of helping you?" He freshened his teacup. "The knowledge that I've helped someone like myself, I suppose. That's all."

And Cesare felt his worry begin to disappear. He smiled. "Then, Mr. Blaschke, if you would, please. How do we find this man who can sneak us across the line?"

CHAPTER 7

Monday, March 18, A.D. 1889
The White House
Washington, District of Columbia

Custer thumbed through the sheaf of letters as he walked briskly down the corridor. Congratulations, felicitations, and wishes of goodwill were still pouring in from all corners of the country, as were the lamentations and complaints. Just as with the votes in the election, the papers in his hand were slightly weighted toward the latter sentiment. He paged through them, reading the first lines, but neither the positive nor the negative sentiments made any difference to him.

"Idiots," he labeled them all. "Idiots." He folded the papers in half and turned the corner, only to run spang into Jacob Greene and Gen. John Meriwether. Letters spilled to the floor and Jacob stumbled backward. Meriwether saved Jacob from a fall, but Custer slipped on a piece of paper. His foot went out from under him and he hit the hardwood, expelling a loud "Oof!"

"Mr. President! Are you all right?" Jacob, despite the familiarity that came from being Custer's longtime friend and now his Secretary of War, paled at having upended his commander in chief. "Good Lord, are you hurt? I'm terribly sorry. I just didn't see you. I—"

"Calm down, Jacob. It's not a treasonable offense." The letter on which he'd slipped was stuck to his heel. He reached down and plucked it free. "Now isn't that a shame," he said after reading the first line. "They'd hoped for so much more."

Jacob knelt down and helped Custer collect the strewn papers. Meriwether joined in as well.

"What are you doing here, Jacob?"

Jacob was sheepish. "We had an appointment, sir."

"Did we?" Custer thought back over his calendar. "Oh, yes. You and John. I've been so muddled of late. I'm sorry. Let's go up to the workroom, shall we?"

"Samuel was looking for you as well, sir."

"He'll find us up there."

They walked down the corridor to the cross hall. The first floor was busy with men in white shirts with dark sleeve-protectors: aides and clerks moving from office to office, handling the day's correspondences and running errands for senior staff members. They all greeted Custer with a polite "Mr. President" or a simple "Good morning, sir," and to them all Custer simply nodded as he made his way up the stairs to the second floor, where he kept his own offices.

An open door led to his workroom. It was a large, high-ceilinged room with one large window opposite the door. Several small tables and straight-backed chairs provided seats for guests, but the main furnishing was Custer's work-table. It was made of oak, heavy with Federalist carvings on the skirt. The legs, fluted and vaguely cabriolet in style, each ended in a taloned claw gripping a large glass sphere. Custer, however, had chosen it for its surface.

The dark oaken top was six feet wide and nearly twelve feet long. Rubbed smooth by thousands of hands and a hundred years' service, it provided ample room for either the maps of a campaign, a full week's worth of papers, notes, and telegrams, or a meeting of twenty men, with room left for libations. Though it was obscenely heavy, Custer had insisted on carting it along during his last years in the military, had used it during his tenure up at the Capitol, and had brought it with him to the White House. He offered Jacob and General Meriwether a seat and looked out the open door.

"You," he said to a passing clerk.

"Mr. President?"

"Go tell Douglas that I'd like some coffee brought up here."

"Yes, sir," the clerk said, and disappeared down the hallway.

"So," Custer said to Jacob, opening the discussion. "You

wanted to talk about John here as a replacement for Herron."

"Yes, sir. I've reviewed the records and interviewed all of the prospective officers. I feel John is the best choice."

"I've never questioned your choices for posts in the past," Custer said. "Why come to me now?"

"I'll answer that, if I may," Meriwether said.

Custer regarded the general. He was a Southern man by birth and by disposition. His face was haggard and dour, as if he'd spent years posing for family portraits and couldn't drop the habit. He beard was closely trimmed, but his mustaches he left long. He was meticulously attired, the brass buttons and gold braid bright against his army blues. Custer had known Meriwether since the Kansa campaign back in '76. The general had always proved to be a man of both dignity and honesty.

"I asked for this meeting," Meriwether said. "I can bring a great deal to this command, but I know that you and I have been on opposite sides in recent years. I wanted to give you the opportunity to quash the appointment."

Custer bristled. "I always have that option, General."

"Yes, sir. But I wanted to give you the opportunity to do it here, privately, before the press heard of it. Afterward, it might prove more . . . difficult. Some might see a public refusal as punishment for past deeds."

"You're referring, of course, to the incident with the Indians up at the Capitol Building."

"Yes, sir."

"You think I might harbor some ill will toward you."

"I did fire upon your son, sir, as did General Herron. And Herron's command is now in the hinterlands of New England, where the closest thing to an enemy is a rogue moose in November."

Custer frowned and rubbed a thumb across the nicks and scratches in the tabletop. "What we have not made public," he said, "is that General Herron did not just fire upon my son. He killed him. Initially, I myself tried to deny the reports made by the general and the few surviving witnesses, but now I have accepted them. However, General Heron's current assignment is unrelated with that fact."

Meriwether shifted in his seat, uneasy with Custer's sudden revelation. "Of course, sir. I didn't mean to imply—"

"Herron failed in his duty, and in his command. That is why he was reassigned."

"My apologies, Mr. President. And my condolences."

Custer subsided, but the emotions still rolled through his breast like a summer storm.

Jacob leaned into the conversation. "The president would be grateful, General Meriwether, if you kept this knowledge in confidence. I'm sure you can appreciate the potential for renewed grief, should this information be brought to the newspapers."

"Naturally," the general said. "I would consider nothing less."

The rattle of china announced the arrival of the coffee, and Custer looked up from the table's scars in genuine relief. Douglas, the house's old but eminently capable colored butler, wheeled a serving cart in through the open doorway, preferring to take care of his president's needs personally than trust them to an underbutler. He set out cups and saucers, sugar bowl and creamer, a platter of treats, blue linen napkins, and a steel pot of scalding-hot coffee.

"Thank you, Douglas," Custer said.

"My pleasure, Mr. President." And the old man wheeled his cart out into the hall. He began to close the door when Custer stopped him.

"Leave it open," he said. "Mr. Prendergast is looking for me."

"Yes, sir." Douglas bowed and left.

Custer poured himself a cup of coffee and took it to the window. Spring had routed winter early this year and the air was balmy. The trees wee beginning to bud, and the lawns had put on their bright emerald colors. Robins poked under hedges, searching for grubs and worms, and the billowed clouds scrubbed the sky to a fresh, clean blue. In the distance he could see the dome of the Capitol Building, where, three years ago, Gen. John Meriwether had fought invading Indians, their beasts, and Custer's own son.

"You remind me a lot of myself, Meriwether."

"Sir?"

"When I was your age. Passionate, cocksure, clever, strong-willed." He turned. "What is *your* assessment of the Territory?"

"Sir," Meriwether said, "it's a mess."

Custer raised his brow and looked at Jacob. The Secretary of War shrugged. "Well," Jacob said, "it is, you know."

Meriwether pressed onward. "It's near chaos, Mr. President. Take the Land Rush staging area, for instance. You've got cartloads of Sooners sneaking out into the Territory every night. You've got mobs of every ignorant stripe piled up behind the starting line. You've got snake-oil salesmen and confidence men every fifteen yards, and in between them you've got thieves, pickpockets, and plain everyday thugs. Graft and racketeering are commonplace, and when you throw canvas-covered saloons and sheet-draped whorehouses into the mix, it all builds up into a mighty froth."

"Sounds pretty bad," Custer commented.

"It is," Jacob offered. "More important, though, it's putting the legitimacy of the Homestead Act at risk. Our implementation requires a stronger hand."

Meriwether cleared his throat. "That's really only half the story, though, sir."

"Oh?" Custer motioned to the general. "Continue."

"There are the Cheyenne."

Custer frowned and gritted his teeth. He turned and looked back out the window. "What about them?" he asked. "Hasn't it been quiet out there?"

"For a while, now, sir, yes, it has," Meriwether said. "But for how long? In a month we will be flooding that land with settlers. We can't wait until then to act."

"All right, yes," Custer said. "But how?"

"I know you hold the Cheyenne in high regard," Meriwether said, "but with all due respect, sir, I believe that we simply need to treat them like the beasts that they are."

Custer took a long, slow breath to calm his heart and settle his nerves. "The Cheyenne have been a thorn in my side—both as a commander and as a president—for many years. Many generals, myself included, have gone up against their Alliance. Ultimately, we all failed. I have found them to be clever in tactics, sly in negotiation, and ruthless in battle."

"But that's just it," Meriwether said. "You ascribe them these virtues not because they are better, but because they

have bested you. You would not do so had you been bested
by a bear or a wolverine. They're beasts, sir; beasts of their
environment and no better than Negroes or some of the
European refuse that fill our slums. They use the tools
available to them, and use them well, but we can be better,
if we allow ourselves. The Almighty has made us so." He
took a sip of his coffee and reined in his enthusiasm. "I
realize that this view is unpopular here in Washington and
near to heresy up north. I must tell you, however, that in
the Carolinas, where I grew up, and in the western areas
like Missouri Territory, where I have served for most of
the last decade, it is considered plain horse sense."

"I cannot deny that," Custer said, "and you are not the
first general to speak so. Herron had similar ideas, though
he did not share them so freely. I should like to know,
though, why you will succeed where others before you
have failed."

Meriwether nodded. "Fair question, and in answer I'll
say that we must fight the Indian as the Indian fights."

Custer furrowed his brow and was about to object, but
Jacob held up a hand. "Hear him out, Autie. Please."

Meriwether waited for Custer's nod before he went on.
"We can't fight a defensive war, not over so much territory.
Nor is this like the Mexican War back in 'sixty-one. We
can't fight them with set pieces and rules of engagement."

Custer coughed. "I'd point out that we lost that war,
General."

"The United States merely chose to forfeit the conflict
in favor of attending to her own internal difficulties. We'd
have gained the Tejano Coast and probably all of Alto
California had we fought it out."

"Bah. You didn't go up against those Creole command-
ers," Custer said, and went to the table to refill his cup.
"Those men had something to prove. Ah, well, it's all moot
now. The whole of it is back in Spanish hands." He chuckled as he went back to the window and looked out at the
beauty of the day. "Now how ironic is that?" he asked
them. "The Mexican Federals were so busy trying to keep
us out of the Tejano coast and Alto California that they
left their back door open for Spain and France to walk
right into Mexico City. *We* gave Spain the opportunity to
take it all back!" He shook his head. "You'd think they'd

have learned a thing or two, after that fiasco with Maximilian and Carlota, but no. They just turn around and crown a king while he's still in his mother's womb. What an idiotic way to run a country."

There was a knock and Custer turned to find Samuel standing in the open doorway looking very uncomfortable. Behind the attaché was a finely dressed elderly gentleman—silk cravat, starched shirtfront, brocade vest, pinstriped cutaway—who was more than uncomfortable. The waxed tips of his gray mustaches practically quivered with rage.

"Mr. President," Samuel said. "I have been looking for you. May I present to you His Excellency Alejandro Miguel Tomás Silveira-Rioja, the newly appointed ambassador to the United States from New Spain."

Custer felt the blood drain from his face. "Mr. Ambassador," he said. "We were just . . . em . . . we were just discussing some of the vicious rhetoric being tossed about in the Senate."

Silveira said nothing, and Custer knew the damage had been done.

"I . . . I did not expect the viceroy to appoint a new ambassador so soon. . . . And for you to come so quickly . . . all the way from New Spain. . . ."

Samuel stepped in to help fill the conversational gap. "His Excellency was the chief assistant to the former ambassador, Mr. President. He was in New York when the ambassador met his tragic demise. The viceroy took your invitation to heart and appointed Don Silveira at his earliest convenience."

"Ah. Yes," Custer said. "Of course. And please, Mr. Ambassador, accept our deepest condolences over the untimely death of your predecessor."

Finally, Silveira showed a sign of life. With a click of his heels he stood straight and gave a slight bow, accepting Custer's commiseration. The ambassador's precise movements told Custer that he was formerly a military man like himself.

"Samuel, do I have an evening open next week?"

"Yes, sir. I believe next Thursday evening is available."

"Good. Mr. Ambassador, if you are not engaged next Thursday evening, I should like it if you and your family came here to dine with me and mine. Just a small gathering, and I can formally accept your credentials then."

Silveira bowed again. "Mr. President, due to the speed of my appointment, my family is still in San Francisco and will be unable to attend. I, however, accept your invitation and will look forward to meeting with you under more . . . cordial circumstances." He turned and walked briskly down the hall. Samuel, torn between staying and following the retreating ambassador, looked at Custer with vexation.

"You really should keep your door closed, Mr. President."

"Yes, Samuel. I know. Now go after him. Try to smooth those ruffled feathers."

Samuel trotted off. Custer closed the door.

"Aw, Hell," he said. "I'll be paying for that for a while, I think."

Jacob shrugged and Meriwether pretended nothing had happened. Custer walked back to the window. He saw the ambassador's carriage heading down the graveled drive of the Ellipse.

"Mr. President, about this post," the general said.

Custer sighed and waved a hand in surrender. "Yes, well, I see no reason to doubt Jacob's recommendation."

"Thank you, sir. And do I have your consent to apply a more stringent hand to the situation in the staging area?"

"Yes."

"And to deal harshly with the Sooners?"

"As you see fit, yes."

"And the Cheyenne, sir. I'd like to restructure my offensive units so that they might employ the Indians' own tactics against them."

Custer turned. "Are you going to put them on giant lizards, General?"

Meriwether smiled. "Whatever is necessary, sir. Whatever is necessary."

CHAPTER 8

Monday, April 15, A.D. 1889
Staging Area
West Bank of the Missouri River
Unorganized Territory

"There's another one."

Fortuna pointed. Cesare looked across the wide swath of mud that served as a road. Everything in view was in motion. Drivers whipped their teams. Mules pulled their carts through the fetlock-deep soup. Lengths of dirty canvas—the walls, roofs, and awnings of makeshift storefronts—billowed in the ceaseless wind. Men argued over wares, women haggled over prices, and children dodged both sharp-eyed proprietors and slowly turning wagon wheels.

"I don't see it," Cesare said.

She pointed again. Cesare squinted and then he saw it. Across the muddy road, a piece of paper was tacked to an awning pole of a dry-goods supplier. It fluttered in the wind. Cesare could not read, but he had learned in the past few days how to recognize the threat that called for him in large black letters: WANTED.

He glanced up and down the road, saw only shopmen and customers to either side. He nudged his sister in the ribs.

"Well? Go get it."

She punched him in the arm but stepped out into the road. Squelching her way across, she casually inspected the sacks of beans and coffee. She walked over to the awning pole, put a hand on the fluttering notice, and while feigning interest in a stack of skillets, nonchalantly pulled it down. Then she turned and came back across the road.

She handed over the wanted notice and Cesare uncrumpled it. "This is not a picture of me," he said.

Fortuna leaned closer to look. "Oh. No, it's for a man named Hawkins."

"But it's not for me." He showed her the notice. "This man looks nothing like me. He's got a beard and a bald head. You should have left this one up."

She glowered, angered by the criticism. "You told me to get it. You didn't tell me to look at it."

"Well, look at it first, next time. If we take them all down," he explained, "the soldiers will get suspicious. Just take down the ones with my picture. Understand?"

Fortuna pouted, but nodded.

"Good," he said. "Now where did you see that gunseller?"

"That way," she said, pointing.

Cesare steeled himself. "Let's go."

"Do you really think we should do this?"

He laughed. "So now *you* are the one who doesn't trust Blaschke? Fortuna, look around you. All these people are here for the same reason. They want land. How will Mama and Papa fare in a race against them?" He shook his head. "We can't afford *not* to trust Blaschke's word."

Fortuna's lips thinned into a prim line as she considered taking this final step. "I suppose you are right."

"You know I am," he said. "It was your idea, anyway, wasn't it?"

She smiled shyly and she took his arm. "Let's go, then."

They headed down the road, and as they walked Cesare looked out beyond the limits of the newborn hamlet. Great white billows rolled across the sky, boiling up from the southwest and the great inland sea that birthed them. In between the scrub-brush clouds, the sky was a deep blue. The land to the west was green with springtime. It was not the dark, tired green he knew from the Old Country, and it was not the cramped green that sprouted in the cracks of New York City. It was a brilliant green. It was deep. It was vital. He took a breath and could smell it in the air. He could feel its dew on his skin. Born of sunlight and air and rich, sandy soil, it was a green filled with life. It made him smile in a way he did not remember smiling. *Grazie a Dio,* it made him hope.

"There," she said.

The gunseller's was one of the few places that had wooden walls and a real roof. It was also one of the larger shops on the dirt track, sporting a wide storefront with shuttered windows and two small storage buildings around back. Everyone wanted a gun.

Two horses were tied to a post near the open door, and Cesare could see a shopkeeper within, showing rifles to two others. He started across the street.

"Shouldn't we wait?" Fortuna asked. "Until it's empty, I mean?"

Cesare shrugged. "It may never be empty," he said. They crossed the road and walked into the shop.

Fortuna gasped as the one of the customers turned around, a rifle in his hands. The brass buttons of his dark blue uniform winked in the light from the windows. The soldier touched the wide brim of his slouch hat.

"Afternoon, miss," he said with a friendly smile. "Afternoon, young man."

"Good afternoon," Fortuna said, recovering her composure.

Cesare forced himself to nod and smile in return but could not bring himself to speak to one of the men he'd been trying so hard to avoid for nearly a week.

The soldier returned his attention to the rifle. He worked the lever forward, then back. The clacking action was loud in the small shop, and Cesare felt ready to leap out of his own skin. "Do you have it in a carbine?" the soldier asked.

"Not on hand," the owner said. "But if you put down a deposit of, say, ten dollars, I can have one brought out for you special. Be here in about a month."

"Holy doodle," the other soldier said. "We might not be here in a month, Jake."

Jake handed the rifle back to the owner. "I'll pass on it, I think," he said. "Carbine works better on horseback."

The owner nodded. "If you change your mind . . ." he said, and as they left he turned to Cesare. "And what can I do for you?" he asked.

Cesare swallowed with a mouth parched by near panic. "I'd like to buy a gun," he said feebly.

The owner was shorter than Cesare but broader of shoulder. His features were rough—a wide nose, a broad mouth, a scraggly rough-trimmed beard, and dark eyes beneath dark brows—but all came together in a way that put Cesare at ease. He smiled and his eyes gleamed above his furry cheeks. He walked over to the display rack, glanced back at Cesare, and then pulled out a long, bolt-action rifle.

"How about this one?" he suggested.

Cesare glanced at Fortuna for support. She nodded, and Cesare spoke the phrase as Blaschke had instructed him. "I need a pistol," he said. "A Smith and Wesson Schofield six-shooter with an etched barrel and pearl handgrips. Do you have such a gun?"

The owner's smile disappeared and he put the rifle back in the rack. "What do you want with . . . such a gun?" he asked.

"I need it for my family," Cesare said. "My parents, my sister here, and three other children."

The owner craned his neck to peer out the doorway. "That would be an expensive pistol," he said.

"How expensive?"

He looked Cesare up and down. "I doubt you could afford it."

"How expensive?" Cesare asked again.

The owner shrugged. "Two hundred dollars," he said. "At least."

Cesare felt weak. He and Fortuna had been frugal with the rich man's money; it had brought them out here, had purchased the required permits, and had bought them a mule, a cart, some tools, seed, and three months' worth of provisions. Two hundred dollars was more than they had left.

"One hundred," Cesare said. "And you throw in a gun."

The owner's smile returned, accompanied by a belly-born laugh. "A hundred? And I throw in a gun?" He laughed again, harder, bending over. When he stood up again there were tears in his eyes. "One-eighty," he said between breaths.

Cesare gulped. "One-forty," he said. "And we get a gun." He pulled out the last of the rich man's folding money and smoothed it out on the table. Seven bills, each bearing on one side the man with the pigtail hair, on the other the woman with the shield, and between them the large number 20. Letters may have been beyond Cesare's skill, but money he knew.

The owner stared, then laughed again, even harder this time. He went over to a table and picked up a pistol.

Fortuna grabbed Cesare's arm. She pulled. "Let's go," she said as the owner came toward them, pistol in hand.

"Calma, cara," Cesare told her.

The owner, still chuckling, put the pistol down next to the bills. "Good enough?" he asked.

Cesare picked up the pistol. It was an old Colt six-shot revolver. It was nicked and scratched, and the wood of the butt was chipped and scored and looked like it had seen a war or two, but the chambers spun and it looked clean. Cesare nodded. "This will be fine," he said.

The owner reached for the bills on the counter but Cesare held on to four of them. "The rest when we're on our way," he said, "and might I have some bullets for the gun?"

The owner grinned and handed over a small wooden box of ammunition. "On the house," he said, wiping his eyes. "I'm Ballard. Have your family ready by the cottonwood grove just before midnight. A man will meet you." Then he started to laugh anew.

After sunset, the clouds had yielded the sky to the moon and stars. A silvery crescent painted the world with blue while the family's mule cropped at the fresh spring greenery with a *clomp-crunch, clomp-crunch* that Cesare was sure could be heard at the homesteader camps that lay beyond the crest of land to the south.

The cottonwood trees released their seeds to the lingering heat, sending forth ghostly filaments that floated on the night's gentler breeze. The leaves rustled peacefully overhead: a whispered lullaby for Vincenzo and Lucia, who lay atop the sacks of flour and feed, fast asleep under their blankets.

"Why so late?" groused their mother. "Why must we do this in the dead of night?"

"Mama," Cesare said, wishing she would simply leave it alone, wishing she would once—just *once*—not worry at it like a dog with a bone.

"Why?" she insisted. "Why are we out here at night?"

"Because it must be done at night," he said sharply, knowing his pique would only spur her, but unable to completely contain it.

"Ah-ha. It must be done at night. Then it must be wrong. Sitting out here like criminals. Like thieves in the night." She humphed and a cough rattled through her frame. "Like Emilio," she said.

"*Mama,*" Fortuna said.

"Just so," she said.

Cesare turned and looked up at his mother, working his utmost to master his ire. Why does she anger me so? he asked himself, but then knew the answer.

Because she is right. He took a breath.

"Mama," he said. "We are breaking the rules. We are waiting for a man to help us sneak out into the free land. If we can get out to the free land early, we won't have to race against all those other people back at the camps. Fortuna and I"—he reached out and grasped his twin's hand—"we decided that with one mule and all we have to bring, we had little chance to get a good piece of land for you and Papa. With this man's help, our prospects are better. That's why we are out here at night. It is not right, but it is our best chance."

His mother straightened and looked up at the sky. Cottonwood featherlets drifted among the stars. "Like thieves," she said, implacable. She made the sign of the cross. "Papa, do you approve of this?"

Cesare felt Fortuna squeeze his hand. When Mama turned it over to Papa, she was ready to be done with it. If he spoke in support, she could acquiesce without actually giving in.

Giuseppe took a deep breath of the night air and let it out slowly. He patted his wife's knee. "Nothing is honest in this country," he said. "America, she expects us to bend the rules, I think."

Cesare sighed and said a silent prayer to the Holy Virgin. He'd barely finished thanking her when he heard hoofbeats from the southeast. The mule lifted its head and swiveled its ears toward the noise. Cesare gripped the handle of the pistol stuck in his belt.

"Is it he?" Fortuna asked.

Cesare listened closely. "One horse," he said. "It's our man."

The rider reined in. Cesare could not see his face beneath the shadow of his hat's wide brim, but he saw the gleam of his rifle's barrel and the steel of his eyes as he looked the family over.

"Ballard sent me," he said. "You ready?"

"Yes," Cesare said.

"Let's head out." He pointed northward. "That way."

They turned the mule and wagon. Lucia and Vincenzo came awake with complaints.

"Hush," everyone told them.

Cesare and Salvatore walked alongside and pushed while the rest of the family perched atop the creaking rattletrap. The ground was gentle to the eye but not to the wagon's wheels. It rocked and jounced them as they made their slow way past the grove of trees and out into the empty space of the prairie. Ballard's man rode ahead, guiding their route around rocks and brush. After a long mile, he came back to Cesare.

"You take them north for another mile or so. Then you can turn west-by-northwest. There's a lot of fine farmland about sixty miles out."

"Is the land like this?" Salvatore asked.

"No, it settles down pretty quick," the man said. "There are a couple of creeks you'll have to cross, and you'll hit a river about forty miles out. There's a ford upstream from a tall hump of granite. You should be able to get there sometime after sunup. You have the rest of Ballard's money?"

"When we get there," Cesare said.

"Hell, kid, you think I'm going with you?"

"But . . . yes. Why? Where are you going?"

"I'm going back."

"Back? Then what am I giving you money for?"

Cesare's mother leaned forward. "What is it?" she demanded in Italian. "What's the problem?"

"Mama, momento," Cesare said, and then to the man, "I'm not paying a hundred and forty dollars for a one-mile escort."

The man pushed his hat back on his head and scratched

his scalp. "Ballard told me you were full of piss and vinegar." He smiled in the darkness. "But don't worry. You're money's well spent."

Behind them, small pops of gunfire echoed along the rolling land. It came from the vicinity of the homesteader camps.

"What's that?" Salvatore asked.

"That," said their guide, "is what will be keeping the soldiers and the marshals busy all night while you head out into the territory."

"What?" Cesare said. "A couple of gunshots in the night?"

"Yes," the other said. "That and . . ." He was silent for a moment, looking back over his shoulder. Cesare followed his gaze.

A bright light blossomed like a dandelion. Fortuna gasped, and then the boom of the explosion reached them.

"That," the man said. "That will keep them busy."

Cesare, still staring back at the rising cloud of fire and smoke, reached into his pocket and pulled out the rest of the money. He handed it to Ballard's man without a word.

"See that star?" the man said, pointing to the cloudless sky ahead of them.

Cesare nodded. "*La stella del nord.* The North Star."

"Head on toward it for another mile or so. Then turn west and keep it over your right shoulder. Then straight on till sunrise."

"Till sunrise," Cesare echoed.

"Take the best land you can find," he said, and then wheeled his mount and rode off. Back at the camps, fire lit up the pillar of smoke, and gunshots snapped in the night.

Cesare followed the instructions Ballard's man had given him. A mile north, then west-by-northwest. The mule did its best, but the wagon was too heavy for it to manage by itself. Cesare kept the polestar near his right shoulder as he put his left against the rear of the wagon.

They met the two small rills and easily pushed the wagon across their gravelly beds. The river, however, proved a greater problem. Though they found the ford just where Ballard's man had said it would be, the springtime rains cut deep and the water swirled up near the buckboards. Cesare, Salvatore, and Giuseppe all worked feverishly to unload their goods before they lost wagon and all. Then, with women, children, wagon, and mule all safely on the far shore, they carted all their worldly goods across on their own backs.

They had made it. All they had to do now was find a parcel of land and lie low for a week until the gun started the Land Rush and legitimized their Sooner claim.

Cesare watched his brother lean against the wagon, sleeping as he walked. His mother and father sat on the buckboard, holding each other up as they, too, slept. Fortuna and the two youngest all lay in exhausted slumber among the sacks and bundles. Cesare, still pushing the cart, let the mule lead the way.

Hours later, the sun began to put color back into the sky. Clouds floated in—stately steamships on the morning air—serene until the sun broached the horizon and lit them with orange fire. He thought of the explosion in the nighttime campsite and of the soldiers and marshals it was supposed to occupy. He looked back over his shoulder, but saw neither smoke from the camps nor sign of pursuit.

The growing morn showed him the world. To the east lay the rolling hills of the Missouri banks. To the south rose the disordered headlands that led to the cliffs and the inland sea. But to the west and the north, the land surged toward the horizon, fast and easy, as if smoothed by the divine hand.

When the sun was well up into the sky, Cesare brought the wagon to a halt. The land sloped away slowly, gently, down to a crease that held the curves of a small river. Along its banks was a wood of tall trees that spread their limbs to create an inviting shade. Beyond the wood, antelope grazed on the nascent grass.

Cesare heard his father groan and stretch as he awakened. His mother, disturbed by his movement, woke with a gagging cough, and that brought the others awake as well. They all stared at the sights around them; the land, the river, the trees. Birds chattered and chased each other through the ankle-deep grass. The air was fresh and new. The city that they'd suffered for so many years—the only home the two youngest had ever known—was gone; a memory, a fading nightmare in the face of the beauty before them.

Cesare's father got down from the wagon, staring at the vista. His jaw was tight, his lips pursed. He held his hat crumpled in knob-knuckled fingers and walked with the stiff-legged steps of a man still asleep. He walked around the wagon, looking in every direction, until he came up to Cesare. He reached out and put a hand on his son's shoulder, and Cesare saw his father's face was wet, his eyes full with tears. He looked at his son, then up at his daughter, Fortuna, who sat atop the bean sacks eager to hear her father's judgment.

"*Bene,*" Giuseppe said. He nodded, and smiled. "*Molto bene.*"

They lived cautiously for several days, staying near the cover of the trees, cooking little and only over small fires. The men built some simple lean-tos that provided shelter from the sudden rainshowers that came and left with neither preamble nor fanfare, and also gave the women a place of privacy—something their mother had greatly missed and something Fortuna had never known. Soon their encampment took on a sense of permanence both physically and in their minds. Cesare and Salvatore walked with their father, tramping up and down the small river trying to decide exactly where to stake their claims. They decided to set their parcels on either side of the river, Father's on the eastern bank, and Cesare's on the west.

"We should have lied about Salvatore's age," Cesare said. His father laughed.

"Him? Eighteen?" He chucked his second son under the chin. "Hairless as a maiden's bosom," he said. "No one would have believed him a man of eighteen. No, two forty-acre parcels will be sufficient for this family."

"Where shall we plant the grapevines?" Salvatore asked.

"There," Giuseppe said, pointing. "On the east bank of the river, where it will have the sun all afternoon. Two vines this year will become more next year, and even more the next."

They turned back toward their camp and Cesare spied something out to the east. His blood froze and his bowels melted as he made out two dark figures riding their way.

"Trouble," he said, and they raced for home. As they ran into the tiny camp, he shouted a warning. "Riders coming!"

Fortuna ran to him, grabbed his arm, and pulled him

away from their circle of shelters. "You must hide," she told him. "They may be out here looking for you."

He remembered the wanted notices posted back at the staging area. "But Mama and Papa. They don't know—"

"I'll tell them something. But you must hide. Once it is safe, or if they're just Sooners like us, you can come out."

"I don't like it," he said, but she tugged on his arm, insisting. He handed her the pistol. She refused it but he forced it into her hands. "Keep it," he said. "And if it is danger, use it."

She nodded. He kissed her cheek and ran off into the cover of the brush beneath the nearby trees.

He lay down in the underbrush, far enough away to be hidden from sight but close enough to hear what transpired. His heart was pounding his chest, trying to punch its way out, and his hands trembled like the leaves on the branches overhead. His parents stood together, watching the riders approach. Next to them stood Fortuna with little Vincenzo, and Salvatore with a hand on Lucia's shoulder. The children were quiet, sensing the fear that their elders felt.

The men rode over the last rise of land and down toward the family. They did not wear the blue wool uniforms of army soldiers, but longcoats and dark, wide-brimmed hats. As they rode closer, Cesare caught sight of the sun glinting from a metal badge—worse than soldiers: marshals. He ducked down closer to the ground.

The two men reined in outside the circle of lean-tos and dismounted. One was short and bandy-legged while the other was tall and lean as a scarecrow. The short man held the horses' reins while the tall one took a step forward.

"Well, well, well," the tall man said. "What do you know, what do you know?" His manner was confident, almost jovial. He smiled as he sauntered toward them. "Snuck out here early, didja? Thought you were pretty clever, huh?"

"Like shootin' fish in a barrel," the bandy-legged man said, and snorted as he laughed.

The tall man swept his arm in a wide semicircle. "All right, then. Come on. Let's go."

Cesare's father was confused. "Go?" he said in his thickly accented English. "No. We estaya here. Thisa our land. We hava papers." He fumbled in his coat pocket and pulled out the homesteader's permits they'd bought. "You see?" He walked toward the man to show him. "Papers. We hava papers."

The tall man slapped the papers out of Giuseppe's hand, slugged him in the gut, then in the face. Giuseppe fell to one knee, surprised by the attack.

"I don't give a Goddamned fart if you've got a golden cock, you dumb dago. I've got a paper, too." He pulled a paper out of his own pocket. "This says that if we find you we can bring you back and collect the bounty. And we aim to do just that." He reached for Giuseppe, but Giuseppe surged upward with the strong legs of a pushcart peddler, butting the tall man in the stomach. He fell back. Giuseppe made ready to swing but the bandy-legged man stepped forward and cracked him across his head with the butt of his pistol. Giuseppe moaned, a hand on the back of his skull, and fell to the dirt. The tall man stood up and kicked Cesare's father in the stomach.

Cesare was on his knees. He heard a shout and saw Fortuna struggling with Salvatore. Salvatore pulled himself away from her. He had their six-shooter. He turned and pointed it at the men.

"You leave him alone!" Salvatore shouted. The tall man held his hands out to his sides.

"Whoa, little man. You just calm down, now."

"You leave him *alone!*" He pulled back the hammer.

"I won't touch him," he said. He took a step toward Salvatore. "I swear I won't." Another step.

Salvatore fired a shot and dirt flew at the tall man's feet. The horses shied and whickered. The mule hawed, pulled free of her tether, and fled off into the wood. The tall man stopped in his tracks.

"All right. All right. Let's not get crazy."

A second shot discharged, but not from Salvatore. The bandy-legged man smiled a bucktoothed smile, his pistol leveled. Salvatore looked down at his chest, saw the blood spilling down his own shirtfront, and fell dead to the ground.

Francesca screamed. The children cried out. Cesare gripped the earth in his hands, frozen by his indecision of where to run, what to do. Fortuna reached down to Salvatore. Another shot cracked and his sister gasped. Cesare fought his own muscles, wanting to shout, wanting to move.

Fortuna, clutching her side, looked straight at him, her lips moving in silent petition.

No, my love, he saw her say. No. Stay where you are. Live.

The tall man whirled on his cohort. "What in tar-heel Hell you doin', Vern?"

Vern grinned some more. "He was fixin' t'shoot you," he said. "Her, too. She was goin' for the gun."

"And what do you think the others will say when we bring them in? *Huh*?" Vern's grin faded. "They'll say you murdered those two kids. And with your record them soldiers'll believe 'em. You'll end up in jail. Or hanged, more'n likely." The tall man shook his head. "Momma'll kill me if I let that happen." He took his own pistol from its holster and pulled back the hammer. "I hate to lose the bounty on this group, but I sure as Hell don't want Momma mad at me. C'mon. Let's clean up this mess you made."

Vern's grin returned.

Cesare watched in horror as the two men began firing. His mother's scream was cut short. Lucia died in silence. Vincenzo cried until a bullet pushed the life from his body. Cesare heard it all, even the shot that killed his unconscious father, but he saw none of it. He saw only his sister's face, her eyes, and her lips speaking to him as she died.

Stay there, *cara mia*. Stay there. Stay there.

He watched her face until the light in her eyes died and he heard the men mount up and ride back the way they'd come.

A lifetime later, he sat among the burial mounds. Dirt caked his arms and blackened his hands. It was beautiful soil—dark, deep, loamy enough to hold the water yet fine enough to drain off the excess. His father would have loved to plant it, work it. He smelled its life and could not keep the tears from his eyes, thinking of the death the fertile soil now enclosed.

Six graves. Five bodies.

Father. Mother. Salvatore. Vincenzo. Lucia.

And now one more: Fortuna.

Her eyes, once so large and dark, and her beauty so fair, lay ruined beside the last empty grave. He had kept her to be buried at the end—or had he been avoiding the duty? From around her neck he took the thin silver chain and baroque crucifix she had always worn. He wrapped her in the sackcloth that they had carried with them, cloth bought with a murdered man's gold. Then he kissed her cold lips and kissed her eyes a final time. As he stepped down and laid her deep in the earth where nothing would disturb her rest, something within him fluttered and twisted against its bonds. As he put the final length of cloth over her face, he felt the thing within him struggle. It grew frantic as he climbed out of the grave, and as he shoveled the dirt over his twin's shrouded body, it reared up and lashed at him, bursting forth in a torrent of emotion. It raged with his every breath, came out in shouts and howls as each shovelful thumped down upon her body. The grave filled, and the surging tide weakened until, finally, with the last spade of black soil, he felt it die. He did not know what it was, but he knew it had been the gentler part of him, the better part; the part that had been tied to her, the part they had shared.

Empty now, hollowed out, he felt nothing. Grief suffused him, numbing his every dimension. He stared at the mound, feeling the sun hot on his head, feeling the sting of sweat in his eyes. The wind freshened from the west, touching the back of his neck and cooling the hair plastered to his brow. He stared, and did not move for a long time. He looked at the graves and remembered Emilio's funeral. On that day, a priest had come to speak words over the dead, words to comfort the living. But Cesare wanted no priest. He wanted no advocate of God in this place. He did not want comfort.

And in that moment there was born within him something new. It grew, hot and sharp, in the empty place only so recently vacated.

He looked at the silver cross; so delicate against the dirty roughness of his hands. Sunlight glinted from its ornate edges. Near his feet, the pistol lay on a piece of paper. He picked up the paper, and looked at it again.

With an illiteracy forged by heavy truancy and a minimum of time in the schools of New York City, the words were little more than hen scratchings. Large and small, they meant less than nothing to him; the only part of the paper that made any sense was the darkened corner where his sister's life had bled out and stained it.

And that was all that Cesare needed to know. He took

his sister's cross, laid it on the paper, and folded it carefully around the cross and its thin chain. He folded it like an envelope, capturing the cross inside the words, and then put the packet in his shirt. He tucked the pistol into his belt, and then lifted to his shoulder the haversack in which he had put the few things he would need. He wanted to look back at the grass and the trees and the fine land that had almost been his, but he knew he would see the graves and he didn't think he wanted to see them again. But the thing inside him, the new thing that burned and cut, made him turn, forced him to look.

Six graves, in a circle.

And planted in their center, a grapevine.

CHAPTER 9

Moon When the Whistlers Get Fat, Waxing
Fifty-six Years after the Star Fell
Where the Elk River Meets the Big Greasy
Alliance Territory

George sat astride his walker, kept his gaze fixed straight ahead, and tried to ignore the argument that Mouse Road and Picking Bones Woman were carrying on behind him. The debate had begun two days prior and had adopted an odd, interrupted form. Miles would go by, hours would pass, in which neither of the combatants said a thing. And then, without any preamble whatsoever, one would speak, and a fusillade of words would ensue. Back and forth they'd snap and quip until suddenly the silence would resume. More time and miles would pass, and when the other began anew, the quarrel continued.

George had tried to interpose himself: at first with words—he quickly learned the error of that method—and then physically, positioning himself between Mouse Road on her whistler and Picking Bones Woman in her whistler-drawn travois, though in that case his walker only exacerbated the tensions. Normally, whistlers and walkers got along as well as sheep and sheepdogs, chickens and farm cats, but when the people around them were agitated, anything could happen.

Eventually he retreated to the vanguard, let the two women have at one another in their own intermittent manner, and tried to pretend he could not hear them.

It did not help that they were arguing about him.

"I can only imagine my grandfather's words," Mouse Road said in a raspy whisper that she thought George could not hear. "I can hear him now, when my father came asking to court you. 'Hmph,' he must have said. 'What do you want with my daughter, old man? She's too young for you. Go home.' ''

George sighed and stared ahead. The hills that rolled down to the Elk River were bright with flowers and deep-colored grass. Purple blossoms of little-grape-weed competed in wide patches with the blazing red tufts of the taller feather-flower. Between them, swaths of bluestem grass added depth to the green blades of wild grain. He could not see the river yet, but he knew they were in the lands used by the Closed Windpipe band for their winter camps. He hoped that the band had come down out of their mountain fastness and prayed that they had not continued on, heading south toward the summer rendezvous with the other bands. Between the women's bickering and the persistent pain of his wounds, he was not sure he could remain civil for that much longer.

"Leave your grandfather out of this," Picking Bones Woman said. "That was different."

Mouse Road challenged her. "How was it different?"

"Your father was the son of a chief."

"So is—" Mouse Road lowered her voice again. "So is One Who Flies. His father is the chief of all the Horse Nations."

"His father is Long Hair," Picking Bones Woman said, "and that is not the same thing."

George winced. For two days, the end of almost every barrage had come down to that, that or something like it. Sometimes it was Long Hair, his father. Other times the complaint was reduced to one word: *vé'ho'e,* the People's word for whiteman. He wondered if Picking Bones Woman would be critical of him had he been born of the People. His alien birth might be nothing more than a convenient excuse, but he was not sure.

"We will see," Mouse Road said. "My brother will understand."

"Hmm," her mother said. "An old woman can only hope."

George sighed quietly. His walker sensed his mood and rumbled, a vibration he felt in his knees, and he tried to settle her with a soft word before she riled the whistlers. He wanted to look back, to steal a glance at Mouse Road, to tell her without words of his feelings for her and that all would be well, but he knew that to do so might put him in line of the steely gaze of her mother. Ever since Mouse Road told her mother of her and George's growing attachment, Picking Bones Woman had not set aside a kind word for him.

He found it a very unusual situation. Never before had he been a suitor. As a colonel's son, he had received more than his share of attention from the leading families of the local frontier culture, but had been too young to take an interest. Later, when his father served in Congress and it was the cream of D.C. society that was willing to march its daughters into the fray, George's romantic endeavors had been restricted by the demands of a West Point education, which, apart from the occasional dance with a debutante at an evening cotillion, gave him neither the time nor the energy to develop amours.

In the army, though, that had changed. His posting back out on the frontier at Fort Whitley had thrown him into the company of a very different breed of men. After years in the protected, upper-crust world of generals, officers, senators, and politicians he found himself down among the ranks, face-to-face with men of common stock, and he a mere lieutenant forced at every step to substantiate his worth and right to command. Being the son of a legend only made matters worse.

It had not been long before he found himself in a frontier brothel in Candide, surrounded by the men of his company, confronted with the choice between bedding a flaccid, disinterested whore and building a wall between himself and the men of his command. He tried to think of what his father might do; wondered if in fact his father had ever been in the same situation. He remembered the good humor with which his father commanded; the pranks and japes he'd played on men and fellow officers alike. It had been with a weak smile that George looked back at his men before leaving the brothel's tawdry parlor and climbing the stairs to follow his partner's swishing skirts.

"Your first time?" she'd asked him after closing the door. His blush and stammer gave answer enough, but her whiskey laugh was not unkind. That evening began the latest chapter of George's education in the ways of women.

Until now.

With one gentle touch, Mouse Road had opened an entirely new book on the subject. Now he found himself befuddled and unable to make a straight-headed decision. While he knew precisely where she was at all times and was attuned to her every breath and word, he felt curiously out of touch with his own body. He bumped into things, continually fumbled with his gear, and had almost lopped off a finger while cutting a rope. It was as if he'd been asleep all his life and was now awake, or perhaps more accurately, that he was still asleep and was now dreaming for the first time. He had never been in love before. He was not sure he liked it.

But love, he knew, did not solve all problems. The People were strict in matters of the heart. Courtships could last for years, and a successful offer of marriage depended on the approval of the girl's father or eldest brother. While Mouse Road's brother was also George's friend, Storm Arriving's endorsement of his suit could not be taken for granted.

Not that I know the first thing about courting Cheyenne-style, he chided himself, and was stuck by his own thoughts. Am I really considering marriage? To Mouse Road?

He imagined the scene wherein he brought Mouse Road to meet his family.

She comes from a fine old family line, Father. You probably met a few of them in battle. A dowry? Well, Mother, she would bring twenty whistlers, fifty elk's teeth, a seventeen-skin lodge, and three wool blankets to the union of our families. A sizable sum, don't you agree?

The tableau of his mother's horror and his father's undoubted disgust filled him with a sudden futile melancholy. The encounter between Long Hair and George's Cheyenne sweetheart could never be anything but a disaster. But such a meeting was impossible, and that knowledge magnified the isolation of his position: standing between the worlds of the whiteman and the red, belonging to both, belonging to neither.

I have lived among the People for years, but I am still *different,* and will always be. Nothing can change that. Nothing.

It was a sobering realization, and one that might well

make the question of courtship moot. But if he did want to know about courting, he wondered whom he might ask. Not Storm Arriving, surely—a man never asked such things of the woman's brother. But then he remembered a conversation he had had with Three Trees Together. The old chief seemed to care about George and his life with the People. Maybe, when the People gathered for the summer hunting season, he could talk to him and ask his advice. If she was still interested in his suit by then . . .

He sighed, and was surprised to find himself wishing fondly for the well-traced pathways of white society. There he would know what to do, with whom to speak, and where he stood. Perhaps the paths were as well defined here among the Cheyenne, but they were unfamiliar to him, and he was lost searching for them in a sea of grass.

He gave in to his impulse and stole a look over his shoulder. Picking Bones Woman reclined atop the pile of folded lodgeskins on the packed travois. She was curled up beneath a buffalo robe, coughing quietly, staring westward, and keeping an eye on the rest of the household's belongings and whistler flock.

Mouse Road sat atop her mount, arms crossed and a frown pulling at her features. She stared at the ground as it passed slowly beneath her. Despite her petulant mood, her beauty and her dogged resolve made him smile, and he took in a gentle, restful breath. Again, his walker perceived his change of mood, rumbled deep in her keel-like breast, and looked back at him with an immense, golden eye. George scratched between her shoulder blades and returned his attention to the trail ahead.

It was a few hours later when, as they were climbing up a slope in the rolling landscape, they heard the first sounds from the Elk River. It was a faint shrieking, a high-pitched stew of sounds that grew louder as they crested the rise. The river snaked out of the hills and curved around a low ridge, laying a wide sandbar along its inner bank. Pale sand shone brightly beneath the sun, and above the beach flew a swirling cloud of small, gray-winged terns; a twisting legion that called out in *skrees* and *skirrs* that blended together into one great dissonant song. Hundreds filled the air, and hundreds more sat on the sandbar, keeping their eggs warm and safe. The river itself was alive with them, as well. They fell from the sky, sharp as dropped stones, pierced the surface, and came up with their wriggling reward. Then they spread their wings and returned to the screaming cloud above.

The whistlers began to trill and warble to each other, and as the wind shifted, George caught the scent of woodsmoke. It was only a few moments later that they came around a bend and saw, a mile ahead, scattered along the banks of the Elk River, the Closed Windpipe band's springtime encampment. Lodges dotted the sweep of land that lay inside a gentle curve in the river's course, and flocks of whistlers rested in the grass of the western hills, soaking up the sun.

"We are here," Mouse Road said, relief lightening her voice.

"Hmph," was all her mother found to say.

Riders—soldiers guarding the perimeter of the camp— came out to meet them, all seriousness and duty until they recognized George's pale hair.

"One Who Flies!" said Burning Stone. He was a mature man with gray in his braids, a Red Shield soldier long past his most effective days on the path of war. But he was still a bachelor and, reluctant to lose the companionship of his soldier society, he remained an active soldier. "Welcome back! It seems you were just here a day ago."

George smiled and indicated Mouse Road and her mother. "I bring the family of Storm Arriving for a visit. Is he in camp or out on patrol?"

The riders all laughed at that, though George did not understand the joke. "He is here," Burning Stone said. "Come, we'll ride in with you."

They nudged their whistlers into motion and headed slowly down toward the riverside camp.

"What was so funny?" George asked the elder soldier.

"About Storm Arriving? Not even Ma'heo'o could get him to leave camp during this moon." He laughed again. "I have never known a more anxious father-to-be." In a quieter voice, he asked, "What is wrong with the mother of Storm Arriving?"

George looked over at Picking Bones Woman. Though his own wounds still pained him, and though the journey had weakened him more than he had expected, he was thankful he had not asked her to wait another moon for their visit. The old woman was almost ashen in her weariness, and her heavy-lidded eyes showed no fire at the mention of her son.

"It has been a long trip," George said diplomatically, but saw that Burning Stone understood what he really meant.

Lodges had been set up in family groups, and were scattered along the river's course for the better part of a mile. Like most winter and springtime camps, families camped where they wished, instead of in the more orderly fashion of the great summer gatherings. The Closed Windpipe band was one of the largest of the ten bands of the People, numbering more than a thousand souls. George saw lodges hiding back up among the trees, tucked in among the hilly clefts, as well as down on the floodplain.

The river chattered as they rode downstream. Masked plovers piped among the reeds in the muddy shallows, fish broke the glimmering waters, and children played and swam along the shore. George and Mouse Road greeted friends with waves and smiles. He heard his Cheyenne name in the air—Ame'haooestse, One Who Flies—as news of their arrival ran before them. He looked over and saw that Picking Bones Woman now slept on the piled lodgeskins. He saw no reason to awaken her. She'd be awake soon enough.

"There," Burning Stone said, pointing. Through the new leaves of maples and alder, George spied a tall lodge, its feather and foxtail over-the-smokes swinging from the tips of the lodgepoles. Two whistlers were staked outside, and a meat-drying rack stood nearby, its bars heavy with venison. A woman emerged from the lodge, carrying a basket. She peered in their direction, then dropped her bundle and ran back inside. She returned with others, and George recognized the faces of his second family among the People: Magpie Woman, One Bear, and the family matriarch, Healing Rock Woman.

He led his walker to one side, keeping it away from the household and the whistlers tied nearby. Mouse Road woke her mother and greeted her brother's in-laws. George told his walker to lie down, and as he cautiously slid off her back, he heard a shout.

Storm Arriving came running at him, arms outstretched.

George tried to warn him off, but his impetuous friend grabbed him about the body and lifted him in a great bear hug that pressed a shout of pain from George's lungs.

"Great spirits!" Storm Arriving said, letting George gently to the ground. "I forgot. I am sorry, One Who Flies. I forgot."

George could not find his breath. He saw the shock and remorse on his friend's face and tried to reassure him, but had no air for it. The pain wrapped around his heart, tied to the twin wounds in his side, and each tiny movement of his ribs tightened the noose. He could only gulp at the air until suddenly Mouse Road was there, cradling him, laying him down on the grass, his head in her lap.

"Softly," she said to him, her hands caressing his brow. "Softly. Smooth breaths." He looked up into her face, felt her gentle touch wipe the sudden sweat from his brow. Her braids draped down over him, and he felt their silkiness against his neck. "Smooth breaths." He tried to comply, forcing his gasps to lengthen, to flatten out. He gazed at the serenity of her flawless skin, and the sweep of her jaw. He followed the curve down her neck. In the tradition of the People, she wore the left sleeve of her deerskin dress untied, exposing the shoulder and bow arm, and George let his sight travel across the bareness of her left shoulder, down her arm, to the hand that caressed his cheek. Her sweetness and care calmed him, and the jabbing pain receded, easing the noose around his heart.

"Good," she said, and George saw her smile. He looked up, past her, and saw Storm Arriving. The tall warrior's face was a cloud of mixed emotions as he watched his sister's intimate ministrations.

George blinked and took a deeper breath. The pain was still there, but bearable now. He started to sit up, and though Mouse Road protested, Storm Arriving was there to help him. Eventually he stood, one arm holding his side, the other leaning on Storm Arriving for support.

"Forgive me," his friend said sincerely, but George saw, too, his sidelong glance at his sister.

"Nothing to forgive," George said, and he managed a weak smile as he limped toward the family's common lodge. Picking Bones Woman was awake, and One Bear had lifted her down off the travois.

"Mother," Storm Arriving said, and held out his free hand to her. "I am glad you are here."

She took his hand in hers. "So am I," she said with an unmistakable *we will talk later* look. Then she smiled and turned to the others. "Where is she?" she asked. "Where is the woman who will give me my first grandchild?"

"Here," said a voice, and Speaks While Leaving stood by the doorflap to the family lodge. She was large with child, her deerskin dress stretched across a belly full and high beneath her swollen breasts. Both Picking Bones Woman and Mouse Road alike abandoned the men and went to her. George chuckled. Storm Arriving caught the good humor and laughed as well.

That evening, in the family's main lodge, skewers of fresh venison crusted in herbs spat and hissed over the coals and filled the air with the perfume of sage and roasting meat. Mouse Road sat near the doorflap on the guest side of the lodge, while George and Picking Bones Woman had both been installed on beds of furs and hides. To their right, One Bear, as head of the family, sat in the *vá'ôhtáma,* the place of honor farthest from the door. Next to him was Storm Arriving, and then the three generations of women in the family: ancient Healing Rock Woman, her daughter Magpie Woman, and granddaughter Speaks While Leaving.

Though immensely pregnant, Speaks While Leaving still carried out her duties as youngest daughter. George watched as she waddled about the lodge, tending the fire, trimming the turniplike tubers for the evening meal, but when she got up to fetch more water, George spoke up.

"And who shall help me?" she asked him with a smile. "You?"

"I'll help," Mouse Road said.

"Guests don't fetch water," Speaks While Leaving said.

"I don't mind," Mouse Road said with a glance back at George. "Besides, I am youngest daughter."

Speaks While Leaving checked with her mother. Magpie Woman shrugged and smiled, and Speaks While Leaving held out the waterskins. Mouse Road took them, smiled demurely in George's direction, and followed Speaks While Leaving outside. Then George noticed that Storm Arriving was looking at him, his face inscrutable.

Walk with me, Storm Arriving signed. Then he stood and quietly left the lodge.

George wondered what custom he'd trodden on this time. After three years with the People, he still tripped over unknown points of etiquette now and again. He made to rise but winced in pain. He waved off Magpie Woman's offer of help, got to one knee, then to his feet, and slowly made his way outside.

The sky, between clouds of gray wool, had deepened into a bowl of cobalt and lapis. In the east a few stars had awakened, and in the west the hills were indigo mounds. Storm Arriving stood in the gloaming, his deerskin tunic preternaturally pale in the fading light. His skin was so dark he seemed to be made of shadow, and George could not see what expression he wore. He turned as George reached him, and headed off between the lodges, uphill, away from the river.

"I'm sorry," George said as he struggled to catch up. "Was it wrong to ask if she needed help?"

Storm Arriving stopped and looked at George. "What?"

"Your wife. She just looked so uncomfortable. Was it wrong of me to speak of it?"

He waved a hand. "No. I'm glad you did. She insists on doing everything. Her mother has been trying to help her for nearly a moon now."

George was puzzled. "Then . . . then what is wrong? What did you want to talk about?"

He started walking again, but slower this time so George could keep up. He stared at the sky as he walked. George looked up as well but quickly looked back down again, unwilling to risk a fall in the dark.

"How long has my mother been that way?"

George sighed. "Most of the winter, from what Mouse Road tells me. She was a little better for a while, but the trip took a lot out of her."

"Then why did you bring her?" Storm Arriving asked sharply.

"She wanted to come," George explained. "It was her idea. She's afraid she's going to die, and she wanted to see you first."

"It was foolish to bring her all this way." His tone was

brusque, his features angry. "The baby may not come for weeks, and even when it does, babies often die. It would have been best for her to wait. You should have made her wait."

George stopped. He yanked the taller man's arm to turn him around. "You aren't listening to me. She wanted to see *you* before she died. She may make a big fuss over the baby, but she's here to see you. And she didn't care if she killed herself getting here—or me, for that matter—she wanted to see *you*." He looked up at the sky and let his irritation fade in the beauty of stars glimmering between the pallid clouds. "You know how stubborn she is."

Storm Arriving expelled a breath into the cooling night air. "Yes, I do," he said, calming himself. "When she wants something, no man can stop her. I'm sorry to have dragged you out here. Let's get back to the fire."

George considered bringing up the subject of Mouse Road, but seeing his friend's edginess, he decided to leave it alone for the moment. There would be plenty of time to discuss it later, during the summer. So, instead, he changed the subject. "Have you heard anything from the south?"

"Some news," Storm Arriving said. "None of it good. Several patrols have come back with tales of *vé'hó'e* lodges all over the lands south of the Sudden River, and the eastern bands tell of bluecoats raiding in small groups, just as we used to raid the bluecoat forts and supply wagons. It is worrisome, especially this news of settlers. Black Cloud says that the *vé'hó'e* have sprouted in the land overnight, like fireweed after a burn."

"And he says they are *vé'hó'e?* Regular families, not bluecoats?"

"Yes," Storm Arriving said. "Families. Not bluecoats. I had hoped that when we destroyed their bridge over the Big Greasy, it would have kept them out of our lands."

"So had I," George said. "I guess we only kept out the iron roads. The people have come anyway." They came back in sight of the lodge. "What do you think should be done?"

Storm Arriving shrugged. "I do not know. The *vé'hó'e* . . ." His voice trailed off as he searched the sky for the words he wanted. "They never stop. I think we could kill every one of them, and by morning there would only be more." He glanced at George briefly, then looked away. "How can we stop them, One Who Flies? How can we keep them away?"

George halted a few yards from the lodge. The firelight filled it up like a Chinese lantern, and he could see the shadows of the family as they sat around the hearth. Their cheerful voices and laughter seemed at odds with his feelings.

"I don't know," he said at last. "After all we've done, and with all the killing and danger, I don't understand them."

"Then we are lost," Storm Arriving said. "If you cannot understand them, the rest of us have no hope."

George heard the despair in his friend's voice. He forced a smile on his face. "Don't worry. We will think of something. Together, we will think of something."

They turned to enter the lodge when out of the darkness, Mouse Road came running. Her eyes were wide with fright. Storm Arriving grabbed her by the arm.

"What is it?" he asked, but Mouse Road only stammered a few syllables and ran inside. "What is it?" he demanded as he and George stepped through the opening. George saw Mouse Road whispering to Magpie Woman, saw them both begin gathering items together: a blanket, a waterskin, a small painted parfleche. Storm Arriving kept querying as his sister took the items and dashed back out of the lodge, leaving him standing there, flustered and sputtering.

"Sit down," Picking Bones Woman said. Her voice was thick with fatigue, but there was a smile on her face. "Come. Sit with me as my son for this last night. Tomorrow you will be a father."

Storm Arriving stared at her, dumbfounded, until slowly a grin crept across his features.

"Yes?" he asked her.

"Yes," she said. "Now come and sit by the fire while we wait."

Mouse Road juggled the bundles and tucked them up under one arm. She unstaked the halter that kept the whistler near the lodge, and led it toward the river. Halfway there she realized that riding the whistler back to Speaks While Leaving would have been smarter. Just as she was chiding herself for not thinking more clearly, she stumbled and her parcels went flying. The whistler shied and she had to coo and coax it back to placidity before she could kneel in the grass and gather up the things she'd dropped. She wrapped everything in the blanket and started off again.

Despite her clumsiness, she found Speaks While Leaving just where she had left her when the first contraction gripped her in its sharp fingers. Her sister-in-law was kneeling in the water at the river's edge, her hands on her thighs, her face wrapped in a grimace of pain. Mouse Road could see the starlit sheen of sweat on her brow.

"I am here," Mouse Road said. "I brought the things you wanted."

Speaks While Leaving signed her thanks, unable to find the breath for words. She struggled to rise and Mouse Road came to her side. The whistler crouched at a command and Mouse Road helped Speaks While Leaving climb atop its back. Then she tied the blanket's corners together. Speaks While Leaving took the bundle and slung it over her shoulder.

"Let me come with you," Mouse Road said.

Speaks While Leaving frowned. "What? No," she said. "This is the way it is done."

"But I could help—"

"No," she said firmly, then took a breath. "Forgive me, my sister, but no. This is a private thing, and it would not be proper. This is the way it is done." And before Mouse Road could protest, she touched the whistler's flank and set it walking.

Mouse Road watched the whistler head off toward the dark hills. She looked back toward the lodges, saw their warm glow among the trees. The drumbeats of the legend-songs, of game-songs, of medicine-songs, thrummed like a hundred hearts through the deepening night, and she felt her own bloodpulse—still strong in her breast, still rapid with unspent fear—an echo to the drums. She imagined her brother waiting at home with their mother, anxious, worried, but trying to be cheerful, trying not to speak of the one thing on his mind. Women had died bringing their children into the world; she had known one, Little Bird, wife of Sweetgum Tree, who had given birth while out digging for roots. By the time anyone found her, she had bled out her life on the ground, and the babe had been carried off by coyotes.

I don't care if it isn't proper, she said to herself. What if something happens to her? What will my brother say? And Mother, who thinks me too young to be woman to One Who Flies, how much less will she think of me if Speaks While Leaving has trouble and I have done nothing to help?

The whistler was still visible, a waddling moonlit shadow near the last of the lodges. Out past the camp perimeter, a coyote yipped and yowled. The choice was simple. To be safe, she couldn't abandon her brother's wife. She crouched and started off, following the whistler's swaying tail.

Speaks While Leaving rode up and over a ridge, sitting sideways on the whistler's back. Mouse Road could hear her singing a soft song, a song of welcome for the baby. She followed silently, keeping low and as far behind as she could. If Speaks While Leaving didn't know she was there, she wouldn't be upset by her presence. If something happened, though, she'd be able to help at once. It was dark out beyond the light from the lodges, and Mouse Road struggled as her eyes slowly adjusted to the light from the sliver of moon. She followed them out a half mile or so to a tree-lined ravine. A creek gurgled down the deep track and Speaks While Leaving rode up into the shelter of the wood.

Mouse Road tried to keep silent as she trailed them in among the brush and undergrowth. She followed in the whistler's path, timing her own footsteps to match the beast's. The whistler warbled and looked back in her direction, but Speaks While Leaving moaned in pain and urged the whistler onward.

They came to a small clearing beneath a large tree. The light was very dim, and Mouse Road could barely discern the whistler as it crouched down to let Speaks While Leaving dismount. She tied the whistler's halter to a branch, and then squatted down against a large, smooth boulder that stood beside the creek. Mouse Road stayed low and sidled behind a bush.

Speaks While Leaving was breathing rapidly, holding the

largeness of her belly in her arms. She moaned again, seemed to relax, took in a long breath of air, and let it out slowly.

"You are eager," she said to her unborn babe. "That can be a good thing, but you will need patience, as well. Let me tell you a story about patience."

As she spoke to the child in her belly, she knelt and unwrapped the blanket she had brought. She took out the waterskin and the parfleche and set them to one side.

A pile of sticks lay nearby, firewood that she had collected earlier against her birth pains coming at night. She began laying the wood for a small fire, stacking twigs over dried leaves. From the parfleche she removed a flint and steel. The sparks filled the clearing with flashes of silent lightning, and soon the seed of a fire lay in the tinder. She blew on it gently, nursing it, capturing it with bits of dry moss. Smoke threaded upward into the blue night and the glowing seed began to flower. Mouse Road saw her sister-in-law's face lit by the burgeoning flames. Speaks While Leaving was a handsome woman, with high cheekbones and long, deep-set eyes, but now, with her pregnancy, her features were fuller than they had been; Mouse Road thought she looked less like the revered seeress, oracle of the People, and more like a woman and mother.

The fire crackled as it bit at the twigs. Speaks While Leaving fed it with larger pieces, and when those had taken, she spread them out to keep them from burning too fast. Opening the parfleche once more, she took out a long braid of dried grass, and touched one end to the flames. The grass sizzled as it caught and began to smoke.

"This is sweetgrass," she told her babe. "Can you smell it? Can you smell how sweet the smoke is? It is a wonderful smell that cleanses the spirit and the mind." With one hand she held the smoking braid, while with the other she pulled the smoke toward her, bathing herself in its scent. Mouse Road knew that scent, could imagine it in her mind; it was like honeyed sunlight, and just the thought of it calmed her.

Firelight filled the clearing with its lively light and its smells of home and family. The boulder against which Speaks While Leaving rested was a huge, moss-covered mass with a humped spine and one flat side. The creek was shiny and black as it flowed before her in its stony bed.

The maple next to the boulder was so old that its trunk
was wider than two men could encompass with their arms.
Its lowest branches reached out into the thin column of
smoke with deeply lobed leaves larger than a man's hand.
In the treetops high above, the western breeze blew, but
down here, protected by brush and the ravine's steep sides,
the air remained still and hushed. The rustle of the canopy
was a sigh above the prattling of the cozy fire and the idle
gossip of the creek. The whistler, comforted by the closeness of the fire, settled in and laid down its head for the
night.

Mouse Road watched the flames—orange, yellow, sometimes green or blue—and shivered. She wished she had
thought to bring a blanket for herself. She tied up the left
sleeve of her dress, sat down on the soft forest floor, and
hugged her knees closely to conserve her warmth.

Speaks While Leaving sucked in a hiss of air. She bit her
lip and her face twisted up into a knot. She moaned—a
low, guttural thing like the snarl of a cornered dog—and
bared her teeth. Her breathing grew stronger, faster. It
came out in forced punches, each with a grunt, as if she
could breathe in but couldn't get it out. She writhed, her
arms stroking her belly and her back in turns. Then Mouse
Road saw her sit back and spread her legs. She reached up
under the hem of her dress, up to where the baby would
eventually emerge, and began to rub herself in a way that
Mouse Road had sometimes done herself. Suddenly embarrassed, Mouse Road hid her face in her arms, her cheeks
burning. She listened as Speaks While Leaving's moans
slowly changed from pain to pleasure. It was an old wives'
wisdom that such pleasure eased the coming of a child, but
it was something that Mouse Road and her girlfriends had
whispered but never believed. Her thoughts turned unbidden to One Who Flies and she felt her own lower lips grow
wet. Her heartbeat ran wild as she tried to think of something else, tried to hear something else, but all she heard
was passion, and all she could think of was the man she
loved, with his kind voice, his gentle touch, and his hair
like summer grass. Finally, when Speaks While Leaving had
reached her peak, Mouse Road allowed herself a quick
look up.

Speaks While Leaving sat with her back against the rock.

The pain was gone from her face, but she looked tired. She reached for the waterskin and took a sip, and then wrapped the blanket around her shoulders. Across the creek, beyond the limits of the fire's light, something moved in the undergrowth. Speaks While Leaving picked up a stone and tossed it into the darkness. The coyote yipped in surprise and scrabbled up the creekbed.

In time, the waxing moon disappeared behind the ridge and the night settled down upon the trees, kept at bay only by the light from Speaks While Leaving's tiny fire. The coyote howled from the lip of the ravine, and far away, the night answered. The birthing pains rose and fell, each gasping crest closer than the last, each respite shorter than the one before. Mouse Road shivered through each locus of agony, feeling her ignorance of such things, and wondering how she'd ever know if something was really wrong. The next wave came and Mouse Road grimaced in sympathy. Her sister-in-law began to seethe with the pain but then cried out. Mouse Road looked up and saw Speaks While Leaving wide-eyed. Her hands explored the shape of her belly and firelight shone from the sweat that beaded her brow.

"No," she moaned, and Mouse Road heard the desperation in her voice. The time for secrecy was over. Speaks While Leaving needed her. She rose from her hiding place, her legs stiff and clumsy from inactivity, and went down toward the circle of firelight.

Speaks While Leaving looked up in surprise, and then broke into tears. She beckoned Mouse Road close, grabbed onto the leather of her dress when she got within reach. Her face was slick with sweat, her nostrils wide, and the dark irises of her eyes nearly swallowed by huge black pupils.

"The baby has not turned," she said. "Help me." Mouse Road stared at her. "I need you to turn the baby," Speaks While Leaving explained.

"How?"

Speaks While Leaving swallowed with difficulty. Mouse Road offered her water and she sipped at it, then waved it away. "I will tell you. I will show you. Feed the fire."

Mouse Road did as she was told. Speaks While Leaving lay back on her blanket. She had taken off her leggings and pulled her dress up, exposing her legs and her abdomen. An angry red line ran down the middle of her belly, and her navel stood out from the otherwise smooth skin like a pebble balanced on a riverworn stone. She still wore her rope—the talisman of virtue worn by every woman among the People. It was tied around her hips, passing low under her distended belly, and from it two smaller ropes twined down between her legs, coiling about each leg until tied off just above the knee.

"Take off the rope," she told her. "It will only get in the way."

Mouse Road complied. Her sister's skin was hot to the touch. Across the creek, the coyote whined, drawn by the scent of birthwater and sweat.

"Now," Speaks While Leaving said. "We must turn the baby."

"Show me."

Speaks While Leaving showed her where to push, where to pull. Mouse Road could feel the outline of the baby within her sister's womb. Its legs were underneath it, the knees pointing upward, its head beneath Speaks While Leaving's ribs.

"Turn it," she said.

Mouse Road took a deep breath and then began to apply pressure as Speaks While Leaving had instructed her. Speaks While Leaving grunted with the effort.

"Harder," she told her. "Stronger underneath."

Mouse Road pushed, but she was afraid. "I don't want to hurt it," she said.

"Harder. I'll tell you if you need to stop."

Mouse Road pushed, cramming the heel of her hand down into the curve above the pelvis, pulling at the top beneath her ribs. Speaks While Leaving yowled, her fists gripping Mouse Road's dress in white-knuckled bunches. Mouse Road kept up the pressure, rocking the baby within the womb. Speaks While Leaving yelped and cried, tears mixing with the sweat that covered her entire body. Mouse Road pushed, rocked, pressed, pulled. Speaks While Leaving gasped.

And then it moved. In a single, fluid movement, the baby moved and spun, turning and slipping into a new position. Mouse Road pulled back. Speaks While Leaving's gasps became sighs of relief. Mouse Road saw her smile, and when they both felt for the baby, it was fine, kicking and ready to enter the world.

Mouse Road stayed with her sister-in-law, tending the fire, giving her sips of water from the skin, and tossing stones to keep the coyote beyond the fire. The contractions were constant now, and Speaks While Leaving's breath was short and rapid.

"The baby is coming," she said between gasps. She pulled herself up into a squat, facing Mouse Road and bracing herself on her shoulders. Mouse Road looked into her face. She sensed that Speaks While Leaving was very far away from their place by the fire. Her gaze was unfocused, her every muscle bunched and tight. Mouse Road felt her sister's fingers digging into her shoulders, she could feel the heat that radiated from her, and she felt her own skin tauten as she smelled the thick aroma of blood and sweat. The whistler raised its head, its eye alert. The skin along its muzzle rippled pale ash and bright crimson in apprehension. Mouse Road looked behind her and saw the coyote on the far side of the fire, a ghost at the limit of light. It lifted its nose and sniffed the air, then sat down to wait. Its eyes glowed with borrowed light. The wind had died, and the forest around them was silent but for the incessant babble of water over the stones.

Speaks While Leaving's eyes opened wide and her grip relaxed. Mouse Road grew fearful but then her sister smiled. "Yes," she rasped, and tensed once more. She grunted like a man lifting a buffalo—a long, powerful building of strength. Mouse Road felt the hair on her arms stand up. She reached down beneath Speaks While Leaving and felt the crown of the baby's head. It was slick and wet and did not feel like any baby she'd ever known. Speaks While Leaving took a deep breath and grunted again, her face turgid as she pushed and pushed. The baby's head emerged, eerily pale and ghostly. Mouse Road reached out with both hands and caught the baby as it came out in a single, wet surge of arms, legs, and liquid. Speaks While Leaving gasped with the release and her next breath came out in a laugh.

The baby was still covered by the birth sac. Speaks While Leaving took the infant from Mouse Road's hands. She pierced the caul with her finger and stripped it away from the baby's face. Its features were round and swollen, but its head was covered with silky black hair. As she pulled the rest of the sack away, they saw that it was a girl.

"A daughter," Mouse Road said.

Speaks While Leaving smiled. "Your brother will be pleased." She grimaced again in pain.

"What is wrong?" Mouse Road asked.

Speaks While Leaving tensed and pushed, and after a moment the afterbirth splashed to the ground, soaking the air with the scent of blood. She sighed then, and sat back on the blanket. She massaged the girl, rubbing her chest and cleaning her face. Mouse Road heard the baby mew, then cry. Finally the girl took a shuddering breath and let it out in a high, tremulous wail, a bleating cry that sounded part laughter, part shivering fear. Mouse Road laughed and realized that she was crying, too. Speaks While Leaving simply smiled.

"My things," she said, and Mouse Road retrieved the parfleche. Speaks While Leaving tied a piece of leather around her daughter's birthcord and then severed the cord with a knife. She placed the cord with the caul and the rest of the afterbirth near the edge of the fire. "We will leave it for our friend," she said, and Mouse Road saw the patient coyote lick its lips as it sat at the edge of the firelight.

The little girl squalled and fussed as her mother swabbed her clean and swaddled her in a soft beaver pelt. Mouse Road buried the fire with dirt, and then helped Speaks While Leaving to her feet and thence onto the whistler's back. She gathered up the blanket and other items, and took the whistler's halter in hand.

"Up," she bade the beast, and smoothly—as if sensing the fragility of its riders—it stood. The baby, warm again in her furs and close once more to her mother's heartbeat, became quiet. Mouse Road saw her sister's peace and felt it fill the clearing. In the east, the morning star was a silver ember in the paling sky.

As Mouse Road led the whistler back down toward the camp, she began to sing a quiet song of welcome.

The celebration was in its third day, and George was more exhausted than when he had arrived.

The first day—from the dawning morn when Mouse Road finally returned with a tired but smiling Speaks While Leaving and her swaddled babe—had been marked by a continuous stream of well-wishers. Word spread fast. Neighbors, friends—everyone in the entire band, it seemed to George—took the time to come by the lodge of Speaks While Leaving and Storm Arriving. As favored friend, George was invited to stay with the families and greet the guests, but in truth he did little more than sit back and smile.

The women who came by cooed at the new addition, said how beautiful she was, and how much she looked like her mother. Their husbands stood back, usually with a quiet smile, or they sat down next to Storm Arriving and told tales of their own firstborn. George found the intense curiosity of the youngest children the most entertaining aspect of the entire day. The People did not have many children: a couple might parent only two children during their marriage. Births, therefore, were rare and instilled a wide-eyed fascination in the visiting toddlers that proved endearing and often quite humorous as the unnamed infant cried out or wriggled. That first day had been filled with arrivals, congratulations, stories, and friendship, and though he had done nothing, George was worn out by the time the sun set. Seeing that Picking Bones Woman was even more tired than he, he offered to walk her to her lodge and thus excused himself for the evening.

The second day was a day of preparation. Storm Arriving and a few of his fellow Kit Fox soldiers headed out at dawn to hunt for the next day's feast. George, still weak and bruised from the trip, his wounds, and Storm Arriving's exuberant greeting, was told that he should stay; a directive that was, he admitted, perfectly acceptable. Mouse Road spent her day running errands and delivering invitations, and all the other women headed out to collect wild roots, berries, and herbs for the feast.

On the third day, the excitement began to build. The men returned with an elk for the banquet feast. When the sun was at the top of the cloud-studded sky, guests began to arrive. A fire was built in a space in front of the family's lodges. Speaks While Leaving sat in a place of honor near the main lodge, on a fine buffalo skin. She held her new babe in her arms, and was the focus of every attention. Mouse Road had been given a place of importance to her right, and her grandmother, mother, and mother-in-law sat close by. The rest of her female relatives began to prepare the game and food for the feast, and the smell of roasting meat soon filled the air.

The men kept themselves occupied with games and competitions. Burning Stone began to define an impromptu racecourse.

"We start here," he said, pointing to the central clearing before the feast's firepit, "and run straight down to the river, then over to the trunk of the sweet-gum tree where my father killed a bear." He looked around for another suitable marker. "Then up the hill—"

Men grumbled and groused.

"—*up the hill*," he continued, "to the rock where Two Fingers always sat and played his flute, then down around the Kit Fox lodge, and back here. Agreed?"

It was. "And One Who Flies shall start us," Burning Stone said.

George laughed. "What if I want to run?"

"You will not run," Mouse Road said, and then hid her face from the looks of surprise her edict engendered. Speaks While Leaving patted her companion's arm.

"She is right, One Who Flies. You are still healing. It would not be wise to run a race."

George held up his hands in mock surrender, smiling. "I cannot deny the wisdom of our honored hostess," he said amid the teasing laughter of the other men. "So when you are all ready . . ."

The runners gathered at the starting point—boys of thirteen summers, men of forty years; soldiers, fathers, and brothers—about three dozen contestants in all, and every man shoving and jostling and laughing as he waited for George to say—

"Run!"

And they ran, off in a cloud of laughter and dust heading down toward the river. Out in front: the young boys, shouting as they ran. Behind them the soldiers and young men ran in a pack, pacing themselves for the two-mile course. And, in the rear, the elder runners, men beyond their fighting years but still strong and easily able to complete the race. They ran, and George watched them go, not wishing to be with them, but simply satisfied in being part of the proceedings; happy at being included.

"Who do you think will win?" George turned to find Healing Rock Woman standing at his side.

"I don't know," he said. The boys were already fading into the pack as the energy from their jackrabbit start began to wither. "I suppose the others might let Storm Arriving win."

"Psh," the old woman said. "That would be rude. No, the winner will be the fastest. You should know that by now."

George shrugged. "There are a lot of things I don't know," he said. "About a lot of things."

"Like about courting?" she asked in a manner so pococurante that George had to smile.

"Who have you been talking to?" he asked as the racers set one foot in the river and then headed up toward the sweet gum grove.

Healing Rock Woman chuckled. "I don't have to talk to anyone to see a love match brewing on my doorstep. Nor to see that her mother is not pleased."

"No," George said. "I suppose not."

"Have you spoken to her brother?"

Excited shouts could be heard from the sweet gum grove, and the first of the runners appeared from within its green bower. The younger soldiers were in the lead, the boys having lagged behind them. Storm Arriving was with the leaders, but now they faced the long climb up the hill.

"I was going to speak to him," George said, "but I didn't know what to say. And then" —he nodded back toward Speaks While Leaving and her new baby— "other things took precedence."

Healing Rock Woman looked back at the women gathered around her granddaughter. "Yes," she said, suddenly serious, "and I fear there will be other things, too." But she brightened a bit as she turned back to George. "There will be no good time to talk to him, One Who Flies, so talk to him soon. Talk to him tonight."

George shrugged. The pack of runners thinned as they struggled up the hillside. "I have never courted anyone before, not even among the *vé'hó'e*. What do I say? That I love his sister?"

Healing Rock Woman laughed. "That sounds like something One Who Flies would say," she said. "You *could* say that, but I suggest you just ask his permission to court her."

The runners were silent now as they ran down the slope toward the lodge where the Kit Fox soldiers held their society meetings. Yellow Rock and Standing Elk, two men in their early twenties, were in the lead. Many of the young boys were still limping up the slope, holding their sides, gasping for air as the more mature runners passed them by.

George glanced back at Mouse Road. The young woman was asking something of her mother, but Picking Bones Woman waved away her concern and leaned against her backrest to nap. Mouse Road looked up and saw George. She smiled and her eyes turned up into happy crescents before she looked down in proper modesty. Asking permission to court Mouse Road was low on the list of things George ever wanted to experience—he had no idea how Storm Arriving would react to such a request—but not asking was an option unworthy of consideration.

"And if he allows me to court her? What then?"

Healing Rock Woman gave him a sidelong glance. "Don't you know anything about women?"

"Among the People?" George protested. "No. I don't."

Healing Rock Woman squinted and pursed her lips. "Ask him tonight. Talk to me about the rest later." She turned and went back to the other women.

The runners were coming in from the Kit Fox lodge. Yellow Rock and Standing Elk shouted and laughed, pulling at each other to gain the lead. A hand on a shoulder, a bump with an elbow, and then a headlong dash to the end. George watched closely as they crossed the line, and when the others came pelting in, he declared Standing Elk the winner by a single step.

Other games kept everyone occupied while the food finished cooking—gambling games for the women, wrestling and stick games for the men—and at last Magpie Woman called everyone back to eat.

The elk had been roasted in a sage and red-berry crust. Diced white-apple roots, spring onions, and cracked corn had been stewed in clay pots to make a savory porridge. And, as at every gathering of three or more of the People, there were piles of hot, golden skillet-bread: disks and triangles of dough fried in fat, crispy on the outside and steaming hot on the inside. The laughter and conversations waned as the food was served and hungry guests fell to, but as the sun began to set and the edge of everyone's hunger had abated, Speaks While Leaving's father stood up and went into the lodge.

One Bear returned with a large whistler-skin drum and several beating sticks. The drum was almost four feet across, and he took it over to some of the older guests. Each man took a stick and they sat in a circle surrounding the drum. They began their beat—a slow, sonorous pulsation that rang and quavered—and then they started to sing.

They sang of grass. They sang of the cool bluestem, of the warm red of buffalo grass. They sang of broad blades and seed-heavy heads. They sang of the carpet of life that covered the prairie and fed the buffalo, the People's provider spirit. Their music rose and fell as would the wind across the land, and their voices warbled like meadowlarks at dawn.

It didn't take long for the younger men to get up and begin to dance. The drummers closed their eyes as they sang. The drumbeat filled the twilight with its steady thrum, and the men's voices joined in tremulous concert. The dancers' movements were rapid, their hands as quick as buffalo grass in the wind. It was a fine dance and, George knew, only the first of many that would take the celebrants well toward morning. He saw Storm Arriving seated near his wife, and wondered if he should speak to him now. The first dance drew to a close and George finished his piece of skillet-bread. He was about to rise when Storm Arriving himself stood up and asked for everyone's attention.

"Friends," he began, "I thank you for coming to our feast." He turned to Speaks While Leaving and she handed to him their daughter in her bundle of furs. Storm Arriving cradled her in his arms. "This is my firstborn's naming day, and I am proud to share it with all of you. To mark this day, I will give one whistler to Red Cloud and two to Swift Water Woman, who lost her husband to the cold of winter. I will also give a buffalo pelt to One Who Flies, who did me the kindness of bringing my mother here in time for this happy day."

The guests all murmured at Storm Arriving's show of

generosity. Burning Stone sat next to George. "It is a giving worthy of a chief," he said.

Yellow Rock sat on George's other side. "Storm Arriving is much like his father," the soldier said in approval.

Storm Arriving held his daughter out in both hands, presenting her to the guests. "I name this woman after one who went on into the spirit world before her time. I name this woman after my sister, now departed. I name her: Blue Shell Woman."

"It is a good name," Burning Stone said.

"She was a fine woman," George said, remembering the day that she had died at the hands of the American soldiers. "With a strong will and a brave heart."

"High praise," Yellow Rock said with a pat to George's shoulder.

Storm Arriving gave the newly named Blue Shell Woman back to her mother's arms, and before George could even think of getting up, the drumbeat started once more and Storm Arriving had joined the dance.

Speaks While Leaving retired for the evening, as did many of the elderly guests. George spied Mouse Road leading her mother away; Picking Bones Woman looked ashen, and she leaned heavily on her daughter's arm. For his own part, George did not feel too strong either, but he was determined to speak to Storm Arriving before the night was out. His opportunity did not come until well after moonset.

Storm Arriving took a rest from dancing and went to the side of elk to get a rib to gnaw. George made his way through the crowd of smiles and grins until he reached his friend.

"One Who Flies," Storm Arriving greeted him. "I haven't had a chance to talk to you today."

"No," George said. "It has been a busy day. May I speak with you now?"

"Of course."

"Alone?"

Storm Arriving sensed the change in situation, and George guessed that his friend already knew what it was he wanted to discuss. "Are you fit to walk awhile?"

"Yes," George said.

Storm Arriving stripped the last thread of meat from the

rib and threw the cleaned bone into the fire. He beckoned George to follow him out beyond the circle of music and dance.

They walked toward the river, the moon high overhead. A bat chittered through the darkness, and across the river a screech owl sounded its rough-edged call. Now that the opportunity was present, George found himself unable to speak his heart. Frantically he searched for the words that would unlock his tongue, but none came until, finally, all his thoughts united in one name.

"Mouse Road," he said.

"Yes." Storm Arriving did not sound pleased.

"I would like . . ." George had been through so much with Storm Arriving: happiness and tragedy, joy and anger. The man who had once wanted to kill him was now his most trusted friend, but George had seen several times— at the Point, in the army—how love could change a friendship. To ask his question might risk that friendship, but to deny it . . . what happiness lay down that road? "I would like your permission," he continued, "to court your sister."

Storm Arriving stopped and looked out over the river's smooth flow. Starlight tipped the wavelets with silver. The air was filled with the shush of water and the distant pulse of the drum. The two men stood there, watching the scene. George waited until his friend finally chose to speak.

"I have seen the way she looks at you," he said. "I know that look. It is not the look of a girl's summer fancy. She looks at you with a woman's eyes." He sighed.

George imagined how he might have felt if one of his old West Point comrades had become enamored of Maria or Lydia, and he did not envy Storm Arriving his predicament. Nothing he could say could mollify his friend's feelings, so he opted for silence.

"My heart wants to say yes and be joyful," Storm Arriving said, "but my mind wants to find a reason to say no. There are others who have asked after her. In the past, I always said she was too young, but that is no longer true." He turned his back on the river and looked back toward the glow of the banquet fire. "Our women are not like some *vé'hó'e* women I have heard of. A courtship is a lengthy and serious undertaking. Forgive me for speaking

plainly of matters that should be left unsaid, but there will
be no quick pleasure with my sister."

"I would not think of such a thing," George averred.

"I remember several moons past," Storm Arriving said,
"when you were not sure if your path lay with the path of
the People. What do you say now?"

George thought of his family, his parents and sisters, and
of his desire to see them. But when he thought of them he
remembered his visit from the Thunder Beings—or was it
only a dream?—and he remembered the one who had
pointed to the world just outside the lodgeskins.

Your family is here, he had said.

"My path lies with the People," he said.

"And Mouse Road? Are you sure about her?"

"No," George said truthfully. "But that is what a courtship is for."

Storm Arriving stood for a long silent moment. "I will
consider your request," he said at last. "I will let you know
in the morning."

But George and Storm Arriving did not talk in the morning. Upon their return to the camp, George excused himself
and went to his lodge. He lay in his furs, listening to the
heartbeat of the drum, the tramp of the dancers' feet, and
the wailing tales the singers wove through the night. As he
lay there, drifting in and out of a painful sleep, he heard
in their songs the rising note of the wind. He saw—or
dreamed he saw—the two black-skinned spirit men dancing
unseen with the celebrants, apparent to him only by their
shadows on the skins of his lodge. He heard their voices
as thunder over the horizon, and wondered if that was why
they had not spoken to him in words.

Your family is here, they had told him. *Family is important.*

Yes, he answered them silently. But what is "family"?
Who is *my* family?

At some point he slept, and when he awoke the dawn
was still young. The skin of his lodge luffed and rippled in
the wind that had come up overnight. He heard something
outside, someone, someone coughing—no, someone crying
quietly, sobs stolen by the wind. He got up, shrugged on
his tunic, and tied on his leggings. He stepped outside and
saw Mouse Road.

She lay on the ground outside the lodge she shared with her mother, her hands on the ground before her. She dug her fingers into the earth, pulled up a fistful, and trickled the dirt over her head. George had seen enough deaths among the People to know what had happened. He walked over and knelt beside her. Inside the lodge, Picking Bones Woman lay curled peacefully on her side as if asleep. But she was not asleep.

Mouse Road wept. The wind brought the scent of a storm. His own grief he swallowed, keeping it within himself. Picking Bones Woman, though crotchety and even spiteful at times, had been a kind neighbor and a patient friend, but no matter how he might grieve her passing, George knew his emotions could not compare to what Mouse Road felt or to what Storm Arriving would soon feel. And so he did nothing more than hold her, cradling her in his arms, giving her the only thing that might help at all: the closeness of another human being. And he waited.

Soon enough, Speaks While Leaving emerged from her lodge. She saw them and slowly sank to her knees. She closed her eyes and George saw her body heave with sorrow. Then she stood and returned to the lodge to tell her husband.

The banquet fire still smoked, the wind breathing wisps of life into the last coals. By the end of the day they would be on their way, bearing the body of Picking Bones Woman southward toward the Sand Hills on the shores of the inland sea. They would take her there to speed her journey to the River of Tears, to Séáno, the land that lay in the star-filled sky above the Big Salty.

Beyond the horizon, thunder.

CHAPTER 10

Wednesday, June 5, A.D. 1889
Palacio del Gubernior
Ciudad de La Habana, Cuba

Alejandro picked up his wineglass and rolled the red wine along its crystal curves. He brought it to his nose and closed his eyes, inhaling deeply of the *tinto's* fragrance. There came the sweetness of roses, the deepness of oak, and the dark sharpness of black pepper. With them he smelled the memory of long youthful summers in Alto California, where the sun baked the vineyards with God's own warmth and where the rivers ran fast and cool and green. He opened his eyes.

The dining hall at the governor's palace was sumptuous. The ceiling soared twenty feet above his head, with foliage of carved plaster that framed scenes busy with cherubim, nymphs, and clouds. Twisting pilasters of turned, polished wood supported the vaults above, and between the columns, along the green lacquered walls, hung framed oils depicting landscapes, hunts, and the glories of Spain. Liveried footmen stood at their stations beneath the gilded frames, ready to assist the diners at table.

The table itself was remarkable: solid oak with heavy legs carved with vines, leaves, and incongruous lion's-paw feet. The chairs echoed the table's ornate features, adding the governor's family crest to the high backs. The warm polish of the tabletop was visible through the fine lace of the cloth that covered its impressive length. Fifty guests could easily have supped along its borders, but tonight, they were only three.

Across from him, Doña Olivia Esperanza Baca de Gutierrez, his sister-in-law and wife to one of his oldest friends, was resplendent in a dress of gray silk, black lace, and seed pearls. Her necklace and earrings were platinum and emeralds, as were the combs that held up her silver hair. Her husband, Don Roberto Alonso Mendez-Gutierrez, Governor of Cuba, sat at the head of the table, attired in formal waistcoat and tailcoat. His silk necktie was copper moiré, and his silver stickpin was tipped with a ruby.

Alejandro sipped from his goblet, feeling the rippled edge of the hand-blown glass and the softness of the wine on his tongue. He breathed gently through pursed lips, aerating the *tinto,* spreading its flavor through his mouth. The roses blossomed to cherries, and the scent of oak gave way to the subtle taste of granite.

"I know this wine," he said, and Olivia smiled.

"I should hope so," she said. "It is yours."

"It's the '72," Roberto added in his usual clipped style. "We've a few bottles left."

"I must remember to bring you more on my trip back to Washington," Alejandro said.

"How long will it be before you return?" Olivia asked.

Alejandro put down the wineglass. "A month at the soonest, I should think, and probably closer to two." He skewered the last piece of lamb from his plate and daubed it with the dark sauce made from mushrooms, amontillado, and crushed chili pepper. "I'd like to avoid the worst of this wretched yellow-fever season. I'd hate to put your sister at unnecessary risk."

"Victoria is returning with you?" Olivia asked. Alejandro could hear the excitement in her voice, and he shared a smile with her husband.

"Yes," he said. "She will be coming back with me. As the new ambassador to the United States, I intend to refute every evil habit in which my predecessor indulged. One of his most unseemly habits was living the bachelor's life, while leaving his dear wife a virtual widow back in Ciudad Mexico."

Roberto chuckled. "You will change that. You will restore honor and dignity to the office. No one is better suited."

Alejandro nodded toward his host, accepting the compliment. He ate the last morsel and put down his silverware.

"That, my dear sister, was the best meal I have had in months. My compliments to your staff."

Olivia bowed her head, modest pride gracing her features. Alejandro felt a sudden pang of heartache. But for her silvered hair, Olivia was nearly the twin of Victoria, her younger sister. Deep-set eyes of walnut brown, with high and arching eyebrows that accentuated the whiteness of her skin. The little lines that crinkled at her eyes and defined the limits of her broad smile spoke of years both happy and sad.

"How long has it been since you were home?" Olivia asked, divining his thoughts.

Alejandro laughed. "You know me well, sister." He shrugged. "Too long. It has been more than a year, and as you know, at our age even a year is precious."

"Indeed," Roberto said. "I wouldn't survive. I need my family around me." He folded his linen serviette and put it on the table. "But the meal! I second the compliments. Excellent. And now, *con permiso*?" A footman stepped forward to pull back Roberto's chair as he stood.

"Of course, my dear. I have some correspondence I would like to complete, if our new ambassador would deign to carry a few letters?"

Alejandro stood and bowed with all formality. "*Un placer,* Doña Gutierrez."

The two men left the dining hall and walked down a long, windowed corridor. Roberto pulled open a thick wooden door and ushered Alejandro inside.

The smoking room was paneled in dark wood, as shadowy as a cave. The carpet was red; the walnut furnishings were nearly black with age. The gray stone mantel and hearth were made of white-veined granite, mottled and cloudy. Alejandro declined a cigar, but accepted the offer of a splash of Pedro Ximénez. He took the cut-crystal glass in hand and walked to the window.

Outside, the firelit clouds of sunset hung over Havana's sheltered harbor. The air had refused to move all day, the heat and moisture united to create a dead, syrupy atmosphere that sapped every morsel of energy.

He sipped the thick, sweet wine. Currants and molasses filled his palate. "I wish I could take your wine cellar with me," he said.

Roberto chuckled as he puffed his cigar to life. "I am glad you cannot," he said. "But it is good that Victoria comes for a visit. Olivia has missed her."

"I only wish that it was for a different reason," Alejandro said. "The thought of my sweet wife consorting with those boorish Americans—" He cut off his own tirade before it got started.

"Are they really so bad?"

"Not all of them," he said. "But that president of theirs . . ."

"So. The American president doesn't respect our queen. María Christina will survive. She does not need his admiration."

"But you did not hear him, Roberto. His words, his *attitude*. He was . . ." Alejandro sought the word that described his feelings. "He was vulgar."

"Come now," his friend scoffed. "We're not children. Let it be."

But Alejandro could not let it be. "No, we aren't children," he said. "We are a great nation. The history of Spain stretches back a thousand years. Our empire spans the globe!" His anger boiled within him and he paced the length of the room with hard-heeled strides. "Why, it was Spanish courage and Spanish gold that explored and fostered the settlement of this continent. America owes its very *existence* to Spain. And now this, this . . ." He wheeled and headed back across the room. "This *Custer* comes along—"

"I don't believe it," Roberto said, amazed. "This isn't about an insult to our queen. This is about the war."

"It is not!" Alejandro was near to shouting.

Roberto laughed. "It *is*! You still hate him. For what happened at El Brazito."

Alejandro restrained his passion. He sipped the last of his wine and let its sunshine taste calm him. "You do not know how much that man has cost me."

"But it's been thirty years since—"

"Thirty years of humiliation! Thirty years of shame!" He put down the wineglass before he threw it into the fireplace. "I was to be a general until that man outflanked me at El Brazito. A *general*! And instead I was demoted." He sat down in one of the velvet-covered chairs. "And when the Royalists finally returned to power, it was all I could do to acquire a post in the diplomatic offices and play *alcahuete* to that old lecher's goatish wants. My poor, sweet Victoria. She deserved so much more. Instead I've spent thirty years climbing back to the rank I should have had all along."

"But look at you now," Roberto encouraged. "You are a respected man. *You* are the ambassador. You can turn it all around. I meant what I said, Alejandro. You will bring honor and dignity back to the office. We all know what you have suffered."

Alejandro nodded. "Yes. Everyone knows what I have suffered, which only adds to my dishonor. And I suffered it because of Custer. Oh, how I wish for vengeance."

Roberto sat down in the chair opposite. "So take it," he said simply.

"Take my vengeance? On the president of the United States?" Alejandro's laugh was bitter. "I must have forgotten to tell you. I am the ambassador to the United States. Dueling with the leader of their country . . . well . . . it might be considered a breach of protocol."

"I don't mean personally," the governor said. He puffed on his cigar, releasing clouds of blue and gray smoke. "Just make him miserable."

Alejandro considered the notion. "Very well," he said with an academic air. "Let us say that I wish to make Custer miserable. What is your notion? How do you propose that I accomplish this feat?"

"Simple," Roberto said. "Start a war."

Alejandro was glad he was not holding the crystal wineglass, for he was sure it would have fallen from his fingers. "Don't joke, Roberto. Not about such things."

Roberto raised a lazy hand, unconcerned. "Who says I am joking?"

"What are you talking about?"

The governor stood up and poured himself and his guest another glass of the thick brown wine. "Alejandro," he began, "you know these things as well as I. War is the *true* sport of kings. It is a game. A contest. And the first man to flinch loses."

"Make yourself clear," Alejandro demanded as he accepted the refilled glass.

"I will." He walked to the window. "Remember this morning. You saw the fires?"

"You know I did. You said the rebels had fired an arsenal up above the battlements."

"Indeed. The rebels. Rebels who have for decades fought for an independent Cuba. For decades. How do they do it? Have you ever wondered? Small groups of men hiding in the hills? How are they supplied? How are they armed?"

Alejandro was suspicious. "What are you trying to say? That the rebels up in the Cuban hills—"

"—are funded by American gold," Roberto finished. "Of course. Who else? *How* else?"

Alejandro's head had begun to ache, though he was more apt to blame a superfluity of wine than the course of the conversation. He put his unfinished Ximénez down on the teakwood side table. "This is ludicrous," he said, patting at his brow with his handkerchief. "I am not going to foment insurrection among the Americans. Nothing can come of that."

Roberto leaned forward, sitting on the edge of the carved-back chair. He smiled; it was a cunning, almost gleeful expression. "Not among the Americans," he said. "Something even better. The Cheyenne."

Alejandro had to laugh out loud. "Now you *are* joking," he said, but the shrewd look on his friend's face did not waver, did not crack. "My God. You *aren't* joking."

"Look at it," Roberto said. "The perfect opportunity. Minimum application of capital and supplies. Maximum disruption to American policy."

"But, Roberto . . . the Cheyenne. They're just savages."

"Savages kept Cortés at bay. For years."

"Against swords and lances, maybe, but against rifles?"

"Haven't you read the papers? They have rifles."

"Of course I've read the papers. So they've won a few skirmishes, even a battle here and there. But against modern weapons? Against artillery?"

"Then give them some. Even the odds. Let them do the rest. It's not as if they'd win. But it would hurt Custer. You can be sure of that."

Alejandro could only gape and stammer. The idea was madness. Madness! His brain would not accept it, but neither could he reject it. Arm the Cheyenne? His head began to swim. "It *would* be perfect," he said as he thought it all through. "Custer . . . even now he is vilified in the press for the smallest misstep in the Frontier. The split in public sentiment over his Homestead Act is deeper even than the one between Democrats and Republicans." He chuckled, and patted his brow again with the kerchief. "I can't believe I'm even considering such lunacy. I wouldn't know how to contact these Cheyenne, and I certainly don't have the time to lead a clandestine war in the American frontier. No, it is a nice dream, Roberto, but I am afraid that it will remain only that."

Roberto sat back in his chair. "Ah, well. It was entertaining, nonetheless." He raised his glass. "To dreams," he said.

Alejandro picked up his own and raised it as well.

"To dreams," he echoed.

Alejandro retired for the evening and spent a restless night tossing in a plush, canopied bed. The heat did not abate, and when morning rose in gray robes above a gray sea, he was glad to see it.

The clouds had thickened overnight, and the warm ocean breeze, heavy and humid, stalked along the walls of dockside stucco with an unexpected bellicosity, tugging at dresses, pushing at hats, and tossing dust in people's faces.

He stood on his balcony, his dressing robe tugged by the wind's rough hand. Like the heat, the pounding in his head had not eased with his troubled night's sleep. Too much wine, he conjectured, or a combination of the wine and the heat, perhaps. He looked out over the plaza and harbor, taking deep breaths of the salt-scented air to clear his senses.

Palms swayed, fronds twitching like ragged pennants. Down at the quays, masts of the smaller fishing vessels swung back and forth, as constant as giant metronomes, but each to its own tempo. He could see the masts and smokestack of his own ship, the *Cabeza de Vaca,* standing tall above the fishing fleet. Already, the stack fed smoke up into the wind as the engineers brought the boilers to life, preparing for the morning's departure.

Alejandro's valet, a small, quiet man named Vasquez, packed up his master's belongings. "Do you wish to wear the gray or the brown, Excellency?"

"The gray," Alejandro said, regarding the somber sky. "I would hate to clash with the rest of the world."

"You sound sad, Excellency."

"Sad? No. Just preoccupied, I suppose. Too many things on my mind."

Vasquez hung the gray jacket on the dressing rack and went to the armoire to select a shirt. "Ah, I see," he said. "Perhaps if you concentrated on one thing?"

Alejandro turned and regarded his valet. "And what do you suggest I concentrate on?"

Vasquez grinned as he inspected the cuffs of a linen shirt. "Why, Excellency, the same thing I am concentrating on. That we are heading home, and soon we shall see our families. That is a good thing to concentrate on, is it not?"

Alejandro managed a weak smile. "Yes, it is. Thank you for the suggestion, Vasquez."

"Un placer, Excellency."

Within the hour he was dockside, watching his luggage being carried aboard the steamer. He turned to make his farewells.

"Thank you for visiting," Olivia said. "I only wish it could have been longer."

"As do I," he replied.

She pressed into his hand a small bundle of wax-sealed letters tied with red ribbon. "For my sister," she said, and kissed him on both cheeks.

"I shall deliver them," he promised her. "And when I return, I shall bring her with me."

He bade Roberto good-bye as well, and then boarded the *Cabeza de Vaca.* The whistle sounded and they pulled away from the docks. The bow swung to starboard, and they headed out of the harbor into the choppy sea.

The *Cabeza de Vaca,* named after one of the more enigmatic explorers of the New World, was a hybrid between a true steamship and an old sailing vessel. Its boilers and steam engine were of middling size, and were used to maneuver the ship in and out of harbor, and in the event the ship was becalmed. Most of its voyaging, however, was done under the power of the wind. Schooner-rigged, its two masts rose from the main deck, both towering a giddy sixty feet above the waterline. Using sails meant less space was required for fuel for the boilers, and that meant a greater cargo capacity.

Alejandro stood on the elevated poop deck, facing aftward, watching the mountainous spine of Cuba recede into the distance. The wind was off their port beam, and the captain was bellowing orders from the wheelhouse. The crew, a collection of Creoles, blacks, and coastal Indians, scrambled to obey, clambering up rigging, pushing the spars, unreefing the sails. The engine rumbled below deck, a throbbing that Alejandro could feel up through his feet and into his bones. Pulleys creaked, capstans ratcheted. Callused hands worked together, hauling sheets, working lines as thick as a seaman's thumb and just as rough. The aftermost mainsail was borne aloft, one heave at a time. It ruffled and flapped in the wind, as curved as the wing of a gigantic bird. Other sails were hauled up, tied off, and trimmed. The captain, a dark, round Creole with a thick beard and a shiny, bald head, called for a northwesterly course. The helmsman cranked the wheel and the deck canted beneath Alejandro's feet. He grabbed the rail and held on. The ship put her rear quarter to the wind and the sails filled with a *crack*! of canvas thunder. The deck slewed the other way as the masts shouldered the pull of the wind. Another command was given, and the engines were tamped down. The mechanical rumbling died, and in its place were the sounds of rushing air, cresting waves, stretching ropes, and the salty insistence of gulls.

The ship rocked and settled into her balance between sea and wind. Alejandro closed his eyes. He did not like sea voyages—his stomach was never up to it, and with today's headache it was a rough start to the second leg of his trip from the United States to New Spain. There was, unfortunately, no better way to travel from Washington to San Francisco. The Spanish railways reached from Veracruz north to California and east to the Tejano coast. The American railways, however, had been brought no farther than the Frontier, especially since the disastrous bridge collapse of the previous winter. Since then, rail companies had been reluctant to consider further expansion without federal assurances regarding the Cheyenne Alliance.

Alejandro sighed. The Cheyenne. He thought over last

night's conversation. The Cheyenne had already caused Custer a great deal of trouble, but any fool could see it was just a matter of time. The Indian's way of life was doomed. Alejandro tried to imagine how much more trouble he could cause with a steady supply of weapons, artillery, and explosives. How far would a little training and advice go? What about tacticians? How much longer would the hidden hand of Spain allow the Cheyenne to survive, if he chose to use it? And how much personal pain would it actually bring to Custer?

"Don Silveira."

Alejandro opened his eyes to find the hirsute Manuel Reposo coming up to the afterdeck. The captain's thick, dark beard started high up on his cheeks and flowed down his face, over his jowls, and down his neck before it dove beneath the collar of his shirt, only to reappear on the backs of his hands. The only part of Reposo that did not seem to be covered with hair was, ironically, his scalp. The captain's bald head gleamed with sweat and the white linen of his officer's jacket was wrinkled and limp in the humid air.

"Have you have settled into your quarters, Don Silveira?"

"Yes, thank you, *Señor Capitan*. Vasquez has tucked everything in its proper place."

"Ah, good," he said, and then noticed his passenger's pallor. "Are you ill, Don Silviera?"

Alejandro touched his brow and shrugged. "A headache. Nothing more. Not yet, anyway."

"Ah, yes," said the captain, who had become fully aware of Alejandro's lack of seaworthiness on their voyage down from Washington. "That is what I came to speak of." He pointed to the sky behind them. "We are in for a bit of a blow. Not today, perhaps, but certainly before we make the Tejano coast. It will start getting rough, I think, probably by this evening. I thought you might want to . . . prepare yourself."

Alejandro smiled apologetically. "I appreciate the warning, *Capitan*. Though I don't know how I might 'prepare myself,' as you say."

"Drink water," the captain said. "And lots of it. You'll lose a lot in the hours ahead. And I've asked the galley to prepare some salted biscuits for you. They won't cure the *mareo,* but they might make it bearable."

"I appreciate your concern," Alejandro said. He glared at the sky behind them. The gray clouds roiled above a gunmetal sea, and whitecapped waves tossed warm spray into the air. Havana had long ago disappeared in the wind-borne mist, and the island itself was fading with each rise and fall of the ship's bowsprit. Their passage was going to be rougher than usual. "Perhaps it would be best if I go below. I expect I'll need as much rest as I can get, as well. If you'll excuse me?"

His quarters were small, but were the roomiest that the ship had to offer. Alejandro ducked his head to enter from the tight gangway into the quarters. His trunks were in cargo, but Vasquez had made sure that his valise and his necessities had made it into the cabin. There was a dry sink attached to one wall and a writing desk and side table attached to the other. On the farthest wall was the sleeping platform, piled high with blankets and a duvet that Alejandro was sure he would not be using on this voyage. Above the bed was a small bookshelf with a railing to keep its contents from sliding off during heavy weather. Everything in the room was either affixed to the heavily paneled walls or latched to the scarred wood floor. Only the wall lamp was free to react to the ship's movement, swaying on its gimbaled joints to remain level despite the pitch and roll of the deck.

Vasquez knocked at the open doorway, carrying a tray with biscuits and a large carafe of still water in his hands. Alejandro motioned him in, and he placed the tray on the side table and locked it into place. "Will there be anything else, *señor*?"

"No. Thank you, Vasquez. I'm still feeling unwell. I think I will try to rest a bit."

"Yes, señor. I am right across the hallway, if you need me."

Alejandro loosened his shoe buttons and his necktie. Then he lay back on the softness of the bunk. His head pounded and his heart beat as fast as a bird's. The bed was a cradle, rocking with the ship in the sea's still-gentle arms, but it did not soothe him. He had seen the sky, and he knew that there was a storm coming, and soon.

He drank a long draught of the water with its slightly brackish flavor. The biscuits were salty but not overly so, and they helped settle the beginnings of sourness that were already rising in his stomach. He removed his coat, took another glass of water, and lay back down on the bed, feeling hot and flushed.

The rest of the day he spent below deck, reading from his books, writing in his journal, and trying to rest. Taking Reposo's advice, he picked at the cook's biscuits and drank water until he felt ready to burst. Later, after a bland supper of chicken and a flask of tepid *blanco,* he stripped the heavy covers off the bed and passed the uncomfortable night in a haze of discomfort, heat, humidity, and motion.

By morning, he could hear the wind's song through the rigging, and the ship's tender sway had intensified. Lying in bed was no comfort. He was tossed from side to side, his gut sloshing around within him like a half-filled wineskin. Finally his nausea awoke. He had learned from dozens of previous sailings that keeping to his quarters while seasick, rather than improving his condition, actually aggravated it. Thus he resigned himself to go up on deck and, despite the ignominy and the sport he would provide the crew, spend the rest of the trip at the rail. At least the sea air might cool him.

He rose, aching from head to foot, and tottered his way to the door. "Vasquez," he shouted, and his valet came rushing, stumbling as the ship took an unusually strong pitch. "I wish to dress."

Vasquez, looking a little green himself, laid out a fresh shirt and underclothes and then set about brushing the lint from Alejandro's brown suit. Alejandro splashed water on his face and took a tentative sip from the carafe. His gorge reeled and he swallowed to maintain control, deciding that he should concentrate instead on dressing. He was slow in his movements, fighting nausea and his aching muscles at every step, and Vasquez helped him at the last.

"Don Silveira!" his valet exclaimed. "Your skin, you are burning!"

"Of course," Alejandro said. "What do you expect? Cooped up here in this rat-hole. It's like a Turkish bath in this cabin. Finish with the damned necktie, will you?"

Without another word, Vasquez did as he was instructed,

and Alejandro fought his nausea as he quickly made his way down the pitching gangway and up the ladder to the deck. He pulled himself upward, wincing as he came into the light of overclouded day, and threw himself toward the leeward rail. All need for control past, he let his gullet have its way. He stiffened, the paroxysm wrenching his torso into a horseshoe of pain. Once, twice, and then on the third spasm, he felt as if he were tossing everything including his heart out into the sea.

He retched for a full five minutes before his body was ready to rest for a bit. He took out his kerchief and wiped his brow. He could feel cold sweat paste the shirt to his back and trickle down from under his arms. He looked up and saw the sea heaving as well.

Immense waves, walls of green, glistened in the wan sunlight. They crested higher than the deck, and he saw the *Cabeza de Vaca* plow through them, shipping green water to either side in fonts of foam and sargasso. The sails hummed, a bass note of depth and power, and crewmen pulled at hawsers beneath the towering masts.

Another convulsion turned him back to the sea, and he spewed a gout of noisome liquid into the roiling waters. A moan sounded from off the starboard beam. He looked up and saw a head—immense and spade-shaped—lift itself above the sea. A dark, snakelike neck as thick as a man's torso pushed it upward, curving and sinuous, increasing in girth as it emerged. The head turned its gaze upon the ship, its eyes dark and coal black, and then it opened its mouth. Alejandro saw teeth, many teeth, and he heard its call again, a mournful *rooor* that rattled the bones in his skull.

In answer, a second head rose, dark like the first but larger. The neck, as it lifted above the towering swells, was a full twenty feet above the water, and Alejandro could see the colossal hump of its body as it swam through the shadowed troughs.

Shouts rose from the crewmen as the monsters were spotted. Alejandro could do no more than grip the rail and stare, all sickness having fled, every discomfort forgotten. Reposo appeared beside him, slamming into the railing like a loose barrel. He carried a shotgun and, hooking one leg among the rails for balance, shouldered the weapon and fired at the gargantuan beasts. The report sounded puny against the wind and the roar of the sea, but Reposo let loose another round, then cracked the stock to reload.

"Damned monsters," he said as he fumbled cartridges into the weapon's breech. "They'll dog us now for sure. Go on! Off with you!" He fired two more rounds of shot in their direction, and the two leviathans returned to the water. They dove, and Alejandro saw their ridged backs rise and fall, like keels of capsized ships, followed by pairs of long, oarlike flippers that saluted and then disappeared beneath the surging green.

"You'd best get below," Reposo warned. "It'll get worse before it gets better, and I'd hate to report the new ambassador was swept overboard with those beasts prowling along our gunwales."

"How long," Alejandro managed, "until we make port at Puerto de Luna?"

"Port?" Reposo said with a gritty smile. "Begging your pardon, Excellency, but you must not have noticed. We're in the thick of it, we are. This storm is about to break open, and when it does, we'll have all hell down upon our puny heads. My first concern is to keep us dry side up. Once that's done, I'll see where it's blown us and *then* I'll worry about making port at Puerto de Luna."

Alejandro clenched his teeth but could find no strength to argue. He felt the touch of a raindrop on his face and looked up into the angry sky. "As you say, *Capitan.* As you say."

"Will you please go below, Excellency? I've enough to worry me without having to set men to watch you at the rail."

Alejandro could only nod, and as he turned, the skies opened up. Rain fell with a fury, like shot from Reposo's gun turned back upon them. It drummed on the deck and pelted Alejandro's unprotected back as he made his way to the hatch.

Hours passed and darkness filled the world. Alejandro sat on the floor of his cabin, nearly insensible, one arm wrapped around the post of his bunk, the other keeping the lidded bucket close by to catch his next wave of sickness. Vasquez fluttered around him as a moth to a weakening flame, swabbing his brow and emptying the fetid spew.

Alejandro could barely keep his eyes open. His heartbeat, no longer the frantic pattering of a caged bird, throbbed with a slow, deliberate rhythm, like the pounding of a drum. The thrum of the engines played an ostinato of power, while the wail of the wind sang eerie coloratura, and the colossal beasts beyond the ship's hull gave full throat in their deep, sonorous bass.

By midnight there was nothing loose in the cabin. All items had either been stowed away or smashed in the ship's violent motion. Alejandro and Vasquez sat across from each other, holding on and sliding back and forth as the ship tossed. The bow pitched up in a slow, inexorable rise that sent everything sliding aftward. Barrels boomed against bulkheads, shards of glass hissed across the decks. The bow reached its zenith, the wind howling all around, and the ship hung in a sickening moment of vertiginous peace. Then it was falling, descending into the trough to crash down with a bone-jarring *boom* that sent everything forward again. Crates smashed open. Oranges and lemons raced each other down the corridor outside the cabin. Thunder ripped the air, and Alejandro held on, fighting his sickness, his pain, and his fear.

The ship lurched—not a pitch or a roll, but a thudding lurch to the side. Beams groaned and the shouts of men penetrated the deck. Vasquez's eyes were white-rimmed with fear.

"We're going down!"

"Vasquez. Stay calm." Alejandro could barely form the words.

"We're going to sink. We'll all drown!" The thin valet began to rise as the ship took another staggering blow.

"Vasquez! Control yourself!"

"We've got to get out of here!"

Alejandro let go of the bed and let the pitch of the deck propel him forward. He slid into Vasquez, grabbed onto his belt, and pulled him back down to the floor. Vasquez stared at Alejandro as at a stranger, then blinked, and reason returned to his face.

"Forgive me, Excellency. I lost my head."

The hull was struck again, and the *rooor* of the leviathans was so close as to be right atop their heads. Alejandro wanted to shake his head to clear it but his neck was too stiff. The pain sufficed to achieve the same end, though, and he blinked in a sudden clarity of sensation.

Water was flowing beneath the cabin door. He tasted it: salt water, not spilled water from the galley or stores. The ship no longer tossed with its usual fore-to-aft punishment, but had instead begun pitching side to side in treacherous degree. He could no longer hear the shouting of men from up on deck, and the rumble of the engines, while still audible, carried none of its previous strength.

Alejandro came to the abrupt realization that Vasquez was correct: the *Cabeza de Vaca* was foundering. That thought came paired with the notion that, in all probability, he was going to die. He would meet his end here, in the dark waters of the gulf, set upon by storm and beast, and would never again see his wife, Victoria, or his daughter, Isabella—the two bright stars of his existence.

He held on as a shuddering boom rang the ship like a bell. "Gather my papers," he told Vasquez. "And the letters from Doña Gutierrez. Wrap them in some leather or wax-cloth, to keep them dry. Put them in my valise."

Vasquez nodded and crawled across the cabin to comply. Alejandro looked around for a length of rope or a strap of leather. Nothing could be had. Vasquez found some oil-cloth and wrapped the papers and letters in it. He placed them within the leather valise and latched it shut.

"Good," Alejandro said. He took off his necktie and tied a noose in it. He slipped the noose around his wrist and threw the other end to Vasquez. "Tie that to the handle of the valise."

"I will be glad to carry it for you, Excellency."

"No," Alejandro said. "I promised to deliver those letters to my wife. I *will* deliver them. Tie it."

Vasquez obeyed and then they pulled open the cabin door. A crewman's body lay at the base of the companion-ladder. They stepped over it and began to climb. The hatch to the deck was open and water poured down it with each roll of the ship. Vasquez helped Alejandro through it up to the deck. They emerged, blinking salt water from their eyes.

The churning dawn flared with lightning. Thunder tumbled from the clouds, the storm wailed, and loose canvas snapped freely in the keening wind. The ship was broadside to the weather, her bow nearly underwater, her beam rolling with each tempestuous swell. Waves crested over the deck, and a dark river ran ankle-deep across the planking.

"Where is everyone?" Vasquez shouted above the gale. The ship jounced again and the two men lost their footing. Alejandro grabbed a rail and held on, the valise dangling from his wrist and Vasquez holding on to his arms. Off the leeward side, a great head appeared. The sea beasts roared and craned their great necks, searching for morsels. One moved toward the mainmast. Alejandro saw a gunshot flash and the beast recoiled, twisting away from the pain.

Alejandro shouted, calling out to the gunman. Vasquez joined in, and Reposo peered around the mast. He motioned for them to stay where they were. With ropes around their waists, Reposo and another crewman made their way across the madly tilting deck.

"Where is everyone?" Vasquez shouted. Alejandro, now spent, could barely move.

"Lost," Reposo said. "We lost half the crew when we struck the reef, and the rest have gone to either the storm or to those devil-beasts out there. What is wrong with the ambassador?"

"His Excellency is ill," Vasquez said. "He has a fever and is in great pain. We must get him to safety."

Alejandro was still alert enough to understand Reposo's appraising gaze. "If you live, *Capitan,* and I do not, there will be the Devil to pay for it."

Reposo squinted past the blowing wind and rain. "As you say, Don Silveira. But if we don't get off this ship, none of us will have a chance."

They tied up to one another in pairs—Alejandro to the captain, and Vasquez to the crewman—and in a long, nightmare procession, slipped and overhanded toward the foredeck. The morning light combated the storm, adding blue to the gray waters. Through the growing light, they could see the waves roll past them, curl, and disappear with muted thunder.

"Another reef ahead!" Reposo shouted. "We've no time. *Move* your asses!"

The foredeck was underwater, waves washing over the rails untroubled. A small dinghy was tied up alongside the cargo boom, and the captain and crewman struggled to free it without losing it to the rushing waters.

Alejandro was dumped into the boat. He held on blindly as water slapped him in the face. The others shouted and swore, their oaths as cutting as the wind. Two pairs of oar-staves slipped between the tholes and Reposo yelled, "Pull!" as he and the crewman put their backs to the oars. "We've got to clear that reef!"

The boat was caught between the reef and the sinking ship. The seamen struggled to escape the trap, pulling with a strength spawned by fear and desperation. The roar of the breakers grew nearer, and Alejandro could see the billowing white of the spume. A wave rose behind the ship. It picked up the *Cabeza de Vaca* and shoved it reefward. The cresting water nearly swamped the tinier craft, and everyone moved to bail. The steamship edged toward them. A boom sounded, and the *Cabeza de Vaca* shuddered as her submerged bow struck the reef. The mainmast snapped with a report as from a cannon, crashing to the water astern of the lifeboat. Alejandro and Vasquez did their best to bail while Reposo and the crewman returned to the oars. The reef hissed as the waves broke over it, and Alejandro could see its dark jagged back exposed between the crests. An explosion from the steamship ripped a hole in the aft deck, sending planks and metal hissing through the air. Vasquez cried out from the bow. His belly was open, torn by a flying shard, his guts spilling out into the flooded boat. Alejandro moved to help him but Reposo shoved him back in the stern.

"Leave him! You can't help him!"

Alejandro gripped the gunwale with pale fingers. The next roller picked them up and threw them toward the sharp-toothed coral.

"Hang on!"

The rowboat came down on the reef, catching a glancing shock along its spine. The frame twisted and wood cracked, but the boat stayed together. The next wave carried them forward, off the narrow ledge and ahead into deeper water. The boat began to fill with blood-tinged water, and Alejandro realized that the wind had lessened, the sky had brightened. Ahead, the waves continued and the men heard the gentle rumble of breakers on a beachhead.

"We are safe!" Reposo crowed. "Pull, Carlos! Let's get this boat to shore!"

Alejandro slid down along the gunwale and said a prayer of thanks. He held on to his valise, his precious letters within, and felt his own heart thudding in his chest as he watched Vasquez hold his innards in his hands and slip silently into death.

CHAPTER 11

Moon When the Whistlers Get Fat, Waxing
Fifty-six Years After the Star Fell
Sand Hills
Alliance Territory

George lay alongside his whistler, wrapped in the heavy fur of the buffalo pelt that Storm Arriving had given him on his daughter's naming day. But despite its protection and the warmth of the hen against his back, he shivered with the cold, his body setting up a tremor that began in his gut and radiated outward to every limb. The hen stirred at his movement and he patted her side to settle her back down. He was wet through from the night's stormy deluge, and even the morning's gentle wind took a bitter bite. He stretched stiff muscles and sat up.

He was cold, yes, but even so he felt better than he had in nearly two moons. The naming celebration had provided him with several days of rest, and even the long, slow ride across the prairie to the funerary grounds—though a silent and somber trip—had restricted him to the minimum of activity. Now if he could just get warm.

He stood. The storm had abated during the night after striking suddenly at twilight, coming up from the south and dumping salty rain down upon them as George, along with Storm Arriving and Mouse Road, had struggled to erect the burial scaffold. Afterward, the violent wind and lightning had kept the trio pinned down through the rest of the night. Storm Arriving and Mouse Road lay nearby, close beside their own mounts and still curled beneath their own protective buffalo-skins. Speaks While Leaving had remained behind with the Closed Windpipe band to care for her newborn. The other whistlers they had brought to the shores of the Big Salty—the ones that had borne the body of Picking Bones Woman and the articles they had needed for her funeral—ringed the sleepers in a tight circle, their bodies making a living, spice-scented windbreak around them.

Beyond the whistlers, tufts of sedge grew in the sandy soil, and the tall, feather-headed plumes of razorgrass turned their backs to the wind. George saw that, a few yards away, the lash-and-lodgepole funeral scaffold had survived the night's weather. The trinkets tied to the cross-braces swayed on their leather thongs, strips of fur and foxtail riffled in the wind, and atop it, the body of Picking Bones Woman still lay whole and undisturbed. George looked skyward. That would change soon.

This was his second funeral on the giant horseshoe of cliffs surrounding the Big Salty. Two years before, after their ride on Washington, he had come here to send the soul of his friend, Laughs like a Woman, to Séáno. During the funeral he had seen the People's death rituals for the first time, and had come away shocked, awed, and moved.

Séáno was the place where souls went after their bodies had died. It was the river of light that ran across the midnight sky—the Milky Way of George's youth—and to aid the souls on their journey, the People brought their dead here, to the shores of the Big Salty. At night, when the stars shone down upon the waves, the shimmering water stretched out to the horizon and continued onward, upward into the heavens, forming a road of light for the departed souls to follow.

But while the grandeur of the scene had awed George, it was how those souls were released from their mortal form that had shocked him. That particular task required the aid of one of the local denizens.

The People called them little-teeth, after the serrated ridges of their long beaks, but to George they were just flying lizards, and big ones, too. They lived along the seaside cliffs and usually filled the evening sky, but the violence of the summer storm had kept them drawn up in their crevices and grottos. Dawn, however, was showing a calmer face. Gossamer clouds, lit by the approaching sun, were brushed by the breeze and stretched across the sky in a veil. The flying lizards had returned to the sky, soaring on leathered wingspans six . . . eight . . . even ten feet across. Most hung motionless out over the sea, riding the constant wind, watching the dark waters for the flash of food, but a few had noticed the funeral scaffold. George watched as two of the bat-winged creatures twitched their paddlelike tails and turned their crested heads, changing course to get a closer view and wait for the humans to move off. Soon enough, the little-teeth would descend upon Picking Bones Woman, tear open her corpse, and release her soul for its final journey.

George was about to awaken his companions when something out along the cliffs caught his attention. He squinted into the wind and, thinking himself mistaken, he rubbed the last of the sleep from his eyes. He stepped back to his whistler's side, opened a parfleche, and took out his pair of U.S. Army binoculars. Leaving the circle of whistlers, he walked to the edge of the cliff. The binoculars were cold against his face as he peered into their circular darkness. The view hop-skipped as he steadied himself against the breeze. Peering over and then through the glasses, he brought them into focus.

"Aw, Hell," he said simply.

A half mile to the west, two men stood at the edge of the precipitous drop. They were dark-skinned men—dark like the night, dark like the belly of a thundercloud. Their hair flowed loose in the wind, and the feathers that trimmed their lances fluttered and twirled. George knew who they were, or was afraid he knew. He had hoped that his memories of them were remnants of a dream, the effects of exhaustion or delirium. But seeing them here, clearheaded and alert as he was, belied that possibility.

The Thunder Beings saw him and raised their lances in greeting. Then together they swept the tips of their weapons in an arc that traced up to the top of the sky, across to the sea, and down to the shore below. George looked over the binoculars toward where they pointed.

From the cliff edge it was at least two hundred feet down a sandstone escarpment to the level of the inland sea. At the foot of the pale cliffs was a thick forest—the dark green belt of fern trees that thrived on the moist air, the sandy soil, and the frequent rains. George had never been down there among the primordial boles, but he had heard tales of

great beasts that lived in the dense foliage. Beyond the forest
lay the white sand of the shoreline, the turquoise waters,
and the foam of the surf where it met the hidden reefs.

He brought the binoculars to bear and saw, sticking up
out from the water beyond the nearest reef, what could
only be a ship's mast. He found the bowsprit, too, stabbing
up from the waves. It had been a large ship, and he wondered how long it had been there.

George looked back up at the clifftop. The Thunder Beings were still there. They pointed again, first at him, and
then down to the sea, the shore, and the ship. Their meaning was unmistakable, and George gritted his teeth.

"I'm tired of doing your bidding," he told them. "Why
should I go down there?"

The faint report of a distant shot told him why.

With the glasses' aid, he found them out on a spit formed
by the confluence of two riptides. Two men, *vé'hó'e* sailors
by the look of their clothing and build, standing over a
third man who lay supine on the sand. One sailor held a
shotgun to his shoulder and was pointing it this way and
that at the forest's dark limits. The other stood in front of
the wounded man, crouching, one arm at the ready as if
he held a knife. George could almost see his hand shake
from the clifftop. They faced the forest, but George could
see no threat from there; the coverage of the trees was
complete. The first sailor swung the gun to one side and
fired. George looked in that direction and saw a large creature go down at the water's edge, thrashing in the surf. It
was one of the lizardlike creatures of which George had
heard many tales: shadow-hunters, the People called them.
As tall as a man, and stealthy as a breeze, they lived in the
deep forest and hunted in packs. They walked on two legs
like walkers, and while smaller, were no less deadly. The
one that had been shot fell still, and George could see its
long neck, avian frame, whiplike tail, and viciously curved
claws. The sailors turned their attentions back to the forest.

"Aw, Hell," he said again. "Hellfire and damnation!"

"What is it?" Storm Arriving had awakened and was
rising from his makeshift bed. George pointed. Storm Arriving came up beside him and squinted down at the scene.

"Vé'hó'e," he said. "They are no concern of ours." He
started back to the whistlers.

"I think they are," George said.

George looked over to the point of land where the dark-skinned men had stood. They were gone, leaving him with only the question of what—or whether—to tell Storm Arriving.

"I have to go down there," he said.

Storm Arriving halted. "Why?" he said. "They are *vé'hó'e*. The shadow-hunters will rid us of them soon, and that is three less that we have to drive from our lands."

"I have to help them."

"Why?"

"I can't tell you, or . . . well, I don't want to tell you. But I have to go down there."

"No," Storm Arriving said. "I will not allow it."

George looked at his friend, surprised by the tenor of his edict. The Indian stood tall, staring right at George with a gaze that challenged. George could think of only one thing to say, the phrase that the People always used to assert personal autonomy.

"You cannot tell me what to do."

Storm Arriving let his gaze drift out toward the sea. "One Who Flies," he said. "You are still weak from your injuries. These men mean nothing to us. There is no reason to help them."

"Yes," George said. "There is."

"Then tell me what it is," Storm Arriving said.

There was no more time to waste. They had to get down there if those men had any chance at all. He had to convince his friend to help him or at least to let him go on alone, and though he did not fully believe it himself, the truth was the last tool he had.

"I have had a vision," he said.

Storm Arriving stared, disbelieving, manners forgotten.

"The Thunder Beings came to visit me," he went on. "Just this morning. They stood over there, and pointed down to the *vé'hó'e* on the shore. I have to go down there."

"Thunder Beings? You are sure?"

George signed in the affirmative.

Storm Arriving turned and leaped back inside the circle of whistlers. He nudged Mouse Road with a toe. "Get up, my sister." Then he began readying two of the mounts. George moved to help.

"What is it?" Mouse Road asked them.

"You must take the whistlers up to the bluff," Storm Arriving told her. He pointed to the sky. "The little-teeth will be here soon to free our mother's spirit."

"Where will you be?" she asked blearily.

"One Who Flies and I must go down to the shore. There are some men in trouble. We must help."

"But One Who Flies—" she began.

"Please. Take the whistlers," George said to her. "I think this is very important."

Mouse Road looked worried, almost afraid, but she set quickly about the task of linking the whistlers' halter ropes.

George took his rifle out of its sheath and checked the magazine. The Winchester repeaters had shown the People good service since they had taken them from the army. Storm Arriving checked his as well.

"I will be glad to have ten shots instead of one," Storm Arriving said. "Aim for the body, One Who Flies. Between the breastbone and the foreleg."

George nodded, then caught himself and signed his agreement. He had met men in battle, had commanded troops in the field, and had stormed garrisoned fortresses. Each time, he had felt the rush of the blood, the tightening of the limbs, and the anxious possibility of death. But now, though he was facing creatures no less savage, he feared them so much more. Their wildness, their reputed ferocity, set his fingers to trembling.

"We'll need other mounts," he said. "For the survivors."

"No," Storm Arriving said. "We cannot afford to be slowed down by whistlers on tethers. We will have to make do with our own mounts. Take your drake. He will be stronger."

They mounted. George looked back at Mouse Road as they turned to go. She noticed his regard and stood tall. George took in her slender form, the open shoulder of her dress, and the look of worry in her eye. "We will be back soon," he told her, promising himself that he would.

They rode to the east, to a place Storm Arriving knew of where they could descend the cliffs. George looked back toward the shore and the reef, but the men were now lost to his view behind the shoulder of land. They led their mounts down toward a low point that led to a brush-lined ravine that sloped ever more downward. The whistlers shied at its steepness, but the men prodded them onward.

The brush became thicker, wetter. The air became moist and still, and soon they were ducking under branches. The ground mercifully began to level off. They rode down under the feathered fronds of the giant fern trees, and entered a world of green.

They raced through the forest, and the whistlers colored their flanks to match the verdure of their surroundings. The ground was carpeted with moss and thick with broadleaf plants. They crashed through smaller ferns merely the height of a man, and dodged between the scaled trunks of their giant brethren. George saw birds and orange and blue in the branches high overhead, and heard the far-off call of some deep-throated beast. They splashed through the shallow pools, scattering wildlife, and George smelled the brackish tang of stream-fed marshes. It was a long, serpentine way through to the shore, but eventually George saw its brightness through the trees ahead.

The beasts whistled as they emerged from the forest and onto the bluffs that trimmed the shoreline. They paled their skins as they charged down the sedge-grass slopes toward the white sands, leaping streams every twenty yards. George saw the mast of the sunken ship out in the surf, and the white breakers that marked the reef that had taken her down.

"There!" he shouted.

There was only one man standing now. He stood before his fallen friends and held the shotgun like a club, facing four shadow-hunters. Two of the hunters lay dead nearby, and George could hear the chatters and hisses of the others as they encroached. George unlimbered his rifle and levered a round into the chamber. Storm Arriving did the same.

He rose up onto his knees and kept them tight along his whistler's spine, wincing at the pain it caused him. As they rode over the dunes, his thighs acted like pistons, keeping his aim steady. He squinted down the barrel, remembering Storm Arriving's advice. The shadow-hunters split up in an attempt to encircle the sailor. George sighted, let out a held breath, and fired.

Sand flew at the hunter's feet and the sailor looked in their direction. The hunters saw the distraction of their prey and lunged. Storm Arriving fired and one beast spun. George took another shot and hit another, but too far back along its flank to matter. The hunters saw the threat but to George's amazement did not flee. They turned and attacked.

Coming straight onward, the hunters were a narrow target. George and Storm Arriving both fired as they closed the distance, but only one went down, leaving two more to close the gap. The hunters held out their arms, and a small part of George's mind saw the ripping claws and the needle teeth.

"To the water!" Storm Arriving shouted, and George followed him without question. The whistlers saw the oncoming danger and yodeled in fright. Their skin rippled with ashen colors as they tried to camouflage themselves. The hunters swerved to cut them off, and George got off a final shot that sent a spray of sand into their faces.

They hit the surf in a shower of warm salt water. The whistlers pushed against the incoming waves, their fear of the hunters overcoming their fear of the unfamiliar sea. When the beasts were hip-deep in the surf, Storm Arriving turned them about. The hunters stood on the kelp-strewn beach, unwilling to risk their light-boned bodies against the surge of the tide. The waves rushed up and the hunters shook their feet like cats at a river's edge.

George and Storm Arriving raised their weapons and fired. The shadow-hunters had learned the threat that rifles carried, and sprinted back up the beach and into the safety of the trees. The two men urged their mounts back toward shore. The whistlers reluctantly complied, keeping close watch on the shadows beyond the trees.

The sailor with the shotgun was on his knees, cowering, afraid to look up. George heard his imprecations and saw him cross himself several times as they rode up to him. He was a roundish, balding man with a rough, windburned face and heavy hands. The man who had held the knife lay dead several yards away. The white sand around him was laced with the crimson scrawlings made by his blood as it had spurted from fatal slashes to his body and arms. The third man—a gentleman by his clothing—lay unmoving on the sands. His skin was pale, but George saw his chest rise and fall in long, slow breaths. The surviving sailor continued to babble his prayers, in Latin and Spanish, neither of which George spoke.

"He is of the Iron Shirts," Storm Arriving said, using the People's term for the Spaniards. George looked at his friend, but the Indian only shrugged and pointed to the men on the sand. "You brought us here," he said. "What do *you* think we should do?"

George turned to the cringing sailor and wondered what it was that the Thunder Beings expected of him. "Do you speak English?" he asked. The words brought an immediate cessation of the man's heavenly petitions and the sailor looked up, seeing them for the first time. He stared at George, puzzlement wrenching his features.

George attempted another tack. If not English, then perhaps French. *"Parlez-vous français?"* he inquired, and the sailors eyes widened and his face split into a slow, unbelieving grin.

"French," the sailor said roughly. His gaze switched between George and Storm Arriving, between hope and fear. "Yes. I speak French. A little."

George sheathed his rifle and bade his whistler crouch. The sailor jumped back, as if seeing the beast for the first time.

"She will not harm you," George said.

"W-what kind of man are you?" the sailor asked. "You dress like a savage, but you speak like a man."

George held up a hand. "Have a care," he warned. "We both speak the tongue of the Trader Nation. Who are you and what are you doing here?"

"I am *Capitan* Reposo." He glanced behind him, at the curling breakers and the reef. The mast of the broken ship stuck up out of the roiling waters, rigging hanging loosely from its spars. "That was my ship," he said. "The storm . . ." He struggled for words. "I was headed for Puerto de Luna. This gentleman is bound for San Francisco."

George gave the unconscious man another look. He was dressed in the remnants of a fine suit, the cotton of his shirt smooth and white where it was not soiled or torn. He held a leather satchel beneath one arm.

"What is wrong with him?" George asked.

"He is ill, señor," the sailor replied. "But I must take him to San Francisco. He is very important."

Another moan. George checked back to make sure that Storm Arriving still had his rifle at the ready and then walked over to the ailing gentleman.

His skin was an unhealthy pallor, but his beard and whiskers were closely trimmed and his hands were as soft and delicately boned as any East Coast aristocrat. His eyes rolled behind fluttering lids. Slowly the lids opened and the eyes attempted to focus. The man's mouth moved as he looked up at George, forming words inaudible above the rush and hiss of the surf.

George knelt, looking into the man's face. "Who are you?" he asked him, still speaking in French.

The man's first sound was a croak like a wounded raven, but George saw him concentrate his attention and form the words. "I am," he said between deep breaths, as if even the simple activity of speaking required the greatest of effort, "Alejandro Miguel . . . Tomás Silveira-Rioja . . . ambassador from New Spain to . . . to the United States of America."

George could not help but smile at the revelation. He looked back to Storm Arriving, but the Indian did not seem to understand the implications.

"And who . . ." the ambassador asked, his eyes closing again in fatigue. "Who do I have . . . the pleasure of addressing?"

George stood. "Excellency," he said. "I am One Who Flies; of the people you call the Cheyenne. But you might better know of me as George Armstrong Custer, Junior, former captain of the U.S. Army, and son of the President of the United States."

The Spaniard's eyes opened and he stared up at George. Then, incredibly, he began to laugh—weakly, and without any real humor—and then he subsided, though he managed to lift his right hand from the shell-strewn sand.

"It is . . . an unexpected pleasure," he said.

George reached down and shook the ambassador's hand. "Unexpected is hardly the word, Excellency."

Storm Arriving took the sailor up behind him on his whistler, and George took the ambassador before him, holding him upright. A few rifle shots fired into the depths of the forest kept the hungrier denizens at bay, and the whistlers pushed back up the slope to the cliffs above. As they came up onto the crest, George and Storm Arriving saw the flapping, raucous collection of wings and beaks that had conglomerated at the funerary bier. The little-teeth were at their work, opening the body of Picking Bones Woman and releasing her spirit. The sight reminded George of why they had come here, a fact he felt shame at having forgotten, even for so short a time.

Storm Arriving looked up at the sun—a glowing disk of light halfway up the cloud-covered sky. "She has a bit longer to wait," he said, "before she can climb the star-road to Séáno."

"She could be patient," George said. "When it was something she wanted."

Storm Arriving smiled. "That is so," was all he said.

In the distance, they saw the silhouette of Mouse Road and the rest of their whistlers. She waved enthusiastically and they waved back to her. George caught Storm Arriving looking at him and realized that he was grinning.

"We never did have that talk," Storm Arriving said.

"No," George said. "Perhaps later. Right now we have other things to concern us."

"What are you saying?" Captain Reposo asked, concerned that the conversation had switched into a language he did not understand. "What are you going to do with us?"

"Do you think the Thunder Beings were interested in this one?" Storm Arriving asked.

George chuckled and indicated the limp ambassador. "I don't even know if they were interested in this one."

"What?" Reposo asked. "What is it you are saying? What will you do with the ambassador?"

"Silence," Storm Arriving said over his shoulder, speaking in the Trader's Tongue. "Be silent or we leave you here for the beasts."

Reposo subsided and looked suddenly uncomfortable with his choices.

The ambassador could not ride unassisted and they had no travois on which to drag him, so they set him together with the captain, Reposo, on one of the gentler hens. The

ambassador, pale and feverish, did his best to remain both
conscious and on the back of his mount. He rode nearly
prone along the whistler's spine while Reposo, riding behind him, held him up when necessary and kept him from
slipping to the ground.

Within a day it was clear that Reposo, too, was ill. Mouse
Road regarded their new companions with unabashed
suspicion.

"Why do we take them with us?" she asked. "They are
Iron Shirts, and bring their sickness with them. You should
have left them."

Storm Arriving looked over at the ailing *vé'hó'e*. "She is
right," he said. "It is clear that they both have the swamp
fever. We risk the health of the People by bringing them
in with us."

"Swamp fever?" George asked.

Storm Arriving looked out at the plains before them.
"The *vé'hó'e* have brought many illnesses to us, but none
more than the Iron Shirts. A hundred years before the star
fell they brought the small pox and nearly killed the Snake
People with it. They brought the winter aches and the flux.
To those whose women are less chaste, they brought the
great pox, and the slow rot. The People—and all the other
tribes as well—lost many to these illnesses in centuries past.
Now we are stronger, and lose only a few each year. But
swamp fever . . ." He looked back at Mouse Road. "My
sister is wrong to blame the Iron Shirts for the swamp fever.
That illness has always been with us."

He pointed to the south, back to where the haze and
clouds marked the expanse of the hidden sea. "The tribes
who lived along the warm waters of the Big Salty have
dealt with swamp fever forever. When it comes, it comes
in the summer and stays until the first frost. It travels from
lodge to lodge, creeping along the shores and banks, killing
whole families. We don't see it much up on the plains,
where the air is always moving and the water clean, but
sometimes it comes, and then it is very dangerous."

George felt a pit open up in his stomach. Yellow fever.
They were describing yellow fever, killer of thousands, and
the scourge of the southeastern and the gulf coasts. He
looked over at the two ailing Spaniards.

And I'm bringing it into the heart of the People.

"We have to leave them here," George said. Storm Arriving turned in his seat and stared. Mouse Road smiled primly. Reposo, still awake despite his illness, sensed the change in mood.

"What is wrong?" he asked in French.

"Quiet!" George ordered.

Storm Arriving stopped his whistler and turned. "One Who Flies," he said. "What are you doing?"

George pointed at the men. "What am *I* doing? What are *you* doing? We can't bring this fever into the gathering of the People?"

"But what about the Thunder Beings?"

Mouse Road moved closer. "What about the Thunder Beings?" She looked at George and then at her brother. "What haven't you told me?"

Storm Arriving pointed. "He saw the Thunder Beings," he said. "They told him to help these men."

"I don't know that," George protested. "I *think* that's what they meant. I could be wrong."

"Truly?" Mouse Road asked of her brother. "The Thunder Beings came to One Who Flies?" Storm Arriving signed that it was true. She looked over at the men once more. "If the spirits want us to save these men—" she began.

"No," George said. "We *can't* bring them in among the People."

"You can't ignore the voice of the spirits," she countered.

Storm Arriving held up a hand to silence them both. "I understand what you are trying to do, One Who Flies. But we cannot ignore the vision—"

"It wasn't a *vision*—"

"I do not care what you want to call it; we cannot pretend that it did not happen. It happened. And now we have these men."

The Spanish captain looked on, struggling to concentrate through his fever. The ambassador leaned back against him, all but unconscious. Reposo could tell that there was a disagreement, and that the point of contention was them. Lines of worry creased his brow as he looked from George to Storm Arriving and back.

"How can we bring these men among the People with the fever that they carry?" George asked.

Storm Arriving glanced at his sister, and she signed an answer to his unspoken question.

"Speaks While Leaving will know what to do," he said.

They continued homeward, each of them keeping a distance between themselves and the fever-ridden *vé'hó'e*. Each day, the captain worsened until he was as bad off as his charge. The men ate nothing, and could keep down only little water. They traveled in a state of semiconsciousness, mumbling, fretting, sometimes sliding from their perches on whistler-back.

In two days' time, they drew near to the place at the Red Paint River where the People had set their first encampment for the summer. Storm Arriving sent Mouse Road ahead to talk to Speaks While Leaving and prepare for the *vé'hó'e*.

When the men came over the last ridge, they saw the camp laid out in its traditional manner. From their southern vantage, they could see the lodges of the Closed Windpipe band nearby, and beyond them, the central clearing where the sacred lodges stood tall above the lodges of the soldier societies. The camp stretched out for more than a mile, enclosed by the river and the creeks that fed it. Their whistlers called out in welcome and George heard others sing in response. Walkers, too, chuffed their warnings, like the harsh barks of monstrous dogs.

But they saw no people. George peered into the distance, searching for children at play or women on errands or men at work in front of their lodges. No one walked or ran or sat. The camp appeared to have been deserted.

"Where is everyone?" Storm Arriving asked.

George pulled out his binoculars and looked again. He searched the paths and the meeting places. Then he looked at the lodges themselves. Smoke still rose from cookfires. Meat still hung from drying racks. Whistlers sat near the lodgefronts, tethered to stakes in the ground. All seemed normal.

Then he looked at one of the east-facing openings and saw three faces peering out. He checked the next lodge, and saw there, too, people hiding inside their homes, peeking out to see the threat that had come riding in to visit.

"They are there," George said, and handed the glasses to his friend. "They are hiding from us. It seems that Mouse Road spoke to more than just Speaks While Leaving."

Storm Arriving grunted as he saw what George meant. Then he pointed down near the edge of camp. "Here comes my sister."

Mouse Road rode toward them from the southern edge of camp, waving and shouting. She reined in her whistler a few yards from them and grinned.

"We are all ready," she said.

"Ready?" George said. "It looks like everyone is terrified."

Mouse Road shrugged. "Maybe a little," she said. "But I told them that the Thunder Beings had spoken to you, and then Stands Tall in Timber said that this was not the first time. He said that they came to you back when you were digging for the yellow chief-metal, too."

Storm Arriving glanced over at George. "Twice?" he asked. "They came to you twice?"

George grimaced. "Three times, actually. Or four, depending on how you count the visits."

Storm Arriving gaped for a long moment, then remembered his manners and looked away. "You should speak up about such things, my friend."

Mouse Road laughed. "That is why everyone agreed to let the *vé'hó'e* come. Speaks While Leaving told us what was needed. We have set up lodges on the eastern side of camp, but far away from all others. They can stay there while they recover."

George looked over at the two Spaniards. "If they recover," he said.

"Let us hope that they do," Storm Arriving said. "I have to admit, I am very curious as to why they are here."

Mouse Road, following the instructions of her sister-in-law, had set up a lodge for the Spaniards on the downwind side of camp, a hundred yards away from the nearest family. The lodgeskins were old and dirty, obviously castoffs donated for the purpose of housing the contagion—George expected that the whole lodge would be burned when the men recovered. The skins were staked to the ground, which was unusual for the summer time. During the heat of the day, the skins on many a family lodge were hitched up like a saloon girl's dresses to allow the breeze to flow through the interior while still providing shade from the sun's strength. But not only were the skins of this lodge staked down, but George saw, too, that dirt had been scooped up against the bottom to keep any wind ? ?ll from entering.

Smoke rose from the smokehole, and against either side of the doorway George noticed large piles of sticks and brush for fire building. Mouse Road saw his puzzlement and explained.

"Speaks While Leaving spoke of how we must help keep the fever from spreading from lodge to lodge. The sick men will stay inside, and a low fire is to be kept burning at all times, and always with some sage or juniper smoldering on the side. It has to be smoky inside the lodge. She says it keeps the fever from leaving the lodge."

George trusted that Speaks While Leaving knew what was needed, and he and Storm Arriving took the men down off the mount and took the captain first into the lodge.

The air was close and warm and heavy with the sharp scent of juniper and the earthy aroma of sage. Sunlight came down through the hole at the apex of the lodgepoles and lit up a lazy column that was filled with the slow curves of dancing smoke. Flames flickered along the smoking coals in the hearthpit and on a clay platter nearby, smudge-sticks made of dried herbs smoldered and added their own thick smoke to the air. There was not so much smoke that it was impossible to breathe, but it was enough to make George's eyes burn.

"How are they going to stand it in here?" he wondered aloud, but when he helped Reposo down onto one of the two piles of bedding and old furs, he realized that the smoke was much thinner down near the ground. The invalids would sleep down in the clearer air.

They brought the ambassador in next and laid him down on the other bed. To George's untrained eye, the ambassador still seemed worse off than the captain, though Reposo's condition had degraded steadily during their last day on the trail. Storm Arriving tapped George on the shoulder and they walked out of the lodge, closing the doorflap behind them. Mouse Road was waiting for them.

"I guess I'll be staying here with them," George said.

Mouse Road looked shocked by the suggestion. "No," she said emphatically. "Not you."

"Then who?" he asked.

"I don't care," she said. "Anyone else, but not you."

He stared at the doorflap to the lodge, thinking of the men that lay behind it, and of how he had found them. The possibility that there even *were* Thunder Beings made him uncomfortable. He had never even admitted that Speaks While Leaving's visions and her prophecy concerning his appearance among the people had any possible basis in reality, much less that there were spirit men who walked the earth and affected the lives of mortals.

But how else? he asked himself. How else did he come to them in their need? Or—he considered, thinking of the storm that had ravaged over their heads the night before— were they brought to us? Cause and effect; how far back did it go? To Picking Bones Woman's death? To her sudden desire to see her son before she died? He sighed, unable to find any answer but the memory of what he saw and the men who lay inside the lodge, sleeping beneath a blanket of sacred smoke. And as to the purpose that might be played by a Spanish sea captain and the viceregal ambassador from New Spain? More questions without answers.

He glanced at Mouse Road and her brother. "It is hard to believe that the Thunder Beings would go to all that trouble, just so I could die of a fever. Someone must tend the fire and bring them water and food. I'll bring my lodge here and stay nearby."

Mouse Road frowned, unhappy with the idea, but she realized that it was a reasonable compromise, and with a quick flip of her hand she agreed.

"Good," he said, and then, "Let's find Speaks While Leaving so she can tell me what I need to do for them."

During the next few days, his role was simple one: Tend the fire, keep it smoky, give them water. Speaks While Leaving came to the edge of camp twice a day to hear of their progress, but as a mother of a newborn, she would not come nearer. On the second day Reposo was whimpering with delusions while the ambassador was sleeping peacefully.

"The seaman will likely die," Speaks While Leaving told

George. "Probably tonight." She cradled Blue Shell Woman in her arms and stared out at the lodge.

"Oh," George said. He wondered if she was seeing anything other than what he saw—his assessment of her visionary talents had altered in light of his own experience.

"The ambassador will recover, though," she added. "He will wake from his sleep within a day. He will be very hungry."

"When will it be safe?"

"When the sailor is dead we will burn his body. When the ambassador wakes, we will burn his clothes and the lodge. Then it will be safe." Her gaze was hard, almost unkind.

"What is it?" George asked her. "What is wrong?"

She did not look at him. She just stared at the lodge. "This is part of the vision I had two summers past: the vision of the yellow chief-metal. But I do not know how it all fits together," she said at last.

George chuckled. "You and me both," he said.

"No," she said. "We are different. You do not believe in the spirit world. You do not know the truth of that place; you have never felt the rightness of the vision or the power of the dance when the two worlds touch." As she spoke, her fingers absently stroked her daughter's fine black hair. "I have had visions all my life, and each one has come true. Each time, I saw the truth of the vision; I felt it coming, and then it came in full clarity. This one, though . . ." She squinted at the distant lodge. "I know it is true, but it is vague. I do not know how it will work out."

She turned, then, and walked back toward the circle of the Closed Windpipe band. George did not watch her go. Instead he turned and faced the east. The lodge where the men lay—one dying, one recovering—seemed small and insignificant beneath the immensity of the cotton-cloud sky. He looked up at those clouds, scanning their rifts and slopes for men out of allegory. He saw nothing except for one cloud shaped like a leaping hound, like Tuck, one of his father's dogs.

He wasn't sure if that meant anything or not. He did not want it to.

Alejandro dreamed of burning trees, of wildfires in the tawny hills above his beloved Sonoma estate. He dreamed of smoke rolling across the land, and he heard the screams of his wife and daughter.

He awoke with a start, heard a gunshot, then several more. Screams both distant and near, of both women and children. His eyes burned. He clenched them shut and rubbed them. His heart clanked; his breath was short and panicked. He sat up and coughed in the smoky air.

Where am I? he wondered, and then remembered the ship. The ship and the storm. The surf. The beach. Reposo and his shotgun.

There was slice of light to one side. He crawled toward it. He heard people running, shouting, shouting in a language he could not understand. He heard horses. More gunfire. He heard . . . music.

The light outlined a leathern door. He pushed it open. White pain engulfed him, flooding his eyes. He shut them but still it hurt. An upflung arm held off the worst, and he stepped outside and squinted at the world.

A vast prairie raced out toward the horizon: an eternity of rolling land covered with a golden pelt that rippled like the sea. A sudden yell made him jump, and men rode past in a storm of shouts and hammering hooves. Their horses lathered, their rifles belching smoke, they rode out onto that vastness. They rode in cavalry formation—Alejandro knew it well—groups of four in diamond configuration, each firing to their rear in succession as they rode. They rode like soldiers, but were not dressed as such. They wore shirts and chaps and wide-brimmed hats like the *vaqueros* of Alto California. They rode, and Alejandro dove to the dirt when a few of their shots came his way. More rode past, shooting and shouting, three more groups that followed the first two.

From his prone position in the dust and broken grass he watched them ride, and wondered who they were, where he was, and why they were attacking. The riders headed straight out onto the prairie, coursing a mile dead-away and then, as they crossed over a delicate rise, they split up into quartets and—he could find no other word for it—simply disappeared. The land ate them up, taking them into unseen clefts and hidden watercourses. They were gone.

He had just gotten back up onto his knees when he heard the music again. A song of massive flutes, it was a dissonant choir that grew louder. He turned and cried out in alarm as great beasts nearly ran over him, huge striped creatures that ran on two legs and blared with cacophony. He stared after them, watching their stripes shift as they ran. And then he saw the men who rode them.

Indians!

He fell back to the ground and finally took a look behind him.

The structure from which he had emerged was a conical tent made of animal skins—a *tipi,* he'd heard them called—and beyond it he saw hundreds more. Thousands more. They filled the plain, crowding the distances between him and the shaggy mountains that rose up behind them. Some of them had been pulled down and others were burning, results he presumed to be the work of the horsemen. Pillars of smoke rose from various points around the vast congregation of homes. People ran to douse fires or simply sat and cradled the wounded and the dead. He heard more music: an eerie singing that made the hair on his arms stand upright. As he watched, he saw other Indians ride out on their fearsome beasts, the men yipping and howling like dogs while the lizards blared like strangling trumpeteers. One of the men saw Alejandro and veered toward him, his crested lizard pulling up sharply, ripping turf and scattering stones as it skidded to a halt.

"Ne vous déplacez pas," the savage said, unbelievably, in French. Alejandro stared at the man. His clothes were made of animal skins. He carried a rifle festooned at barrel and stock with feathers and fur. His hair, shorn close on one side, hung down his back in a braid and earrings hung from an inch-long rip in his ear. *"Comprenez-vous?"* he demanded. *"Je vous ai dit de rester ici!"*

Jolted from his shock, Alejandro nodded. "Yes," he said, also in French. "I understand. I will stay here."

The Indian showed his teeth in a snarl of emotion. He turned toward the encampment and shouted something that didn't even sound like a language to Alejandro's ear. Then the savage kicked his horrible mount into motion. The giant lizard kicked up dirt as it sped away, stripes of brown and white moving along its flanks. Alejandro looked back toward the village.

Another animal was headed his way. This one was larger

than the others. It had no bony crest on its head, and the subtle stripes of russet and tan that raked its flanks changed neither shape nor color. It ran toward him on two long legs, its spine nearly parallel with the ground, its long tail counterbalancing a terrible head. It roared, and Alejandro was glad he was already on his knees. He saw the fearsome maw of a hundred finger-long teeth, saw the muscles bunch and pull beneath pebbled skin. It halted twenty feet from him and roared again—a sound like the tearing of metal and pure rage—and it cocked its head and pinned him to the earth with a large yellow eye. Alejandro looked down at the ground and held on to the grass beneath his hands with a strength born of sheer terror.

"Excellency?" someone said in French.

Alejandro looked up. An Indian sat astride the monster's back. With a touch, he commanded the beast to settle to the ground and dismounted. The rider wore brightly beaded moccasins and long leggings with green fringe down the sides. He wore a breechclout of red cloth under a long leather tunic. The breast of the tunic was ornamented with a patterned yoke of blue and white, from which hung animal teeth. A wide belt, also beaded, cinched the savage's waist and held a large knife and a pouch. The man's hair—

—was as pale as cornsilk in the summer sun, and his eyes were the color of the aquamarines on Victoria's favorite earrings. Alejandro sat back on his heels and stared.

"Excellency," the man said again, his expression angry but his words calm. "I am glad to see you are feeling better. I do not know if you remember me; you were not well at the time. My name is—"

"Custer," Alejandro said dreamily, able to do little more than stare at the young man. He could see the father in the son that stood before him, at least physically. Not tall, but lithe and even a bit wiry. His hands, not pretty, but long-fingered and heavily knuckled. A strong, almost aquiline nose and high cheekbones, and the eyes, those blue eyes so sharp, so agile. Alejandro could see the cunning in those eyes, his father's cunning.

"Yes, Excellency. I am George Armstrong Custer, Junior. However, among the People, I prefer to use the name they have given me: One Who Flies."

"One Who Flies," Alejandro said. "I had thought you a dream. A fiction of my fever."

"I am quite real," the young man said.

"But how?"

"There will be time for that, Mr. Ambassador. But right now, as you can see"—he motioned to the fires among the homes behind him—"there are other matters that demand first attention."

Alejandro stood up on his fever-weak legs. "What has happened?"

"An attack, Mr. Ambassador. An attack on my people by the United States Army."

"Those horsemen I saw?" Alejandro asked. "Those were not soldiers. Deserters, perhaps."

"I don't like to disagree with you, sir, so early in our acquaintance, but I assure you that they were indeed soldiers. They were well-trained cavalrymen in active service of the U.S. Army."

"But they weren't in uniform. That is against all articles of war. I do not understand."

"I do not doubt it, sir." The young son of the American president stared back toward the camp. "Perhaps in time, you will." He turned back to Alejandro. "In the meantime, I welcome you as a guest of the Alliance. I have been selected as your liaison to the People and the Great Council."

Alejandro nodded, accepting the welcome. "Pardon me, Mr. Custer, but my memory is hazy about the events that brought me here. If I may ask, where are my companions? The captain and the young man from the ship?"

One Who Flies made a sign with his hands. "The young man you speak of died in the attack by shadow-hunters on the beachhead. If it is any consolation, he died in defense of you as well as himself. Captain Reposo survived the attack. Unfortunately, he contracted the same illness you did—yellow fever. He died a few days ago."

"Yellow fever? ¡Dios mío! I had no idea. I thought it a simple ague. Poor Reposo. Yellow fever."

"Yes, Mr. Ambassador. So you will understand when I tell you the healers of my people instruct me to burn everything you have been in contact with during your recovery."

"Everything?"

"Yes, sir. The lodge, the bedding, even your clothes."

"My clothes? But what shall I wear?"

"New clothes will be provided." One Who Flies plucked at his own tunic. "It will, however, be of a slightly different sort."

"I see," Alejandro said, suddenly seeing that his years of diplomatic experience were to be put to good use. "I understand your concerns, and thank you for your generosity. Naturally, I shall comply with all precautions your healers prescribe. I wonder, though . . . I had a valise with me during the shipwreck."

"We have it here," One Who Flies said.

"There are some letters inside, personal letters for my family. Must they be burned as well?"

Alejandro saw a small smile of empathy touch the lips of One Who Flies, the first gentleness he'd seen on the young man's features. "I believe I can arrange that they be saved from the fire."

Alejandro bowed. "Again, my thanks," he said.

Once the fires were doused and the wounded seen to, his "liaison" escorted him down to the riverside. It had been many, many years since Alejandro had bathed in a river, but he was glad to do so now, both to scrape the salt and scum of a two-weeks' fever dream from his body and to remove any possibility that the miasma of yellow fever somehow still clung to him. As always, young Custer—One Who Flies, he corrected himself—kept watch nearby. The attentions of his liaison seemed part protector, part guardian, making Alejandro suspect that his presence among these Indians was not entirely welcome. One Who Flies had kept him far from any of the natives, traveling on the back of his incredible beast, circumventing the entire encampment.

Now, One Who Flies stood on the riverbank at a distance that allowed modesty, but not privacy. Alejandro used his fingers to rake through his stringy hair. River sand and a crooked stick sufficed to scrape the dirt from his skin, and the living water rushed around him, cold and refreshing and tasting of stony cataracts. He felt quite weak after what One Who Flies had told him was more than week of semiconsciousness, and he wondered when he might get some food.

"The attack," he said to One Who Flies. "Why do you think your army was responsible?"

"Not *my* army, Don Silveira. *My* army is out there, among the lodges of the People."

Alejandro cursed himself. "Of course," he said, attempting to navigate around his *faux pas*. "The American army, I should have said. What makes you so sure those men were soldiers?"

One Who Flies kept his back turned and spoke over his shoulder. "After we destroyed their forts and their bridge, the military leaders shifted their tactics. Instead of marshaling large numbers of troops, they now send out small raiding parties—twenty to fifty men on light horse—a small enough number for them to disappear within the landscape."

"Has it been working?"

One Who Flies shrugged. "It is hard to say. From their vantage, probably so. Smaller parties suffer fewer losses, and being more mobile, they are able to find us more easily. Likewise, it is harder for us to find them when they retreat and scatter. From our side, though, I would say that their successes are limited. We also suffer fewer losses, and so far their raids are neither numerous nor severe enough to force any change. Frankly, I do not understand the intent, though I suspect it has something to do with the sea of immigrants they are ferrying into our lands. By traveling without uniform or guidon, the army can claim they have nothing to do with these raids. But it is still early. In a few months, the strategy of my father's generals may become apparent."

My father's generals. That took Alejandro aback. He had not known what to make of One Who Flies, this son of a famous father. He had assumed that he was dealing with a starry-eyed idealist. But with those last few statements, Alejandro glimpsed a mind much more closely attuned to the realities of the situation. This was not some misguided youth on a crazy adventure, no, nor was he just a rebellious son out to spite his father. This man had the calm aspect and lucid eye of a seasoned commander.

This man, Alejandro thought to himself, could be of use.

He stepped out of the river and skimmed the water off his chest and arms. His limbs were thinner now than when he was in his prime, and his stomach rounder; another vestige of his years playing the toady for the old goat. He walked over to the pile of clothing One Who Flies had left for him and began looking at the articles.

There was one garment that was a recognizable shirt, as well as a pair of leather moccasins and a belt. Then there was what seemed to be an unfinished pair of trousers and an extra piece of cloth. He was about to say something when he noticed exactly what it was that One Who Flies was wearing. The young man still had his back turned, to protect his guest's privacy. Alejandro noticed that the young man's leggings did not go all the way up to the waist, but stopped under the buttocks. Were it not for the length of his tunic, he would have been bare-assed to the world. One Who Flies sensed his hesitation.

"I found you a tunic that was longer than others," he said. "It will cover more of the . . . deficit . . . that comes with the usual clothing we wear."

"My thanks," Alejandro said with sincerity.

With some coaching, he was eventually successful in donning the Indian garb. Despite being made mostly of deerskin and thick cloth, it was loose and surprisingly cool under the summer sun.

"How do you feel?" One Who Flies asked.

"All in all," Alejandro said, "I feel rather well. A bit hungry, perhaps, and still quite tired, but well overall."

"Good. Follow me."

For the first time—perhaps because he was now dressed in a manner these people considered "acceptable"—they finally entered the camp itself. Women glanced at him as they hurried their children out of sight, and older men stared in unmistakable anger. One man came out of his lodge with a heavy-ended stick in his hand. Without a word, he ran toward Alejandro and raised the club, but the blow was warded as One Who Flies stepped between them. The wild Indian, a man of perhaps Alejandro's own age, spoke in angry words of sibilants and whispers, with gestures sharp and pointed. Slowly, One Who Flies calmed the man and turned him back toward his home. As the man stepped inside the skin-covered domicile, Alejandro saw several people caring for a teenage boy who lay moaning on a bed of furs.

"His son was wounded in the raid," One Who Flies said matter-of-factly. "I explained that you were of the Iron Shirts and not from my father's people."

Alejandro's heart was still trembling behind his ribs like a rabbit behind a hedge. It had been a long time since he had been that close to hand-to-hand combat. "Iron Shirts?" he asked, more to cover his discomfiture than anything.

"Yes. The People still remember you Spaniards as the men who rode up from the south wearing iron shirts and hats—the armor of the conquistadors. Blue Feather, a man from the Broken Jaw People, still has the chainmail shirt his great-great-grandfather won in battle. The People have a long memory."

"So it seems," Alejandro said, not entirely sure that that was a good thing. "But I thought you said the raid was not serious. Were many people wounded?"

"A few dozen or so," One Who Flies told him. "And five dead. A sixth may die as well."

"By all that is holy," he said, shocked, and stayed One Who Flies with a touch on his arm. "Five dead is not severe?"

One Who Flies did not look at him but only cocked his head in a gesture that blended imperiousness with impatience. "No, it is not,' he said as he started walking again. "Not compared to what we have known in the past. When the bluecoats—the American soldiers, that is—when they came at us in force, we sometimes lost up to two hundred men, women, and children in a single attack. On those days, however, they lost more. Now it is only a handful dead. Though we regret the losses, they are a war price we can afford to pay for now."

They had been walking among the lodges for what seemed a mile when, as men leaving a dense forest, they came suddenly into a great open area. Two or three hundred yards across, the huge circular clearing was surrounded by the multitude of lodges. In its center stood three huge lodges, each perhaps twenty feet tall. Two of them, both painted red and black, stood apart. The third gleamed in the sunlight, its bleached hides as bright as the sands on the shore that Alejandro remembered only through a fevered haze, and around it sat and stood a large crowd of people. The skins of this white lodge were cinched up to the height of a man, and within its timbered circle was a gathering of old men. Everyone was silent, and Alejandro had the uncomfortable realization that they were all looking at him.

"The Great Council," One Who Flies announced. "The People's ruling body. They would like to speak with you, if you feel up to it."

Alejandro knew he could not refuse, though what he might say, what they might ask, was a mystery he only hoped did not resolve itself into disaster. "Of course," he said, and followed One Who Flies toward the Council Lodge.

He was ushered in past the throng of people that surrounded the meeting place, in under the umbrella of the lodge's raised skins, and on to an empty place near the center. Acutely aware of the bareness of his backside, he managed to sit without too flagrant an exposure. He noted how the other men sat and crossed his legs likewise, tucking the breechclout down to cover as much as possible. There was some sniggering by a few of the nearest, but he chose not to notice it. One Who Flies sat down next to him.

"I shall interpret for you. Some of the chiefs understand French, though, so do not say anything to me that you do not want them to hear."

"I understand."

The Council consisted of more than fifty men; the youngest appeared to be around thirty-five years, while the oldest of them was of an agedness that surpassed any obvious numbering. Such a latter one was the old man who seemed to be the chief among chiefs. A withered creature, he sat near Alejandro in the inner circle. His back was bent with his years, and his white hair had been coaxed into two wiry braids. His face was lined, and his lips and tongue played with the gaps in his teeth while his hands played with a small fringed bag that hung from a leather thong tied about his neck. Alejandro sat as straight as his cross-legged position allowed him and looked at the venerable ancient in respectful silence, waiting for him to speak. Time passed, and Alejandro heard some of the other chiefs whispering amongst themselves. As the moments dragged, the whispering grew louder, more urgent. One Who Flies touched his arm.

"Quickly. Look down at your hands," he said.

Alejandro did so.

"Do not look a man in the eye," One Who Flies explained. "It is considered very rude, even a challenge. I am sorry; I should have thought to warn you. Do not stare, and do not speak until the person talking to you is finished."

"Anything else?"

"Yes. Don't get up until I tell you to."

Alejandro nodded.

"And don't nod. It makes you look stupid."

Alejandro glanced up at him.

"Ah-ah . . ."

He looked down at his hands again but not before he saw the young man smile.

"It makes you look stupid to us, I mean."

With his eyes respectfully lowered, the angry whispering subsided, and when quiet had returned, the old man spoke. His voice was calm and even, and he spoke in a slow, peaceful rhythm like a Schubertian andante.

"Three Trees Together speaks, welcoming Speaks for the Iron Shirts among the People. He regrets that your companion did not survive his illness. How are you feeling? he asks."

"I am much better, your . . . What do I call him?"

"You can call him 'Grandfather.'"

"I am much better, Grandfather. I would like to thank you for your hospitality and your gracious generosity. I owe you nothing less than my life."

One Who Flies translated his words while Alejandro struggled with *not* looking at the man to whom he was speaking, or anyone else for that matter. His hands filled his vision. He twisted his wedding band around his finger, concentrating on the bright piece of gold in the gloom of shaded summer.

"You are far from home," One Who Flies translated. "How is it you came to us?"

"A storm, Grandfather. A storm that rose from the south and blew me to your shores." He fingered his gold band and felt the bare breath of an idea begin to blow across his mind. "It was almost as if I was meant to come here," he said.

Murmurs could be heard from some of the chiefs, and

One Who Flies balked at translating. "What are you doing?"

"I am answering his question."

Three Trees Together spoke, and One Who Flies made a sign with his hands and then resumed his translation. "Three Trees Together asks you to explain."

Alejandro saw that he was treading delicate ground. One Who Flies was very protective of his adopted people, and wasn't about to let any flummery pass by without comment. Still, it was obvious that Alejandro had touched a chord that resonated with these savages.

"Well, it is just that the night before I left Havana, the governor and I were speaking about your people. We were talking about how bravely you had been fighting, and of your remarkable victory against the soldiers of the United States." He glanced at One Who Flies but the young man simply passed his words onward. "That night I said to my friend how I wished I could help you in your struggle against the soldiers, but"—he chuckled and hoped it sounded genuine—"I had no idea of how to contact you." He held out his hands. "And then the storm, and now here I am, talking to you. It just seemed . . . fated."

After One Who Flies passed his words along there was a long moment of quiet in which Alejandro heard only the whispering of the crowd beyond the poles that marked the perimeter of the lodge. The day was hot, but not nearly as hot as Havana had been, and with the breeze that waltzed through the interior, it was actually quite pleasant. Still, he missed the cool stucco of his San Francisco home and the evening fog that kept the air moist and fresh, even during the warmest weeks of summer. How he would ever get home from this place he did not care to guess. If it were to happen, though, he felt sure that the man he knew as One Who Flies would play a part.

"Why do you wish to help the people?" the old chief asked.

Alejandro suppressed the urge to glance at One Who Flies. This was the moment when the impression of deception could be deadly. "I have spent many years in the United States as a messenger between the leaders of that country and mine. I have heard of the great struggle you have waged against them, and I have heard many of them speak out in your defense." There was a reaction to this news—the Indians obviously had not known that they had supporters in the northern states. Alejandro noted this and continued.

"From what I have heard, from what I have read, and from what I have seen, I believe that you deserve to keep this land. I believe that the United States should withdraw its claim to your territory, and I am not alone in this belief. There are those in America and, more important to our discussion, there are those in New Spain who believe this as well. Your bravery and perseverance in this fight to retain your homeland have won you the admiration of many. Such courage deserves assistance, if it can be offered. And now, it seems, I can do just that."

As the translation ended Alejandro glanced up at the old chief and saw him sitting there, toying with the beaded bag that hung from his neck. He realized that the chief was listening—to the other chiefs and even to the crowd outside—taking in all the whispered comments and barely spoken opinions, judging his people by the mere tone of their words.

"What kind of assistance?" was the simple question that he finally asked, deftly maneuvering Alejandro into a corner of words, but Alejandro had learned his craft well, both at the negotiation table and in the brothels of New York. He knew how to answer a pointed question.

"Whatever can be provided," he said vaguely. "Once the nature of our relationship is agreed upon, the details will come naturally."

Several of the chiefs laughed quietly as the translation was passed along. Alejandro turned to his interpreter. One Who Flies turned up his palms.

One of the other chiefs stood and spoke. "One Bear says that you didn't say anything. He says that is just like a *vé'ho'e*—a white man—to speak with words that are as water in a man's hand. We have heard the same from Long Hair—President Custer." One Bear sat down. Alejandro heard the agreement in the whispers of the other chiefs and felt his cheeks flush with embarrassment. Irked at having been compared to Custer, he spoke before he thought.

"New Spain is a nation of great wealth and power. Tell me what it is that you need and it shall be provided." The silence that followed his words was different from the previous moments of reflection. This was a chilly silence, a fair response to his arrogance. But Alejandro's greater fear was not of giving offense.

¡Dios mío! he thought in exasperation. What have I just promised them?

The words of Three Trees Together were passed to him. "The nation of the Iron Shirts has many great and wonderful things. They are just as rich in things as are the men from the Horse Nations to the east. I am sure that whatever we want, the Iron Shirts have. What worries me is the price for these things. What price will the Iron Shirts ask for these things?"

Alejandro released a held breath, grateful that the Indians had not taken his words as a pronouncement of national policy. "The price," he replied, "would be friendship, an alliance between our governments, and trade between our peoples. This is the way of civilized nations. It is the way of New Spain."

"Your recent illness must have left you tired," Three Trees Together said. "You have our thanks." And then he rose to leave.

The sudden end to the proceedings could only mean that something had gone very wrong. "Wait," he said. "If you would agree to send some of your men . . . I'm sure the viceroy . . ." But the chiefs were leaving. Alejandro looked at One Who Flies.

"Do not worry, Don Silveira. Three Trees Together has heard enough for today."

"Oh, yes. I see." But he was not convinced.

"Tell me," One Who Flies said as they walked away from the Council Lodge. "How can you negotiate with both America and the People at the same time?"

"You can't," he said with an edge of exasperation in his voice. "You lie to one while you treat with the other." And then he heard the words he had just uttered as if they had come from someone else's mouth. He had let his befuddlement brought on by the afternoon's quick turns cloud his judgment. His illness must have weakened his mind as well as his body. "My apologies," he said, trying to retrace his steps. "That was unkind as well as untrue. Perhaps I am a bit more tired than I had thought. If I might try to answer your question again, I would say that it is very possible to negotiate with two opposing factions. It is done all the time. One must ensure, however, that the principles of the one dialogue are not in conflict with those of the other. It can be a delicate undertaking."

One Who Flies did not respond for a few moments. Finally he said, "I like your first answer better."

Alejandro had been afraid of that.

He spent the next few days resting and fretting while, as One Who Flies told him, the Council—and thereby the People as a whole—deliberated on what to do about their new guest. Having spent a lifetime within either a monarchical or a military command structure, he found the Council's methods both unreliable and unwieldy.

"How can they get anything done?" he asked on the fourth day. "How can they ever come to a decision?"

One Who Flies shrugged as he sat outside his lodge cleaning his rifle. "It does take time," he said. "But don't confuse the methods of the peace chiefs with those of the war chiefs."

Alejandro shook his head. "What do you mean?" he asked. "I have never heard of a peace chief."

One Who Flies put down his weapon and picked up a stick of firewood. He drew a circle in the dirt. "The Council is made up of peace chiefs. Four chiefs from every band." He drew ten small circles outside the larger one. "That makes forty chiefs. Add to that the four principal chiefs, like Three Trees Together, and you have the Council of Forty-Four. When the four allied tribes join up with us during the height of the summer, they each add four more chiefs to the council, for a total of sixty chiefs in the Great Council. These sixty chiefs are peace chiefs. Together in the summer, they decide matters of policy and politics. They decide with whom we shall trade, when to hunt, and when we shall move. They are the judges, the senators, the congressmen, and the aldermen of the People. They take about as long as you might expect to come to a decision, but when they do, it is always the best course of action."

He drew six other circles on top of all the others. "And then there are the soldier societies. Unaffiliated with any band, they are led by war chiefs. They are the generals and colonels of the People. It is the war chiefs who determine against whom we war, and when, and whether we fight just to count coup and steal whistlers or in an all-out fight to the death. They make their decisions quickly, as is often required, but sometimes they make mistakes. Sometimes bad ones."

He picked up his rifle stock again and resumed his cleaning of the action. "Be glad it is the peace chiefs who are deciding your fate. You wouldn't like what the war chiefs come up with."

"As you say," Alejandro conceded. "I can be as patient as the next man, when pressed."

One Who Flies glanced up from his work. "It looks like your patience will no longer be required."

Alejandro followed his host's gaze and saw four elderly men and a large collection of younger men making their way toward them. Families came out of their lodges as the elder chiefs and their retinue passed. The old men stopped to visit, to touch a child's cheek, to share a smile and a word. Alejandro recognized Three Trees Together among the four older chiefs, and it was he who set the slow pace. One Who Flies calmly continued to clean his weapon as the voice of the Council slowly made its way toward them.

When the chiefs were just a few lodges away, One Who Flies reassembled his rifle, stood, and stepped toward his lodge. "Come," he said, and Alejandro followed him inside.

He pulled the lodgeskins up to let in the breeze and poked a stick into the coals of the morning's fire. The coals responded, reaching up to touch the wind with a wizened finger of smoke. One Who Flies invited Alejandro to sit near him at the back of the lodge, and then pulled out a long bag from behind his wicker backrest. As the old chiefs arrived, One Who Flies stood, greeting them in their own language and inviting them inside. The invitation was accepted, but only the four elder chiefs entered to sit around the cooling hearth. The younger chiefs and the others with them all sat down outside the lodge, beyond the pinetree lodgepoles.

One Who Flies translated the introductions and opening pleasantries. Alejandro was familiar with the somewhat lengthy and circuitous protocols observed by certain statesmen, and so he was not surprised when, rather than getting to the point, One Who Flies took out of his bag a long, hand-carved pipe decorated with leather windings and pendants of feathers and shells. He proceeded to fill it with tobacco.

One Who Flies lit the pipe, but before he drew on it, he pointed the mouthpiece to the compass points, the sky, and the earth. Then he pulled a few mouthfuls, and passed the arm-long pipe to Alejandro. Alejandro took the pipe, drew on the stem, and found the smoke remarkably palatable. While he could taste the sharp resin, the Indian tobacco still produced a smoke that was sweet and flavorful. He followed the example of One Who Flies, and passed the pipe onward without word or comment, letting the bowl rest on the ground and handing the stem to the next man. The pipe traveled first clockwise around the circle, and then counterclockwise back toward One Who Flies. Some of the men let the smoke trickle upward from their mouths and wafted it up into their face and hair with a gentle wave of a hand. The pipe completed the circuit in silence, and when it was emptied and put away, Three Trees Together began to speak.

"We have thought about what you said the other day," he said. "We have thought very hard. It is difficult for us to believe the Iron Shirts want to be friends of the People. The Snake People tell of how the *vé'hó'e* of the Iron Shirts are no better than the *vé'hó'e* of the Horse Nations. The viper may shed its skin, but it still bites. The arguments against you were many."

Alejandro began to speak but One Who Flies moved a finger, reminding him to let the old man finish and not interrupt.

"But it seems as though the Thunder Beings have brought you to us, and that is a weighty thing. And then there is the vision that some think foretold of this." The old man began to toy with the little leather bag that hung around his neck. "It is hard to be sure of such things. The spirits do not speak the same language as men, and sometimes we get it wrong." He let go of the little bag.

"We have decided to send you home, Speaks for the Iron Shirts. One Who Flies will go with you, and fifteen of our soldiers. We will hear what the Chief of the Iron Shirts has to say about an alliance with the People."

Alejandro could not keep from grinning. He would be

returning to New Spain with the prospect of an alliance with America's most hated enemy, *and* with the son of their president. The revenge he could wreak, and the boost to his family's reputation—the viceroy could not ignore them now! Alejandro would be restored to his rightful place, and Custer would be put in his!

"Thank you, Grandfather. You don't know how much I appreciate this opportunity."

CHAPTER 12

Saturday, June 29, A.D. 1889
En route to Monongahela House
Pittsburgh, Penn's Sylvania

It had been a solemn and silent trip down from the coal-dark slopes of the western Alleghenies. Custer sat next to Libbie and wished she were not there, not because he did not take comfort in her presence—the interlaced fingers of their hands was evidence enough of that—but more so because he wished she had not seen what they had seen today.

Johnstown had been a thriving town with a rail junction, a healthy coal transportation industry, and a lovely resort community on the dammed waters of the Conemaugh River. The rainstorms of May 31 had ended all of it when the dam burst, hurling a violent flow of water upon the town. Custer, at the governor's request, had agreed to view the devastation in assessing the county's need for federal assistance in the reconstruction.

The air had been thick with moisture and the smell of decay. After four weeks, the odor of death was heavy in the air: a brutish, animal sweetness that lay beneath every taste, every smell he encountered. He stood on the tall embankment, looking down on the remnants of the town. Libbie had been at his side, perfumed lace held to her nostrils and an expression of ghastly understanding in her eyes.

The banks of the riverbed had been scoured clean, excoriated by a monstrous hand that left only the muddy nakedness of the water-soft earth. Houses and shops, hotels and meeting halls, anything that had stood along the riverside was gone, but the riverbed was glutted with debris. Custer scanned the bed and saw piles of wood planking, a cartwheel, whole trees, and scraps of iron trestlework. The flood had taken out all of the upstream bridges. Amid the refuse he saw dead livestock—horses, pigs, and dogs. A woman's brightly colored dress, half-stained with mud, hung from a branch. As they walked farther downstream, the silence that would accompany them back to Pittsburgh began to settle upon them. He saw railway cars piled together, a tractor bent and twisted like a broken insect. Piles of splintered wood and crooked metal littered the way where men had tried to clear their way to survivors and the dead. And then, past the town, stood the old stone bridge with its low, heavy arches—the only bridge that had held against the thousands of tons of watery might—and piled up against it three whitewashed houses, each tilted at a different angle, leaning against each other like furloughed soldiers, and each of them incongruously whole.

Custer had stared at those houses for a long time, noting especially the middle one's third-story window; unbent, unbroken, the rippled glass of its panes still intact. Inside that window, a curtain of blue lace hung at an angle.

That image haunted him more than the numbers: nineteen hundred dead; three hundred still missing and unaccounted for. Eighty percent of the town's economy wiped off the earth. Reconstruction? He couldn't imagine it. There was nothing to rebuild, no base from which to begin anew.

But the devastation was, for him, a thing that could be understood, something that could be put into perspective. Two thousand dead was a terrible number, but no more than he had known during his years in the military. The wars for the Kansa coast had shown him losses of comparable numbers, and the War of Secession had shown him much worse.

For Libbie, however, who had never seen battle firsthand and for whom such numbers had been only black ink in a newspaper headline, the sights of Johnstown were nearly overwhelming. Custer had felt her hand creep into his as they viewed the results of Nature's power. Mindful of the dignitaries, she had not wept nor exclaimed in any fashion. But throughout the rest of the afternoon, her hand had never left her husband's.

Now, in the carriage, jostling down the rain-rutted road toward Pittsburgh, the funereal silence continued, and Custer had found it not unwelcome. Sitting across from him and Libbie were his attaché Samuel and James Beaver, the governor of Penn's Sylvania. Beaver, his feelings of responsibility for the First Lady's state distressing his refined features, finally decided to breach the silence.

"You are sure you won't follow me up to Philadelphia, Mr. President? The missus hoped I might prevail upon you to join us for a late supper. I'm sure Mr. Prendergast here could rearrange your schedule to accommodate it, that is, if you cared to visit."

Custer smiled but it was Samuel who stepped in with a response.

"It is possible, Governor Beaver, as are most things, but perhaps not desirable. The President has several meetings scheduled this evening with the leaders of the railway and steel industry. Strikes, as you know, may be imminent, and we must try to reach a stable solution before the union leaders call the workers to act. I don't think I need tell you the effect such a work stoppage could have on the entire seaboard."

Beaver nodded. Custer knew him to be a fair-minded man, but also a man of a different age. Industrialization had come as a surprise to Jim Beaver, whose main political strategy had been to run a decent and honest administration for the public good. "I understand," the governor said. "I had heard, too, that some of the labor factions had planned to stage a . . . what did they call it? Ah, yes . . . a 'demonstration of solidarity' outside your hotel this evening."

"What?" Samuel said indelicately.

"Yes," Beaver went on. "And quite a show they had intended, too. Not to worry, though. I took the liberty to ensure that the so-called 'demonstrations' would fail to achieve their desired effect."

"Oh?" Samuel said with a worried glance toward Custer. He had his walking stick in hand. He leaned forward on its knob and looked directly at the governor. "Ensured how?" he inquired.

"Why, I simply secured the services of the Pinkertons."

"Aw, Hell!" Custer said.

"Autie," Libbie chided, breaking her silence.

"But Mr. President. The Pinkerton National Security Agency is known for their ability—"

"I am well aware of the Pinkerton Agency's reputation," Custer said. He nodded to Samuel.

Samuel rapped on the carriage ceiling with the knob of his walking stick, and the carriage came to a quick but controlled halt. The carriage lurched as Higgins, one of the two men always within reach of the president, descended and came to the window.

"Sir?"

"There's been a change of plans," Samuel said. "It seems some of the labor groups intend on protesting outside the hotel this evening."

"Yes? That shouldn't be a problem. We have the local constabulary at our disposal."

"The Pinks are in play," Custer told him.

Higgins frowned. "Yes, Mr. President. That changes things."

"Send someone ahead," Custer instructed him. "Wire Villard and the others. Cancel the meetings. We can't have them riding into a hornet's nest."

"Yes, Mr. President. Do you wish to head home tonight?"

Custer glanced at Libbie. Her eyes were still hollowed out by what she had seen. "No," he said, contriving an excuse to avoid the long nighttime trip. "I don't want to appear to be running away. Can you secure the hotel?"

"Indeed, Mr. President. Monongahela House is already sealed off to the general public."

"Good." Except it wasn't good. It wasn't anything *like* good. "We will leave in the morning, as planned."

"Yes, Mr. President."

Governor Beaver was as pale as birch bark. "I . . . I can't begin to apologize, Mr. President. It just seemed the right course of action."

"Of course," Custer said.

Higgins cleared his throat. "I'm sorry, Governor. I need you to switch to one of the other carriages." He opened the carriage door and held out his hand to assist the gentlemanly politician.

Beaver looked puzzled.

"For your safety," Custer explained. "And for mine. They'll take you directly to the railway station. Easier to protect us separately than together."

"Yes," the governor said meekly. "Of course." He gathered his hat, gloves, and stick, and with a weak smile stepped down. After a few moments the carriage rocked once more, and Custer heard Higgins order the driver to get them going.

"I'm sorry, sir," Samuel said.

Custer waved it off. "It wasn't your fault," he said. "Let's look at it as a boon, shall we? How often do Libbie and I get an evening alone with no business to perform? What do you say, sweet? A quiet dinner in our room? We could read aloud afterward. We haven't done that for ages."

Libbie's smile told him all he needed to know.

Spring steel creaked as they made their way over the country roads that rose and fell with the folded land. The sun traveled far ahead of them, heading for the clouds along the western horizon. An endless hour later, the sun had slipped down below the clouds, shining beneath them with a warm, even light. Custer looked out and saw that they had reached the last of the hills. The sun lit the valley of the Monongahela River like a lantern on a hobbyist's toy town, ricocheting off the river and glimmering through the haze of industry. The towers and steeples of Pittsburgh stood bright and tall in the last of the day's light. Beyond the waterfront buildings he saw the tall smokestacks of riverboats, dark as pitch, belching coal smoke up into the gathering clouds.

A quiet evening, he hoped silently. Pray that the Pinkertons don't create too much havoc.

As they came down through town, down Smithfield toward Water Street, it became apparent that Custer's prayer had gone unheeded by higher powers. Small groups of working-class men, shoulders hard and gaits stiff, stumped along the boardwalks and the mud-rutted streets. They carried torches and lanterns; a few had placards high over their heads. From around the corner appeared bowler-topped Pinkerton agents, their long batons in hands prepared to crack a few skulls. A group of union men stood their ground and placards became lances, torches became clubs. Eventually they all scattered, but all were headed downhill, toward the riverbank, toward Monongahela House.

Higgins leapt down onto the running board and poked his head inside the window. "It looks bad, Mr. President. I'd like to take us around the back."

"Of course," Custer said. They passed through an intersection where another brawl had broken out. An onlooker noticed the presidential carriage, stared after it, shouted, and pointed. Men began to run after them.

"Damnation," Custer muttered. He grabbed Samuel's walking stick and struck the ceiling. "Let's get moving," he ordered. The carriage responded to his command, thundering across the cobbles and rails.

Every entryway to the hotel was guarded by a pair of dark-suited constables The two at the rear entrance, not expecting any duty other than rebuffing the too-brazen or the overly curious, stared as the President and First Lady stepped down from the shiny dark carriage and moved quickly toward them.

"Look lively, you two," Higgins said as he prepared the way. The constables recovered, snapped to, and put hands to their nightsticks.

Custer and Libbie passed them without a word and climbed the back stairs to their second-floor apartment— the same rooms that had been used by Lincoln and Grand Duke Alexis. It was a fine room, and well deserving its rarified clientele. The plastered ceilings rose high overhead, surrounded by a two-foot-tall cornice molding. The walls and windows had been covered with a fabric of rich red and maroon, patterned in a large design that struck Custer as something between a scallop shell and a phoenix. The furnishings, all heavily carved in dark walnut and cherrywood, did their utmost to not appear dwarfed by the room's height, assisted by the ten-foot-tall, oak-arched mirror that stood atop the whitestone fireplace.

It was a grand room and would have provided them with an evening's ease except for the raucous shouts and jeers that came from outside. Custer walked to the tall windows and peeked through the split in the heavy drapes.

He looked down onto Water Street, the riverbank, and the two low gridiron arches of the Smithfield Bridge. The intersection below the hotel was filled with men from curb to curb. Vying factions had set up podia on either side of Water Street, decorated with bunting and banners that proclaimed their opposing views.

On the near side of the street, thick-thewed laborers from the iron and steel mills called for solidarity in a "National Strike for Fair Wages." Across from them, the banner for the textile and manufactory unions demanded decent hours. And at the corner, a flock of suffragettes and northern freethinkers brandished their placard signs mandating the establishment of equal rights for all, including self-determination for the Indians of the territories. The ironwrights shouted, the factory workers hollered, and the suffragettes joined hands with their existentialist comrades and sang "Nearer My God to Thee."

Custer *tsk*ed.

Libbie came up behind him, her perfume of orange blossoms enfolding him. "What troubles you, dear?"

He gestured outside. "Them," he said. "They don't know what they want."

She put a hand on his right shoulder and peered over his left, looking out the narrow slit he held open in the drapes. "How so?"

Custer became aware of the warmth of his wife's breath on the nape of his neck, the pressure of her bodice against his back. "They want us to expand the railways into the territories, but don't want the Indians to suffer for it. They want us to stop fighting the Indians, but don't want to lose anything." He pointed to the labor groups. "They want higher wages and shorter hours, but don't want to pay more for their goods. They say they'll strike in order to get what they want, but don't want to lose their jobs. It's hard to believe these unionizers really have the workers' needs at heart."

"The speakers do seem much better fed than those they represent," she said, and he heard the smirk in her voice. "But I'm sure they will suffer mightily in heart while the workers suffer in body."

Custer chuckled. "True enough. And of course, the business leaders don't want anything to change. They grow rich on the status quo and will do anything to maintain it."

The speaker for the steelworkers stopped exhorting his constituents and began hurling epithets at his counterpart across the street. The rhetorician for the textile union responded with likewise fervor. It was only moments before the first punch was thrown.

As if it had been a signal, around the corner marched a double rank of men in dark coats and rounded bowlers. Each man carried a yard-long length of wood.

"The Pinkertons have arrived," Custer said dismally.

The agents from Pinkerton National Security moved on the crowd. Holding their batons lengthwise, they pushed at the protesters, trying to sweep them forward and down the street. Ladies from the suffragette brigade met them headon, standing firm for a breath of time. Too minute a threat for Pinkerton concern, they quickly either broke and fled or were callously shoved to the rear.

The line of batons quickly met the roiling mass of workers. The shouts of a dozen brawls became the roar of a building riot. Batons began to rise and fall as the Pinkertons began their work. Custer heard the sound of breaking glass from the floor below.

There was a quick knock and the door opened. Higgins came in. "Please, Mr. President," he said, coming to his side. "We're only on the second floor, sir."

"As you wish," he said. He let the drapes fall closed on the chaos. It did not keep out the sounds.

"Thank you, sir. Would you or Mrs. Custer care for supper?"

Custer glanced at his wife and saw the tiny contraction of her brow. "Later," he said.

"Thank you, Mr. President," Higgins said, and departed.

Custer walked to the fainting couch and fell back onto its tuck-and-button upholstery. "What an immortal muddle. Meriwether is flummoxed in the Territory, able to merely keep the Alliance at bay. The only headway we make is by throwing open the doors and flooding the plains with homesteaders. Meanwhile, the unions here threaten the moguls, who then shy away from investing out in the Frontier. I can't see a way to win on both fronts. The two factions are too far apart."

Libbie followed him to the couch and knelt beside it, the flounces of her skirts pillowing up beneath her. Her face was crowned by a dark sunburst of chestnut curls, and the long sweep of her slender eyebrows quirked upward with an idea. She smiled with an almost impish expression.

He questioned her with a look. "What are you thinking, I wonder?"

She looked at him frankly, tenderly, resting against him. He felt her soft, cool fingers take his hand and caress his knuckles. "I am thinking," she said, "that you have never been talented in the art of compromise."

"Why, I thank you for the compliment," he said with friendly sarcasm.

"I meant it as one," she said. "Drawing men to consensus is simply not your way. You are my Beau Saber, my Golden Cavalier, and you are ever the man of action."

Custer sat up a bit on the couch but took care to keep hold of his wife's hand. "I'm afraid I don't follow your drift, my dear."

She looked down at the hand she held with such tenderness. "You know I don't like to give you advice. . . ."

"But when you have, I've always listened, haven't I?"

"Yes . . ."

"Well, then?"

"Now don't get cross," she warned, "or I shall say nothing."

"You exasperate me at times, Libbie Bacon. You honestly do." He took a deep breath. "My apologies. You were saying?"

Libbie glanced up at him again, this time in seriousness. "I do not believe that compromise is the best path for you to follow," she said. "You aren't good at it, and it is not the proper solution."

"And what is?" he said, and when her brow twitched with mild annoyance, he added quickly, "I really want to know."

She nodded, reconciled on continuing, and met his gaze. "You are a man of war, not politics. I've always said that, but right now I think it can be to your benefit." She glanced at the window to indicate the throng in the street beyond. "You are in a battle, Autie—you just said it yourself— fighting two foes: Industry and the Frontier."

"Yes," he said, understanding her.

"And you cannot win on both fronts."

"No," he agreed. "I don't see that I can."

She shrugged, as if it were the simplest thing to solve. "Then you must give ground on one flank, in order to achieve a victory on the other."

"What are you saying?" he said slowly.

She rose up on her knees and leaned toward him, resting her corseted breast on his torso. "What if you gave way on the Territory, even ceded part of it to the Cheyenne, and then turned a hard hand against the unions? You could win back the businessmen, please the freethinkers, and overcome the labor parties in a thrice."

He was shocked by the suggestion. "Give up the Territory?"

"Why not?" she asked, and then with an icy calmness said, "You could always take it back later."

"Libbie," he said, "I didn't think you could surprise me anymore." He smiled. "I seem to have been wrong." He pulled her closer.

Outside, shrill whistles and the clop of hooves announced the arrival of mounted police on the scene. The cries and havoc began to die down and drift away into the night. Within minutes, the cobblestones were empty save for discarded placards, crushed hats, and the unconscious victims of Pinkerton excess.

CHAPTER 13

Sunday, September 15, A.D. 1889
Westgate
Yankton

Cesare jumped down off the wagon and spat into the dust.

The dust, always and ever, the dust. Yellow, gritty, dry as stone in a man's mouth, sharp as glass in his eye. He hated the dust as he hated few other things. It rose with the morning's breeze, flew with the noonday air, and settled into a man's every crack and orifice by the evening calm. It was a dust so dry that when it rained, water beaded up on it and ran off, seeking easier ground. And now, returning from another back-cramping day spent digging trenches, hauling dirt, and wrassling with foot-thick ties; now, with the sun nearly set and the first stars winking down upon his pain; now the dust covered him, covered every man head to toe, skin and clothing, turning them all into men of dust and clay. They descended from wagons and cars, each man alike regardless of his birth: pale and pasty, red-eyed and stoop-shouldered, beaten and bitter, golems of exhaustion.

He and several other men went to the trough and splashed water on their faces, revealing skin beneath the grime. The water sluiced past ears crusted with sweat and dirt, over brows gritty with salt. From moving statues, Medusan warriors, they emerged: African, German, Irishman, Swede. Men they became again, and human.

Cesare unhooked the tin cup he carried on his belt and dunked it into the water. He did not care that the trough was already foul with dirt, for the water was not for him to drink. Someone shouldered against him, causing him to

spill. It was Murphy. The broad-faced Irishman had taken
Cesare as his own personal whipping boy, and stinted no
opportunity to use him. He sneered, silently inviting violence, but Cesare had learned many lessons since his own
tragic Spring, not the least of which was to choose his battles with care. The obvious fight was usually most easily
lost.

He dunked the cup again and turned away without meeting the Irishman's challenge. Murphy chuckled and said
something audible only to those still washing at the silted
trough. Laughter, derisive and cruel, followed Cesare as he
walked toward the tents.

The railworker camp was a few large tents surrounded
by a sea of small ones. The large tents—the mess, the
stores, the infirmary, and the bosses' barracks—glowed in
the early evening with yellow lantern light, the canvas walls
alive with shadows of men. The tents stood close together,
facing inward toward one another, as if to deny the existence of Cesare and the throng of workers at their backs.

But they did exist. Men from a dozen countries walked
from the wagons and railcars toward the unlit canvas shells
where they would lie, crammed four or six to each army
surplus tent, through a short and dreamless night only to
rise sometime before dawn—voluntarily or with encouragement—to begin another day of toil.

The men of the camp were built for labor—rough, uned-
ucated, and poor as the dust that coated them. There were
hundreds of tents, over a thousand men. The camp was a
town unto itself, a town built of dust, with nothing for
leagues around them except the sharp-edge prairie grass,
and the long, vanishing lines of the iron road that bisected
the camp. Cesare stood for a moment, staring eastward
down the shiny-railed road that led back to the big rivers
of the civilized world. In the distance, he could see the
lights of homesteads such as the one he had imagined for
his own family. Beyond those lights he thought he could
see the glow of Mansfield, one of the dozens of towns that
had sprung up literally overnight after the Land Rush had
opened the gates.

Looking west, however, he saw nothing. Beyond the dark
railcars, the shadowed stockpiles, and the hissing, pinging
bulk of the camp's black locomotive, there lay nothing but

emptiness. It was as if the world did not exist in that direction and he stood at the edge of the earth, a cliff roofed over with a canopy of strengthening stars.

He began walking again, wending his way through the sloppy ranks of tents. He heard music—to his left a concertina, to his right a harmonica, and somewhere ahead a jaw-harp and spoons twanging and clacking like strung bones. The odors of strong urine and stronger whiskey wafted between the shells, and Cesare knew some of the men would forgo the unsatisfying food at the mess for a more fulfilling evening with a bottle purchased with half a week's wage.

He came to his own row, followed it down past a dozen shells, ducking clotheslines and overstepping guy ropes, until he found his own tent. Petursson and Ingvarsson were already there, as was the man they all knew only as Coffee—a huge black who spoke no civilized tongue but who understood English well enough to keep his head on his shoulders and a meal on his plate. Cesare had never seen Coffee sleep, and therefore he considered the black giant a good man to have around.

Petursson and Ingvarsson did not like sharing their tent with an Italian and a Negro, but put up with the arrangement because they were only four to a tent instead of six, due in no small part to Coffee's size and fearsome aspect.

The two Icelanders looked up as Cesare approached but said nothing. Coffee raised a giant pale-palmed hand and Cesare returned the greeting.

"Cavendish put me on cleanup," he said to the Negro. "Had to stay out until the last run."

Coffee nodded, meaning he understood. He always nodded when spoken to, even if the proper answer was a "no." For all Cesare could tell, the man understood him, but still he had taken to using only phrases that required an affirmative answer when speaking to Coffee.

"Looks like I made it back in time for grub, yes?"

Coffee nodded.

Cesare walked around to the rear of the tent, opened the flap, and sat down on the ground, careful not to spill the water he carried. He reached inside and felt the rough edge of the can he kept near his bunk. Careful of its contents, he pulled the lone surviving grapevine out into the starlight.

The vine's lobed, hand-sized leaves looked like velvet, soaking up the blue night. At the end of one of the broken canes, three new leaves had untwisted from their crèche and were reluctantly unfurling. It was late for new leaves, but the grapevine had been through much, and new leaves were a sign that it was recovering from its difficult summer. Cesare took the can—a replacement for the pot Murphy had shattered weeks ago—and put it on the ground, trickling some of the water he brought into it. The dry soil soaked it up as quickly as a sot consumed gin, and Cesare dribbled in more, here and there, until the soil was saturated and the excess began to drain out the holes he had punched in the bottom of the can.

"There you go," he said to the little plant. "Papa would be proud of you." He put the can back inside near the sloping wall of the tent shell and tossed the small bit of water left out into the dust.

He lay back, half-in and half-out of the tent, resting his head on the roll of his blanket and staring up into star-filled eternity. He reached inside his pocket and took out the palm-sized fold of parchment he always carried. A quick glance told him that the two Icelanders were talking to each other and paying him no mind. He looked back at the folded paper. It was definitely worse for its travels. To its bloodstains, Cesare had added the marks of sweat and dirt. One corner had worn through, which, as he rolled onto his side and unfolded it, revealed a pattern of symmetrical holes.

The words on the paper were heavy and dark. Even in the dim light they looked strong: so deliberate and forceful. For the most part they remained as foreign to him now as they had been on the day of his family's slaughter. He stared at them, then let his finger touch the only word he had been able to sound out.

America.

But he did not care so much about the words on the page. He cared about what was held within the paper's folds.

He tipped the paper to one side and the chain hissed as it ran out into his hand. It was so delicate, so fine that he could not feel it when it dripped across his palm like quicksilver. But he felt the crucifix. He felt the edges of its filigree against his fingertips, felt the limits of its four ends, and felt the smoothness of the tiny Christ who hung pegged to its crosspiece. He stared at the cross, brilliant with starlight, and said a tiny prayer for the souls of his family.

"Fortuna," he said softly. "Tell the angels about me. Ask them to pray for me." Then he kissed his sister's crucifix, refolded the paper around it, and tucked the packet away. He looked up to see Ingvarsson and Petursson watching him.

"Did you see the Indians?" he asked, distracting them from the silver cross. "Belvoir said his gang saw some off to the north."

"I don't believe him," Ingvarsson said. His voice was guttural and ugly, though his features were crisp and Nordic.

"You can ask him yourself," Cesare said. "He said they saw about twenty Indians on those big lizards, just standing out on the prairie, watching."

"I don't doubt he said it," Ingvarsson said. "I just don't believe he saw anything."

"We haven't seen an Indian in months," Petursson chimed in. "Much less twenty. Besides, Belvoir cannot speak without lying."

Cesare shrugged. "If you say so, but some of the others in his gang—" The mess bell interrupted him. They all swore and scrambled to get their plates and cups before jumping to their feet.

The bell—no more than a suspended bar of iron that the cook's assistant beat upon with particular flair—pealed as the men ran toward the center of camp. Its sound was sharp and urgent. As they neared the tent, they joined up with other men until at the end they were a mob on the move. They shoved and pulled at each other, pushing for position in the four large lines that formed up out of long practice. Cesare, with Coffee at his side, both being large of frame and heavy with muscle, walked past the frenzy at the end of the line, past the men who did not dare complain. The trick, he had found, was not in taking advantage of weaker men, but in discovering which of the stronger men he could cow. He walked to the middle of the line and scanned the faces.

The line formed a spectrum of strength, the mighty at

the front, the weak at the rear. With no more than a glance, Cesare was able to find where in that continuum he fit. The stronger ignored him; the weaker looked at him with anxious deference. Between these were the men who met his gaze frankly, and it was in amongst these equals that Cesare and Coffee stepped into line.

He caught sight of Murphy, up ahead of him in the other line. The Irishman smiled, showing lost teeth.

"What's the matter, guinea?" he shouted above the din. "Too busy sayin' yer prayers to come to dinner?"

Cesare took a breath but felt a hand on his shoulder. He looked back to see Coffee's calm face. *Patience,* that countenance told him.

"Praying," Cesare said with a nod. "Took me a long time. I asked the Holy Madonna to have pity on such a stupid sinner as you. You should thank me. Without prayers like mine, you're going to be buggered by the Devil himself."

Murphy bared his remaining teeth and lunged but was held back by his men. Cesare had painted him into a corner, for as a good Catholic, he could not in fair conscience beat another for entreating the Holy Mother on his behalf. The Irishman dismissed Cesare with a wave of his hand, and Cesare felt the tension drain out of him. He turned to share the good humor with the others in line and saw a man leaning against a tent pole. The man was watching the scene with interest. Cesare turned away.

"Who's that?" he asked one of the others in line.

"Hm?" the other said, glancing over. "Oh, that's Cooper. Gang boss. Usually works the stores and shipments. Easy work, if you can get it. Seems to have noticed you."

Cesare grumbled. "I don't want to be noticed."

"Then you shouldn't chafe the biggest mick in camp."

He kept his mouth shut after that, and waited for the line to crawl forward to the slop troughs. Then, with a heel of bread, a cup of water, and a tin plate full of a spicy stew they all called simply "red," he went in search of a peaceful spot to sit and eat.

He and Coffee went over to the stacks of food crates, where they could lean back and enjoy their meal. Other men followed them and soon the short length was occupied. They had all just started to eat when around the corner came Murphy and his toadies. Kicks and curses cleared a space for the newcomers, and with a few meaningful glances toward Cesare and Coffee, they sat down beside them.

"Mary, Mother of God," Cesare said under his breath. "Why won't he leave me alone?"

Once again, Coffee patted his arm in gentle encouragement. Cesare sighed, and went back to his meal.

"Red" was usually called so because of the deep, garnet sauce made of oil and ground chili pepper that coated the beans and made palatable the occasional chunk of overaged meat. Sometimes, though, and especially when Cook's assistant had charge of the preparations, the appellation came from the color of men's faces as they ate. Tonight was such a night, and as Cesare took his first mouthful of the thin stew, he felt the heat rise in his mouth. After months of such culinary assaults, he—like all the old hands—had built up a resistance to the spice, but tonight's attack was especially fierce. The color rose in his cheeks, his eyes watered, his nose began to run, and sweat beaded on his forehead, but he was able to suffer through and even—in an odd, almost perverse way—enjoy the experience. Others, however, were not so fortunate, and shouts and laughter bloomed in the night as the newer laborers had their first taste of the other "red." Cesare even heard some stalwarts coughing at the heat.

At the other end of the crates, one of Murphy's men had had enough.

"God *damn* it!" His plate clanged as he threw it to the ground. Murphy and the others laughed at their comrade's distress. "Shut yer gobs! We work, day and night, f'r a penny-pittance, killin' ourselves f'r the Man, buildin' his railroad, makin' him rich, and all he sees fit t'feed us is this *shite*." He swilled water from his cup and spat it out in a spray. "I'm sick of it, I tell you. I'm fekkin' sick of it!"

The others of his crowd applauded the litany of woe, seconding the sentiments with complaints of their own.

"I had a better bed when I lived with me seven brothers in a one-room shed. We're stacked up like cordwood out here."

"And he charges us for the blankets!"

"Surprised he doesn't charge for the food."

"I wouldn't pay, I wouldn't."

"I can't save a dime here. How can we send money home if we can't save?"

" 'Tis a shame, it is. A fekkin' shame."

Cesare ignored them as best he could and ate his bowl of spice. He remembered his mother's cooking on Sundays, the smell of *pasta e fagioli* filling their small house, and the taste of raw, new Chianti—the best his father could afford but a luxury he would not do without. "To break bread on the Sabbath without a splash of the red," his father used to say. "Now *that* would be a sin."

But the red Cesare had before him now was as different as he could imagine. Idly, he wondered if it was Sunday. It had been a long time since he knew what day of the week it was.

"You!"

Cesare looked up, startled out of his reverie by the man who stood before him. It was Murphy's man, the one who'd tossed his meal away.

"Yeah, you. You're awful quiet. Your nigger's too fekkin' stupid to speak up, but what about you? You think it's so grand here, eh? You think I'm just a little whining girly or somethin'?"

Cesare felt his pulse begin to surge, felt his breath go slow and deep. His torso pulled itself taut as muscles prepared for battle. Murphy and the rest of his men looked on in fierce attention, waiting for his assault, waiting for the moment when they would all jump him and beat him into a bloodied mass of meat that even Cook's assistant wouldn't touch. He fought his urges, forcing himself to break away and look back down at his meal. He took another spoonful of meat.

The man's foot caught Cesare's plate and sent it singing through the air. Red spattered up into his face and eyes.

"I'm talkin' to you, y'guinea *gobshite*. You think you're better than me? You think you don't have to answer me when I'm talking to you?" He snorted. "Get up, y'dago bastard." The man was ready, fists clenched, legs bent slightly at the knees.

Cesare, sitting on the ground, holding his dripping spoon, his eyes stinging with red, sighed.

"Get up, fekkin' dago."

He moved to rise but Coffee held him back. He saw his friend's warning glare, but beyond him he saw Murphy's gleeful anticipation.

"Some battles," Cesare said to Coffee, "a man cannot avoid."

He held up a hand to ask for a moment to rise, and the Irishman backed off a step. He got to his feet and shook his head to clear it. He was tall and broad, but the Irishman matched him pound for pound. He put up his left hand and pulled his right in close, palming the long-handled spoon. Murphy and his men surged up and formed a circle around the combatants. Coffee rose and joined the circle, for which Cesare was thankful. When they all jumped him, they'd have to deal with Coffee, too.

The Irishman began to dance like a Hell's Kitchen pugilist while Cesare simply walked the circuit, keeping the other in view, at a distance, and with his left hand between them. The other threw a punch, hitting Cesare's shoulder, and another that grazed his jaw.

An eye on his opponent, he watched the circle as well. Murphy egged the fighters on, wanting blood—wanting Cesare's blood—but the others were watching Murphy. They watched the fight, to be sure, but it was from Murphy that they were taking their cues. A few held cudgels or saps, while in Murphy's hand he saw the gleam of lamplight off a dirty blade.

You see how it is, Fortuna? he prayed. Tell the saints, *cara*. Tell them that I am not a bad man.

He leapt in with a left-handed feint. The Irishman ducked it, not realizing that he was not the goal. Cesare continued onward, toward the men in the circle. He flipped the spoon in his right, the handle of the spoon now protruding from between his fingers. He hit Murphy in the face, the spoon's handle sinking deep into his eye socket. Cesare spun, swinging widely with his left, smashing the nose of the next man in the circle. Murphy fell backward, dead before he hit the ground, his knife still in his hand and the spoon deep in his brain. Cesare turned back to his opponent. The Irishman stared at the deadly violence that had erupted before him. Cesare snapped his fingers and the man looked at him.

"Just because a man doesn't speak up," Cesare said, "it

doesn't mean he doesn't agree with you." Then he kicked up into the man's groin, booting him up off his feet. He fell to the ground in a gasping ball of pain. Cesare turned again and found only Coffee, two other men moaning at his feet.

Cesare bent and picked up his plate and his cup. From one of the others he took a spoon. He motioned to Coffee.

"Best we go," he said.

They stepped quickly around from behind the crates and came face-to-face with the man Cesare had seen earlier. The gang boss. Cooper.

Cooper glanced over Cesare's shoulder. "Have a little tiff with the big mick?"

Murder had happened in camp before—it was inevitable with such a large collection of vulgar men, many of whose last bed and board had come beneath a penitentiary roof—but it had never been a punishable offense. The bosses had always turned a blind eye and let the men sort it out. But Cesare was nervous. This was the second murder he had committed, and here was a boss taking an especial interest.

"Wasn't anything, sir," Cesare said as he tried to step by.

Cooper held him back with a hand on his chest. "Don't sell yourself short, lad." He nodded toward the bodies—alive and dead— that lay on the ground. "That was most definitely something. Something indeed."

Cesare exchanged glances with Coffee, but gleaned no ideas from his silent companion. "Just a workman's fight, sir. We sorted it out."

Cooper's mouth was wry with the trace of a smile. He let his hand drop. "If you say so," he said as he turned and walked back toward the mess tent.

Cesare felt his knees go weak as the rush of battle drained out of him. "Let's get out of here," he said.

Coffee nodded.

By the morning, word had swept through the camp. Cesare awoke before dawn to find the two Icelanders missing, their pallets rolled up and taken, and every evidence of their existence having disappeared in the night. He and Coffee looked at each other in disbelief. They looked at the expanse of vacant space beneath the canvas shells, looked at each other again, then broke out into grins and rearranged their belongings so as to take up as much acreage as possible.

When the morning meal bell was struck, they ran—just as usual—to collect their bowl of slop and gulp of coffee. But as Cesare came in to find his place in line, he found the point of equilibrium had shifted. Men who had previously faced him now only glanced nervously in his direction. Others, who before had never paid him a moment's mind, now met his gaze with rough-hewn respect. Cesare and Coffee stepped into line a full twenty feet closer to the fires than before. They were even early enough to get a slice of bacon on their grease-soaked bread.

"I tell you," Cesare said as they sat down to eat. "If I'd known that we'd get *this* kind of treatment, I'd have killed that dog's prick two months ago."

Coffee smiled, but behind him Cesare once more saw Cooper, leaning against a pole, eating his meal, watching. The gang boss skewered a sausage link from his plate, and raised his fork in morning salute. Cesare picked up his slice of undercooked bacon and greeted him in kind. Together the men ate their meat, each eyeing the other.

Coffee noticed the exchange and scowled.

Cesare smiled around his meal. "Don't worry," he said. "If we were to be in trouble, we would be in trouble by now."

Coffee scrunched up his face but subsided and went back to his meal. It wasn't until they were sopping up the grease with their crusts that Cooper came over, and by then Cesare was ready. He'd dealt with *padroni* before.

"You seem to have come up in the world," the boss said.

"Yes, sir. Quite a bit, sir," he said as he stood to meet their benefactor. "I would like to thank you for stepping in on our behalf. I can't begin to think of how I might begin to repay such—"

"Hold it," Cooper said. "You think I'm responsible?"

Cesare stammered and looked to Coffee for help. "Y-yes, sir. Of course."

Cooper shook his head. "I did nothing. What you earned today you earned on your own merits."

Cesare was confused. "Then . . . then why . . ."

"Why am I interested?"

Cesare nodded. So did Coffee.

"I'm interested because I think I *can* do something for you. Me and Mr. Wood. That is, if you're willing to do something for us."

Cesare stood up straight at the mention of Mr. Ellerby Ignatius Wood, a man whom no laborer had ever actually seen but of whom all had heard. "Yes, Mr. Cooper. What sort of 'something' are you talking about?"

And Cooper told him. He told him of Wood's efforts to unionize the railworkers, both here and in Chicago, and of why that was a good idea. He told him how, just as the smallest twig could lever an iron rail into position, a little muscle applied in just the right place could coerce even the strongest man.

"I think that we can help each other," Cesare said. "But on one condition." He hooked a thumb over his shoulder, pointing to the silent giant at his back. "Him, too."

Cooper thought about it. His eyes glanced from Cesare to Coffee. He turned and paced off a rail length, came back, and paced it off again.

"Wood won't like it," he said. "He won't like a nigger at all."

Cesare sensed a need to press the advantage. "Mr. Cooper," he said. "You saw what happened last night. You know that if Coffee hadn't been there, today you would be looking down on my grave instead of Murphy's. Coffee and me, we are a team. I can't do what you want without someone I trust. No offense, sir."

"None taken." Still, Cooper looked disturbed by the notion. His mustache writhed beneath his nose as he tried to figure the odds. In the end, he decided. "We'll try it out," he said. "But he's *your* nigger. Not mine."

Cesare understood precisely. "Yes, sir."

Cooper frowned for a few moments more, then seemed to think that they were done. "Come see me tomorrow morning."

"But Cavendish, my boss. He'll want—"

"Come see me tomorrow," Cooper said again, and in a tone that brooked no counter. "Both of you."

"Yes, sir," Cesare said.

It did not take long to build up a reputation with the workers. Within a week, Cesare walked in the company of men he used to fear. The mere mention of Cooper or the shadowy Mr. Wood was usually enough to turn around even the most stubborn of men, but for those who remained resistant to the union leaders' desires, a more personal demonstration of power was arranged.

Cesare and Coffee would loiter in the firelight as Cooper spoke to men he wanted to turn to the union cause, plying them with beer. When the meeting broke up, Cooper would tip his hat if the discussions had gone well. If he didn't, Cesare and Coffee would head out to the latrine pits and wait.

Through experience and tips from Cooper's other strong-arms, Cesare learned how to bend but not break a man, as well as how to break him if he so desired. He learned how much force meant a two-day stay in the infirmary, how much more meant a week's stay, and just how much more meant a ticket back east. And each day, he found his place in the meal line had moved forward a few more feet.

For Coffee, however, instead of bringing safety, their new notoriety brought danger. When Coffee arrived back at their tent beaten and bloody, Cesare demanded to know who had done it.

"Tell me!" he shouted. "I'll kill the bastards!"

But Coffee refused to speak, even to name his attackers. The next day Coffee lagged behind when Cesare went to meet with Cooper for their morning discussion.

"Hurry," Cesare said. "He's waiting for us."

For the first time since he had known him, Coffee shook his head.

"If you just told me who did it—"

Coffee grimaced and shook his head again.

Cesare looked up into his friend's face; coal-dust skin, blood-pink teeth, vein-shot whites around irises the color of stone, the bloody knot on his forehead, and the purpled swelling beneath his left eye. "Had enough?" Cesare asked, understanding.

Coffee nodded.

Cesare held out his hand. "If you need anything . . ."

That night, Cesare had the tent to himself.

His reputation grew as his "education" continued. Which of a man's joints was the weakest. How to disable with a penknife. How to set a fire that would frighten but not kill.

And how to kill. Most definitely, how to kill. He took to it quickly; but though his soul was already consigned to Hell, his easy acceptance of the work worried him. His grief had frozen, fossilized, but the rage in his heart still burned, and the violence helped to release the rage. When his own acts disturbed his sleep, all he had to do was touch the folded paper that held the last remembrance of his dearest twin.

Among Cooper's enforcers, he became an outcast: too brutal even for them to accept. Soon he was at the front of the food line, regardless of when he arrived, and every morning ham and links were waiting for him. It was not long after when Cooper came up to him with news.

"Mr. Wood wants to meet you."

Cesare tried hard not to show his trepidation.

"Mr. Wood is coming here? To the Territory?"

Cooper laughed. "Hardly. You're going to Chicago."

His jaw fell slack. "Chicago?" he managed. He barely remembered Chicago. It had been a blur of smoke and elbows and cattle and machines and brick-walled canyons. He and his family had sped through it on their way to Yankton and the dreams of the Land Rush. But he remembered the reason for their flight. Though it seemed a lifetime ago, the image of his bloody hands, Fortuna's screaming mouth, and the foreigner's crushed-in skull still haunted his nightmares.

"Mr. Cooper," he began, not wanting to say too much but feeling that something had to be said. "Before you take me to Chicago, I have to tell you . . . I had some trouble, sir. Back in New York."

"What kind of trouble?"

"Bad trouble, Mr. Cooper. I killed a man."

Cooper folded his arms and squinted. "A policeman?"

"Oh, no, sir. Not a policeman. A Spaniard."

Cooper chuckled and slapped Cesare on the shoulder. "You had me worried, son."

"But he was a rich man, Mr. Cooper."

"He could be the king of Spain for all I care. Just so long as he wasn't a cop, we'll have no problems. Now come on. We leave tonight."

The train trip to Chicago took five days, during which time Cesare was transformed. Physically he was washed, scrubbed, shaved, clipped, oiled, trimmed, and pomaded. His clothes were ceremoniously sent forward to the engineer for incineration in the firebox, after which he was given new clothing from the skin outward. The attention to his body and the new suit of clothes affected him. He felt stripped of his own harshness, as if the oils and perfumes and the soft touch of fine cloth were sinking inside, soaking into him. And when the train stopped at Cairo and let on some additional guests—female guests who were already closely acquainted with Mr. Cooper and very willing to include Cesare to their circle of friendship—he began to realize that his life had changed in almost every way.

He sat in a private car with Cooper, who sat on the divan, a redheaded woman named Florence close beside him. Aromas of richness filled the room. Cooper smoked a cigar, filling the dark-paneled room with its sweet smoke. Cesare smelled the leather and wood of the wing-backed chair in which he sat, smelled the soapy scent of his own skin, and smelled—most intensely of all—the flowery fragrance of Justine, the dark-haired beauty who sat on his lap, leaning against his chest.

"Don't you turn his head, now," Cooper warned Justine. "He's been out on the Frontier a long time. I'll wager he hasn't seen anything as fine as you in a year or more."

"Ever," Cesare said as he regarded the young woman. She had fine, pale skin, a small mouth, and a delicate chin. As she leaned against him, he felt the boning of her corset beneath her dress, and saw the rise and fall of her upthrust bosom in the glimmering lamplight. "The finest I have seen ever."

Justine smiled, playful but kind. "Monsieur Cooper," she said, her French accent thickening as the evening wore on and the champagne grew low. "It is not his head you should be worried about being turned, but mine."

Cesare still had the virtue to blush at the compliment.

"Well, you be good to her," Cooper advised. "She's one of Mr. Wood's favorites."

Now it was Justine's turn to blush, and Cesare was glad when Cooper stood to turn in for the evening, asking Florence to accompany him.

"Is that true?" he asked Justine after they had gone. "Do you work for Mr. Wood?"

Dark lashes covered Justine's eyes. *"Oui,"* she said.

Cesare considered her: a young woman from a foreign country, beautiful and caring, much like his sister used to be. If she had turned to whoring, who was to say that her reasons were not as pure as Fortuna's had been?

She glanced at him. "Do you want me to go now?"

"It would be rude to turn away the finest that Mr. Wood has to offer." He blocked the slap that she sent his way. "I apologize," he said. "I meant that as a compliment. I don't care if you belong to Wood or Cooper or anyone else. It doesn't matter to me. You *are* the finest thing I have ever seen, and I would like you to stay. If you want to."

Justine smiled. She took his hand in hers and led him back to his private compartment, where he learned just how many layers of clothing a well-dressed woman wore, and where he learned that Justine was just as fine beneath it all as she had appeared on the surface. They made love, blending together their disparate forms—his power with her fragility, her supple curves with his tightly muscled limbs, and afterward they lay nestled together, listening to the heartbeat of the train over the rails.

Cesare's own heart was light and free, and he felt the knots of his worry untying beneath his flesh and in his mind. Somewhere behind him, as if from a far distance, he recognized the voice of his sins baying in the night, but the softness of Justine's skin, the curve of her breast, and the way her hair fell down across her cheek and onto his torso enabled him to ignore his recent past, if only for the moment. He could not help but smile as he looked down upon her quiet features. The gentle rocking of the car set up a rhythm in his mind that sidestepped his memories of poverty and pain, and leapt back across the ocean to a place of white stucco along the Ligurian seaside. The rocking reminded him of the boats along the bright-watered quay, the splash of waves against the Tuscan shore. He smelled the salt in his own sweat, heard the gulls in the creaking of the car. A tune crept into his mind. He began to sing, quietly, the song of fishermen and long days and sweethearts left behind. His tenor voice rose with the melody that he had not heard since his childhood. He felt tears spill down his cheeks, and when the song was done, he saw Justine's eyes were open and full with tears of her own.

She lifted herself up along his length, kissed him, and began to love him anew.

When Cooper pounded on his door just after dawn, Cesare was alone. He looked around in confusion.

"Don't worry," Cooper said. "You'll see her again. But get dressed now. We're due at the offices by nine."

They departed the station as soon as the train pulled in, and Cooper led Cesare through the maze of Chicago's south side. Cobbled streets were filled with horsecarts and delivery vans. Men of every type—from silk-scarved dandies heading home to suspender-and-belted butchers heading to the slaughterhouses—made their way down the boarded walks. The sun had barely begun to reach down into the northbound streets, but already the wet heat of early autumn had begun to rise. Cesare followed his boss up boulevards and down avenues, through courtyards and alleyways. They stopped at a shoeshine stand to have the dust brushed from their boots. At a barbershop they reclined for a shave. At a bakery they bathed in the scent of fresh bread and enjoyed a quick bite to eat. At each place Cooper was met by name, and at each place Casare was introduced as "Mr. Uccido, from New York and the territories." Each time, proprietors and customers alike deferred to them, giving them preferential treatment and a quick trip to the front of the line.

"I feel like I am a king," Cesare confided to Cooper as they headed back out onto the street.

"Kid, just wait."

It did not take long for him to understand what Cooper meant.

They crossed a bridge over a broad, green river, the sun grinning in a hazy sky, and entered in among tall, stone-faced buildings that towered ten, even twelve stories above their heads.

"Crap," Cooper said, and pointed to the clock in a tower down the street. It was nearly nine o'clock. "Come on."

They ran across the street and passed into one of the buildings, its marbled columns like the entrance to a modern temple. Cesare's footsteps echoed through the granite foyer, bouncing from his shiny new shoes to the arched ceiling and back. They hurried up the stone staircase, climbing two flights, then three. When the clock in the tower outside began to toll the hour, Cooper began to run and Cesare followed. On the fourth floor they headed toward the big double doors ahead of them. The doorman put his hand on the brass handle as they slid to a stop.

"Mr. Cooper," the doorman said with a tip of his hat.

"Charlie," Cooper replied, straightening his collar and slicking back his hair. Charlie opened the door just as the clock finished its chime and Cesare walked into a room of sheer opulence.

It was the largest room Cesare had ever seen—bigger than an entire apartment back on the Bowery—perhaps twenty feet square. The ceiling was made of carved mahogany joists supporting squares of embossed tin, and beneath his feet was a plushy red-and-gold carpet that soaked up every sound. A bronze statue of a woman holding a bow and arrow stood on a pedestal near one wall, and near the other was a large desk at which sat a young man. The young man stood.

"Right this way," he said. "Mr. Wood is expecting you."

If the last room had been large, the next room was huge by Cesare's standards. Easily twice the length of the antechamber, Mr. Wood's inner office was bright with sunlight and gold. Gold framed the pictures that nearly covered the walls with scenes of mountains and people and running horses. Gold bordered the inlay in the dark marquetry squares that paneled the walls. A dagger-leafed palm stood tall and narrow in a footed pot decorated with golden fruit. And gold glinted from the pen, and the cigarette case, and even the ashtray that sat on the huge, oak desk.

"You are late," said the man at the desk.

Ellerby Ignatius Wood was a large name for a small man. Cesare struggled not to stare, failed, and knew it.

"Mr. Wood," Cooper said. "May I present Cesare Uccido. The man I've told you about."

The man who stood up from behind the grand desk was no more than five-foot-three with his hair mussed, which it wasn't. He walked around the desk and held out his hand. Cesare clasped it; it felt like a woman's hand, lost in his own massive grip.

"You thought I would be taller," Wood said. Cesare sputtered and looked at Cooper for help. "Don't worry," the small man went on. "Everyone does." He walked back to his desk and picked up his cigarette case. He offered one to each of them, which they politely declined, and then struck a match and lit one for himself. "Everyone thinks that only a big man can be a 'big man,' if you follow me. To most, it is as if strength were the only attribute that mattered." He breathed smoke and blew a gray cloud into the streaming sunlight. "What about you?" he asked Cesare. "Do you think that only a strong man can be a powerful man?"

"N-no, Mr. Wood," Cesare answered, sure it was the correct response.

"What else then? What else might make a 'big man'?"

Cesare thought about the powerful men he'd known: the *padroni* from the Old Country, and the men who virtually ran the wards around New Italy. What did they have that set them apart?

"Smarts," Cesare answered, and Wood smiled, nodding.

"Very good, Uccido. 'Smarts' is indeed a very useful attribute. But let me tell you another, one more important even than smarts." He put a hand up next to his mouth, as if he were imparting a well-kept secret.

"Fearlessness," he said, and winked.

Cesare glanced at Cooper and saw him smile as if he knew precisely what Wood was talking about.

"Fearlessness, and its corollary, ruthlessness, are paramount," Mr. Wood said as he walked back around behind his desk. "And that, Uccido, is what Cooper here says you have in abundance. Sit down, you two. Relax."

They took seats in claw-footed chairs, and Wood leaned back against his own leather upholstery.

"Cooper tells me that you've almost single-handedly demolished the antiunion sentiment out in the Territory," Wood said.

Cesare shrugged. "If Mr. Cooper says so."

Cooper and Wood exchanged a glance and a smile. Wood took another drag on his cigarette and with delicate fingers picked a piece of tobacco from his tongue. "He does say so. And I've seen the evidence." He paused and regarded Cesare through an eye-squinting haze of smoke. "I may have work for you, Uccido. Are you interested?"

"I don't know, Mr. Wood. What kind of work?"

"A fair question. I want you to do the same thing you've

done for Cooper out in the Territory, just here in Chicago. You'd have rooms of your own, spending money in your pocket, and all the comforts and inducements you enjoyed on your journey here."

The image of Justine came to Cesare unbidden, but the thought of her confused him and he banished her from his mind. Of all the comforts and inducements he might continue to enjoy, Cesare was sure that one of Wood's "favorites" would not be among them.

"And if you do well here," Wood added, "there might be other work, back east. We could always use a man like you. So tell me, Uccido. Are you interested?"

He knew what this choice meant for him. If he took the offer, he would become a hired thug. If he turned it down, he'd be back in the territories, killing and maiming still, but doing so to merely survive. He was on a path now, and it was a dark one, darker than a moonless prairie night, darker even than the twisting back alleys of Mulberry Bend. Behind him was the only light he ever knew, but he could not go back to it. That light was gone. Forever buried.

"What have you got there, Uccido?"

Cesare blinked, having been lost among his possible futures. Wood pointed with his cigarette and Cesare looked down at his hands. He held the folded paper, having taken it out without thinking, a reflex to the tumult in his mind. He felt the form of Fortuna's crucifix within the blood-stained paper and heard the chain hissing inside. The sight of it, instead of comforting him, filled his heart with pain and his head with hot rage.

"It's nothing, sir," he said. "It belonged to my sister."

"Ah. I see," Wood said, though Cesare could tell that he didn't, nor did he care to. "So, what shall it be? Do you think you have what it takes to be a big man in the big city?"

He returned the little parcel to his coat pocket and tugged at the collar that suddenly seemed to throttle him with every heartbeat.

I do not deserve the light, he reminded himself. The dark is where I belong.

"I'm your man, Mr. Wood."

CHAPTER 14

Plum Moon, Waning
Fifty-six Years After the Star Fell
Southern Reaches
Alliance Territory

George's walker jogged along in the vanguard, leading the riders ahead into a land he did not know. The party of sixteen was comprised of ten Kit Fox soldiers, four scouts, Storm Arriving, and George himself. Sixteen was a symbolic number—four times four—and the Council had insisted on it (the ambassador, ostensibly, was not pertinent to their calculations). In his turn, George had insisted that Storm Arriving—whom he valued as an adviser and as a translator of the Trader's Tongue—be one of the soldiers selected, and the Council had agreed.

As the gathering of the People had headed north to follow the buffalo, George and his party headed south, toward the Moonshell River and the contested lands. They rode through the low hills beyond the Sudden River. Their scouts, riding back in from their advance positions, reported homesteads scattered throughout the land to the east and, at one point deep in Alliance Territory, the entire party came upon a large force of men working on a rail road.

George and Storm Arriving had stopped with the rest of the party on a low ridge to watch as the workmen rolled barrows of dirt and gravel to build the rail bed. Behind the workers, others hefted huge timber ties, sinking them into place. On the ties, still others laid the long, shiny rails, and behind them came men with levers and sledges and spikes. From a mile away on the low rise where they had stopped, George heard the rhythmic songs as the men worked, heard the thrum and hiss of the locomotive that stood behind, impatient as a thoroughbred at the gate.

"What are they doing all the way out here?" Alejandro asked.

"Invading," George said.

"But I heard that you had beaten them back beyond the Missouri."

"We did," Storm Arriving said. "But now the *vé'hó'e* have brought their war to the north, and we are forced to concentrate our soldiers there. It is more important to protect the People than the southlands."

Alejandro shrugged. "Then you will lose the southlands, I fear. You must occupy a land in order to hold it." He pointed to the rail workers. "And that is what they're preparing for: people, living on the land."

Storm Arriving frowned, but George looked at the rail road that grew every minute, and sensed the seed of an idea.

People, he thought. To keep this land, we need people who will live on it. People who don't roam. People who live in one place and raise their crops and their children. People who will live like the *vé'ho'e* settlers.

"Earth Lodge Builders," he said to Storm Arriving in the language of the People. "The Ree and the Mandan. And the others who have come to us from across the Big Greasy and the rivers of the north: the Sweetwater People, the Sauk, the Fox. Even the Wolf People."

Storm Arriving signed that he did not understand.

"They come to us," George said, "fleeing the new *vé'ho'e* laws and the *vé'ho'e* rail road up in Grandmother Land. They want a new home." He pointed to the rail road that stretched back through Alliance lands. "Let us invite them to come here. Here, and everywhere along our borderlands."

Storm Arriving pursed his lips as he thought about the suggestion. "Hm," he said simply. "It is worth considering."

A shout from the workers and a shot from an outrider convinced them to move onward. They continued south and west, heading toward the Alliance borderlands.

The border between Alliance lands and the Tejano coast of New Spain was more than a line on a map; it was very nearly a physical thing. The prairie did not melt away or slowly transmute from one environment to the next; it simply stopped. First they were riding along, coursing over the undulations of tough bluestem, avoiding the occasional hummock of razor-grass or sagebrush, and then, within the span of a few miles, they were in a desert land filled with paddle-shaped prickly pear, dark-leaved mesquite, and dry, dry earth. They led their beasts up onto a broken tableland torn by deep ravines. George's walker jerked and snorted as sudden wildlife broke cover. Quail drummed up into the air from beneath thorny shadebushes, and jackrabbits hared off, their absurdly long ears listening for pursuit as their long legs created puffs of dust at each twenty-foot bound.

"This is the land of the Snake People," Storm Arriving told George and Alejandro. "They live up there." He pointed to the steep, dun-colored mountains to their right. "They are good traders, and fierce fighters. Isn't that right, Ambassador?"

"Yes," Alejandro said. "Quite fierce."

The ambassador's smile was prim, and George could see that the question nettled him no little bit. Perhaps Storm Arriving held more rancor against the Iron Shirts than he knew.

On George's left, downslope from the rocky heights and past miles of treacherous badlands, he could see the haze of the Big Salty. Where the inland sea's northern and eastern coasts were bordered by lush forests fed by the water-birthed rainclouds, its western limit was dry and barren rock and scree. It was hard to believe that people were able to eke out an existence on such land, much less wanted to.

"Is it all so parched here?" he asked.

"For many miles, yes," Alejandro answered. "The mountains that are the home of the . . ."

"The Snake People," Storm Arriving supplied.

"Yes, the Snake People. Thank you. Well, those same mountains hold back the rain from the west. No cloud makes it over them to this side. It is a near desert, from here to Socorro and beyond."

George sighed. "And we went to war over this land?"

"Ah, my young friend," the ambassador said, "you see only the surface. Compared to the hills of Virginia or the grasslands that feed your buffalo, this stretch of the Tejano coast must seem a wasteland. But there is water here, beneath the surface. It bubbles up in springs and trickles down through limestone caverns large enough to house a cathedral. And there are sites of wondrous, austere beauty here: deep canyons striped with rainbow colors, pools the color of turquoise, and places where precious stones lie in the dirt of the chaparral. Farther to the south, at El Brazito and down the Rio de las Palmas, there are dense forests of oak and broad expanses of grassland, just like your northern prairies." Head inclined, he shrugged. "It is a harsh land that marks its people, to be sure, but those who live here love it. It is one reason why those who came here from the United States wanted to annex it."

"Did you fight in the Mexican War, Excellency?" George asked.

Alejandro looked off into the distance. "The Mexican War? You will excuse me, but when we New Spaniards speak of 'the Mexican war,' we mean the war that France and Spain fought against a rebellious Mexico. I was not in that war. What I am sure you mean, however, is the short conflict between your father's country and mine that took place here, along the Tejano coast. If that is the case," he said, "then, yes. I fought in the Tejano conflict. I was at the battle of El Brazito."

"Really?" George said. "My father was there, too, you know."

"Yes, we met in battle, he and I," the ambassador said. He seemed distracted, as if his mind was far away, but then he snapped back like a bit of India rubber. "But that was a long time ago. I hope that your visit to New Spain will be less—what is the word—volatile?" He laughed. To George the laughter sounded hollow.

They rode on for two full days at the best speed their mounts could manage in the tumbled landscape. The animals disliked the withering air—George's walker most of all—and the riders were forced to stop whenever water presented itself in a catchpool or arroyo.

"They're going to be trouble," George said as he stood with the others at the rim of a canyon pool. His walker tipped her head back to let another mouthful of muddy water trickle down her throat and then proceeded to roll in the slop to coat her skin. "She's already as cranky as a mule. The whistlers are nearly as bad. I still say we should send them back when we reach the railroad."

"I really wish you wouldn't," Alejandro said. "Please, the viceroy *must* see what you can do with these animals. He will not believe it if I merely tell him what I have seen; he must see it for himself. It will show him how your people have been able to master the plains."

George frowned, knowing how much trouble the animals would be on a train trip.

"Besides," Storm Arriving said. "We must keep our number to sixteen. The council was very clear on that point."

Others among the party—all men with whom George had ridden years ago in the raid on the Capitol Building— signed their support of this. George's frown only deepened. His walker rose up out of the slimy mud and shook herself, forcing men and whistlers alike to shy from the spatter.

"As you wish," he said, reluctant but resigned.

By the fifth day beyond the border, the land began to smooth out and fill in the cracks. Ravines became valleys. Grasses returned in low, scraggly patches. The men were even able to rest in the shade of a copse of oaks, though the prickly leaves that littered the ground beneath this southern variety eliminated any hope of a nap.

Not long after that, the meandering deer- and peccary-paths that they had been following drew together into a trail. And later, as the sun slowly drifted down toward the hilltops that still commanded the west, one of the outriding scouts whistled. Men snapped to alertness and rifles appeared from their sheaths. The scout whistled again, and George saw him pointing. Down along the seashore, still miles ahead, they all saw the smudge of a village.

"La Puerta del Norte," Alejandro said, naming the sad stain. "And up there," he said, pointing up to the darkening hills and the mountains beyond them, "we will find Cimmaron. We can reach it tonight." The ambassador was grinning, obviously pleased at the prospect, but his enthusiasm did not affect any of the others. George understood them well: This was the end of the trail, the end of what they knew. From here on out, it was a strange world ahead of them.

The moon was rising lopsided and gibbous as George,

Alejandro, and Storm Arriving walked into the town of Cimarron. The whitewashed walls of the mud-brick homes gleamed with azure light, and windows and doorways pulsated with the warmth of yellow hearthlight, illuminating neighbors and families who gathered to spend a cool hour in the evening air. George and his companions had left their mounts with the rest of the party at the limits of the town, but as they walked along the street, George wondered if that had been a good idea. While the animals were not there to cause alarm, the mere presence of three men in native costume seemed enough to frighten; and now they had no quick means of escape.

Housefront conversations ceased as they approached, and porches and patios were abandoned, the menfolk hurrying their women into the stuccoed courtyards. Shouts could be heard in the sidestreets as the locals conferred, and it was only a little time before the fear and surprise in the voices was replaced by belligerence.

"We should stop here," Alejandro said. "I will speak to them."

They stopped in the middle of the street. The ambassador raised his arms and turned around, speaking to the shadows and the faces that hid in them.

George's Spanish was poor, based solely on the attenuated similarity it bore to French. He listened, and did not know what the ambassador was saying. With a cold fear and a pounding heart, he realized the immense trust he had unwittingly placed in Alejandro. What if he was betraying them, calling the townsfolk to attack the party? He hissed quietly to get Storm Arriving's attention and brought his hand closer to the strap that held his rifle over his back. Storm Arriving signed his readiness to act.

Alejandro continued his speech and they waited. George, prepared for an attack, prayed silently to the spirits until, from around the corner of a plastered portico, a torch emerged, held high above the gleaming pate of its owner. A question was asked, an answer was given, and men stepped out from every shadowed niche and doorway. The amazed looks on their faces told George that his prayer had been heard, and he relaxed with an easy breath.

Introductions were made, telegraphs were sent down the wire, the town's mayor grinned at them with tobacco-stained teeth, and in the morning the viceregal response was delivered.

"He will see us," Alejandro told George and the others at their camp outside of town. The ambassador reread the message to them. " 'Viceregal audience first priority. Proceed immediately to San Francisco. Train accommodations for ambassador and Cheyenne delegation dispatched to Albuquerque. The Viceroy Lord Serrano-Ruiz.' " He looked up from the page smiling. "Are you ready?"

George looked to Storm Arriving. "Are we?" he asked.

Storm Arriving looked in turn to his fellow Kit Fox soldiers. "Are we ready?" he asked them. The answer was immediate.

"A Kit Fox is *always* ready."

They left Cimarron, riding fast and hard through the high mountains. The terrain was rocky, dry, and the wind—honed sharp by the altitude—chilled them despite the season. George hoped to meet no other travelers during their journey. The road was so narrow that an encounter would have been impossible to avoid, and any encounter between local travelers and sixteen Indian soldiers on whistler-back was bound to end badly. So far the road had been empty. Oddly so, to George's mind.

"Is there another pass through these mountains?"

"No," Alejandro answered him. "This is the quickest way through the Sangre de Cristos."

"Then why are we alone on this road?"

Storm Arriving, riding close by, touched George on the arm. He pointed up at the heights to their left and right. "We are not alone," he said, speaking in French so the ambassador could understand as well.

George looked up at the rocks and scrub and stunted, twisted trees that studded the land above them. He could see no one, but that meant nothing—his scouting skills were severely lacking. Glancing over his shoulder at the soldiers behind him, however, he saw that all eyes were trained on the hillsides.

"Do not worry," Storm Arriving said, sensing George's anxiousness. "So far it is only the Snake People who shadow us through these mountains. They know the People, and will not bother us."

George saw that the ambassador was glancing nervously

toward the heights on either hand. "I am glad to hear it," he said. "But while the Comanches control this road during the day, it is *banditos* who rule it at night. We must make haste, ere the sun falls and we come under the gaze of less friendly eyes."

They made it to the summit and picked up their pace, heading down the switchback trail with the rays of the westering sun shining in their eyes at every turn. Ahead, the land showed signs of vitality, and down beyond the mountains' feet, a haze of fields and greenery could be seen. Soon they saw their destination.

Lazing in the afternoon sun far below was a town. It lay on the gentle slope above the serpentine coils of a broad, green, tree-lined river.

"Albuquerque," Alejandro said, "and the Rio de las Palmas." He sighed and smiled, as if spying an old friend. "From here we will take the train to Alta California and thence to San Francisco, where you will see the viceroy, and I will see my family."

George heard the longing in the ambassador's voice. "How long have you been away?" George asked.

Alejandro shrugged. "Not long, as one counts the days. Perhaps a year. A little more. But it feels much longer."

George thought of Mouse Road, back home with the People, all on her own, with mother dead and brother here with him on the road of politics. He thought of her and then of his own family, so much more distant than she might ever be. Both seemed so out of reach at that moment. "I envy you," he said to the ambassador. "Family is important."

Albuquerque had heard of their coming, but was not prepared for what actually arrived. From a distance, George could see people—men with broad smiles beneath broader hats, and women with pale skirts and dark mantillas—and they lined up along the small thoroughfare that sped down from the mountains to bisect the town. Children ran in the street, and the sour notes of a four-man brass band floated weakly in the desert air. As they rode into town on fearsome, nine-foot-tall beasts and one immense, toothsome monster, men paled, the timid music faltered, and children were snatched back close to their mothers' skirts. But the harsh land had made a tough people, and the townsfolk stood their ground to greet the unparalleled sight of nearly a score of Cheyenne soldiers in their hometown streets.

They were greeted with formality and dignity, and though the elite of the town extended their hospitality, George could see the relief in their faces when Alejandro—citing the viceroy's instruction to come with all speed—politely declined their invitations, staying in town only long enough to reprovision himself with clothing more befitting a man of his station. They were taken to the rail spur on the far side of the river, where there had recently arrived a small train for the ambassador's private use.

Three passenger cars had been provided, along with several cattle cars with open tops and walls made of heavy boards. These worked well enough for the whistlers, and though unfamiliar with corrals and fences, the smaller animals took comfort from the closeness of their flockmates.

For George's walker, however, the situation quickly proved problematic.

When she stood, her head and shoulders would be well above the limits of the car's walls. If she wanted to get out, George knew that the board-and-timber construction would prove no real obstacle. But those considerations all proved to be academic as the strong-willed walker simply refused to walk up the creaking ramp. George tried leading her up by her halter rope and tried maneuvering her up while astride her back. He tried coaxing her, shouting at her, pushing and pulling at her. Each time she came right up to the ramp, placed one three-toed foot on the bottom edge, eyed the enclosure, and roared her defiance.

"I don't know what else to do," George said to Storm Arriving and Alejandro. "She's never been this stubborn before."

"Someone will have to take her back," Storm Arriving said.

"Please, my friends," Alejandro said. "There must be something else we can do. We must bring this magnificent beast to the viceroy. He must see her in action."

George and Storm Arriving gawped at one another, stunned by their own stupidity. They looked at the walker. She stood near the rail car, shifting restlessly from foot to foot. George watched as her gaze roved over toward the whistlers, as the length of her striped tail switched and snapped like a pennant. He stood and went to her. She leaned down and sniffed his hair. With one hand he reached up and caressed the bony narrowness of her muzzle. Her breath was warm on his face, its smell sharp and acrid. He sensed her impatience, her desire. It wasn't fear that kept her from boarding the rail car. It was hunger.

"Excellency," George said. "I need one of the largest steers you can provide."

The ambassador had seen walkers in maneuvers and races back at the camp, but he had never before seen them eat. With the arrival of the fine, long-horned steer, he was given a short and intense education in the more sanguinary aspects of walker husbandry. With its blinders removed, the steer sprinted away from George's ravening mount. In five long strides she was upon it, snapping her jaws about its neck and jerking back to break its spine. Felling the long-horn within a minute's time, she was ready to feed, but her long-established training stepped in to halt her. She looked back at George, her bloodstained jaws agape, and waited.

George walked slowly to the steer over which she stood. The kill had not tired her, not in the least, but yet her sides heaved as she breathed in the delicious scent of blood. She was ready, but still he made her wait. He withdrew his knife from its sheath and turned to the carcass, showing his back to the towering beast.

The ambassador groaned audibly, and George saw pale fear on Alejandro's face. He chuckled.

"This is the crucial moment," he told the ambassador. "If she eats without my permission, I lose all control over her." He cut into the steer's side, just under the ribs, and reached in to slice off a piece of the liver. "If I let her eat too often without touching the kill for myself, she forgets for whom she hunts." He took the slab of meat and inspected it. It was firm, dark purple, and unmarbled: the steer was healthy. He cut off a small piece and popped it into his mouth. He turned and lobbed the rest of it into his walker's waiting maw. She snapped it up, and George saw the iris of her yellow eye widen. He stepped back from the carcass.

"Eat," he said, releasing her.

The ambassador, groaning more, could not make himself look away as she began her meal.

Afterward, her belly now full, the walker now comported herself with a more docile demeanor. She waddled after George, peaceful as a lamb, and though she eyed it warily, she climbed the creaking ramp up into the rail car, and lay herself down for a long, long nap.

"We might want to bring another steer or two along."

Ashen-faced, the ambassador nodded and wiped his brow with a white handkerchief. Within the hour they were underway: whistlers, walker, men, and two very nervous longhorns.

The viceroy had sent accommodations fitting for use by the ambassador of one of the richest nations in the world. The three cars were appointed with the most sumptuous of fixtures and furnishings. Two of the cars were divided into compartments for sleeping and privacy, but the third car was designed like the meeting room at a gentleman's club. Everywhere George looked there was polished wood, burnished metal, velvet, silk, or leather. Upholstered chairs were flanked by end tables and ash stands, and the corners were commanded by divans and couches. At the forward end of the car, a red-jacketed servant stood ready to carry requests to the galley.

George could not remember the last time he had sat in a soft, velvet-covered chair. At Alejandro's invitation he settled himself into one, sighed, and prepared himself for a pleasant five-day journey.

Storm Arriving hated it.

He was very ill at ease with these new surroundings. Aside from being inside a big box that rattled and clanked, he hated that everything *moved*. For as long as he had lived, he'd never known anything but walking, running, and riding; none of them had. The People never used wheeled vehicles, preferring instead the simplicity of whistler-drags and travoises. This was noisy, and everything seemed to be in motion—the chairs, the raised sleeping platforms, the glassed lanterns that hung from the walls, even the walls themselves and the wooden floor on which they sat. *Everything* moved. The ground shouldn't move.

The other Kit Fox soldiers were just as uncomfortable. They looked about them at every sound, eyes wary and brows creased. They refused to touch anything but what had to be touched, and eschewed the chairs and other furnishings in favor of the floor. One Who Flies had shown them the sleeping boxes in the other car, but Storm Arriving doubted any of them would use such a thing. The bedding was too soft, there were no furs to cover oneself, and it was so small, it would be worse than sleeping in a sweat lodge.

When the food came, however, it was a welcome thing. Even though it was sliced thin and covered in sticky sauces, the aroma of roasted meat and fowl overcame even the most disinclined. The meal also provided bread, beans, and other familiar foods, and though the thin-handled spoons and knives proved a challenge, there was more than enough to satisfy everyone.

Afterward, Storm Arriving sat on the floor and leaned back against one of the many chairs. He pretended to doze, but surreptitiously he watched One Who Flies at the far end of the car. One Who Flies sat in a chair near Speaks for the Iron Shirts, leaning back into its plush embrace. He sipped coffee from a tiny cup and saucer that chirped whenever they touched as if they were made of a seashell. The two men spoke the Trader's Tongue in low, friendly tones, a conversation intersticed by smiles and gentle laughter. Speaks for the Iron Shirts asked One Who Flies about his younger days, and One Who Flies told of his father, Long Hair, and of his life on the prairie with the bluecoats. He was quite comfortable with these new surroundings, and Storm Arriving realized for the first time that this was how his friend had lived for all those many years before they had met.

It was silly not to have seen it before, not to have even thought of it, but Storm Arriving had never seen his friend in such an environment. Even when they had traveled to the City of White Stone, Storm Arriving had never been in a room like this one. He had always pictured One Who Flies as a man of the prairie—first as a bluecoat, and then as a man of the People—sun and sky above his head, and nothing to either hand but the entire world. This place, this cramped box filled with soft seats and hard floors, where all the colors were dark and where every space held a picture or a dish or a book, this was also part of the life that One Who Flies had left behind him. He had never spoken of this part of his past, had never voiced a regret for having left it behind, and yet, as restless as Storm Arriving might feel in this place, One Who Flies seemed to feel right at home.

He looked at how One Who Flies sat in his armchair, and wondered if it really was as comfortable as his friend made it look. He rose from his place on the floor and went to a similar chair next to one of the glassed windows. Gingerly, he sat down on the sat. The fabric was cool and as soft as a whistler's hide. The upholstered cushion compressed beneath his weight, managing to be both soft and firm at the same time. He bounced on it, surprised by its springiness, and leaned back. The chair accepted him like a lover. His legs felt odd, draped uselessly from the edge of the chair, but it *was* comfortable.

"Do you like it?" One Who Flies asked.

"Yes," Storm Arriving said. "It is like lying down while sitting up." He put his hands on the chair's arms, snuggled back into its depth, and looked out the window.

Their private train was taking them he knew not where as it traveled through a land burned red by the sun. Plump spires of treelike cacti pointed upward with accusing fingers while mesquite and coyote bushes shrugged their dusty, leather-leaved shoulders and endeavored to survive the day. All was light and pale hardness until, at sunset, the sky came to life. Blue infused it, and coral pink painted the clouds that had been invisible while white light had ruled. Purple appeared, first in the now-distant mountains and then in the eastern sky itself, while to the west the horizon delayed the ball of orange sunfire, holding it up until it rolled slowly off the edge of the earth, leaving in its wake streaks of red and yellow and green. Cobalt and indigo sped across the heavens, and through his lamplit reflection in the window's glass, Storm Arriving saw the first stars appear.

He awoke with an aching neck and feet as lifeless as stones. The other soldiers had brought in blankets and bedded down on the floor of the main car, while One Who Flies and Speaks for the Iron Shirts were absent, having retired to the sleeping compartments.

Beyond the window's glass the world still moved past, but overnight the desert had been washed away by fields of green and gold. Storm Arriving looked out on an immense valley, its defining mountains nearly lost in the haze of distance. On the valley floor, crops grew in huge squares of perfect homogeneity. He had seen cropland before, had seen the mixed plantings of the Earth Lodge Builders, but never had he seen anything like this.

It consumed every handsbreadth of land, excepting only the roads that delimited deep green from pale green, yellow from gold. Sometimes, amid the verdure, he spied a complex of large, low buildings of white stone and red clay, lonely as islands in a vast lake. The train continued, bringing even forests that grew in an orderly fashion: trees standing rank upon rank, row upon row. After a time the croplands returned, and he stared at the miles of greenery, watching the triple aisles of uniformity race through the acreage, one straightaway, one to the fore, and one to the rear, all keeping pace with him as the train sped down the track.

"The Gardens of California," whispered One Who Flies, settling himself quietly in a nearby seat. "Some of the most fertile land known to Man. We could do this, you know, out on the prairie. A little bit of irrigation, a handful of plows, some seed . . . the Ree and the Mandan already raise crops. This wouldn't be so different."

Storm Arriving stared at the immensity beyond the window. "We do not need this much," he heard himself say, as if giving voice to a crime.

One Who Flies leaned toward him. "I know," he said quietly, so as not to wake the soldiers sleeping nearby. "We do not need a tenth of this. We don't need anything more than what we have. What we have keeps us from being hungry." He touched Storm Arriving on the shoulder, forcing him to turn and meet his challenge. "But we need to do more than stave off hunger, my friend. We are talking about survival of the People."

"To grow more than you need is to waste. How can wasting food save the People?"

"It would not be wasted," One Who Flies insisted. "It would be sold. To the Iron Shirts. To the Horse Nations. To the men of Grandmother Land. Even as far as the Trader Nations. It is one of the things that makes the *vé'hó'e* so strong. And Alejandro can show us how."

Storm Arriving blew air in disgust. "We do not need to

be like the Iron Shirts. We do not need to grow and sell food like they do. We have the yellow chief-metal, and we can always dig more if—"

One Who Flies grabbed Storm Arriving by the arm. "Say nothing of that here. Especially not in the Trader's Tongue. The Iron Shirts must not know of our hidden wealth."

Storm Arriving pulled his arm away. "Yes," he said, disliking his friend's domineering tone. "I see that. I will not mention it." He looked out the window again. "But I still do not see why we need to grow crops the way the Iron Shirts do."

One Who Flies sat back and sighed in exasperation. "It's another tool," he said. "Even if we can make this alliance with the Iron Shirts, it will only take us so far. If we are not careful, we will simply exchange one tyranny for another. We must find a way toward true independence."

Inwardly, Storm Arriving chided himself. Having seen One Who Flies so friendly with Speaks for the Iron Shirts, having seen him take so easily to the *vé'ho'e* ways . . . he felt shame at having thought so little of his friend. "I am sorry," he said. "I misunderstood. We should consider anything that helps strengthen our independence." But as he sat back in his chair and looked out at the cropland that continued past the window, he was unable to eliminate his doubts about One Who Flies.

The world was changing beneath his feet. He was at the vanguard of this mission, and yet he knew neither where he was going, nor what he might accomplish. Once again he found himself following the man who sat beside him— One Who Flies, the Man who Fell from the Clouds— onward into an unknown land. Their last adventure had ended in a great coup, but it had cost the People much. Storm Arriving wondered what the cost of this trip would be.

The train switched tracks and within a day they came to a coastline where Storm Arriving and the other soldiers caught first sight of what One Who Flies called an ocean.

"Like the Big Salty," he told them, "but a hundred, hundred times bigger. They call it the Pacific: the Peaceful Ocean."

They stared at its immensity. It owned the horizon. "It's like the end of the world," Storm Arriving said.

"That's what the Iron Shirts thought," One Who Flies said, "a long time ago. But they found other lands out there. Beyond the horizon."

More of the superiority of the Iron Shirts, Storm Arriving thought with an edge of bitterness.

"We will soon arrive at our destination," Speaks for the Iron Shirts announced. "From the rail station we will travel to my family villa, where we will spend the night. Tomorrow, we will meet with the viceroy."

"Wonderful," One Who Flies said with a smile.

Storm Arriving gritted his teeth. His displeasure with his friend grew with each ingratiating grin and comment. One Who Flies *said* he was thinking of the good of the People, but only a fool would fail to see that he preferred the world of the Iron Shirts to the more austere existence of prairie life. While Storm Arriving was fascinated by the way these *vé'hó'e* put their stamp on every aspect of their world— from the unnatural farming methods to changing the very course of rivers—he found more wondrous the sweetgrass of home, the deep arroyos of the Snake People's land, and the limitless expanse of water to his left. He was not impressed by fine furnishings or unidentifiable foods or massive machines like the one that pulled him toward an unknown destiny, and he was determined never to be so.

The locomotive hissed into its final destination in the middle of the night. Storm Arriving, still in his chair near the window, awoke to see a dozen tracks of gleaming silver and, beyond them, a series of hillsides speckled with the diffuse jewels of fog-shrouded street lamps. The men descended from the train into the cool, salty air.

"Welcome to San Francisco," Speaks for the Iron Shirts said.

The whistlers fluted and sang. The drakes flashed aggressive stripes of white and red while the hens, more interested in survival than competition, mottled their flanks with splotches of gray and charcoal. The night was full of odd smells and unfamiliar sounds, but they disliked the railcars more than they feared any threat from the ground, and so descended the ramp in a tight-knit flock, hens alert, drakes in the forefront, protecting. The soldiers went among their mounts, soothing them with words and caresses. Storm Arriving calmed his own elder hen, scratching the hump of her spine. Her flutings became less urgent and her eyes lidded half-over with pleasure at his ministrations. Her tranquillity calmed the younger mounts—his war drake and his other pack whistler—and soon they were all disembarked, rigged, packed, and ready to ride.

The train tracks were fronted by a pair of long, low buildings joined by a tall archway. Through the arch, Storm Arriving saw a cobbled street and heard the hooves of horses. Iron-shod wheels grated on mist-slick stones, and a carriage pulled up across the gap. The driver climbed down and opened the door, extending a gloved hand. A woman emerged and stepped down to the pavement. A younger woman followed her, and together they walked through the archway.

The women wore long dresses and cloaks that hid their shapes, turning them into gliding mounds of rustling fabric. Their heads were covered by shawls, but Storm Arriving saw the older woman's face: regal, heart-shaped, pale, dark-haired, and dark-browed. They approached, leaving the shadows and striding purposefully toward the assembled men and beasts. A servant man touched the ambassador's arm and pointed to the pair. His face beamed, and he nearly ran to meet his family.

The elder woman embraced him, her cheek upon his shoulder, and he kissed his wife's hair. The younger woman—a daughter, Storm Arriving could see—hung back and awaited her father's notice. Her face was a youthful mirror of her mother's: beautiful, fair-skinned, and with hair like a raven's wing. Speaks for the Iron Shirts released his wife and embraced his daughter. The three spoke in low tones, the father reassuring his family as they regarded the soldiers and their collection of animals. The ambassador looked about—for One Who Flies, Storm Arriving had no doubt—when a bellow tore through the night. The women jumped in fright and everyone turned toward the rear of the train.

The tall walker still stood in its railcar, unwilling to step foot on the ramp, and roaring fury down on the head of One Who Flies. One Who Flies stood his ground, staring up into the creature's maw. He held on to the halter rope, though if the walker chose to leave, no man or rope could hold it back. Still, One Who Flies tugged at the halter.

"Let's *go!*" he shouted at it. "Now." He turned and walked down the ramp, pulling the rope taut as he did so. The walker roared again—the screech of a giant eagle—and chuffed up at the shrouded sky.

"Walk," One Who Flies commanded. The walker looked down at him, at the ramp, and Storm Arriving could hear the thunder rumble in the walker's chest.

"Careful," one of the soldiers said.

One Who Flies heard her threat. He looked up at her, then looked down at her feet. She stood on her two rear legs, as walkers always did. Her upper body was cantilevered out over the ramp, her twelve-foot-long tail a counterbalance out behind her. It was dark, and her own bulk and the railcar's slatted walls cast shadows on the bed, on the ramp, and on her feet.

One Who Flies walked up onto the car and disengaged the ramp, leaving a clean edge of light and dark that she could see and navigate. He jumped down onto the railbed and turned back to her.

"Let's go," he said again.

She sniffed the air, inspected the edge, and chuffed once more in his direction. Then she hopped down to the gravel with a thump that shook the ground. The ambassador's family gasped. One Who Flies looked up and spied the new arrivals, and Storm Arriving watched as Speaks for the Iron Shirts, ignoring all others, brought his wife and daughter to meet the son of Long Hair.

Storm Arriving turned away, and saw that several other soldiers felt the building pressure of the ambassador's obvious preference.

Be calm, he said with a gesture. *Vé'hó'e* only see other *vé'hó'e.*

Soldiers smiled in toleration, and Storm Arriving endeavored to do the same. He thought of Speaks While Leaving at home with their newborn child and, as he watched One Who Flies kiss the hand of the ambassador's daughter, he thought of his sister, who was facing her first winter alone. He smelled his whistler's spice-scented skin, and a current of homesickness swept around his heart. It was all he could do to compose himself as One Who Flies turned to introduce the entire party to their hosts.

*   *   *

George and the others rode behind the ambassador's carriage, following his nervous horses through the sleeping streets. The ambassador's villa was atop a high ridge that bestrode the peninsula on which the city lay. As they climbed, the lamps of the city slowly swelled and merged beneath a gauzy veil of fog, their light diluted to a faint glow that soon disappeared altogether.

Affluence increased with the altitude, with larger and larger grounds enclosed by ever-lengthening walls, their guardian tops rising higher and higher off the well-maintained cobbles, the buildings behind them standing farther and farther back from the street, screened by shrouded gardens. Eventually the riders came up out of the fog, and the slivered moon rode low in a star-spangled sky, while below them was but a pale mist. When they arrived at the ambassador's hilltop villa—a grand two-story structure with broad, tiled roofs, covered balconies, and an enclosed court with palm trees that stood taller than the eaves—there were only a few hours of night remaining. They had enough time before the sun rose to see their animals ensconced in hastily emptied stalls, and then head to the detached cottages, where they were able to catch some sleep on beds that did not shudder with the train's metallic pulse over the rails.

But uncaring of their exhaustion, morning dawned at its usual hour, brilliant with light and filled with sound. George rose reluctantly from the softness of his borrowed bed, wrapped a blanket around his body, and stepped out onto the veranda. The small cottages were set in a shallow arc around the tiled veranda and a gurgling fountain. From the tended flower beds at the patio's edge, George looked down upon the villa's terraced gardens, its riding oval, and its stables. Beyond the stables, Alejandro had assured them, lay a view of the city and its sparkling bay, but fog still blanketed everything, and the brilliant sun of the clear autumn morning lit it with white light.

But it was not the light but the noise that had pulled George from beneath his feather comforter. The morning was alive with sounds erupting from the stables below. Whistles and shrieks rose above the serenity of the view. The challenging trumpet of drakes and the three-note "gather close" songs of the hens wrestled with the high-pitched whinnies of horses made nervous by the scent and sounds of the large lizardlike beasts. The cacophonous medley continued, only to be silenced by the roar of George's walker. When the echo of the beast's challenge had faded, the others renewed their furor.

Some of the other men had pulled their blankets and covers out onto the close-clipped grass, preferring to sleep beneath the stars than under the close ceilings of the cottages, but George did not see Storm Arriving among them. He reentered his own cottage, dressed, and was braiding his hair when he heard a knock at the open door. He looked up to find Alejandro at the threshold.

"Did you sleep well?" the ambassador asked as George came out and joined him in the morning sunshine.

"Like on a cloud," he said, and pointed to the fog that lay like piled fleece. "It's like we are in a city in the clouds."

Alejandro nodded and motioned toward the main household. "The viceroy will be here soon. Would you care to come up and join us for a morning meal before he arrives?"

George looked at the soldiers, who were beginning to stir and emerge from their short night's sleep. Alejandro seemed to sense his question.

"I will have food sent out here to your men," he said.

George swelled with the ambassador's implied compliment but felt compelled to amend it. "Excellency," he began, "I apologize if I have given the wrong impression, but these are not *my* men. They are soldiers of the Cheyenne Alliance and as such outrank me by any measure we might use. I am not a member of any soldier society, much less a war chief or a peace chief. I am simply the only one among our number fluent in English and French, as well as our own language."

Alejandro listened politely. When George had finished, he smiled and put a paternal hand on George's shoulder. "My young friend," he said. "I apologize for having to disagree with you. Whether you know it or not—whether you admit it or not—these are indeed 'your men.' They follow you; they look to you. I have watched them. And though you will deny the assertion, I will say that it is you who are leading this delegation." George began to correct him, but the ambassador pressed onward. "However, I know what it is you mean to say. You want me to know that you are not the leader in any official capacity, yes?"

"Yes," George said.

"Good. In that we are agreed." He looked around the veranda. "And yet I fear that so many at our breakfast table will send my serving staff into apoplexy. Perhaps you would care to invite a few key members to join us. In, say, half an hour?" And with a curt bow, he left, walking along the path of pale tiles that meandered through the gardens toward the main house.

George was glad they had smoothed over that difficulty. Alejandro had been incredibly kind and understanding so far, and George felt a growing esteem for him. He had come to enjoy the company of the elder statesman, but did not want any misconceptions to give rise to difficulties during their stay. The offer of an alliance still held a great deal of promise, but the Spaniards needed to understand fully with whom they were creating this agreement; that it was not with him, but with an entire nation.

Storm Arriving came out of one of the cottages, blinking at the morning light.

And there's another problem, George thought.

He knew that this had not been easy on his friend. Storm Arriving was not practiced in diplomacy or politics; he was a man of action who had spent many years on the path of war. And while George was glad Storm Arriving had come with them on this trip, he saw, too, that he had been neglecting his old friends in favor of cementing relations with new ones. He wondered if a meal at the ambassador's table would help, and went to extend the invitation to him.

Breakfast quickly became a disaster. With the ambassador at table were his wife and daughter: the Señora Victoria Isabel Baca de Silveira and Señorita Isabella Enriqueta Silvera. George, acting on the ambassador's suggestion, had invited Storm Arriving as well as Grey Bear and Limps, but while all four of the guests could speak passably well in the Trader Nation's tongue, it was primarily to George that conversation was directed. The daughter, especially, seemed intent on speaking only to him. She sat twisted in her chair so as to face him more directly, the starched percale of her blouse making tiny comment with her every movement. Her dark hair was swept up in shining curves and pinned with combs of silver and abalone shell. The eyelet lace at her wrists accentuated the pale softness of her hands, and George found it hard not to stare at her fine, porcelainlike beauty. Her dark eyes were captivating, as was the sensuous lilt of her Castilian diction. Her obvious interest made George uncomfortable, not in the least because of his guilty enjoyment of her attentions as she asked about every detail of his life.

"My father tells me that your arrival among the Cheyenne was quite dramatic."

"One might call it so," he said. He could not help but smile at her enthusiasm, but he wanted to include the others in the conversation. "In fact, it was Storm Arriving who found me after the crash. You nearly killed me then, didn't you, my friend?"

Storm Arriving did not help. "Yes," he said sullenly, and went back to struggling with his eggs and his silverware.

"And did you know," George said, "that Gray Bear was with us when we rode to Washington? Weren't you, Gray Bear? When we rode to the City of White Stone?"

Gray Bear signed that it was true but said nothing and looked at no one, as was the custom among the people.

"Oh, do tell us of that, One Who Flies," Isabella implored. "Please do."

He looked to Alejandro for assistance, but the ambassador either did not notice or did not care that George and Isabella were monopolizing the conversation. George suspected the latter, and that Alejandro was trying to prove his point, that whether George liked it or not, he was the *de facto* leader of the delegation. The meal plodded onward, and eventually George surrendered. He answered every query the *señorita* could devise, indulging her romantic sensibilities and sensing her growing infatuation. All the while, his companions grew more sullen, more stoic. Storm Arriving, having finished with eating, sat quietly in his chair and looked uncomfortable, shifting his weight from cheek to cheek as the young Isabella rattled on with her questions and expostulations of amazement.

When Alejandro finally mentioned the viceroy's impending visit, George wanted to shout for joy. The women excused themselves, and all the men stood as they left the room.

"I expect you'll want to confer with the rest of the delegation before the viceroy arrives," Alejandro said with a smug smile.

Back at their cottages, Storm Arriving's displeasure was intense.

"What did you expect me to do?" George asked. "You did little more than grunt."

"There was nothing that required anything more. 'What did you do, One Who Flies? How did it happen, One Who Flies? How ever did you manage, One Who Flies?' Shameless. Fawning over you like a woman of the Cloud People."

"And if she did? Why is that of such concern to you?"

"You did not seem to mind it."

George laughed but knew that his struggles against Isabella's attentions had been halfhearted. "She's just a girl," he said, trying to belittle the situation."

"She is my sister's age."

"But your sister is not a girl," George shouted, letting his temper flare in defense. The other men had stopped in their tasks to listen to the argument. "Mouse Road is a woman," he said more calmly. "She has seen death; she has seen sorrow. She took care of her mother and her household for the past year or more. She is nothing like that pampered little girl who goggled at me from across the breakfast table."

Storm Arriving would not be convinced. "But it is the pampered little girl that you seem to prefer," he said. "I think you actually prefer much of this life."

"Prefer? I . . . what . . . you think . . ." George stepped away, raking his fingers through his hair. Storm Arriving's suspicions were far beyond George's own embarrassment at having enjoyed a mild flirtation with the ambassador's daughter. He walked back and forth across the veranda. "I do not believe that we are arguing about this."

"The man whom I let marry my sister must be worthy of her."

George stopped his pacing and felt a true rage rise within his breast. His fingers clenched into bloodless fists as he controlled himself. When he had his anger in hand, he turned and walked to stand shoulder to shoulder with Storm Arriving. He stared straight ahead and spoke in a clear, slow voice that all the men there could hear.

"I cannot tell you what to do," he said, "nor can I tell you what to think. But I can tell you this: I am not here to court Alejandro's daughter. I am here as part of a delegation to the Chief of the Iron Shirts. I am here to forge an alliance between our nation and his. Not between men. Not between tribes. Between *nations*. And if that requires a bit of tact, the use of polite words, and perhaps a bit of flattery, then let it be so." He took a few steps, stopped, and turned back. "If you can't see the importance of that, then you should have stayed at home."

Storm Arriving was fuming, nostrils flared, muscles along his shoulders tense and ready to lash out, but George ignored him, past caring about his friend's feelings. He looked at the men who waited nearby, listening to the argument. "I suggest you prepare yourselves," George said. "We meet with the Chief of the Iron Shirts in less than a hand of time. It would be a sign of disrespect if we are late."

The viceregal visit was preceded by an intensification of household activity. Staff ran from place to place carrying linens, dustbins, and brooms. Smoke and savory aromas rose from the kitchens. Groundsmen swept the paths and walks clear of the leaves that were just now, in the delayed seasons of New Spain, beginning to color and fall.

George and the delegation, too, made ready for their audience. Tried of trying to care for the feelings of each individual, George started issuing orders—though he couched them in terms of suggestions. To his surprise, men moved to comply. He sent several soldiers down to bring the whistlers out into the riding oval. He selected Gray Bear and Limps to join him and Storm Arriving in the core group that would meet the viceroy, and proposed that the rest act as a sort of color guard. The men had brought their finest clothes and jewelry for the meeting, and the final few fingers of time were filled with primping and the arrangement of feathers and headdresses.

Viceroy Lord Serrano-Ruiz and his staff arrived in several carriages. George could hear the horses' crisp steps in the graveled drive. He looked at the soldiers that waited with him on the veranda.

They were lean and ready. They did not speak to one another, but stood still and silent in the growing heat of the afternoon sun. Many wore tunics of bleached deerskin or antelope hide, their fringed sleeves jingling with shells or bits of silver as the ocean breeze moved among them. Wide beaded belts girdled waists with bright colors and dramatic designs in red, white, black, and blue. Breechclouts hung from beneath the tunics, many of red trader cloth hemmed with black ribbon. They all wore leggings, long and dramatic, painted yellow for the sun or green for the land, with fringes down the sides to match their sleeves, and their moccasins were likewise beaded with designs of power and history.

But with those basics, all uniformity ended and each man's individuality began. Limps wore fox tails on each shoulder and carried a lance wrapped with otterskin and hawk feathers. Gray Bear wore a pectoral of blue beads and elk's teeth in a display of personal wealth. Storm Arriving, the right side of his head shaved close, wore a white eagle feather at the nape of his neck and seven silver earrings that jingled with his every move. There were headpieces of spiky badger and skunk fur, a capelet made from a beaver pelt, and necklaces of pounded copper and bear claws. Many had lances similar to the one Limps carried. Some held leather and wood shields that bore the sigils of their dream power. Almost all of them carried a knife in their belt or had a war club hanging at their side.

George dressed himself in a buckskin tunic, beaded belt, breechclout, and long leggings. He bound his braid of pale hair with a strip of red cloth, and stuck a single hawk feather in the knot. He carried only his knife and a small pouch that held a few things of personal value. It was the best he had, and though he was, compared to the rest, virtually unadorned, it suited him. He was still relatively new to the People, and had yet to discover his own symbols of power.

When Alejandro came to escort them back to the house, he was visibly taken aback by George's change in attitude. "Is everything all right?" he asked.

"Yes, Excellency," George replied coolly, dropping all familiarity.

The change in George's demeanor puzzled Alejandro,

but he nodded and accepted it, as George had known he would. "Then I'll take you to His Lordship."

"Thank you, Excellency."

Alejandro began walking back to the main house. The soldiers fell in behind him, two by two, followed by Gray Bear and Limps, and then George and Storm Arriving. But the ambassador did not lead them toward the far wing of the villa, where George knew the grander rooms were. Instead he led them through a series of archways, down a long colonnade, and into the villa's intimate heart: the courtyard.

The walls refused to accept the afternoon sunlight, bouncing it instead from side to side so that it filled the space with radiance. Two palm trees supplied spots of shade under the high sun. A paper-flowered bougainvillea clung to the stucco walls, and small shrubs and hanging vines infused the air with the sweetness of lavender and jasmine. George heard the slippery sound of running water and spied a fountain in the middle of the court. A central pillar rose up from the water. Plump, pale cherubim with stubby wings chased one another around the tapering pillar, and water bubbled from its top, cascading from ledge to ledge, from wing to hand, trickling down to fill the pool around its base. On the ledge that surrounded the pool sat a man in a pale gray suit.

George noticed that Spanish guardsmen—with their ceremonial helmets and modern rifles—were posted at every entry but the one through which they had entered. He motioned to the soldiers of his own delegation and they quickly stationed themselves to either side of their own archway, establishing at least in theory their control over one corner of the courtyard.

Alejandro led the four delegates up to the fountain. The man in the gray suit swished his hand through the pool's green water, sending fat orange fish twitching for safety beneath the plate-sized leaves of water lilies.

"Your Lordship, may I present the delegates from the Cheyenne Alliance: One Who Flies, Storm Arriving, Gray Bear, and Limps. Gentlemen, the Viceroy Lord Enrico Joachim Xavier Rudolfo Serrano-Ruiz."

The viceroy stood and accepted a towel from a servant.

He dried his hand, extended it, and shook George's with a quick snap and a click of his heels. He gave a curt nod to the other three delegates, and then motioned toward a table and chairs that stood nearby.

"Before we begin our discussions," the viceroy said as they all took seats at the table, "I should like to thank you, One Who Flies, and you, Storm Arriving, for returning to New Spain its most valued subject and ambassador."

George inclined his head, acknowledging the compliment, but it was Storm Arriving who spoke.

"You are most welcome, Chief of the Iron Shirts. It makes us glad to be of help."

George glanced over at his friend and saw him motion with his hands.

For the People, he signed.

Yes, George replied in kind, and then turned his attention back to the viceroy.

Lord Serrano-Ruiz was a mature man, though his shiny black hair showed not a hint of silver. His beard and mustache were trimmed and his clothing unwrinkled. He sat straight, feet crossed at the ankles, and his shoulders did not touch the back of his chair. Even his boots were impeccably clean, without dust or mar from his journey up the ridge, and his primness and his habit of straightening the lines of his jacket or trousers gave him a dandified air.

He was, however, an attentive listener and an intelligent conversationalist. Though he sipped tea and tossed cake crumbs into the fountain, watching the copper-sided fish spin beneath reflections of palm and cloud, he never lost the thread of their talk. As the afternoon sun slipped down the roofline and the shadows crept toward the fountain, he spoke to George and the others without evasion. As the rising breeze of evening sent wayward leaves trundling in through the archways, he finally began to talk of alliances, of trade, and of mutual benefit.

"In addition to arms and supplies," the viceroy said, "New Spain might also provide the loan of funds."

"Funds?" George asked. "To what purpose?"

Lord Serrano glanced at his ambassador, and Alejandro took up the thought.

"The Spanish Throne cannot formally recognize your Alliance while your lands are still—technically, at least—a territory of the United States. To do so would be tantamount to a declaration of war."

"Yes," George said. "We understand this."

"Then it must be clear that, before the Crown can recognize you, the Alliance must achieve some level of *pro forma* independence." He shrugged, as if the conclusion were obvious. "One possible way to do that is to . . . well . . . to buy the land."

Storm Arriving sat forward and put his hand on the table—his way of asking for the party's attention. "The land is already ours. We have always lived there, and we have always controlled it. There is nothing for which we need to pay."

The viceroy leaned forward and patted Storm Arriving on the hand. "That is fine," he said, "and I am sure that you are right, but let us not be naïve." He sat back and tossed another crumb to the fish. "The reality of your situation is this: the United States paid money for that land, and they can hardly be convinced to let it go without some recompense. It's simple politics. War can allow you to occupy a land, but in our world, before you can own it, you must buy it."

A silence spread out until all that could be heard was the splashing of the fish after another crumb.

"Food for thought," Alejandro said, stepping into the breach. "I beg pardon, Your Lordship, but if you wish to see these men ride their magnificent animals, I suggest we do so soon before we lose the light."

"Ah, I am glad you mentioned it. Don Silveira, while your eloquence had convinced me of the political usefulness of this proposed alliance, there are those who doubt that our new friends can be viable partners in the military sense." He presented them his open hands, as if he were somehow helpless. He plucked at his lapels. "Though my family goes back for centuries among the *Madrileños,* I am not, as you may plainly see, a military man. And ruling New Spain has become a largely military enterprise. In Cuba, in the Yaqui territory, and in the Philippines, the word of the *generalíssimos* carries great weight. So too will it be as regards the Cheyenne. Therefore, in order for us to successfully advance our plan, I must engage the support of my military leadership and, toward that end, I have arranged for a less private review of your guests' riding and military talents." He rose from his seat and everyone stood with him.

"Tomorrow afternoon," he told them. "At the Palacio de Toros." He gave a curt bow to George and Storm Arriving in turn. "I have enjoyed our discussions, gentlemen, and look forward to the possibility of a more formal relationship. Until tomorrow, at the arena?"

He did not wait, but turned crisply and walked out of the courtyard. The helmeted guards snapped to attention as he exited, and followed him out.

"I apologize," Alejandro said. "This is . . . unexpected."

"There is a problem?" Storm Arriving asked.

"Yes," George said, troubled.

"One Who Flies," Storm Arriving said in his native tongue. "What went wrong? The Chief of the Iron Shirts talked as if he would help us."

"He did," George said. "But he has left himself an avenue of retreat. We must perform this riding exhibition for his war chiefs, so he can judge their reaction. If the war chiefs do not support the alliance—or if he *says* they do not support it—he can say 'yes' to our face, 'no' to our backs, and can walk away from us without a qualm."

"Will the war chiefs support us?"

George turned to Alejandro and switched to the Trader's Tongue. "Will the generals support us?"

The ambassador shrugged. "It is hard to say. Many of our generals are open to innovation, but others will leap upon any excuse—"

"Then we must not give them an excuse," George said. "We must give them an exhibition that will show them that our riders can do everything an Iron Shirt can do."

"Everything," Storm Arriving said, "and more."

Groomsmen set lanterns and chimney lamps on posts around the riding oval. The kitchen kept coffee and savory broth in steaming urns near the stables to help fight off the chill of the evening fog. Messengers ran out into the growing mist bearing instructions, orders, and imprecations, then returned and left again with more.

Alejandro sent for help from old military friends who

came without question, rolled up their sleeves, and took on the task of training the most unlikely cavalry they had ever seen. George and the others, cloaked by the mist and surrounded by the dancing glow of pulsating flames, worked through the night.

They learned formation drills—an unknown skill among the riders of the People—and practiced precision maneuvers. They worked, too, on old skills known to every rider, building the spirit of boyhood games into complex motions. As they repeated and repeated and repeated again the tasks, they changed from fifteen individuals into a cohesive unit of one thought and one instinct. Their speed and accuracy were astonishing, even to George, who knew what a whistler could do.

His own tasks, to be done on walker-back, depended not on teamwork but on honing his control over his own mount. The old man who tutored him in the private paddock separated from the riding oval did his best to adapt traditional Spanish horsemanship to George's large and less graceful beast.

"What color is the turf?" George asked Alejandro during a rest break. They were watching the riders race around the oval in nose-to-tail formation. "In the arena. What is the ground like? What color is it?"

"It is sand," Alejandro said. "Red sand, shipped up here from the southern deserts."

"Can we get some cloth the same color as that sand?"

"I'll see to it," the ambassador promised.

At midmorning, with the sun strong in a hazy sky, they rested. The animals were stabled and the men walked up to the cottages. They lay down on the cool grass or on the warm tiles as was their need. Aching and tired in mind and in body, they found an hour's peace a welcome necessity. Storm Arriving came up to George and sat down beside him on the patio tiles.

The argument they had had was still heavy on George's mind. "How do you think your riders will do?" he asked with a casual air.

"We will impress any man who sees us," Storm Arriving said. "It cannot be helped."

He chuckled at his friend's conscious bravura. "These

are my feelings as well. I only hope I can match your standards."

Storm Arriving laughed, too. "I was watching you. You will succeed." But then he gave his hauteur over to a more serious tone. "At the very least, we will show these Iron Shirts a thing they have never seen."

"We will do that," George agreed. Though they had not apologized to each other for their previous ill tempers, it felt as if they had, and he wondered if that would be good enough. He lay back to let the sun's warmth soothe his tired muscles, and found himself thinking of Mouse Road and guessing at what sort of future lay beyond the morrow.

Alejandro's carriage led the way from the heights over-looking the Pacific down to the rail termini and stockyards south of San Francisco's mercantile core. Though the *corrida* was not among their passions, Victoria and Isabella were with him, and he was glad for their company. They all agreed that they should come to see the day's remarkable exhibition, but Alejandro knew that Victoria's insistence on attending had more to do with his being home after a long absence. Victoria's hand had rarely left his own since his return.

They passed the Mission San Francisco de Asis with its square, stolid face and its three bells under the eaves. Though it was not a tall building, its red-tiled roof still commanded the neighborhood. It had stood for over a hundred years, sanctified before the Americans had sent their letter across the Atlantic, and no businessman had dared construct an edifice that challenged the city's first house of God. For that they had gone to the north end of town, where their impudence might not be so obvious to the Holy Franciscan Fathers.

But it was not the buildings that Alejandro looked for with interest. It was the people. As the cortege headed south for the last mile, the streets began to thicken with throngs of men—and some women and young boys, too—all headed toward the arena. They cheered as they recognized his family crest on the carriage doors, and waved the placards and announcements that he had arranged to have posted around town. As the carriage rattled across the rails and turned onto the Street of Kings, he saw the crowd for which he had hoped.

The plaza in front of the arena was packed side to side with people. He could hear their single voice exclaim in a mixture of wonder and terror as, behind his carriage, the native riders rounded the last corner. The crowd parted before his guardsmen, giving him access to the main gates.

His carriage stopped and he stepped down, turned with an extended hand, and assisted his wife and daughter to disembark. The crowd shouted again and Alejandro saw One Who Flies and his walker come into view, head and shoulders above the whistlers before them. Men on horseback struggled to restrain their fractious mounts, and nervous guards guided the native riders past the front of the arena and around to the participants' side entrance. As the incredible beasts walked out of sight, the crowd turned and headed for the gates, hoping to purchase tickets for at least some seats up high in the stands.

Alejandro and his family walked through to the guest's gate and made their way up to the viceroy's shaded box placed just behind the front row *barreras* at the end opposite the large green gate where the bulls entered the ring. In the box they met the other guests who had been favored with viceregal attention. Lord Serrano's seat, however, remained empty.

The arena was a bowl similar to the Coliseum of ancient Rome, but on a more intimate scale. The Palacio de Toros had not been designed to contain the broad conflicts of chariots and gladiatorial might. In this ring a much more personal battle was played out: one man against one bull, and though the *corrida* did not have the grandiosity of those older spectacles, it more than made up for the lack with grace, beauty, and skill.

And the bowl was filled. Though there was barely a seat to be found outside the viceroy's unoccupied chair, people still streamed in through the *puerta grande*. They pushed and squeezed against each other, they leaned at the *barreras* at the front, they sat on the stairs, and they stood in the aisles. Word had spread quickly.

"This is your doing, isn't it?" asked Señor Generalíssimo Garcia, holding out one of the leaflets that had been distributed around the district overnight. The general was a massive man who imposed on the space of all around him through the bulk of his physical presence, the brashness of his sharp-edged voice, and the poor quality of his cigars. His chair was placed two spots away from Alejandro, but still he bent forward in front of the undergovernor of Alto California, who sat between them. The undergovernor smiled weakly and pretended not to notice that Garcia had a hand on his thigh as he leaned in to speak to Alejandro.

"And if it is, Señor General?" Alejandro said archly. "I can see nothing wrong with inviting the people to share in this exhibition."

"Ah! So you admit it?"

"Why shouldn't I?"

"Because this was supposed to be a *private* exhibition! Military and government officials only. How can we possibly judge these savages with this mob around us?"

A new voice entered the conversation. "The same way you would were you here alone," said the viceroy, coming down the aisle from behind them.

Everyone stood as Viceroy Lord Serrano-Ruiz came to take his seat. He was dressed in a tight-waisted suit of polished, dark green silk, a deep-cut brocade vest that showed the frills of his shirt, a high silk hat, and white cotton gloves. He made his way past his guests, shaking hands, saying a brief word, plying them with his considerable charm. When he came to Alejandro and his family, he stopped before Victoria. She extended her hand, and the viceroy removed his gloves to take it in both of his. "You honor us, Doña Silveira," he said, bent at the waist, and kissed her fingers. "And you, señorita," he said to Isabella, taking her hand as well. "Do you, like Señor Generalíssimo Garcia, come to judge these savages?"

Isabella smiled shyly but shook her head slightly. "No, Your Lordship. I come to see One Who Flies," she said. "He's the son of the American president, you know."

"Indeed?" the viceroy said with an indulgent smile, and the other men nearby chuckled at the young girl's innocence. "We shall have to see if your One Who Flies can ride as well as a Spanish soldier." He turned to Alejandro and cocked his head toward the *generalíssimo* and then at the crowd that packed the stands. "You have had a busy night."

"It is an important occasion," Alejandro said. "They wanted to be sure you saw them at their best. And in my experience, a performance is always improved by the presence of an audience."

The viceroy smiled with sincere good humor. "Touché," he said. "We shall see if your instincts are correct."

They sat down and, at a signal from Lord Serrano, the trumpets sounded to mark the beginning of the exhibition. The crowd stood with a cheer as the gates at the end of the arena opened, but the enthusiasm died in a groan when there emerged from the darkness beyond the gate not the exotic beasts they had hoped for, but merely a cadre of men on horseback—a squad of riders from the Royal Cavalry.

A dozen men on glossy chestnut stallions rode out in double file. They wore red jackets trimmed with gold, and their black leather leggings were buttoned at the outer seam with brass that flashed in the sunlight of early afternoon. They carried pikes over their shoulders and at midfield stopped, saluted the viceroy, and then split into two lines, each curling back around to form two circles. This drill was well known to the spectators and they settled back to wait, shouting for the attention of vendors who pushed their way down the overcrowded aisles with refreshments of wine, fruit, or warm fried *churros* spiced with cinnamon and sweetened with dark sugar.

The riders lifted their pikes—ten-foot poles capped with a four-inch speartip—and rode out of their circles to form up into loose ranks. The metal tips came down and touched the red sand of the arena floor, and the men nudged their horses into a display of riding skill. With tips embedded in the sand and each weapon's butt-end held high by its owner's hand, the horses began weaving in, out, under, and around the pike's shaft. The riders guided their mounts by pressure of their knees, without commands, and the horses performed in perfect unison. As familiar as this was to the crowd, still the expertise began to capture their attention, and soon there was applause with each difficult maneuver. The drills grew more complex, with horses working in pairs, then in fours. Riders held the pikes between them, moving in circles around a central rider, his stallion slowly turning beneath a canopy of speartips.

Then they began to ride back and forth across the bullring. More riders emerged from the gates, and the crowd applauded as the riders headed toward each other. Now over twenty in number, they rode inward from the four directions, passing close, creating a tapestry of men and beasts, shiny speartips and black hooves. They turned, swerved, and repeated the drill. Red sand flew. Manes and tails fluttered like flags. As a finale, the riders split and formed two ranks at either end of the bullring. The crowd was cheering, ready for the last grand maneuver. With a cry the riders spurred their mounts forward. The cry was echoed in the stands as two beautifully straight lines of arch-necked stallions pounded toward the center. Alejandro, though he knew the outcome, felt his heart race with the sheer power of it. The pikes lowered, and speartips now pointed at the onrushing ranks. The voice of the stands rose as the inevitable approached, then burst into a cheer as the riders missed each other, spearpoints grazing harmlessly past.

The mob was on its feet, and Alejandro looked to the side to see if anyone in the viceregal box had noticed the opening of the gate at the far end of the bullring.

The riders reined in to accept the approval of the crowd. They came together at the center of the bullring and put their mounts in a square facing outward toward the stands. Then, as one, the horses knelt down on one foreleg, bowing to the crowd. No one noticed the shadows that had ridden onto the red sand of the arena.

Gunfire burst in a ring of white smoke. Spectators screamed and the horses in the bullring began to panic. Someone pointed, and soon everyone saw what Alejandro had known was there. Around the limit of the bullring, along the wood-planked edges below the *barreras,* shapes were moving, but shapes that defied the eye.

"There!" shouted the viceroy, pointing.

"And there," said a guest.

"What are they?" Lord Serrano asked, amazed.

"A moment longer, my lord, and you shall see."

Pale red ghosts rode round the bullring, ghosts the same color as the rust-red sand beneath them. Only their shadows seemed whole as their bulk seemed to flutter and shift, and then the whistlers dropped their camouflaging colors and the riders lifted their shrouds of dyed cotton. The array of horses in midfield reared and bolted for the gate. The men on whistlers raised their rifles and fired another shot to the sky. The last of the horses fled, some leaving their riders behind. The stands erupted in shouts and cheers as the whistler riders held their rifles aloft and rode around the ring.

The whistlers were bulkier than any horse, but moved with a grace and control that made the finest cavalryman think unkind thoughts. The riders directed their mounts into the now vacant center of the ring. The fifteen riders formed a large circle, and the whistlers began to walk slowly so as to give everyone a good, long look at these incredible beasts. At a command, the whistlers shifted the color of their flanks from brindled gold to obscuring taupe and rust, matching the colors of the light-filled bullring. Riders rode beasts made of illusion, and Alejandro saw not a few spectators rub their eyes in disbelief. Another command and the whistlers lifted their muzzles in song—a hair-raising, trumpeting call that started low and rose into a high-pitched keening that gave the beasts their name.

The riders took their beasts over to the far end and made them crouch down in the sand. Then four of the riders picked up pikes and rode to the center of the arena and, with a salute to the viceregal box, commenced their own version of the pike drill performed by the cavalry riders. Alejandro watched with interest as the large whistlers moved gingerly under the pikeshafts, pivoted around the grounded points, and spun without disturbing their rider's grip on his planted weapon. Their precision was not as great as that of the earlier riders, but it was nonetheless impressive. The crowd, now understanding the purpose of the earlier cavalry exhibition, began to cheer on this new variation on an old, familiar theme. Out of the corner of his eye Alejandro saw some of the *generalíssimos* shift in their seats, wanting, he was sure, to see this as an affront to tradition but unable to challenge both the skill before them and the goodwill of the crowd.

As the pike dance ended, the gates opened. Several whistlers flashed bars of red and white along their snouts and necks as three men rolled a water barrel into the arena. They placed the barrel in the center of the ring and quickly departed.

The riders joined up again and put some speed into their mounts. They formed two circles, one inside the other, and began coursing around the ring. The whistlers ran faster and faster, creating a ring of dust. Men at the rails held up their hands to protect themselves from the kicked-up sand. Then the riders began to shout—a high ululation—and the two circles began to weave in and out like braiding a plait of hair. They circled the bullring, leaning in as they increased their speed and closed their distance, and the riders took out their rifles. On their knees on the backs of their running beasts, they took aim at the barrel.

The danger of this maneuver was intense, as a missed shot or ricochet could hit a comrade. Despite the assurances of both One Who Flies and Storm Arriving as to the talents of these men, and despite the hours of practice at his home, Alejandro was on his feet with the rest of the crowd, fearing disaster.

The first man fired, and water spurted from a hole in the barrel. Another fired. And another. Water streamed from a dozen shots and the riders widened their circle. They all raised their weapons and, as one, fired. The barrel burst into a ball of spray, and cheers filled the ring.

The Indians reined in, whooping in victory, and with a brief salute to the viceroy, spun and ran to the gate. The throng cried out in unparalleled praise, sending their cheers with them into the darkness beyond the gate. The crowd kept up its noise until they saw movement in the shadows at the far end of the arena. Thinking it was the riders once more to perform an encore, they raised their voices in anticipation.

Alejandro smiled.

The riders did not reappear. From the dark maw of the far gate came the only thing that could increase the crowd's frenzy: a bull.

Lord Serrano leaned close, a hand on Alejandro's arm. "What have you planned?" he asked, never taking his eyes off the lone bull as it powered its way into the center of the arena.

"I would hate to spoil the surprise," Alejandro said, and was rewarded by the viceroy's laugh.

The bull, head high, black-tipped horns agleam, ran a circuit of the bullring. This was not one of the steers of the

Tejano ranchers. This was a fighting bull, a *toro de lidia*, and he was ready. His flanks shone in the sun. His throwing-muscles bunched high above his shoulders. He was magnificent, but Alejandro knew he had no chance.

A sound echoed up from beyond the gate, a roar unlike any heard in this arena or any other. The bull turned midfield to meet the challenge, and the crowd surged forward to the rails to see what was coming. The second roar was louder and so fearsome that it was enough to send some spectators back from the railings. When the walker emerged, the crowd's cheers turned to screams. The walker screamed back at them, a hoarse, enraged sound made of feral force and unpredictable nature.

The walker stood in the sunlight, feet well apart. Its tail twirled and waved like a striped pennant in an imagined wind. Its head was narrow, almost birdlike when seen from a distance, except for the teeth. It leaned forward and roared again—a long blast of fury—and its teeth gleamed.

A gasp ran through the crowd as a man emerged from behind one of the barricades near the walker. He wore the fringed and beaded garments of an Indian, but his hair shone like gold in the sunlight. He walked up to the huge beast and commanded it to the ground. Incredibly, it complied, crouching so that he could mount to the rudimentary saddle that was now apparent on its back.

"Our friend?" the viceroy inquired.

"One Who Flies, yes, my lord."

One Who Flies reached behind the wicker saddle and untied a steel-tipped pike. He undid the ties and unfurled a long flag attached to its end. The flag was made of a thick crimson cloth like the traditional capote, the cape used by matadors in the bullring.

The bull had, until this time, waited in the center of the bullring. Now he started forward, as did One Who Flies and the walker, and thus began the most unusual *corrida* ever performed at the Palacio de Toros.

Alejandro watched as One Who Flies pulled the bull into right and left passes. The bull, unintimidated by the immense beast before him, drew cheers of approval from the crowd. One Who Flies speared the bull between the shoulders with the pike, but the bull pushed bravely onward, ignoring the pain and the walker that towered over him.

Alejandro cheered with everyone else as the walker side-stepped the bull's horns, moving with a lightness that belied its size. Every pass drew a roar from the crowd, despite the clumsiness of the rider's maneuvers. Man and bull alike were working at their top ability. Only the walker was being restrained.

Finally, after repeated passes and several moves that brought thrusts from the pike, it was time. The bull had fought bravely, but had been sapped by his wounds. The walker had obeyed every command from her rider, but the scent of blood and the dust of combat agitated her. She stared at the bull across a span of twenty yards, her neck craning, her muzzle pointing right and left, to the sky, to the earth, as she eyed the object of her hunger from one side, and then the next. The bull stood his ground, nostrils sucking air, his sweat-slick flanks quivering with exhaustion.

One Who Flies unhooked his leg from the rope saddle and descended. The walker tensed, but waited. One Who Flies turned toward the viceroy's box and, with a bow, dedicated the kill to Lord Serrano. Then he turned and motioned with his hand.

The walker rasped twice, a coughing call as harsh as torn metal. The bull pawed the ground and charged, head low. His bloody shoulders shone in the sunlight. The walker pushed off with one leg, pivoting. As the bull's horns dashed past her belly, the walker reached down and grabbed him behind the head. The bull bellowed, thrusting with all four legs and twisting, trying to gore her with his black-tipped horns. The walker set her foot in the dust. The crowd gasped. The silent struggle continued until the walker's teeth found the gaps between the bull's neckbones and her jaws came together with a snap. The bull went limp and, after a moment, the body fell to the ground.

It was over.

Flowers rained down onto the blood-red sand. One Who Flies went to the body and took the ears as a trophy; then he stepped back and let loose his monster. She moved in, planted a clawed foot on the body, and grabbed the hind-quarter in her jaws. Crunching through flesh and gristle, she pulled, teeth gnashing, and tore the leg from the hip joint. Then she tossed the haunch into the air, snatched at it, and swallowed it bones, hide, hoof, and all.

One Who Flies bowed to each quadrant, accepting their plaudits, then turned and walked toward the gate at the far end. His walker, half-gorged on her kill, picked up the rest of the bull and followed her master into the darkness. The crowd continued to throw flowers into the ring, cheering their new champions.

Alejandro glanced over at the others in the box. Generalíssimo Garcia sat with his hands folded across his ample belly, the stub of his cigar smoldering away. He was looking out at the empty arena, his eyes squinted and his lips pursed. Other guests were similarly quiet as they considered what they had just witnessed. The viceroy, however, was smiling.

He stood and prepared to leave. "I expect to hear your opinions this evening," he said to his guests. "Well done, Don Silveira."

Alejandro bowed as his lord left the box. As he straightened, he felt Victoria's hand slip into his own.

"Congratulations," she whispered to him as the box began to empty. "You have made quite an impression."

Alejandro squeezed her fingers and smiled, not trusting his voice to contain the varied emotions he felt. An alliance between New Spain and Custer's hated enemy, led by Alejandro himself and Custer's own son. The stage was set. He need only bring the players together for the next act.

"We must begin to pack, my dear. Washington awaits."

George and the others stopped at the crossroads. Before them were the Big Salty and the tiny town of La Puerta del Norte, both dark and lonely beneath the shadow of bad weather. Behind them, the Sangre de Cristo Mountains rumbled with thunder as an autumn storm tossed lightning from cloud to cloud. The wind at their backs smelled of electricity and the promise of rain, but nothing but dust blew past their animals' feet. They heard the rattle of the carriage making its way up the mountain trail, and the men moved their whistlers away from the junction. George and Storm Arriving dismounted.

The carriage came into view, pale with dust and surrounded by armed horsemen. The guards wore the metal helmets and breastplates of an honor guard, but George noticed that they also bore German-made repeating rifles.

The Spanish military was passionate about its traditions but did not let that override common sense and the practicality of new technologies.

The driver brought the carriage to a halt, and a servant jumped down to place the step and open the door. George and Storm Arriving stepped forward as Alejandro was helped down. Behind him, Doña Silveira and Señorita Isabella peered from the carriage windows.

"There," Alejandro said, pointing to La Puerta del Norte. "I will ensure that there is a ship waiting there for you. Come quickly, though. The season's storms will soon arrive."

George and Storm Arriving shook the ambassador's hand. "We will come as quickly as we can," George said. "Thank you for all your help."

"We have really only begun," he said. "But it is a good beginning. And there is something I must tell you." He pulled some papers from his coat pocket. "I received these telegrams in Cimarron. In addition to the promise of military support and cooperation, the viceroy has agreed to loan you up to ten million in gold to help in our negotiations."

George did not dare look at Storm Arriving, fearing to betray his thoughts. "Ten million?" he said instead to Alejandro. "How could we ever repay such a sum?"

The ambassador dismissed his concerns. "As all nations do," he said. "Trade, exchange of services; we will worry about that later." He turned back to his carriage. "I will have everything ready for your arrival," he said as he climbed back inside. "¡Adios!"

The servant latched the door and leapt up just as the driver snapped his team into motion. The carriage lurched forward, and George and Storm Arriving raised a hand in farewell. The large wheels crunched across the rock and hard-packed earth, and the steel springs creaked with the uneven terrain. George and Storm Arriving watched the carriage make its troubled way down the rough road. Young Isabella leaned quickly out the window, waved, and blew a kiss in George's direction. She disappeared as quickly as she had emerged. George felt a smile on his face, but smothered it before he turned back to the others.

Storm Arriving cleared his throat. "How much is ten million?"

"A great deal," George said. "But not nearly enough for what we hope to do."

"We will need more, then."

George nodded.

"He must know that it is not enough," Storm Arriving said.

It was a thought that had not occurred to George. As they turned back toward their mounts, toward the north, and toward home, George suddenly had a doubt where before there had been no doubt.

CHAPTER 15

Cool Moon, Waxing
Fifty-six Years After the Star Fell
Near the Milk River
Alliance Territory

Mouse Road plunged her digging-stick into the dry earth beneath the yellowing leaves of a white-apple plant and sang along with the other women.

> *My sweetheart is coming*
> *Down from the hills*
> *He has spoken to my father*
> *Tonight I will be happy.*

It was a cheerful song, designed to lift the spirits, but it did little for Mouse Road other than to bring into focus what had been for her a particularly bad string of days. She sang, though, and worked her stick in rhythm to the music: dig-push-push-lift, dig-push-push-lift.

When the stick was deep enough, she pulled on it like a lever. From beneath the tired leaves and the dried grass came clods of dirt, small rocks, and a constellation of a dozen white tubers. Most were little larger than her fist, but one was as big as a whistler's egg. It was a lovely size, good enough for a meal by itself. Her tired hands picked up most of them and tossed them into the open parfleche she carried strapped over her shoulder, adding them to the others she'd gathered during the day. She left two of the smaller ones on the ground and pushed them back into the hole whence they'd come, covering them with soil. With her foot she tamped the earth down over the seed-roots, and then searched for another white-apple plant, singing of love as she did so.

> *He has captured many whistlers*
> *He has counted many coups*
> *He has spoken to my father*
> *He wants to make me happy.*

"I think I know who wants to make Mouse Road happy," said one of the women. Others nearby laughed. "Black Swallowtail has been looking at her all day."

Mouse Road frowned and thrust her digging-stick into the earth a little harder than was necessary. Nearly forty women had come out to dig for white-apples, and worked in a loose formation along the hillside, scattered along the slope uphill from the creek. But whether she worked the edge of the group or the center, the old gossips had always seemed to surround her, taking every opportunity to tease.

"I think I know two," said another woman.

"What?" asked the first. "Who else?" the second woman pointed and all the women looked. Mouse Road refused to look and kept her gaze on the ground.

"Ah, Hungry Bear," said the first woman, naming another of the soldiers who rode as escort for them. "Poor man. But it is too soon for him. His first wife passed beyond only two moons ago."

"But she left a newborn," said the second. "And the older child can only do so much. He needs a wife."

The first woman clucked her tongue and set again to digging. "True," she said. "True. Winter is coming and he will need help with the babe. And you, little one," she said to Mouse Road. "How will you survive the winter now, without mother or brother? Surely you aren't counting on One Who Flies."

Mouse Road ducked her head, ignoring the question, and worked her way to the edge of the group. She just wanted to gather some food. She did not want to think about the emptiness she felt every day, nor worry about what the winter might bring. There had been enough to worry her recently.

"Mouse Road," said a shadow that crossed her path.

She looked up and saw Black Swallowtail sitting atop his

whistler. He was one of the four Little Bowstring soldiers the Council had sent out to guard the women while they dug for roots. They always had escorts now. They were only allowed to leave camp in groups; regardless of the errand—to gather wood, fetch water, pick berries, or dig for roots—it did not matter. The raids by the *vé'hó'e* had become too frequent and too dangerous for the women to leave the encampment without guardians.

"Mouse Road, I love you," Black Swallowtail told her.

"Don't tease," she said.

"I'm not teasing," he said in a low whisper. "You are the prettiest girl I have ever seen, and I want to make you happy, like in the song."

She felt a blush rise to her cheeks and she looked down at her work to hide it. Black Swallowtail was a young man of twenty-five summers. He was a good hunter, and his mettle had already been proven in battle and in the scars of sacrifice that he bore on his forearms. But she had no interest in him, nor in any of the other suitors who had come visiting during recent days, emboldened by the fact that she now had neither mother nor brother at home.

"Find another girl," she said solemnly. "And soon, before we separate for our winter camps."

"I don't want to find another, Mouse Road. I am serious. Every time I see you, my heart is glad. I did not want to let another winter go by without speaking to you."

She looked up at him and saw by the set of his jaw and the furrow on his brow that he was indeed in earnest. She saw, too, the gift ring he held out to her—a twisted braid of copper for her to wear as a token of his feelings—and she did not know what to say. She glanced back at the other women. They had all stopped in their digging and were watching Black Swallowtail press his suit.

What should I do? She wondered. Tell him not to bother, that I have already lost my heart to another? Or take the ring, and let him have his hope until Storm Arriving comes home and crushes it? If he crushes it . . .

"I am sorry," she said. "Courting me will come to nothing for you. I love another."

The frown deepened on Black Swallowtail's face. "Hunh," he said. "One Who Flies. I thought you were smarter than that." He looked at her, forcing her to look down at the broken earth at her feet. "You should see things as they are, Mouse Road. You are alone. Your mother is gone. Your brother is married. And One Who Flies? Where is he? When will he be back? How long will he stay?" The gift ring landed in the dirt before her. She looked up and met his gaze. His dark eyes were in shadow beneath an angry brow and the muscles bunched tight along his jaw.

"Who will take care of you, Mouse Road? Not One Who Flies. He is too busy digging for gold in the earth or traveling to visit with *vé'hó'e*. He has no time for you." He struck his fist against his chest—a hollow thumping sound. "But I do," he said. "I would take care of you." There was another hollow thump and Black Swallowtail's face changed. All of the hurt and anger drained away, leaving only a look of surprise. His jaw worked soundlessly and the surprise, too, leaked out of him, just as blood began to bruise his tunic. Mouse Road stared, frozen, as Black Swallowtail pitched forward off his whistler and hit the ground in a heap. She heard another thump. Someone screamed—perhaps it was her—and then havoc descended upon them all.

Whistlers fluted as the soldiers nudged them into motion.

"What is it?" Honeybee Woman cried.

"Bluecoats," one of the guarding soldiers replied. "Get down in the grass."

Mouse Road ducked down. The grass was only knee-high, with an infrequent clump of scrub brush for cover; she hoped it would be enough. She heard the distant pop of gunfire, and incoming bullets hissed through the dry blades.

"Up there," one of the soldiers shouted. "In the trees."

A man grunted and she heard him hit the ground, heard his whistler yodel in confusion. The two remaining soldiers fired toward the far line of dark firs, then kicked their whistlers into a run. Honeybee Woman wailed.

"Quiet," rasped one of the old gossips, and Honeybee Woman stifled her fearful clamor.

The riders fired as they approached the trees, hoping to flush their enemy, but the bluecoats were waiting. As they got to within yards of the trees, a white cloud of smoke erupted. The soldiers were tossed from their mounts and the whistlers went down, thrashing the air. From out of the

trees came six *vé'hó'e,* armed with rifles. They finished off
the soldiers and their mounts and then looked down the hill
toward the women. They raised their weapons and began to
fire.

Women screamed.

"Stay down!" shouted one of the cooler heads, but too
late. Most of the women had bolted in panicked retreat.
The *vé'hó'e* made their slow, methodical way down the hillside, firing at will. Screams chilled the air and Mouse Road
blinked away stinging tears. The *vé'hó'e* would kill them all.

She scrambled through the grass to where Black Swallowtail lay. His rifle was beyond the reach of his outstretched hand, his dead gaze still fixed upon it—his last
duty unfulfilled. She took the rifle and worked the lever.
Using Black Swallowtail's body as a shield, she laid the
barrel across him and aimed.

Her first shot was low, as she miscalculated for the uphill
rise of the land. She worked the lever and tried again. Her
second shot brought a man down. The *vé'hó'e* halted at her
returned fire and crouched. Mouse Road fired up at them,
aiming at heads that bobbed above the blades of grass. She
aimed as well as she could, but her heart merely hoped
that they would flee. She volleyed round after round up
the hill. One *vé'ho'e* stood to fire down upon her and she
dropped him. There were three left. She aimed once more,
and pulled the trigger, but there was no shot. She had run
through the ammunition in the rifle's magazine.

Frantic, she searched the ground near Black Swallowtail,
looking for his cartridge bag. A leather strap ran across his
torso and underneath his body. She pulled at him, rolling
him down toward her. Uphill, the remaining *vé'ho'e* sensed
her predicament and rose above the grass. She scuttled to
one side just as they began to fire. A bullet thunked into
the body and she cried out. The *vé'hó'e* heard, and began
to run toward her. She lay flat, tugging at the strap to the
cartridge bag.

A shot cracked from across the hillside and a *vé'ho'e*
shouted in surprise. A second shot brought another man
down. The last *vé'ho'e* stopped just feet from where Mouse
Road lay in the grass, and turned toward the source of the
new threat. A bullet caught him in the face, punching his

head back like an old doll's. He fell backward into the grass, his body sliding, coming to rest next to Black Swallowtail's, eyes staring past a ruined nose.

Mouse Road felt the pounding of her pulse in her neck, and heard the tremulous sobs of the women nearby. Across the hillside, she saw a soldier holding his rifle. Blood from a head wound darkened the side of his brow and cheek like a red shadow. He staggered, but when a woman rose to help him he waved her away.

"I am fine. Everyone. Back to camp," he said. "Now. Quickly."

The women did as he instructed while he went from body to body to ensure that the *vé'hó'e* were dead.

Mouse Road was collecting her spilled white-apples when the soldier came over to her. "What about Black Swallowtail?" she asked. "And the others?"

"We will come back for them," the soldier said. He was an older man, broad-shouldered and strong of limb. His hair was in a long, single braid wrapped in rabbit fur, and the yoke of his tunic was quilled with finely sewn circles and lines in blue and black. He glanced down at her through the sheen of blood that ran from his brow down past a crooked nose and a scarred cheek. "You are Mouse Road, are you not?"

"Yes," she said. "I am Mouse Road of the Tree People, sister of Storm Arriving."

"I am Hungry Bear, of the Closed Windpipe band. I have heard of your brother, and of his young sister. You did well today, and he will be proud. May I tell him of the kills you made today?"

"My brother is away from the People," she said. "He has traveled to the Land of the Iron Shirts with One Who Flies."

The mention of One Who Flies did not faze Hungry Bear as it did most others. "I know. When he has returned, then? May I tell him when he has returned?"

She hesitated as she put the last white-apples in her parfleche. "You do not need my permission to speak to my brother."

"No," he said. "I was hoping I might speak to him of other things. Of things that . . . I was hoping to speak to him about you."

There was a seriousness to this man that confused Mouse Road. He was not brash or impetuous like the other men who had asked permission to speak to her brother. Like Black Swallowtail. This man was solemn, almost sad, and yet confident. He was older than the others, too; older even than One Who Flies.

"May I speak to him?" Hungry Bear asked.

She thought of what the old gossips had said *How will you survive? . . . Winter is coming. . . . Surely you aren't counting on One Who Flies.* Her future was as cloudy as the storms that loomed beyond the world's western rim, and it promised only heartache and hunger.

"You may speak to him if you wish," she said quietly, and then hurried down the hill toward the rest of the women returning to the camp.

Word of the attack had raced ahead, and soldiers rode out to meet the survivors and retrieve the dead. Word, too, of Mouse Road's kills had preceded them, and people came out to congratulate her. She made her way back to her single lodge among the Tree People, thanking well-wishers and deferring invitations to tell her story along the way. Her knees were weak, but not from exertion. The panic that had tightened her gut during the attack now turned her muscles to water, and she felt the shaking in her legs and arms as she struggled to make it home. Outside her lodge, neighbors clustered, concerned for her well-being.

"I am fine," she told them with a frail smile. "I am just tired." She thanked them and went inside, closing the door-flap behind her. Inside, she sat down near the cold hearth and waited until the footsteps and murmurs of her neighbors turned homeward. Only then—only when she felt sure that she was alone and that no one would overhear—only then did she move to her bed, curl up beneath a buffalo robe, and, with her mind filled with images of the dead and dying, of winter and hunger, quietly begin to weep.

A storm announced itself in the clouds that had piled up during the day, massive pillars of gray and blue that blocked the westering sun. George wondered if he, Storm Arriving, and the others would reach home before the weather came down upon them.

The scouts had come back with disturbing news, and as

they rode over the top of the final hill, they saw that it was true. Miles ahead, the camp spread out in a broad ring, but even from this distance they could see the empty spots in the north and southwest. The People were disbanding. Before even the first frost had touched the land, the bands were separating for the winter, and already the dark specks of families and their flocks stretched out along the southern and eastward trails.

"I cannot believe it," one of the riders said.

"Believe it," Storm Arriving answered.

George heard the bitterness in his friend's voice. "You can't be certain," he said. "You can't know why they are leaving so early."

Storm Arriving touched his chest. "I know what I feel is true, and I know what I have seen." He shrugged. "But that no longer matters. We will know soon enough. I only hope enough of the Council is still here to act on our news."

They rode ahead, waiting for an outlying guard to challenge them, but instead of meeting with a lone picket set out along the perimeter, five rifle-bearing soldiers stood up from behind a breastwork dug into the ground.

"One Who Flies?" one of them asked, recognizing George on his walker. "Is that you?"

"Yes," George replied. He looked to either side and saw similar nests of guards set all along the perimeter. "I am with Storm Arriving and the rest of the delegation to the Iron Shirts. We need to speak with Three Trees Together. Is the Council still here?"

"Yes," the guardsman said. "He and the Council are meeting right now. Do you bring good news?"

"I hope so," George said.

"We could use some good news," the guardsman said, and waved them on ahead.

As they rode in toward camp, they saw that not only were there more guards at the perimeter, there was a second boundary with trenches and breastworks. Storm Arriving pointed, and George saw the positions had been fortified with the Gatling guns captured from the U.S. Army. Up to ten armed men waved as they passed.

"What has happened?" George wondered aloud.

His only answer was thunder from the building clouds.

George and Storm Arriving rode up to the Council Lodge just as fat drops of rain began to fall. They dismounted and walked toward the crowd that surrounded the tall, skin-covered lodge. The chiefs who guarded the door beckoned and the crowd parted to let them through. They were ushered in just as the sky opened up and loosed its rain in heavy sheets.

Inside, a fire crackled and hissed in the hearthpit. Beyond it, George saw Three Trees Together sitting at the *vá'óhtáma*. The old chief's face, usually so placid, was pulled into a frown, and his dark eyes glinted like shards of black glass from beneath glowering brows. One of the younger chiefs was speaking as they sat down near the door with the youngest members of the Council.

"We must consider other options," the young chief was saying. "If we are visible, we are vulnerable, and we are most visible during our summer gathering. If we do not gather in the summer—"

A shout of refutation rose from the assembly. Despite the insult of such an outburst, the young chief politely waited for it to subside before continuing.

"If we do not gather in the summer, we can move faster, and the *vé'hó'e* raiders cannot find us as easily."

The Council members were hard-pressed to remain silent until the young chief finished his comments and sat, releasing a frenzy as others stood to speak their objections. Three Trees Together let the storm rage inside the lodge just as it did in the sky above the wind-rippled lodgeskins.

"What of the Medicine Lodge Dance?"

"And if the Sacred Arrows must be renewed? How are we to do that without gathering together?"

"Not to mention our young people. How are they to court and marry if the bands do not gather?"

Men rose and sat in quick succession, most stating their opposition to the suggestion, but a few, mostly younger chiefs, stood to add their voice to that of the first chief. Rain drummed on the lodgeskins and thunder rumbled, but soon the charged air dissipated, and Three Trees Together leaned forward to regain control of the meeting.

"There are many things we must consider," he said once they had all quieted down. "Matters of the spirit and matters of the soul. Sharp Knife is right when he says that a smaller camp is faster and may be protected more easily; but it also takes less to rub it out. The *vé'hó'e* are very angry at us for destroying their forts and their bridge, and I think they want to rub out all of the People. It is easy to see that something must be done, but if we no longer come together each summer, if we no longer gather to hunt or dance or sing, are we still a people?" He let his words pass through the Council and out to the people standing in the rain. "We must be careful that in saving our people, we do not destroy the People."

There was no sound other than the storm and the hissing gasps as raindrops fell through the smokehole and into the fire.

Finally, Three Trees Together sat back. "It is a difficult question and we must think on it, but I see an easier one that requires answering now. Storm Arriving and One Who Flies have returned. What can you two tell us of your time with the Iron Shirts?"

George and Storm Arriving related the events and the discussions that had transpired during their journeys. The question of whether or not to send a second delegation was quickly raised and answered.

"It is agreed, then," the ancient chief said above the storm's thunder. "We will go." A gust of wind ruffled the skins and made the lodgepoles creak. "But the decision of who will go is a thing for old men. Let us excuse our young friends, with our thanks for their troubles."

The Council, by its silence, concurred with the suggestion of their eldest chief, and George and Storm Arriving made their way back out into the rain.

"One Bear will tell me what they decide," Storm Arriving said above the rush of the storm's wind. "I will send someone to you with the news."

George signed his agreement and made his way toward home. It was not long before he was standing outside the lodge he had dreamed of for weeks. He sat atop his walker, looking down on the familiar designs of dark blue handprints over white circles of hailstones and yellow lines of lightning. Rainwater streamed down his face, soaking him thoroughly. He stepped down from his mount into the thin mud and walked up to the doorflap.

"Mouse Road?" he called.

The doorflap flew open and there she stood, frozen like a deer at the moment of discovery, unable do choose which way to run. She stared at him, all manners lost, eyes squinting against the weather. The rain pattered on her brow, her cheeks, and she blinked her crescent-shaped eyes. He saw her gaze take in his every aspect: his face, his sodden hair, his clothing drenched and soiled from weeks on the trail, returning once more to his face again. He could feel a grin stretch across his face, and he wanted nothing more than to hold her close.

"It makes my heart glad to see you," he said.

But no reciprocal smile touched her lips. Her mouth remained fixed, as if halted in midthought.

"Aren't you glad to see me?" he asked.

And finally she moved, life returning to her features as she said, "Should I be glad? Can I? Will you let me?"

He was stunned by her words. "Will I *let* you?"

"Will you give me reason to be glad, One Who Flies?"

"I am here," he said, feeling resentment kindle within him, and panic, too. "I am home. Isn't that enough?"

She clenched her teeth and blinked against the rain. Her hand rose from her side and slowly formed a single gesture: palm down, palm up.

No.

His gut roiled with the blow of her meaning. "Why not?" he managed to ask.

"Because you are not here to stay."

Relief flooded through him. "But my sweet one," he said with a chuckle, "I am still here for a while—"

"How long?" The sharpness of her query brought him up short.

"I . . . I am not sure. A week, perhaps."

Her eyes were fierce. "And then?"

The rain pelted down upon him. His head began to hurt. "And then I must go with the chiefs. To the *vé'hó'e* city."

"And how long will you be gone?"

"I don't know," he said. "Until spring, if all goes well, but Mouse Road—"

"And then what?"

"What do you mean?"

"When you return from the City of White Stone, where will you go then?"

"I don't know," he said again, trying to think of the words to calm her. "There will be much to do when we return—"

"Where?" she said. "At the mining sites? Among the Iron Shirts? Back up in Grandmother Land? Where?" Her breath was broken by anguish, her face melting into a tearful frown. "How long will you be gone, One Who Flies? How long until you will be *here*? How long until you will be with *me*?" She stepped back inside her lodge.

"Mouse Road, wait," he said, and she did, though she did not face him.

"How long, One Who Flies?" she asked again. "How long will it be before you can be a whole man?"

Now it was he who was transfixed, caught in the swirl between two courses of action—to proceed, or to turn aside. The opposing forces of possibility sapped him of the strength he needed, the strength to choose. He was adrift, helpless before her storm.

"Winter is coming," she said, "and I am alone. This is not what we had planned"—she swallowed past tears that clogged her throat—"but it is the way things are."

The doorflap closed. George stood in the rain, its water running down his face, his arms, and his back in cold streams. The wind pushed him, shoved him. Lightning sparked, rolling thunder down from the mountains. He stood there, staring at the closed doorflap, wondering what had just happened and fearing that he knew. It was a long time before he moved, and when he did, he merely looked up into the sky.

The stormclouds formed a solid ceiling now, and the last gloom of the hidden sun was fading from the world. Lightning bounced across the sky, caroming from thunderhead to thunderhead. He looked for some sign of the Thunder Beings, not knowing what such a sign might be, and saw nothing but the rumbling clouds.

"Is this part of your plan?" he asked the storm and the spirits who sent it.

Family is important, echoed their words through his mind.

Yes, he replied in thought. But you didn't tell me that I would have to give up one to have the other.

Mouse Road did not answer his call the next morning, though he stood outside her lodge for nearly a full hand of time. In the afternoon, one of Storm Arriving's young in-laws, Mockingbird, arrived with her dog, Barks like Thunder.

"Storm Arriving says that the chiefs have decided. They will leave tomorrow."

George, still disturbed by Mouse Road's silence, listened but said nothing. He scratched Barks like Thunder between the ears, receiving a slobbery lick in payment.

"He asks that you come tonight to a farewell feast," Mockingbird continued. "At sunset." And when George remained silent, she added, "Whistling Elk will be there. He is a good storyteller."

"Will Mouse Road be there?" George asked.

"I think so," Mockingbird said. "Will you come?"

"Yes," he said. "I will come." He patted the dog and sent them on their way.

The days were getting shorter as winter began to steal the light of summer, and he did not have much time to prepare himself. The Council had come to its decision more quickly than he had expected, and tomorrow was sooner than he'd thought they'd have wanted to leave. It only made the previous night's argument with Mouse Road more bitter, as it served to prove her point. He'd not even unpacked his belongings, and was already preparing for another departure.

But how could he turn away from his responsibilities? How could she expect him to leave his work to others? Or did she?

He needed to talk with Storm Arriving, and hoped that tonight's feast provided an opportunity. He set about making himself presentable.

As the sun slipped down into the thin space between the clouds and the horizon, it gave the day its first real touch of sunlight. The world gleamed, chased in pale silver. The sun, sinking lower, turned alchemist and changed the silver to gold. Overhead, as a wavering vee of widgeons peeped and whistled its way southward, the clouds tarnished from gold to brass. Brass faded to bronze and thence to burnished copper, and as George headed across the central clearing, the metals merged in the fireless flames of sunset, burned, and went out. The sun departed for the day, and the clouds lidded the world over.

In the new gloom, lodges glowed, alive with warmth and light. They surrounded most of the clearing, but not completely. Already the Hair Rope band and the Suhtai had departed. The allied tribes—the Cloud People, the Inviters, and others—had long ago left the body of the Alliance, driven away by the incessant bluecoat raids.

George cursed his father or whomever had suggested this tactic. It had turned the tables, giving the bluecoats the advantages of speed and mobility while requiring the People to defend established positions. Militarily, it had been an effective strategy. The raids were demoralizing and disruptive. The bluecoats never struck the People on the open plain, where whistlers could overtake the raiders' horses; they only attacked where there was forest or broken terrain in which to hide, and such places were available at every established camp. Out beyond the camp's perimeter, George knew, soldiers waited in trenches, watched from behind breastworks, and sat at gunners' emplacements, ready to protect the inhabitants, for, should the raiders penetrate the defenses, they would be able to wreak a painful toll. He thought back to his own attacks on the U.S. Army's wooden-walled forts. Their methods had been perfectly exchanged by these new tactics. Like the bluecoats of a year ago, the People were now safe only while on the road or on the hunt.

He continued on his way through the empty circle of the clearing, passing by the silent, shadowy cones of the Council Lodge and the two lodges that housed the sacred artifacts: the Sacred Arrows and the Sacred Buffalo Hat, the symbols of the northern and southern tribal groups. Gifts of the spirits, these items were the crux of the People's spiritual identity through summer dances and ceremonies, and the source of much power throughout the year. George remembered the discussion in the Council and considered the possibility of the bands remaining separate during the summer. Three Trees Together had cut to the crux of it all: If they did not gather, would they still be a people?

George sighed and prayed that wiser minds than his could uncover a solution. As an engineer, he was a builder;

as a soldier, a destroyer. Only now was he beginning to realize that he knew very little about the life that was supposed to come in between the two.

The camp of the Closed Windpipe band lay ahead on the southeast side of the clearing. George walked in among the lodges, his moccasin-clad feet squelching on the still-sodden ground. The farther he went, the more he was enfolded by the arms of life. The sounds of meals being served, the gentle prayer of thanksgiving before a meal. The snap of twigs in the fire, and the pleasant voices of children asking questions. From up ahead came the sound of a drum and the rhythm of voices raised in common song, and as he drew nearer, he saw the light of an outdoor fire dance along the skins of lodges. It was the enclave of One Bear's family, of which Storm Arriving was now a part, and a number of people had already arrived for the feast.

George stopped at the limit of the firelight. Storm Arriving and his family—Speaks While Leaving with the newborn Blue Shell Woman, One Bear and Magpie Woman, young Mouse Road and old Healing Rock Woman—sat near the fire in front of the family's main lodge. To either side sat their guests: older neighbors, younger soldiers, and relatives.

Family, George thought wistfully, and wondered if he would ever belong to such a gathering.

To the other side of the fire, the musicians sat in a circle around a wide circle of stretched whistler hide. Two of them held the ends of a length of twine on which beads had been strung, and the beads danced on the painted hide with each stroke of the curved sticks, adding a buzz to the heartbeat of the music. The drummers sang, as did everyone around the fire, and the swaying, back-and-forth rhythm filled the air.

> *Come, you timber-men, come to me!*
> *Come, you timber-men, come to me!*
> *Now the timber-men are coming closer,*
> *Toward me stealing, creeping closer,*
> *Now I hear them, H'mm, h'mm, h'mmmm!*

It was a silly song, and an old one, carried forward from the days before the star fell. Timber-men were the large rats that lived in the northern woods and made for a good snack for a quick hunter. The song came around again and George watched the firelight glint from smiling eyes. Old men and children traded gap-toothed grins as they sang. Everyone seemed cheerful except Mouse Road. She sat next to Speaks While Leaving, leaning up against her sister-in-law; she sang, but took no joy from the happy song.

Speaks While Leaving noticed George standing at the border between firelight and the gloaming. She smiled and waved, and beckoned him to a spot with the family.

"I seem to be a little late," he said, greeting them. He smiled at Storm Arriving, but his friend only nodded the most perfunctory greeting. As George sat down, Speaks While Leaving rose to address the assemblage.

"And now, the two whom we honor are here: my husband Storm Arriving, and our friend, One Who Flies, who tomorrow will both travel once more to the City of White Stone. And with us, too, is Whistling Elk," she said, introducing the man next to George, "who has graciously agreed to sit with us tonight, to bless our departing loved ones, and to regale us with stories and songs."

George glanced again at the man on his right. Whistling Elk was like no person he had ever seen before. Instead of tunic and breechclout, he wore a dress similar to the one Speaks While Leaving wore. His hair was done up as a woman's, in coiled braids with decorations behind each ear, and he sat with his knees together and feet at his side, like a woman, instead of cross-legged as the men usually sat.

His features, too, were unusual, with a smallish nose, a delicate chin, and lips that twitched upward with amusement at George's consternation.

"It is an honor to meet you," Whistling Elk said, gaze cast politely downward. "A person hears many stories of One Who Flies. Perhaps you will share one with me." Even his voice was feminine, soft and expressive. "I'm always looking for new stories to tell."

George realized that he was staring. He looked into the fire and swallowed with difficulty. "Of course," he said, "though I don't have many stories to tell."

"That," Whistling Elk said, "I simply cannot believe."

George glanced to his left, toward Storm Arriving and a hoped-for explanation. Storm Arriving was paying no attention, but Speaks While Leaving, seeing George's confusion, entered the conversation.

"Whistling Elk is one of our greatest storytellers," she said, "and one of our finest healers."

Whistling Elk bowed at the compliment. "Though I have also learned much from you, my hostess."

This discussion, unfortunately, did not answer George's questions, but as the feast was about to begin, he had no choice but to simply wonder at his effeminate neighbor as Speaks While Leaving and the other women of the family rose to bring out the food.

Through the doorway of the main lodge behind, the women brought skewers heavy with roasted meat and fowl. The meat sizzled and smoked in the evening air, and drew *ooh-aahs* of appreciation from the gathered guests. There were baskets filled with steaming skillet-bread, and clay pots filled with a variety of bubbling stews of fried beans, roots, and strips of venison. Mouse Road came out with a large, shallow basket that held the first of the fall fruits: nuts and apples from the river country. Clay bowls and horn spoons were available in plenty for all to use, and the aromas swirled in the air.

George ate with great pleasure, having missed the simple but essential flavors of home-cooked food.

"You have a good appetite," Speaks While Leaving said. "Didn't the Iron Shirts feed you?"

George smiled. "Speaks for the Iron Shirts took great pride in both his palate and his cooks. He showed off both at every opportunity, but the flavor of Iron Shirt food is weak and thin compared to anything eaten on the prairie." He pointed with a rib-bone to the fire, the guests, and the sky above. "Out here, even water tastes better."

"You seemed to enjoy his food while we were there," Storm Arriving said.

"I did," George said, trying to work around his friend's sullen mood. "But food here is better."

Whistling Elk laughed delicately. "Now there is a diplomatic answer," he said. "He can tell you you're right and wrong in the same breath. I can't wait until you marry, One Who Flies. Your wife will never be able to win a single argument!"

Others laughed at the jest, but Storm Arriving was not

one of them. Neither, George noticed, was Mouse Road, who ripped small pieces from a triangle of skillet-bread and ate them, her gaze never leaving the flames of the bonfire.

"One Who Flies, if you are not married, why haven't we seen you at a Sweetheart Dance?"

George was flustered. Whistling Elk seemed overly interested in his romantic affairs. "Sweetheart Dance?" he asked, and looked for help from Speaks While Leaving.

"A Sweetheart Dance is part of a Victory Dance ceremony. It is run by the men-becoming-women, like Whistling Elk."

"I see," George said. "I guess . . . I always seem to be . . . too busy."

Whistling Elk laughed again, as if this were the funniest of jokes. "Too busy for a Sweetheart Dance? How can you be too busy for a Sweetheart Dance?"

"He is," Storm Arriving snapped from George's other side. "He always is too busy."

Whistling Elk leaned forward to glance at the faces of George, Storm Arriving, Speaks While Leaving, and Mouse Road in turn. He seemed to glean something from his inspection, for a look of understanding spread across his pleasant face. "Leave it to me. The next Sweetheart Dance, I will make sure you are not too busy."

George smiled weakly, and returned to his meal, though his appetite was greatly diminished.

At the end of the meal, robes and blankets were handed around for warmth, and thick branches were added to the flames.

"Whistling Elk," said one of the youngsters. "Will you tell us a story?"

"Shall I?" he asked in affected concern. "I would not want to delay the dancing." The response was unanimous, from young and old and in between. "What story, then?"

"Green River-Monster," said one boy.

"The Twins and the Turtle," proposed an older neighbor.

"The Race between Buffalo and Man," said one of Storm Arriving's Kit Fox brethren, and everyone quickly seconded that suggestion.

"A good choice," Whistling Elk said, and waited until everyone snuggled into their furs and their woolen blankets, until the voices fell silent, until the cool night air trembled with anticipation. Whistling Elk half closed his eyes. His hands enscribed a circle in the air.

"Long, long ago," he began, his voice soft but clear, "when Ma'heo'o made the world and put the men and animals upon it, everybody was equal. Men and animals alike lived on the earth, and all enjoyed it. Soon, though, the Buffalo began to grumble. 'We are the biggest animals in the whole world,' they said. 'The others should honor and respect us. This is our due.'"

George watched the others as Whistling Elk spun his tale. Eyes gazed raptly at the storyteller's hands, his words filling the circle with images and creatures. With fists he showed the strength of the Buffalo and their great size as they lumbered into the camp of Men during the Sun Dance. With gentle hands the men pleaded with the Buffalo to live in harmony as Ma'heo'o intended, and with fists again the Buffalo declined and challenged the Men and other animals to a race to determine who was strongest. Children stared, slack-jawed, enthralled by the phantoms that Whistling Elk wove in the air before them, while their parents and elder neighbors smiled, knowing the story's outcome from years of retelling.

George had heard the story before, and Whistling Elk said all the right words in all the right places, but he added to the telling, creating a drama that surpassed mere words. With his vivid voice, his expressive features, and his hands, he brought the story to life.

He told how the animals and men decided upon a relay race, and with deep voices he acted out the parts as a Deer, an Antelope, and an Elk joined with one of the Buffalo to form a team of split-hooves. George laughed with the others as, with high and comic voices, he told of how a Dog, a Whistler, and a Hawk joined with a young Sun Dancer to form a second team. The story had progressed to the start of the race when George saw the stranger come into the circle of firelight.

He did not know who the stranger was, but Storm Arriving obviously did. He rose from his place next to George and went to speak to the new arrival. The rest of the family watched with concealed interest, especially Healing Rock

Woman, who glanced from the two men standing outside the story circle, to Mouse Road, who sat dour and unmoving, and finally to George.

Interrupting the story was out of the question, so George could only sit, watch, and wonder. Whistling Elk had finished telling of how the Sun Dancer lost ground to the Elk in the first leg of the race, and now his storyteller's hands leapt and bounded as the Deer pulled even farther ahead of the Dog. The stranger stole secret glances past Storm Arriving, glances at Mouse Road, and George started to grasp the nature of the discussion.

A suitor, he told himself. A suitor for Mouse Road.

Storm Arriving stood straight and firm, signing *yes* or *no* to the stranger's whispered words. Mouse Road stared at the fire, but George saw the tiny downturn at the corner of her mouth, and saw her rub the outside of her thigh with a clenched fist, a sign of her displeasure that he knew well from her months teaching him the People's language.

In the story, the Whistler had gained ground on the Antelope, coming up even as the race headed into its final leg. "O, how fast the Buffalo ran on those skinny legs!" Whistling Elk told them, his voice aquiver with excitement. Then he moved his arms in slow, exaggerated wingbeats, and said, "And how slowly did the Hawk spread his great wings as he rose from the ground. But as he soared along, using the wind to carry him, he was still even with the Buffalo. He was saving all his strength."

The stranger was listening to Storm Arriving now, standing in respectful silence. George could not see his friend's face and could not tell what was being said, but finally the stranger smiled and George saw him say *Yes, yes, thank you, Storm Arriving*. Then the stranger left, disappearing into the night. Storm Arriving turned and George saw his clouded brow and his surreptitious glance toward him and Mouse Road.

Whistling Elk built to the climax of his tale. "At last the end of the race was at hand," he said. "The Buffalo ran as fast as he could, but the Hawk, having climbed high into the sky, swooped down, passed the Buffalo, and was waiting at the finish when the Buffalo stumbled across with wobbly knees. All the animals had gathered to watch the finish, and now the Men and their friends shouted a victory whoop for the Hawk." The elder guests shouted, startling the children and setting them to laughter. Whistling Elk laughed with them before tying up the story's end.

"The Buffalo and the other split-hooves broke camp and left, for they would never again be the equals of Men and their friends. Now we hunt the split-hooves for food and clothing and shelter, and in honor of the Hawk, the People call the bravest of their soldiers Hawk Men, and we use the Hawk's feathers in our prayer fans and our ceremonies."

Smiles and murmurs of approval met the end of the tale. Storm Arriving took the opportunity to return to the story circle, but he did not sit. Instead he stood next to George and waited for everyone's attention.

"I thank Whistling Elk for his story," he said, "and hope to hear more of his tales later." He shifted on his feet, and George sensed his unease. "Tomorrow, One Who Flies and I leave for the City of White Stone. We travel with our great council chiefs to speak with Long Hair. We hope that, with the help of Speaks for the Iron Shirts, we can convince Long Hair to leave the path of war, and make peace with the People." He looked down into the hot heart of the fire.

"It will be a long trip there, and a long trip back. We will be gone during the winter moons, and must leave behind friends and family. And so I ask you, my family and my neighbors, to look after my wife and my new daughter." He gestured to Mouse Road. "I also ask you to take into our band my sister, and watch over her until we return with the springtime moons."

The guests all signed or spoke their happy concordance, but George saw the frown on Mouse Road's face deepen. As Storm Arriving thanked his guests and sat, Mouse Road stood. Her pale-fingered fists were clenched at her sides and she stared at the ground before her as at a hated enemy. She stood in conspicuous displeasure, her silence infecting everyone. No one spoke. She stood there, trembling. George saw the glimmer of tears in her eyes, but before they could spill, she fled the circle, dashing off into the darkness beyond the fire's reach.

George began to get up but was stayed by a gentle touch. Whistling Elk had placed two fingers on George's arm, and now he leaned in close.

"Whatever it is," he said, "it is between a brother and sister. You should not interfere."

George regarded the peculiar man to his right, and sensed the ill-contained anger of Storm Arriving on his left. Around the circle, he could see other guests waiting to see what he would do, wondering if One Who Flies would act like a real person or like a crazy *vé'ho'e*.

He settled back down. "Could we have another story?" he asked.

The storyteller grinned and patted George's arm. "A fine husband you will make," he whispered, and then addressed the circle with, "What story, then?"

As the guests' smiles were refreshed and requests for favorite stories were made, George tried to contain his own feelings of betrayal and anger toward Storm Arriving. He had separated George and Mouse Road from each other, and had given his permission for another to court her, having never even responded to George's request to do the same. The more he considered the situation, the deeper his pain and anger bit.

The prospect of a winter spent in close company with Storm Arriving suddenly seemed nothing short of unbearable.

CHAPTER 16

Custer pushed back his hair as his guests entered the library. As president, he didn't have to stand for anyone—especially some of the men who had just come in—but he had long ago learned that it was good practice to show more respect than he felt, for the other man was almost surely going to perceive less than he'd been given.

And so he dropped his reading spectacles on the pile of letters and reports he had been studying, and stood. He had wanted to be out on the balcony to enjoy the sunshine, but the chill of an early winter had driven him inside, forcing him to opt instead for a small chair in the light that streamed in through the bentwood and bowed-glass doors that fronted the library's southern exposure. He blinked into the room's unlit half as Douglas showed in the three men who were here to ask for something that Custer would not—could not—give them. He stepped out of the sunshine and into the library's shadows to greet them.

Henry Villard, with his broad brow and thick mustache, led the small group of powerful men. He walked forward without hesitation, hand extended.

"How good to see you again, Mr. President," he said, his Bavarian accent adding crispness to his diction.

"A pleasure as always," Custer said, shaking his guest's hand. A magnate of eastern publishing and western rails, Villard had come to this meeting in person, rather than sending a delegate like the man behind him.

The second man, shorter and broader, was not as well

known as Villard; at least not to outsiders. James Hislop was unassuming and avuncular in appearance, but always had the best table, the largest suite, and the finest companionship in Washington, Philadelphia, or New York; for whenever James Hislop entered the room, the whispered name of Carnegie followed him.

Custer shook the hand of the lieutenant of the steel industry. "James," he said casually.

"Mr. President," Hislop returned. "I'm sorry we missed you in Philly."

The third guest was a relative newcomer to the peerage of business royalty, but he was known to Custer nonetheless. Brig. Gen. Thomas W. Hyde, owner and chief backer of the Bath Iron Works, was, like Custer, a certified hero of the War Between the States, their careers similar even to having achieved the same brevet rank. His walrus mustache rivaled Villard's, and his grip bespoke a man unafraid of manual labor.

Behind the trio of businessmen was Jacob, Custer's Secretary of War.

"Drinks, gentlemen?" Custer asked as they seated themselves around the large library. Douglas served refreshments while they exchanged pleasantries, until Jacob, ever guardful of his president's time, brought the meeting to order.

"Gentlemen," he said, "if we might proceed?"

"Of course," Villard said, taking the lead. "Mr. President, we come to you today to inform you of a most serious situation."

"Oh?" Custer said, sipping his tea. He knew precisely why they were here, but wanted to hear how they would present their case.

"Yes," Villard said. "Surely you are aware of the labor unions and the strength that they are developing among the steel and rail workers."

Custer nodded. "And among miners as well."

"Indeed, this is so. It is about these unions, Mr. President, that we wish to speak. They begin now to garner a large popular support. Our industries have done as much as is practicable to control the spread of this . . . I can call it nothing less than rebellion—but to no avail. The situation has worsened now to the point of economic repercussion."

Custer smiled. "Henry, I've always admired the way you put things. For a man who came to this country without a word of English, you have certainly made up for lost time." He put down his cup and saucer and leaned forward, elbows on knees. "But let's put things a little plainer, shall we?"

"Heah, heah," said General Hyde in flat, New England tones. "The president is a busy man, as are we all. Let's save the fancy words for speeches and get to the point."

Hislop harrumphed at the general's Maine-born practicality. "All right, then. Let's." He tossed off the last finger of bourbon from his glass, rose, and handed the glass to Douglas for a refill. Then, refreshed drink in hand, he spoke, walking back and forth as he did.

"We need your help, Mr. President. Plain and simple, we need your help. The unionizers in New York are stirring up a hornet's nest of trouble: fistfights, brawls, riots. You've heard it all. They're talking about boycotts and strikes, and the papers—if you'll pardon me, Henry; I know you've kept yours pretty well in check—but the papers are whipping the rabble into a froth. We need more than what the Pinkertons and the local constabularies can apply. We need federal assistance."

Custer sat back in his chair. "What can I do that you've not already done?"

"You can send in some troops, for one thing," Hislop said. "Cordon off the mills and the shipyards and the railyards."

"Arrest the scoundrels," Hyde said. "They're interfering with our legitimate business."

"We need to send these malefactors a distinct and unambiguous message," Villard added.

"Gentlemen," Custer said, shaking his head. "You know I can't do any of that. There are strict rules about the use of federal troops. And I can't just go around arresting every union official on the eastern seaboard."

"Well, why not?" Hislop demanded.

Custer chuckled. "Why, for the simple reason that they've not broken any laws. There are rules about that, too, you know."

The businessmen were not pleased, and Custer glanced at Jacob to get his sense of things. Jacob's quick glance heavenward told all. Hyde folded his arms atop his belly, Villard sat back, relaxed but concerned, and Hislop was pacing back and forth across the creaking hardwood floors.

"Mr. President," Villard said, a pleading tone in his voice.

"You mean that's it?" Hyde growled. "Just 'no'? Because if it's just 'no,' then I've got to say I expected a little more for my contribution to your campaign."

Hislop harrumphed again. "as do we all. But I'm sure President Custer will rethink his position when he realizes the ramifications of his decision."

Here its comes, Custer thought, and Jacob's wink confirmed it. "What ramifications are those, Mr. Hislop?"

The representative from the iron and steel industry stopped his pacing and turned to face his president. He drained his second glass, put it down, and began enumerating causes and effects on his fingers.

"In the short term, strikes mean men out of work, and men out of work mean hungry families, and winter's coming, Mr. President. You'll have food riots before January." He began to pace again. "But let's look long-term. If railroad workers out in the Territory strike, it will put any expansion plans you have for the region hopelessly behind schedule. But then again, that won't matter much, because they won't have the steel rails to begin with, because the workers at my mills will have stopped work as well. And if Henry doesn't have steel for his railroads, then neither will Thomas here have iron for his shipbuilding. While you may not feel the pinch when his municipal steamers are late in coming off the line, you'll be sure to feel it in a year or so when he's supposed to begin laying the keel for the USS *Machias*." He stopped and faced Custer. "In short, Mr. President, refuse to help us now and you'll feel it for years."

Custer looked at the three men before him. Hislop was practically gloating over his delivery. Hyde pouted beneath his mustache. Only Henry Villard seemed a tad ill at ease with Hislop's tirade.

Let's see what I can do about that, Custer thought.

He stood and, clasping his hands behind him, walked to the window in an affected performance of sudden introspection. "I suppose there might be something I could do for you gentlemen after all," he said.

"I thought as much," Hislop said, and his supercilious tone wiped away the last iota of sympathy Custer felt for them.

"Yes," Custer said, turning. "I think there is a way we can use federal troops; don't you think so, Jacob?"

Jacob pretended to think about it, acting as if he and Custer had not discussed this possibility in depth the previous evening. "I believe so, sir," he said innocently. "I believe so."

Custer shrugged. "Of course, it means federalizing the steel industry, and the railroads, too, but I think we could make a decent case for our right of eminent domain."

"We need them," Jacob supplied. "If they can't protect them, it'll have to be up to us."

The trio went slack-jawed, but Custer pressed onward. "But as for the shipyards, I don't see much of a case there. At least not yet," he said, quashing Hyde's momentary relief. "Once work on those navy contracts commences, though . . . well, let's just leave that aside for now."

Hislop found his voice. "You can't be serious," he said.

"I can't?" Custer said, and looked to Jacob. "*I* can't be serious?"

Jacob only shrugged, and Custer turned back to the businessmen.

"I assure you . . . gentlemen . . . that I can be and that I *am* serious. Entirely so." He came away from the window and let his rankling anger have its head. "You have come here, expecting that I—the president of the United States—that I, acting as your personal thug, will round up anyone who has the guts to take you to task. You come to me here and demand, in the basest terms, value for your campaign dollar. Well, sirs, I shall not have it. I shall not." He stopped for a moment to recapture his composure. The trio stared at him as at an apparition. He could see that his message had gotten through, but he wasn't ready to let them off the hook.

"I suggest that you gentlemen look for other ways to solve your labor problems. I suggest that you think less about how little you must spend and more about how to keep your workers happy and healthy. Do that, gentlemen, or I *will* send in my troops. Good day."

Villard was the first to move. He rose, dignified and calm, and bowed slightly from the waist. "My apologies, Mr. President." Without another word, he turned and stepped to the door. Hyde heaved his bulk up off the divan and followed, waiting with Villard for Hislop to join them.

Hislop, however, stood stiff as an oaken board. Custer could see the anger in his eyes and the desire to rage and rail in the veins on his neck and brow. He took a stiff-legged step closer to Custer.

"You'll regret this," he whispered so that none other could hear. "You will pay." Then he, too, walked to the library door and left, pulling Villard and Hyde behind him in his wake.

Jacob sighed. "Hislop," he said. "You lost a friend, there."

"No," Custer said. "I merely kept an enemy. What about Henry?"

"He knows you're in a bind. Hislop's the one who wanted federal thuggery. I think Henry was just looking for some political help."

"Well," Custer said, turning back to the window, "maybe I can give him some assistance on that end. Do you believe that Hislop, though?"

"The steel industry has grown, Autie. They're more powerful than even the rails, now."

"I know, and their effrontery has kept pace."

"Good Lord," Jacob gasped.

Custer turned. Samuel stood at the door. He looked shaken and pale. "What is it?" Custer said, crossing the room. "Is it Libbie? The girls?"

Samuel shook his head. "The First Lady and the Misses Custer are fine, sir"

"What is it then? Are you ill?"

Samuel composed himself. "Mr. President, the Ambassador from New Spain is here."

Custer knew that such simple news would not upset his attaché so deeply. There was more to it, and he prepared himself for it while he waited for Samuel to tell him.

"The ambassador brings news," he said, "about young George."

Custer bowed his head and closed his eyes. He swallowed a lump that constricted him, threatening to choke him, and when he opened his eyes again, he saw Samuel's concern.

"Send him up," Custer said.

Jacob came to Custer's side. "Autie, are you all right?"

"I'll be fine," Custer said. "We knew word would get out sooner or later."

From his station at the coffee service, Douglas looked on with a concerned brow. "Do you want me to stay, Mr. President?"

Custer, not trusting his voice to remain steady, said nothing.

"I think that will be all for now," Jacob said.

Douglas waited for Custer's consenting nod before he bowed and left the room.

It took a maddeningly long time, but eventually Custer heard Samuel's shuffling step echo down the corridor. Punctuating it was a long, heavy-heeled stride that trod its patient way to the door.

"His Excellency, the Ambassador from New Spain."

Custer, hands clasped behind his back, bowed to the silver-haired man before him. The ambassador returned the greeting. He held in his hand a large folded parchment decorated with florid writing and a red ribbon affixed by a palm-sized seal of red wax.

"Mr. President," he began, "I am here at the specific and urgent request of the Viceroy Lord Serrano-Ruiz of New Spain. He has sent me to offer my services as an intermediary." He held out the letter he carried.

Custer did not take it. He glanced at Samuel but the old man only shrugged, not knowing what the letter might contain. "Forgive me," Custer said slowly, still trying to master his emotions. "There seems to be some confusion. I was told you had some news of my son."

The ambassador proffered the letter anew. "If you will read this communiqué, Mr. President, all shall be made clear."

Custer eyed the letter. He could see his own name amid the swirls and loops of courtly Spanish script. He disliked taking hold of any missive the contents of which he did not already know—a lesson learned in Congress—but saw no alternative. He accepted the letter.

Even folded, it was as wide as a normal piece of writing paper. He felt the roughness of the parchment on his fingers and felt the weight of it in his hand. *To Colonel George Armstrong Custer the Elder, President of the United States,* he read on the front, noting that it used his commissioned rank and not the brevetted rank to which he was technically entitled.

Before I've even opened it, a snub from the Spanish Crown, he thought.

He turned it over and saw the two ribbons of red silk and the seal of the Western Throne of Spain embedded in the shiny red wax. The seal broke with a crack and the letter unfolded with the sound of heavy canvas.

"I have had the privilege," the ambassador began, "to meet with the leadership of the Cheyenne Alliance."

Jacob was incensed. "You *what*?"

The ambassador calmly and needlessly repeated himself to Jacob, but Custer had stopped listening. The letter engaged his entire mind. He held the parchment at arm's length, squinting through his farsightedness to read the viceroy's message.

Regards from the Western Throne . . . a delegation of Alliance dignitaries . . . courtesies of diplomatic chargé . . . arriving soon . . . protection of New Spain.

Stunned, Custer handed the letter to Jacob and stared at the ambassador. "Just what is it that you think you are doing?"

"Sir," the ambassador said with a short bow, "my only desire is to act as a liaison; to help establish a dialogue, the purpose of which is to eventually establish a treaty between your two nations."

Jacob exploded. "Two *nations*? Autie, this is nothing but a ruse. Why, if you don't throw this scalawag out on his ear right now—"

"Secretary Greene," the ambassador said, calm in the face of Jacob's storm. "Before you 'hand me my hat,' as you might say, I suggest you read the bottom of the viceroy's missive." He was more than calm, Custer noted; he was smug. Custer snatched the letter away from Jacob.

"Down at the bottom, Mr. President, where we have listed the names of the dignitaries who will be arriving shortly, under the flag of New Spain. I think you might find them of interest."

Custer scanned the lower half, where the names of the delegates had been listed in the infuriatingly baroque lettering of the Spanish Court. Finally, he saw it:

One Who Flies, it read, *who once was known as George Armstrong Custer the Second.*

Custer felt his heart trying to push past his ribs. George was alive; alive, and on his way to Washington. He had wondered, and he had hoped, but eventually he had given in to Herron's declarations—*I know,* the general had said, *because I killed him*—and considered his son dead. But now it seemed that his heart—the thing that hammered and beat so violently within him, the thing that shoved the surf into his ears and made all the world go dark but for that one name on the parchment—his heart had never heard those words. It had hoped when there was no hope. And now that hope was fulfilled.

He would see his boy again. Custer's vision swam with tears that burned and cut, blurring the official communiqué from the viceroy. Yes, he would see his son again, but the visit came on very hard terms.

"Mr. President," he heard the ambassador saying. "Can I wire the viceroy and tell him that you accept the meeting? Mr. President?"

Custer waved the parchment at the ambassador. "Yes, yes," he said, not caring if his bitter ire broke through the presidential façade. "I'll take your damned meeting." He looked at Jacob. "Get him out of here."

Jacob complied, and with more enthusiasm than diplomatic protocol either demanded or countenanced, but the ambassador submitted without complaint. Custer saw only the satisfied smirk on his face as Jacob conducted him out into the corridor. Samuel, at the door, took a breath, hesitated, and left without speaking.

Custer sank down into the plushness of an upholstered chair. The parchment slipped from his fingers and rasped to the floor. He saw nothing, heard nothing. He felt nothing, numb to all sensation. His mind was aswirl with possibilities and eventualities, all spinning around a single thought, and that one thought kept all the others inchoate and diffuse. Nothing else in his mind could achieve even a phantom of form. No notion could force its way past the barrier made by that one thought, that one question. As Custer sat and stared into nothingness, he could only think of one thing: What do I tell poor Libbie?

CHAPTER 17

Thursday, December 19, A.D. 1889
Fifth Avenue
New York City, New York

The horse's hooves made sharp, hollow sounds as the cab rattled along the cobbled avenue. It was late, but still the lamps were lit and the streets were filled with carriages and coaches. On the walks, men in high silk hats escorted women whose dresses glittered from beneath fur-trimmed cloaks.

Cesare stared out the window at the finery, fogging the glass with his breath. Justine pulled him back into his seat.

"You told me you used to live in New York," she said with a laugh.

He shook his head, still gawking. "Not in this part," he said.

There were so many lights—street lamps, marquees, shopfronts, and carriage lanterns—they dazzled him almost as much as did the woman by his side. Every object seemed to burn with an inner excitement as if the entire street, even the city itself, were thrilled by its own existence and glad to be alive. People smiled and laughed as they walked from theaters to cafés, from red-carpeted entrances to leather-upholstered coach boxes.

"Everyone is so beautiful," Cesare whispered.

"You are making me jealous." Justine pouted.

He broke himself away from the scene of fascination and turned to her. "Forgive me," he said, taking her lace-gloved hand. "I am a stupid sap. Here I am, sitting beside the finest woman, on my way to the finest hotel in the finest city in the world." He smirked and shook his head. "I still can't believe it."

Justine snuggled up under his arm. "Cannot believe what, *mon cher*?"

He shrugged. "Any of it," he said. "That I'm back here. That Mr. Wood sent me here. But most of all, I can't believe that you are with me."

She looked up at him. "Can you not?" she asked.

"No," he said. "My reason for being here is simple: Wood told me to come, to meet with Halloran about some big job. But why did he send you along, too?"

"You wanted to bring someone else?"

"No! Of course not. It's just that . . . he can't be blind. He must know how much I care for you. If he hasn't seen it himself then Cooper has certainly told him. I just don't understand why he didn't take the chance to separate us. I don't understand why he sent you."

She looked down at his meaty hands that held her own so gently. "He sent me to keep you happy," she said. He raised his eyebrows in disbelief. "*Vraiment*, he told me himself. You have become very important to him."

All the joy drained out of Cesare. He took his arm from around Justine's shoulders and looked out the window. "Important," he said, dismissing the notion. "I'm just a tool to him; no, a weapon. I'm a weapon. I'm . . . I'm a knife in the ribs. A gun in a dark alley. I don't see how you can stand to be around me."

She took his chin and made him look at her. "Because I do not see you that way. I do not see this knife or this gun that you speak of. I see only the sweet man who sings me lullabies at night. I see only the man who prays every night to a keepsake cross before going to sleep." She kissed him, and a hole in the roadway jostled the carriage and they bumped noses. They laughed and she snuggled back up against him until they reached the hotel.

The carriage pulled up at the curbside, and the door was opened by a doorman in a long blue tailcoat. He offered a hand but Cesare declined, stepping down and then turning to aid Justine himself. Together they walked up to the brightly lit entrance and passed through the main doors.

Cesare doubted he could ever get accustomed to such

overt opulence: the woven detail of carpets atop floors of gray-veined marble, the dark polish of wood carved by expert hands, the glint of crystal on chandeliers and door-knobs, the touch of bright brass on hinges and drawer pulls and the buttons of the bellboy's uniform. Everything was clean and precise and perfectly placed, even down to the part in the clerk's hair. As they checked in, the deliciousness of perfume, the whispers of silk, and all of it— every scrap of it—began to oppress Cesare, calling out to him in myriad tiny voices that coalesced into one gargantuan shout inside his head.

You do not belong here.

He stood, transfixed by the urbane setting, while around him the elite of New York hobnobbed and postured. They inspected him frankly: a quick glance—once up, once down—was all they needed. Whether it was his shoes, his stance, or the muscled girth of his arms, they saw enough to know: he was different, out of his class, and beneath their notice. With excruciating sharpness Cesare felt the price of the journey that, after nearly a year and almost two thousand miles, had brought him only thirty blocks from his tenement home in Mulberry Bend. The gash created by his family's slaughter reopened, and he felt beside his heart the vertiginous space that his twin had once filled. He felt her crucifix in its folded paper pouch, burning against his breast. Fire rushed into his brain, and he saw his fury reflected as fear in the faces of those around him.

"*Mon cher,*" Justine was saying, her hands gripping his arm. He blinked. Her eyes were wide. Behind her, the clerk and the bellboys stood with the luggage, waiting nervously to show them to their rooms. "*Mon cher,*" she said. "You are tired. Shall we go upstairs?"

"Now you've seen the weapon," he said, and did not give her a chance to respond. He motioned the clerk ahead. They made their way through the lobby, slicing through the after-theater crowd to the grand staircase, climbing up to a balustrade paneled with silver mirrors wherein Cesare saw Justine: a long-necked woman, her hair piled high atop her head, her blood-ruby dress sparkling with crystalline light. She held on to the arm of a man who was thick-thewed and raw, his face filled with black grief, his soul surrounded by shadow. He stared at his own reflection as they walked past, unable to look away from the turpitude that he wore like a cloak.

In his suite, Justine cajoled him, tempting him with songs and caresses. She failed, unable to separate him from either his mood or the bottle of liquor he'd told the desk to send up. The vision from the hallway stayed with him, and eventually he sent her to her own rooms. He spent the balance of the night at the table, a single candle burning down low, staring into the small hand mirror he'd taken from the dressing room. He searched beyond the glass, behind the silver, looking for the visage from the hallway. He searched until the liquor blurred his sight and the candle guttered out.

Before morning, Justine returned to him. She took him to bed, cradled him against her breast, and sang to him as to a child.

> *A la peche aux moules, moules, moules*
> *Je ne veux plus aller, maman.*
> *Les gens de la ville, ville, ville,*
> *Ont pris mon panier, maman.*

"What song is that?" he asked her sleepily.

"It is only a silly tune, a child's song that my *maman* taught us."

He felt her bosom rise and fall with every gentle breath. "What does it mean?"

"It is about gathering mussels on the shore. Now you must get some rest, or you will embarrass yourself tomorrow."

"Mm?"

"Your meeting tomorrow," she said. "With Monsieur Halloran."

"Mm."

"*Oui*, 'mm.'" She stroked his brow with a satin-soft hand, and he slept.

Late that morning, squinting and hunched, Cesare forced down burned toast and springwater for breakfast. Justine *tsk*ed at his condition but said nothing. With her assistance, he shaved, dressed, and hailed a cab for his meeting.

He gave the driver the address of an office down near the Battery and sat back in the cab. The streets were still wet with overnight rain and the gray sky promised more. The weather was turning cold, and as the horses clopped around Union Square, from Broadway onto Bowery, Cesare thought of his previous winter here in New York City. He had spent his nights shivering, huddled with his siblings for warmth, with Mama forbidding anyone to use the piece-work clothing as a blanket. Mama's cough kept him up at night, allowing for sleep caught only in snatches. He remembered dreams of drowning in a cesspit, and then waking to find the Widow Scottolini's daughter dead in a pool of her own filth.

Sitting in the upholstered cab, he looked outside. On the street, peddlers stood at their pushcarts, calling out their wares. Men with gaunt faces shambled down the walks, already cold in their thin clothes. Cesare could see the fear of winter in their haunted eyes. The elevated train screeched overhead, and as they passed the intersection of Bowery and Canal, he felt his lungs tighten. He pressed himself back into the cushioned seat, fearful of being seen, of being recognized.

He touched the soft wool of his suitcoat and heard the creak of his leather gloves around the knob of his walking stick. The collar of his shirt was starched and stiff, encircling his neck with propriety, and his body was wrapped with a waistcoat of stippled brocade lined with cool silk. He saw the shine in his shoe leather, and smelled the oil that slicked back his hair.

No one would recognize him, he realized. Not unless he gave himself away. He relaxed, then, and leaned forward to watch once more the misfortune on the street beyond the carriage window.

They arrived at the address. It was an unassuming building faced with brown brick, trimmed with sandstone at the corners and along the cornices. It was not, however, the building where the meeting was to take place; it was simply the place where the cab was to drop him. Knowing that his reading abilities were limited, Wood had given him specific instructions on where the meeting was to be held, and how he should get there. Cesare stepped down from the cab, paid the hack, and waited for him to drive away before he entered the third of three small, unmarked doorways and walked down the creaky hall.

The shabbiness of the place did not concern him. His work for the union bosses was usually clandestine and always dangerous—hurting people was not something one did in the broad light of day—and this was proving to be no different from a score of similar meetings he had attended back in Chicago. The only difference here, Wood had told him, was the stakes.

He passed by three doors, all of them closed, walked to the end of the hall, turned left, and exited the building at the rear. The alley behind was narrow and shadowed as the tall brownstones blocked the low winter sun. Even in the crisp air, Cesare could smell the sharpness of urine and the dusty smell of moldering refuse. He turned left, heading back upriver, walked alongside a rotten-wood fence, and turned down a basement stairwell to enter a matchstick manufactory. The chatter of women competed with the grinding of machines above him as he crossed through the dark basement. Exiting the factory, he emerged a block from the waterfront at Old Slip, turned, and headed into a fishmart, walking past stinking stalls to come out in a crowded alley. He negotiated the warrenlike backways and cross-courts as one born to it, moving from sidestreets to storefronts with ease. When he reached his final destination, he rapped on the blue door, tipped his hat to the man who opened it, walked into a large furniture and upholstery shop, and headed up the stairs.

The second story had originally been set aside for offices, but as he climbed the flight, he saw that the offices were empty and had been for some time. Gray winter sunshine seeped through the dirt-veiled windows, dusting the large open area with light. The air was thick with the blended scents of cedar and pine, horsehair and burlap, polish and solvent, wrinkling Cesare's nose and drying out his eyes. The sounds of hammers and mechanical saws made a constant din above which men shouted to be heard. Their voices flew up from the workroom and bounced around the empty loftlike space, filling it with unintelligible echoes.

The area had been divided by chest-high walls and half-doors that hung ajar like gates in an abandoned garden. Far within the third such "room" Cesare saw a plume of smoke rise from the shadows into the shaft of weak sunshine. A man sat forward, leaving the gloom for the ghostly light, and with fat fingers and a stubby cigar, he beckoned.

Seamus Halloran was a thickset man with thinning black hair, piercing blue eyes, a pug nose, and a crease in his forehead put there, rumor said, by his kid brother and a lead pipe. As chief organizer of the Union & Labor party in New York, he was as formidable politically as he was in person. He also never traveled alone, and as Cesare entered the last and darkest area of the loft, he saw two other men in the shadows behind Halloran. A quick glance to either side proved that one of the other corners was occupied as well. An unoccupied chair was in the rectangle of wan sunlight near Halloran; Cesare walked up behind it and waited.

"Sit," Halloran said in a voice like crushed gravel.

Cesare complied.

Halloran sat back and sucked on his cigar. The ember glowed orange in the gloom. "Wood recommends you highly," he said. "Your work has impressed him."

Cesare shrugged. "I do my best," he said. "Mr. Wood makes it worth my while."

Halloran smirked. "You're damned right. I've seen her. But enough of friendly chitchat." He motioned to the men behind him, ordering them away. They left their posts and walked toward the stairs, out of earshot. The third man, Cesare noted, did not leave, obviously allowed to be privy to their conversation.

"We have an important job for you," Halloran said, and Cesare wondered if "we" meant Union & Labor, or Halloran and his shadowed companion. "There are some powerful people who remain dead-set against us, people who have not responded to our other forms of . . . persuasion." The cigar crackled as he drew on it and expelled smoke in a thick cloud. "We need to send these people a message. The kind of message that at the same time will . . . clear the road, as it were."

Cesare thought of the men who had left the room, and of the men who were still here. "Mr. Halloran, respectfully, sir, I am not some dumb guinea just off the boat. I know what's what, sir." He saw Halloran's eyes seek the man in the shadows at Cesare's back, and wondered what the game really was. "You can tell it to me straight. What is the job you want me to do?"

Halloran thought it over for a moment and then nodded. "Do you know the difference between murder and assassination, son?"

The answer was easy. Despite his young age at the time, he remembered well the nation's shock over the assassination of President Sherman after only eight months in office.

"Murders make the newspapers," Cesare said. "Assassinations make the front page."

Halloran sputtered, belching smoke, and coughed repeatedly until the paroxysms slopped together to make a soupy laugh. "Well said, son. Well said." Again the glance to the man in the shadows. "So, Uccido, are you up to it?"

The men at the stairwell, he knew, were just as able as he, perhaps more so. Halloran had an army of thugs capable of doing the job. Then why me? he asked himself.

He turned and looked over the back of his chair at the man in the shadows. The man was tall, well dressed, slender. He could not make out much of the man's features aside from a thin gray mustache, dark eyes, and the silver hair. By his posture, though, it was clear that he was not a rough-born man like Halloran but a creature of breeding and position. A man used to a higher echelon, forced to visit with Halloran on a bit of dirty, dangerous business.

He turned back around to face Halloran, the answer to his question clear. Halloran had chosen him over one of his own men for the same reason that he was staying in a posh hotel and dining in the best restaurants. It was the same reason that Justine was with him.

It's because I'm not supposed to survive.

The darkness seemed to deepen, and the light took on weight, pressing down upon him from the dingy window. He looked up into the sun, glimpsed the white-hot disk, and shut his eyes to see the red glow. He looked back at Halloran.

"I'll do it," he said. "I don't have anything to lose."

Halloran stood. "Usually I wouldn't trust a man who says he has nothing to lose." He stuck out his hand. "But sometimes, that's just the kind of man for the job."

CHAPTER 18

Big Hard Face Moon, Waning
Fifty-six Years After the Star Fell
On the Potomac
Washington, District of Columbia

As the steamer dragged herself upriver, George was sure he had never seen men so hungry to put a foot on dry land. Young and old, soldier and chief, they all stood at the rail, eyes fixed on the shore, waiting with sullen patience for the end of their first seaborne voyage.

Alejandro had sent the *Maria Argenta* to ferry them from the Tejano coast to the isle of Cuba and thence to their diplomatic rendezvous. The ship was a hybrid—half steamer, half sailing vessel. At over a hundred feet long, she was large enough to boast five staterooms but still with a lean enough draft to put into the shallow bay at La Puerta del Norte. She had withstood the weather and open sea admirably. George could not say the same about the passengers.

Three Trees Together, despite his obvious years and seeming frailty, had fared the best of them all, spending the wind-battered days on deck, sitting cross-legged against the foremast, eyes closed, his body rolling with the ship's pitch like a rider atop a gigantic whistler.

Stands Tall in Timber, the delegation's spiritual chieftain, coped less well, spending his days pacing the length and breadth of the *Maria Argenta,* filling his lungs with the crisp, salt air, and keeping one hand at all times on the rail. During the worst moments, however, when the sea was high and the ship rose and fell in maddeningly irregular rhythm, he did more than keep one hand on the rail. Much more, to his chagrin.

And yet he was not the object of any teasing by the others, for he was not the greatest sufferer. That position was held by Two Roads, and it was for him that George held the greatest empathy. As a war chief of the Kit Fox, Two Roads was the military pillar of the chiefly triumvirate. Where Three Trees Together was their wisdom and Stands Tall in Timber their spirit, Two Roads and the dozen Kit Fox soldiers with him represented the body and strength of the People. He was the youngest of the three chiefs, and was surrounded by younger men—of which Storm Arriving was one—who were all fit and action-ready. And yet it was they, almost to a man, who had spent nearly the entire two weeks of their journey lying below deck in their staterooms, filling the ship with their moans. Only the two youngest soldiers had remained unaffected by the ship's ceaseless and unsettling motion. Badger and Shouts at the Darkness had spent their time running races up the rocking deck, climbing ratlines and dancing on spars forty feet above the whitecapped sea. Two Roads quickly gave up attempts to rein them in, and so the ship's captain—a leather-skinned, black-haired man with the gaze of a hawk and little tolerance for boyish pranks—put the two young men to work replacing halyards, hauling on sheets, and performing any chore that got them up, off the deck, and out of his way. The two soldiers proved worthy sailors, and they earned the respect of the crew for their ease aloft in the high rigging.

For George's part, sea travel was one of his favorite modes of transport. As they made their slow way from La Puerta del Norte to Ciudad de La Habana and thence around the belly of the southern United States, he spent most of his time on deck. When the weather was mild, he either laid down along the bowsprit and watched the dolphins at play, or sat near Three Trees Together at the foremast and tossed bits of torn biscuit to the gulls that keened and gyred overhead.

After their stop in Cuba, the weather turned foul, and winter stropped its razor wind. George stayed aft, where he could see the length of the ship as the sea lifted it up and put it down as easily as a child with building blocks.

But when they rounded Cape Charles and finally sighted the mouth and relative calm of Chesapeake Bay, even George was ready to leave the high seas for a quiet room on solid ground. Only Badger and Shouts at the Darkness seemed sad as the slate-colored ocean disappeared behind hills covered by the gray lacework of dormant trees.

The Potomac was even more peaceful, especially when compared to the open waters of the Atlantic. The *Maria Argenta* cut through the current, her boiler rumbling below-decks, her stacks trailing thick streamers of black and white smoke through the clear, cold air. Snowflakes drifted on the wind, adding a bitterness to the breeze of their upriver passage.

Despite the cold and wind, the entire delegation stood at the rail, watching the shore slip slowly past. The brusque air ruffled fur cloaks and made headdress feathers flutter, but not a man moved.

On the shore, trotting horses drew carriages down the riverfront roadway. Passengers leaned out windows and sat on the roof, shouting and hallooing to the *Maria Argenta*. George was thankful that he alone among the delegates spoke English, for the sentiments hollered from the banks were crude, disrespectful, and often obscene.

They surely know we're coming, George thought to himself. The fat's about to land in the fire.

A murmur ran through the men assembled at the rail, and George looked upriver to see a long, low bridge and, on the starboard shore, their destination.

For some of them—George, Storm Arriving, Two Roads, a few others—this was not their first time to Washington. They had come here three years before, had ridden their whistlers and walkers across that very bridge and stormed the gates of the Capitol. For most, however, this was their first sight of what the People had come to call the City of White Stone.

Even through the snow-haze, Washington's Monument gleamed from its place near the foot of the bridge that spanned the Potomac from Alexandria. On the low hills beyond it lay the buildings of government: the Capitol's immense dome; the pale façades of courts, embassies, and offices; and the squared lines of the White House. George wondered if his father was watching from the balcony, and raised a hand in silent greeting.

Closer to them and downstream from the strictly planned streets of the town's center were the low houses, twisting alleyways, and dark-stained piers of the port. It was toward this less lofty neighborhood that the *Maria Argenta* made her way. Other ships stood at anchor in the deeper waters of the channel, but the captain simply wove his little steamer between them. On the docks ahead, George could see the dark mass of a dense crowd. He could hear the mob's voice—a sound like a waterfall or the crash of the sea on the shore—a sound that rose in pitch and intensity as their vessel approached the quay. Several bunting-draped banners were strung between poles, and George made out words such as *Treason, Justice,* and *Equality* in their slogans. As the steamer maneuvered into position, it was clear that the delegation had both friends and enemies on the docks.

A large faction had come to label George as a traitor to his country. Their signs and banners decried his guilt, and the protesters shook fists and flags as they called for his summary execution. George could not find it in himself to blame them; they were right, after all. He had deserted his post and his army, had conspired against his government, and had borne arms against his nation. He was the worst kind of traitor, but he could not see how he might have acted differently except by ignoring the evidence of his own eyes. Still, justification never helped the turncoat, and he was glad for both the viceroy's diplomatic papers in his belt and the line of constables that stood between him and those seeking his death.

But just as numerous and just as vocal was another group gathered beneath a banner that read EQUALITY AND RIGHTS FOR ALL! Judging by their signs and placards, George was in their estimation a selfless hero. CHAMPION OF THE DISEN-FRANCHISED read one man's sign, and FIGHTER FOR UNITY AND DIGNITY read another. George wondered what sort of rhetoric had been flowing across the editorial pages of the northern papers, and hoped that it would prove to be a benefit and not an anchor around his neck.

The steamer's whistle blew three long notes that set George's heart leaping and fed the energy of the mobs. Beyond the constabulary wardens, the end of the pier was empty except for a trio of men. George recognized Alejandro, but did not know the other two. The ambassador doffed his hat to the delegation as sailors scrambled to tie off hawsers and secure the *Maria Argenta* in her slip.

Descending to the end of the gangplank, George handed the viceregal documents to the ambassador. Alejandro inspected them, and turned them over to the man next to him, a short fellow in a plain black suit and bowler. "As you see, Commissioner, this ship is here under the flag of New Spain, and its passengers are all under the protection of the Spanish Crown."

The man Alejandro had titled Commissioner seemed frustrated by the news. He glared at George from beneath eyebrows as big as dormice, his mouth a twisted line of contempt. "Then let the Spanish Crown protect them," he said, tossing the diplomatic papers down on the scarred planks. "I'll have nothing to do with such refuse. Come on, Fletcher. The stench here makes me sick." He turned and the two men started away.

"Thank you, Commissioner," Alejandro said in a tone filled with solicitation. "And I do hope you enjoy your retirement."

The commissioner stopped but did not look back.

"For I'm sure you understand," Alejandro continued, "that should you or Mr. Fletcher provoke an incident by, say, removing the presence of your officers and constables . . . well, I would have no choice but to lodge a formal complaint with the Department of State. Such a stain on your record—and be sure, I *would* be required to mention you by name—could hardly be overcome. A quick review, an early retirement, it would all be over for you. Career, reputation, your future in public service, it would all come to a swift but inevitable end."

The short man looked back over his shoulder. Fletcher, at his side, looked from Alejandro to the commissioner with agitation. Alejandro raised a hand in farewell.

"Have a pleasant afternoon," he said.

The commissioner sneered and stormed off. Fletcher, with a final glance back at Alejandro, scurried to follow. They stopped at the police line and George saw the commissioner speak emphatically to one of the constables. But when the duo left the wharf, the constabulary remained. Alejandro bent to pick up the letters that lay on the pier.

"Sometimes I adore my profession," Alejandro said to George, and then spread his arms wide and addressed the delegation. "It is my pleasure," he said, speaking in French, "to welcome you to the District of Columbia as the guests of New Spain. Our carriages are waiting to take us to the embassy. If you will follow me?" He swept a hand toward the barely contained mob.

"We're going up there?" George asked.

Alejandro shrugged. "It is where the street is," he said. "There is no other route, I'm afraid."

George explained to the chiefs, and Two Roads instructed the soldiers to form ranks around the elders. It was a sound plan, for even the most irate workingman would think twice before challenging the fierce mien and pointed lances of the Kit Fox color guard. Then, with heads up and eyes alert for danger, they walked toward the crowd.

The constables held back the tide, but as the delegation climbed up to the platform that led to the street and their waiting carriages, a score of men ducked the line of linked arms and ran toward them. The Kit Fox reacted, leveling their lances and unsheathing knives, but Alejandro stepped into the gap and the onrushing men skidded to a halt at the foot of the platform. George, his heart pounding, sighed with relief as he realized that the men were only newspaper reporters.

"Gentlemen, if you please" Alejandro said, soothing jumpy nerves with his calm demeanor. "Allow me to introduce the members of this august delegation." He presented each of the chiefs in turn, and then introduced George. "And may I take this opportunity to thank the people of the District for this enthusiastic welcome. I am afraid we only have time for a few questions."

As George and the chiefs stood next to Alejandro, the newspapermen began firing queries, and the mob behind them quieted to hear the responses.

"Is it true that the Indians are here to surrender to President Custer?"

Alejandro smiled and raised a hand. "Hardly," he said. "These worthy dignitaries from the sovereign tribes are here to discuss a future based on the mutual respect due two such honorable nations."

Behind the protective line, the two factions erupted in applause and catcalls.

Sovereign tribes, George noted to himself. That'll get the old man's dander up.

"Do you include Captain Custer when you say 'worthy dignitaries'?"

"Indeed," Alejandro said. "I have found Captain Custer, Junior—or One Who Flies, as I have come to know him—to be the most honorable of men. He saved my life on the shores of the Gulf of Narváez. He and the Cheyenne with whom he lives have proved to be an honest, forthright, and generous people."

"How did Captain Custer save your life, Mr. Ambassador?"

As Alejandro told the story of his shipwreck and illness, the crowd became engrossed. The constables no longer had to push back the protesters, and even George's most vehement detractors shushed each other so they could hear. The suffragettes and egalitarians smiled with genuine admiration, and from the ranks of union workers, a man stepped up onto the base of a lamppost to better hear the ambassador's speech. The man on the lamppost stared at the chiefs as they stood on the platform. Alejandro was telling of how the People had nursed him back to health when George saw the man on the lamppost reach inside his coat. He paused, squinted, and then in one quick movement he drew out a revolver and fired.

The bullet hit the wooden pillar between George and the chiefs. Splinters flew. The crowd screamed, and turned toward the sound. By the time the man fired a second shot, George was in motion, grabbing Three Trees Together and pulling him behind the pillar. The scene exploded into pandemonium. People pushed toward the street. The constabulary was overcome, but a few retreated to help guard the delegation. A third shot was fired.

"This way," Alejandro shouted, and "Follow!" George yelled to the soldiers. The Kit Fox surrounded their leaders like buffaloes around their calves. They ran for the carriages. The street was fifty yards away, and the flood of the panicked crowd already filled the exitway. The constables cleared a path with their sticks and the Kit Fox shoved at anyone who came too close. They reached the street, and the elders were put into the first carriage, the ambassador and George in the second. Kit Fox hung on to the rails and stood on the running boards as the drivers whipped the horses into motion.

Storm Arriving rode the running boards outside George's window. "Are you all right?" he asked the ambassador. Alejandro nodded.

"Was anyone hit?" George asked. The question was passed forward, and the answer came back.

"No," Storm Arriving said. "All are fine."

"I don't understand it," Alejandro said. "I would never have thought anyone would be brash enough to try to harm me."

George eyed his companion and felt the splinters of wood embedded in the side of his neck. "You?" he asked. "You think he was aiming for you?"

Alejandro looked surprised. "Who else?" he asked.

As they clattered through the cobbled streets toward the city's political core and finally entered the embassy gates, George was not at all sure.

That evening, they settled themselves in their suites on the upper floor of the stone-faced embassy. George stood near the whitestone hearth, wrapped in the buffalo robe that had been the gift of Storm Arriving, and discussed the ambassador's interpretation of events with the chiefs. The older men sat on the floor in front of the fireplace. A fragrant fire crackled in the hearth, illuminating their faces with its lively light.

"He thinks *he* was the target?" Two Roads asked.

"Yes," George said.

Two Roads shrugged. "It could have been meant for any of us."

"No," Stands Tall in Timber said. "Not any of us." They waited for him to elaborate but he simply sat and stared into the flames. The old man sucked on his teeth as he worked things through. The others kept silent while they waited for him to speak.

"Not any of us," he said at last. He pointed at George. "Only you."

"Me?" George said. "Are you sure?"

The old chief's eyes glittered with firelight. "Our last night on the Big Salty," he said, "I had a dream. In this dream, it was night and I stood on the deck of the ship. I felt the big water beneath me and I felt the wind blowing above me, and I was filled with power. It felt so good. I felt like a young boy again, and I climbed up the ropes like Badger and Shouts at the Darkness did. I climbed all the way up to the top of the mast, up into the clouds, and up there I met a man."

He paused, but no one dared to interrupt. Even the soldiers who lounged around the room or stood post at windows and doors were silent, anxious to hear the dream of their greatest living spiritual leader.

"I could barely see this man in the darkness," he went on. "He was a man made of mist, but he spoke like any normal person. He said, 'I have come to tell you that someone is going to die.' I asked him who it was that would die, and he said, 'The man who has the most reason for coming.' I asked him if he was sure and he said, 'Pretty sure.'" Stands Tall in Timber looked down at his hands. "One Who Flies, I think you have the biggest reason for coming here, for you have all of our reasons and all of your own, as well. Besides, the *vé'hó'e* knew you were coming. Speaks for the Iron Shirts has been here for more than a moon. If these people wanted him to die, they could have acted a long time ago. No. It is you they want to kill." He sighed. "I am sorry to say it, but I think it is so."

George tried to take it all in. His mind wanted to refuse the idea, but the credence he was willing to ascribe to the People's belief in the spirit world had increased dramatically since his own encounters with the Thunder Beings. He was trapped between belief and denial, between his experience and his desires. His future dissolved and blew away, as easily as smoke carried up to the sky. Dreams, hopes, thoughts, plans—all were destroyed before the single idea of his own death. The potential of his life was demolished and he could see nothing, could feel nothing except a small kernel of heat in his throat. The kernel grew, expanded, and tightened into the grip of loss: loss of life, of love, of everything he wanted for himself and others.

A touch on his shoulder brought him back to the world, the present, and their ornate rooms in the Spanish embassy. He looked and saw a withered hand. His gaze traveled from the hand to an arm, up the arm to a shoulder, and thence up to a face as old as time. Three Trees Together stood beside him.

"Come," the old man said. George stood and followed the chief out onto the balcony. The doors closed behind them, but through the windows George saw that Storm Arriving and Badger kept watch.

The city glowed, yellow lamplight on blue snow. Large, fat flakes drifted down from the darkness, as delicate as butterflies, to settle on the stone railing, the sidewalks, the rooftops. Horses drew clattering carriages down cobbled streets, the sound of their clopping hooves bouncing between marbled façades. The wind sliced past with icy teeth.

George shivered and pulled his buffalo robe closer. "It's cold."

"It's good for you," Three Trees Together said, and turned to face the city. To their right they could see the warmly lit windows of the White House and the dark breadth of the Potomac. "I am going to speak frankly to you now," he said, "but I think it is necessary." He paused for a moment, and then continued. "I know what you are thinking. You are thinking of all the things you want to do. You are thinking about the women you want to bed and the children you want to father. You are thinking about all the victories you will not win and all the feasts that will be held without you. You are thinking of life and love and all the tender things you will miss if Stands Tall in Timber is right about this dream." He tightened his own robe about his shoulders. "But I will tell you something. You have been given a gift."

George chuckled. "It doesn't feel like a gift."

"It never does, the first time," the old man said. "I have been told three times that I would die. The first time is always the worst."

George could not help but stare. Words tumbled around in his skull, but none fell through to his mouth.

"I know," the old man said. "You thought that what Stands Tall in Timber spoke was the truth." He shrugged. "In a way, it is, but it is not the only truth."

Words finally returned. "Then if it is not the only truth, how is this dream a gift?" George asked.

"I have great hopes for our mission here," the chief said. "Hopes that may even be greater than yours. The future of the People depends on what we do, and I had hoped that Stands Tall in Timber would have named me as the one who would die. He says that Death is near you, and he is probably right. But when you know a thing like this, your choices become clear: You can bring yourself shame by fighting it, or you can try to make your life—and your death—a good one."

"But I don't want to die, Grandfather."

"No one does, no one does. But we all will. There is no way around it."

George considered the chief's words. "What do you suggest I do?"

Three Trees Together took a deep breath of the sharp air and let it out in a frosted cloud. "Accept the gift," he said. "Accept it." And in a rare moment, he looked George straight in the eye. "A man dies only once, but he can live in shame for a lifetime." He shrugged again. "And if it turns out that you do not die, then you can get back to"—he glanced toward the window where Storm Arriving stood—"other things."

George smiled ruefully, but he found the old chief's wisdom perfectly acceptable. It was a path that pleased both his doubting reason and his budding faith. "If I am to die," he said, "There is nothing I can do about it."

"Yes," the chief intoned.

"I can commit myself to our goal, and not worry about my future."

"Yes," the old man said again.

"Because my future may not exist."

"Yes," he said, and looked up into the sky. Flakes of snow fell upon his face, disappearing as they fell upon his mahogany skin. Then the leader of the Cheyenne Alliance stuck out his tongue, caught a snowflake, and giggled like a boy.

"Yes," he said again. "Now, let us return to the others. There are many details I want to discuss before we meet with Long Hair."

CHAPTER 19

Sunday, December 22, A.D. 1889
The Spanish Embassy in the United States
Washington, District of Columbia

Alejandro and Victoria stood at the bottom of the stairs and waited for their guests to appear. The Cheyenne delegation had taken breakfast in their suites, preferring, according to the note One Who Flies had sent down, to spend the morning hours finalizing their strategy for the day's meeting.

But now the time had come for them to leave. Carriages waited in the snow-dusted drive, guardsmen stood at attention at door and gate, and despite the cold, the streets were thronged with the angry, the supportive, and the simply curious, all wishing to catch a glimpse of the ambassador, the delegation, and their president's rebellious son.

He gave Victoria's hand a little squeeze as he heard the doors to the guest suites open and the sound of floorboards creaking beneath moccasin-clad feet. His wife glanced over at him, her smile gentle and relaxed. It had been a long time since he had seen Victoria so at peace with her surroundings. Even at their country villa on the sunburned hills above their Sonoma vineyards, he had seen the strain his subservience had brought to his wife's dignity, but now, here, as *doña* of the Spanish Embassy in America, she was finally in her deserved position.

He could hear their guests talking as they approached, their speech of hisses and whispers still alien to his ears. When they emerged from the upper hallway, Victoria gasped and gripped his hand.

"Calmly, my dear," he said softly, but he understood her reaction, for the creatures that appeared at the top of the staircase looked the fiercest sort of men.

The delegates had dressed themselves in their finest regalia. First came a cadre of soldiers, all in vestments of leather and fur, each bearing a shield decorated with arcane symbols of brutal geometry and trimmed with feathers and hammered circles of bright silver. They came down the stairs two by two. Their movements were fluid and graceful but Alejandro saw the corded muscles in their necks, the tautness of their shoulders, and the wary eyes that scanned the room. After the fracas at the wharf, these men were prepared to kill in order to protect their leaders.

After the soldiers came the chiefs themselves. Stands Tall in Timber wore a necklace of elk's teeth, a girdle of brightly beaded leather, a shirt of calico trading cloth, and a headpiece of spiky fur and grouse feathers that danced with his every move. He carried an Indian-style smoking pipe, its arm-long stem carved and decorated with feathers. With him was Two Roads, the braids of his hair hanging long down his back. On his head was a bonnet of white eagle feathers, the cascading tails of which hung nearly as long as his hair. Behind these two came Three Trees Together, stately and dignified, almost kingly to Alejandro's eye. Over his tunic of supple hide was a wide pectoral of finger-long dentalium shells set lengthwise in two placards. In contrast to the ornate headdress of his fellows, standing up tall from his braided, gray hair were only two eagle feathers, white and tipped with down and red threads. In his arms he carried a bundled buffalo robe and, heavy and bulky though it seemed, no one offered to carry it for him.

Last to come downstairs was One Who Flies, Alejandro's greatest hope for retribution, followed by the remainder of the Cheyenne guard. Alejandro tried to imagine President Custer's face when he saw his son enter the meeting dressed as he was now. The young man's hair, bleached by the prairie sun, was pulled back and braided in a foot-long plait. He wore a yellow tunic cinched by a roughly woven sash of red and black cloth. His leggings were brown, with long green fringes, and his moccasins were beaded with white and blue circles. Sticking out from his hair at the nape of his neck was a single, dark feather, stark against his blond hair. But it was his face that Alejandro found the most striking.

Young Custer's face was haunting, his skin tanned and taut, his cheekbones prominent, and his eyes—the Custer blue: glacial, forbidding, daring—held a fierceness that had not been there the day before. Alejandro wondered if trouble was brewing, and if he needed to modify his plans.

Calmly, he told himself, echoing the advice he had given his wife. Keep calm. Today's meeting dictates tomorrow's actions. This must be done correctly, lest everything fail.

The chiefs came up to Alejandro and his wife, stopped, and bowed in near-perfect rendition of current fashion. Alejandro returned the greeting, and Victoria curtsied to their guests.

"I hope the accommodations were to your liking," she said to them.

The eldest chief replied, and One Who Flies, from his place behind the trio, translated. "Three Trees Together speaks: 'Everyplace I look, I see something lovely. It is a place full of marvelous things.' I especially enjoyed the river-inside-the-lodge. He means the plumbing," One Who Flies added in a quick aside.

"I am glad to hear it," Alejandro said. "And I would like to talk more of such things, but time grows short. We are expected up the avenue, and in cases such as these, it is not wise to be late." With a wave of his hand, he ushered them toward the foyer. Servants opened the tall, double doors, letting in a fall of snowy light.

As they all emerged into the frostbitten air, a clamor went up from the gates. Guards armed with rifles stood inside the wrought iron, facing an uproar of men. Shouts and chants were hurled through the gates' bars. Hands shook leaflets, some held banners, and some were just empty, clenched fists.

Alejandro turned to the captain of the guard, who stood beside the front door. "Where is the city constabulary?"

"Nowhere to be seen, Excellency."

Alejandro glowered at the raucous crowd. "Get them away from the gates. And if any of them set foot on Spanish soil, you have my permission to shoot."

The captain headed off, shouting orders. From around

the side of the main building came the sound of hooves, and a phalanx of riders emerged to help restrain the crowd. The delegation boarded the two carriages: chiefs and senior delegates within, guardsmen and Indian soldiers without. The gates were opened and the horsemen pressed into the throng. Pedestrians retreated from the intimidating presence of horses and saber-armed riders, and with the path cleared, the carriages made their way safely onto the avenue.

Beyond the embassy gates, the populace was more mannered. From the walks and curbsides they stared and gawked and pointed at the carriages and at the Cheyenne soldiers that rode on their tailcoats. Between their savage appearance and the flanking lines of uniformed riders, there was no further challenge to the dignity or sovereignty of the Spanish delegation.

Within a few blocks the city's buildings fell back, revealing the expanse of the Ellipse. The lawns were covered with a thin blanket of white, though beneath the sugar-dusted trees, green grass could still be seen. Beyond, on its low hill, stood the White House itself.

Alejandro admired the architecture of the executive mansion. From a distance, and especially from the south, the White House seemed a relatively commonplace building: a low-lying manse on a gentle roll of sward. As one traveled closer around the curving drives, however, the scale of the building changed. It grew, inflating itself against the perspective of the grounds, and what had at first appeared as a rather unassuming two-story affair now stood an imposing three, its simplicity transformed into the grandiose, its bulk conveying a calm but unquestionable power.

They passed the checkpoints and were escorted up the drive to the south entrance hall. An underling with a thin mustache brought them inside, down a broad hall, and into a large room. A fire crackled in the hearth, and chairs had been set in lines along two of the walls.

"If you would wait here, please," the aide said, and departed.

One Who Flies passed word of what was happening, and the soldiers took up posts near the two doors and windows. Alejandro saw One Who Flies look about him with an inquisitive eye.

"Is it odd to be back home?" he asked.

One Who Flies made a motion with his hand that Alejandro had come to recognize as no. "I have never been here before," he said. "I was in the army when my father first took office. When the family gathered, it was always the homestead, up in Michigan Territory. This place . . ." He looked around at the fine furniture, the fabric-clad walls, the antique paintings, and the gimcrack. "This place is not my home."

Alejandro wondered if he was speaking of more than just the room and the building that contained it.

The inner door opened and the soldiers leapt into motion before anyone could say a word. The aide who had brought them yelped in fright as the soldiers caught him by both arms. One Who Flies spoke quickly, and the soldiers released the young man. The aide, bug-eyed, straightened his collar, but aside from the nervous twitching of his mustache, made no more motions than were necessary.

"If the principals of the delegation would follow me, please?"

Alejandro and the three chiefs, with One Who Flies as interpreter, followed the aide through the door and into the room beyond.

This room, larger and longer than the last, echoed with their footsteps. The air smelled of leather and polishing wax, and the draperies had been pulled back to let in the slanting winter light. The floorboards were as dark as coffee, but the sunlight found streaks of red within the grain. Throughout the room, chairs congregated around hearths or window seats. All were empty but two. At the other end of the room, near the marble-faced hearth, two men sat. Alejandro recognized them and bristled. Their presence, though objectionable, was not unanticipated.

The delegates walked behind the aide as he ushered them down the length of the room, and Alejandro took the opportunity to clamp down on his temper. The two men stood as the delegation approached.

"Excellency," the aide said, "and delegates, may I present Secretary of the Interior Mr. Temperance Fullerton, and Secretary Jacob Greene of the War Department."

The assemblies bowed to one another.

"Excellency," said Fullerton with an oily smile. "May I take this occasion both to congratulate you on your appointment, and to say how glad we all were to hear of your rescue and recovery."

"Sir," Alejandro said, not waiting for One Who Flies to finish his translation and not wanting to let Fullerton's obsequiousness blunt his opening gambit, "you may not. What you *may* do is tell me why I am speaking to you and Secretary Greene rather than to the President or the Secretary of State, as is proper for the reception of foreign delegations."

"Mr. Ambassador," the rotund Greene said with a stern face, "this delegation may be many things, but it is not, in our evaluation, foreign."

Alejandro was prepared for this argument. "Even if you disallow the sovereignty of the Cheyenne Alliance, Mr. Secretary, I am still here. Are you saying that this administration now refuses to recognize New Spain as an independent foreign nation?"

"You, Mr. Ambassador, are here as a liaison," Greene said, his tone sharpening. "Even according to your own viceroy you are here as such. A liaison in what is solely an internal matter."

"If it is an internal matter, Mr. Secretary of War, then why are *you* here?"

"Gentlemen," Fullerton interjected. "This tenor is hardly conducive to productive discussions."

"Sir, productive discussions are based on a foundation of mutual understanding and respect. These are things—"

"Respect?" Greene blurted. "What sort of respect do you anticipate with this group of—"

"Mr. *Secretary*—"

"Mr. *Ambassador*—"

"*Tosa'e* Tsêhe'êsta'ehe?"

"These men are the leaders of a foreign—"

"The status of these men is clear—"

"*Tosa'e* Tsêhe'êsta'ehe?"

Alejandro and Greene both realized that someone else was speaking. They turned and found the old chief standing beside them, still clutching his rolled buffalo hide.

"*Tosa'e* Tsêhe'êsta'ehe?" he said again.

Alejandro looked to One Who Flies.

"Three Trees Together speaks: 'Where is Long Hair?' " The chief spoke again. "I have something to tell him."

Greene stepped back into the conversation. "Your . . . your . . . chiefness. The President is not here. As I am trying to explain, it is inappropriate—"

Three Trees Together spoke and pointed at Greene. "Then you will tell him."

"I am not a messenger—"

"Tell Long Hair that I am here. Tell him that his old friend, Three Trees Together, is here, and that I would speak with him, as we spoke so many years ago on the shores of the Big Salty."

Alejandro stared, as unable to hide his surprise as were Greene and Fullerton. Alejandro noted, however, the slight smile on the face of One Who Flies as he saw the reaction the chief's words created.

"But tell Long Hair," the chief continued, "that I will not meet with him while he is murdering my people. Tell Long Hair that Three Trees Together says he must call back his bluecoat soldiers."

"The President of the United States does not take orders from the likes of you," Greene said.

"And let us not forget," Fullerton added, "that a great many settlers were murdered in years past."

"Yes, that was a bad choice," Three Trees Together said. "There was no honor in those deaths. We told our soldiers to attack them no more, and we have stopped killing. But so must Long Hair, before I will speak with him."

Greene and Fullerton looked at each other, jaws slightly agape. "I am sorry," Greene said, "but I cannot change the policy this government has as regards the Territory. Even if I had the authority, which I do not—"

"Then get someone who can," Three Trees Together said.

"What?" Greene said.

One Who Flies did not translate, but simply restated the chief's words. "Get someone who can change the policy, or we are done here."

Greene stared at One Who Flies with open hatred, and One Who Flies stared back with the fierceness that Alejandro had first noticed back at the embassy.

"Jacob."

They all turned. At the door was President Custer himself, his feet apart, his hands clasped behind his back, his head back, and his scowling gaze aimed at his Secretary of War.

"Mr. President," Jacob said, cowed.

"Tsêhe'êsta'ehe," the old chief said.

"Three Trees Together," Custer said, walking forward. "My heart is glad to see you still alive after so many years."

Alejandro watched in open disbelief as the two men—president and chief—clasped hands.

Custer smiled at the man who had been old when they had first met, twenty years before.

"You look well," the chief said. "Your hair is grayer, I think."

"Whose isn't?" Custer replied. Remembering his hard-learned lessons in Cheyenne etiquette, he fought to keep his words quiet, his tone pleasant, and his gaze away from the chief's face. The greater battle, though, was ignoring the interpreter, whose voice was so like his own, and whose every utterance cut him, stabbed him, and flayed his heart.

"I would like to talk with you, my old friend."

"And I with you," Custer said. He turned to his cabinet secretaries. "Jacob, Temperance, would you please wait for me up in the library?"

Jacob looked ready to spit, he was so angered, whereas Custer's Secretary of the Interior was as cool and unflappable as ever. Jacob turned and left. Fullerton bowed first before following.

"Please," Custer said to the chiefs, gesturing to the seats before the fire. "Sit. Rest. I will have food and drink brought."

The three chiefs settled down cross-legged on the lushly patterned rug in front of the hearthtiles. Custer glanced through the open doorway and saw Higgins and Campbell, his bodyguards, standing to either side. Douglas, the butler, stood nearby, waiting discreetly. Custer nodded to his servant; Douglas responded in kind and left to fulfill the President's wishes.

"Please," Custer said again, this time to the ambassador. "Join us at the fire."

The ambassador took a seat in a nearby chair. Custer, without a second thought, tugged at the knees of his trousers and joined the Indians on the floor. Still, though, he forced himself to ignore the presence of the young interpreter standing respectfully behind the chiefs.

Not my son, he said to himself. Not yet. Maybe not ever again.

The ancient chief began to speak. His language was a creation of the open plains—whispered, sibilant, urging—and Custer could hear in it the wind through the knee-high grass. Then, from the interpreter, came English spoken in a voice as familiar as Custer's own, yet with words colored by that same prairie wind.

"Three Trees Together speaks: I am glad that you have come to us, Long Hair. It is better to speak to one's opponent face-to-face."

Opponent, Custer noted, and not enemy. He wondered how much Geo—the interpreter—was shading the chief's words.

"I agree," he said. He reached within his coat and took out a long folded pouch. "I have a gift for you." He handed the pouch to Three Trees Together and saw the chief smile as he opened it.

"Ah," the old man said, smelling the tobacco leaf. He passed it to the other chiefs. "Your people have always made the best smoke-weed," he said. "My thanks."

"Perhaps we can share some later," Custer said, knowing the significance of the smoking ritual.

"And I have brought you this," the chief said as he put the rolled buffalo hide down in the space between them. He began to unroll it and Custer and the other chiefs lent a hand opening the heavy fur.

It was over six feet wide, nearly eight feet long, and still carried the bull's hooves, tail, and scrotum. The fur was long and soft, though worn in places, and the skin itself had started to stiffen with age. The men wrestled it fur-side down, and Custer saw the painting on the yellowed hide.

Down either flank were figures of men—one side Cheyenne, one side army soldiers. On the Indian side were lodges and families; on the army side were the split squares that denoted soldiers' tents. The men rode whistlers and walkers and horses, according to their camp's traditions, and they clashed at the hide's head and rump in great battles that left many of both sides lying dead upon the ground. Arrows flew. Bullets sped. Blood spilled. People died.

In the center of the army side was a knot of darkly clad men, and in the center of that knot was a man with yellow hair. From that man, from that knot, spreading out toward the Cheyenne, reaching out along the hide's backbone, were flames.

"I painted this," came the chief's words in the echo of Custer's own voice, "so that I would remember." Three Trees Together pushed at the hide. "I give it to you now, so that you will remember."

The painting described the day of Custer's greatest victory—and of his greatest regret—when, after all negotiations had failed, his forces had met the Cheyenne in open battle on the rolling hills above Kansa Bay. The number of civilian dead among the Indians had been ghastly and, though they had been unintended, the deaths still haunted his nights. Custer bit the inside of his lip.

"I remember," he said, and heard the interpreter's voice turn his words into the whisper of the prairie. He reached out and touched the knot of men and the figure with the long blond hair. "I have never forgotten that day. I have regretted that day ever since. Do you believe me when I say that?"

The old chief was silent for a moment as was proper for such a question. "*Héehe'e,*" came the answer, and "Yes," came the translation.

The chief continued through his interpreter. "Lives are being rubbed out again, Long Hair. Many lives, both of the People and of the *vé'hó'e.*"

Custer looked up, surprised by the word, a word he had not heard for so very long, and found himself looking into his son's eyes.

Son's and father's gazes met and held for a moment before each looked away, but in that moment, Custer felt his breath catch in his throat. That word—*vé'hó'e*—had been smeared in bitterness, and Custer had expected to see acidic hatred in the eyes of the man who spoke it. Instead he had seen sadness in his son's eyes, a great sadness that stabbed into Custer's own heart.

The chief spoke again and began to stand. The other chiefs stood, too, and "That is all I have to say," young George interpreted.

Ambassador Silveira leapt up as the chiefs turned to leave. "Gentlemen," Silveira said, concerned. "Where are you going?" Neither chiefs nor interpreter gave any answer as they walked back across the length of the room. Silveira stepped quickly to keep pace. "Please," the ambassador entreated. "We have barely begun our discussions. One Who Flies, stop them."

The chiefs walked on but Custer saw his son turn to face the ambassador from New Spain. "The Grandfathers of the People have nothing further to say. Not until our conditions are met."

"Conditions?" The ambassador's whisper was laced with rancor, and the room's hard acoustics carried it to Custer's ear. "Do you realize where you are? What it took me to get you here?"

"Don Silveira," George said. "We are aware of your assistance and grateful for your intercession—"

"Inter*cession*!"

"—but the People have stated their demands and will not engage in discussions until they are met."

"Why you ungrateful . . ." The ambassador struggled to contain his anger. He looked over toward Custer and, with a transparent smile, said, "I am sorry, Mr. President. We will be just a moment." Then he turned his back so that Custer could not hear his words.

He didn't have to. He saw the ambassador's fists, his hunched shoulders, the redness that colored the nape of his neck, while facing him was the interpreter, standing straight, taking the abuse, not flinching, calmly stating his case. The Ambassador from New Spain, perhaps the second most powerful man in Washington, spewed his whispered rage upon the young man, and the young man weathered it, standing like a bulwark against the storm.

That, Custer thought admiringly, is my son. Let's see how he does against me. "Mr. Ambassador."

The older man turned, smile in place, but florid anger still in his cheeks. "Yes, Mr. President."

Custer beckoned. "Send the interpreter here, if you please."

Silveira retreated a step. George looked to the chiefs, who had stopped near the far door. They exchanged hand signals, the meaning of which Custer had no inkling. Then Custer's son turned and walked toward his father. Silveira made as if to follow, but Custer held up a hand.

"Just the two of us, if you don't mind."

The ambassador gave a stiff and shallow bow.

"Come," Custer said to his son. "Let's sit by the fire and talk about these . . . conditions."

George followed him back to the hearthside.

"Please, sit," Custer said, and hid a smile as his son sat cross-legged on the rug as had the chiefs. Playing games with me, are you? he thought. We'll see.

Custer sat down on the floor as well, facing his son.

"It's been a long time," he began.

"Yes, sir."

"I should turn you over my knee."

"I'm a bit old for that, sir," his son said. "And anyway, it wouldn't do any good."

Custer nodded. "How's the hand?" he asked.

George opened his left hand and wiggled the stub of his little finger. "Fine, sir. I don't even notice it anymore."

"We were told you had been killed."

George frowned, his gaze still set upon his wounded hand. "I nearly was, sir. I was shot three times by your bluecoats, at Fort Assurance."

Another shot across my bow, Custer thought. All right, son, let's quit playing around.

"Your mother . . . she'd like to see you."

Stillness. Custer saw his son's pulse quicken at his throat. "Does she know I am here?"

Custer considered lying, but if they did meet he would know soon enough. He glanced down the length of the room. Silveira was inspecting the spines of books with feigned nonchalance while the chiefs, down at the far end, were standing like statues, watching every move Custer and his son might make. "Of course she knows," he said truthfully. "That is one secret even I could not keep. It was all over the papers. Even Maria and Lydia know. Wouldn't you like to see them?"

George swallowed against a hard lump. "Yes, sir," he said, his voice quiet, all the steel gone out of it. "I would."

"Fine." Custer looked out the doorway and caught the attention of Higgins. "Why don't I send for them then, and—"

"No, sir."

Custer stopped midgesture. "It's no trouble, son."

"No," George said again, and looked up. The steel had returned, sharp and ready to cut. "I will see Mother when you recall your forces back to this side of the Niobrara."

Custer was stunned. "For God's sake, George. You're negotiating with your mother's affections."

"No, sir, not I. You. You are dangling a quaint family reunion as a carrot to pull me back to the negotiations, as if I were the one to make such a decision." He leaned closer. "Frankly, sir, I don't know why you bother. If we walked away from here, your problems would be solved."

Custer suddenly tired of the shifting game. "No, son. My problems will not only remain, they will multiply, regardless of what you do."

"Then why?" George asked. "Why try to hold us at the table? Why speak to us at all?"

Custer shied from the question, not wanting to admit that the greatest reason had nothing to do with policy or matters of state. The greatest reason was sitting cross-legged before him. "Why do *you* wish to talk?" he snapped.

"To try to end it. Somehow, to end it." George sighed in exasperation. "People are dying. Every week a dozen die from your raids. Women. Children. Old men. As well as our soldiers. There is no honor in this. It is shameful."

Custer winced, unprepared for such unvarnished honesty. "War is a difficult thing."

"You have seen war, Father, and this is not it."

Custer shook his head. "And yet you walk away."

George sat back, straightened, and stared into the fire. "The chiefs will not speak with you while you are killing the People."

George was playing a harder game than Custer had expected. "And your mother? What shall I tell her? That you won't see her?"

George did not blink. "Sir, you will tell her what you will, but I swear, if you let us walk out of here, she need only read tomorrow's papers to know the real reason."

Checkmate, Custer said silently. Because you'd do it.

You'd splash our family's trauma across the headlines of every paper if it would get what you wanted.

He smiled grimly, recognizing the same passion and grit in the man before him as existed within his own heart. "You're better at this than I thought you'd be," he said. Turning to the door, he shouted to Higgins. "Get Jacob back in here," he said. "And Temperance, too."

They waited in silence as the two cabinet members were retrieved. "Yes, Mr. President?" Jacob asked.

Still sitting cross-legged on the rug, Custer spoke over his shoulder. "Jacob, please wire General Meriwether. Instruct him to cease all hostile actions in the Territory effective immediately. He is to pull his forces back past the Niobrara."

"Mr. President, Meriwether's forces are in the field. It'll take some time before—"

"Then do it quickly, Jacob."

"But Autie . . . we can't just abandon—"

"I cannot express too strongly the importance of this, Jacob. Do it, and do it now."

Jacob swallowed against a bitter taste. "Yes, Mr. President," he said, and stormed from the room.

"And Temperance," Custer said to the Secretary of the Interior, "it seems we might have to revisit our policy regarding the Territory. Please have Samuel set up some time for us to discuss it."

"Of course, Mr. President. I'm always at your service." He bowed, and left as well.

Custer turned back to his son. "Now," he said, "if you invite the chiefs back to the fire, I think we should begin our discussions. Tomorrow we'll see if we can join the family for a visit."

And for the first time, Custer saw his son smile. "Yes, sir," George aid. "I think that's a fine start."

Alejandro sat to the side, sipping port as the afternoon crept toward evening and the wan winter sun faded from gray to gloom. The chiefs—Indian and American—were inexhaustible, speaking of old times and new times, past and future. As he sat and audited the proceedings, he regarded the tableau before him with a gimlet eye.

Custer—the President of the United States!—sat on the

floor like a savage and spoke in quiet earnest to the three chiefs. They told stories of old battles and old meetings. Alejandro had had no idea that Custer had met these men before, nor, had he known, would he ever have guessed that their reunion would be so cordial.

And as for the chiefs, Alejandro was at a loss. They spoke quietly, simply, directly, but without passion. He heard neither fire in their speech nor fury in their tone. Hadn't they come here to negotiate for their people? Hadn't the deaths of hundreds pressed them into action, spurred them to this meeting? If they had, Alejandro saw no evidence of it, for their demeanor was as banal and everyday as a clutch of old men on a plaza bench.

But the biggest puzzle was One Who Flies. He sat between the two groups, hands on his knees, staring into the fire. The words passed through him like water through a sieve. Alejandro had *seen* the zeal of which young Custer was capable, but here, in this most critical of meetings, he was as calm and unperturbed as could be.

In fact, it seemed that, of all the participants, only Alejandro felt any anxiety at this gathering. His personal proximity to Custer was one thing, but to watch the man speak amiably, calmly, to see him smile . . . it was nearly too much to bear. Alejandro wondered if his own plans did not require modification. He could hardly build a war out of these lackluster proceedings.

The evening ended where it had begun. Both sides had ceased hostilities. Both sides expressed a desire for peaceful coexistence. Both sides hoped to achieve a mutually acceptable solution.

And both sides laid claim to the lands west of the Mississippi River.

It was an impasse, but a frustratingly polite one, and Alejandro despaired of any real progress until he heard One Who Flies translate the words of Stands Tall in Timber, the religious leader.

"You *vé'hó'e* place great store in the value of gold, I hear."

"Why, yes," the president responded. "We do. Although we value other things as well."

"But gold," the chief pressed, "is of greatest value. You use it to buy land, do you not?"

Custer seemed mystified by this line of inquiry. "Yes," he said.

"How much did you pay for our land, when you bought it from the French?"

Custer laughed, as if embarrassed by the question. "A great deal," he said.

"How much?" the chief insisted.

Custer sobered. "Ten million dollars," he said. "But that was a long time ago."

The chiefs spoke among themselves and One Who Flies did not translate. Alejandro knew what they were discussing, though: the viceroy's guaranteed loan. He put down his glass of port and waited for the fireworks to begin.

"You will forgive me," One Who Flies interpreted for Three Trees Together, "but an old man grows tired quickly. I think we have said enough for one day."

Alejandro gritted his teeth and watched the opportunity slip away. As the delegates were ushered to their carriages for the short trip back to the embassy, he smiled, acted pleasant, and agreed that yes, tomorrow they could pick things up again.

They passed through the crowd at the White House gates, and then through the crowd at the embassy gates. As his guests climbed the stairs to their suites, he smiled again, and bade them good night. Only when they were all gone did he drop his façade.

"*Encima de la mierda,*" he swore under his breath. He stormed down the corridor to his office, dipped a pen, and scribbled a few words on a piece of paper. He folded it and daubed it with a stick of melted wax but did not impress it with his ambassador's stamp. Then, as the unmarked seal hardened, he walked back down the corridor, turning toward the kitchen. He pushed open the door and found three scullery maids finishing their chores. He hooked a finger at one of them.

"Go out to the gates," he said to the maid. "Ask for the man from the *Herald*. Tell him you have a secret to sell. Don't sell it for less than ten dollars. Give him this." He handed her the sealed note.

She hesitated.

"Do not worry," he said. "You'll be doing nothing wrong. I just don't want him to know it's from me."

The maid took the note and curtsied. Then she headed back into the kitchen and out the side door.

That's enough for a start, he said to himself, and headed back to his office to prepare a telegraph message.

George sat by the window, wrapped in his buffalo robe, and watched snowflakes fall through the light of the lamps beyond the embassy gates.

The evening had been consumed with discussions and strategies and notes, and now, finally, the chiefs had pulled the feather mattresses off the bedframes and laid them out near the fire, while the soldiers slept either on the beds or near the doors and windows. The rooms were filled with the sounds of sleeping men—the quiet rustlings of linen, the rumbling snores of the elders—but it was neither the sounds nor the multitude of strategies and possibilities that disturbed his mind and kept him awake.

In the window glass, a ghostly reflection appeared, hovering in the night. "Trouble sleeping?" Storm Arriving asked.

"Yes," George said as his friend joined him on the window seat. Together they watched the snow swirl down the street.

"What disturbs you?"

George looked down at his hands. "My father," he said with a sigh. "As a child, even in the best of times I felt the pressure of my father's reserve. There was always the unspoken demand, the standard that he set for me to live up to. And when I would finally live up to that standard, I found that the bar had been raised and I had to do even more. I've never felt close to him. I've never felt a part of the family that he says he loves so much. Mother, she is a silent presence, standing behind him. And my sisters . . . I've been apart from them for so long, I barely know them. We—all of us—we're all struggling to keep up, competing for his regard."

"It does not sound like a family to me," Storm Arriving said.

"Of course it's a family," George said, nettled. "He's my father. They're my parents. We are related."

"You may be related," Storm Arriving stated with cold logic, "but that does not make you all a family."

George frowned. "What do you mean?"

Storm Arriving made a sign of equivocation. "I cannot say how it is for you, but for me—for many of the People—what you are talking of is blood, not family." When he saw that George plainly did not understand, he tried to explain further. "When a child is orphaned, he may be raised by people of another band. A boy of the Tree People may find a home with the Hair Rope band. As he grows, we all know that he is of the Tree People—that is the place where his blood lies—but his family is of the Hair Rope band, and this, too, we know." He took a moment to frame his words. "A blood relation knows who you were," he said. "But your family knows who you are. If you are fortunate, the two are one and the same, but it is not always so."

George considered his friend's words, and felt he understood them. "I suppose I had hoped to be one of the lucky ones," he said with a shrug. "I guess I wanted my father to be someone else."

Storm Arriving chuckled. "Long Hair is Long Hair," he said. "People do not change unless they want to."

"Perhaps," George said tentatively, and looked back out the window. "Do you mind if we talk about something else?"

Storm Arriving hesitated. "I never did give you an answer about my sister."

"No. You didn't."

Storm Arriving settled himself up against the frame of the window seat. "I can give you that answer now, if you wish."

Outside, the wind strengthened, whistling through the casement cracks and sending a freshet of chill air into the bay where he sat. George shivered, pulling the robe closer about his shoulders, and realized that now it was he who hesitated. Months ago, he had been impatient for Storm Arriving's approval of his request, but now, he realized, he was avoiding it.

He recalled how Mouse Road had treated him before his departure, and wondered if Storm Arriving's answer was even necessary. His own feelings for Mouse Road had not been diminished by her rebuff; had increased, in fact, with his separation from her. The attentions of Isabella, while enjoyable and flattering, had not touched his heart. But things had gotten so bad . . . would Mouse Road even accept him now?

It did not matter, he realized, until he had permission to court her. Once that hurdle had been passed, he would worry about how to win back into her good graces.

"Very well," he said, suddenly anxious once more for the answer. "I would like your permission to court—"

"No," Storm Arriving cut in.

George stopped breathing and his words stuck in his throat. The blood rushed to his neck, his face; it pounded in his ears, drowning out everything. Everything but the mental echo of that one word.

No.

"I am sorry, One Who Flies, but I must think of my sister and of her future. She needs someone who will provide for her, and who will protect her. I know you care for her, and that she cares for you; that much is plain. But that cannot be the only reason. You spend too much time away from the People—here, with the Iron Shirts, or digging for gold—and you have no wealth to bring my sister. There is more to marriage than love. Much more."

George barely heard the words as Storm Arriving spoke to him. He stared out the window, seeing nothing.

"I know this hurts you," Storm Arriving continued. "And I have been thinking about this for many months. I might have answered you differently, especially since Stands Tall in Timber told us of his dream, but if you *do* survive this journey, and if you *do* return to the People, what will have changed for you? Will you suddenly be wealthy? Will you suddenly be able to provide for my sister and the children she hopes to raise? Will you suddenly live the life of a normal man among the People?" He made a sign with his hand: no. "You are not a normal man, One Who Flies. You are the son of Long Hair. You came from the cloud-that-fell. You are a man of prophecy, singled out by the Thunder Beings, brought from the *vé'hó'e* to the People to change both our world and theirs." He reached out and touched George's arm.

"You have much to do, and you are far from done," Storm Arriving said. "And until you are, you are no fit husband for my sister."

George closed his eyes and dropped his chin to his chest. Storm Arriving released his grasp on George's arm.

"I am sorry," Storm Arriving said. "I know it is not what you wanted to hear." Then he left the window seat and returned to his post by the door.

George stayed where he was, his limbs leaden and cold, his mind frozen. No thoughts came to him, no arguments or countering logic entered his brain. He had no notions of his own; Storm Arriving's massive pronouncement blocked his every cognition, locked him within his own awareness, sealing off the exits. He had wanted answers, and now they were his; but he had never thought that Storm Arriving would deny him.

Eventually he became aware of the lightening of the sky outside the window. Then someone touched his shoulder. It was Stands Tall in Timber.

"Time to prepare," the chief told him.

"Yes," George said, his voice cracking like springtime ice. "Time to prepare."

He washed and shaved mechanically, and ate a few mouthfuls of porridge when instructed to do so. Someone stopped him and began to fiddle with the braid in his hair. He turned and saw that it was Two Roads.

"What are you doing?" he asked numbly.

"Your feather, it needs retying."

George realized that everyone—chief and soldier alike—was handling him like a wounded walker. As he looked around at them, no one met his gaze, and while this was only proper manners, it was the *way* in which they did not meet his gaze that suddenly irked him. They all knew what had transpired overnight, he realized, and then reminded himself that no one was able to keep secrets among the People. Not for long, at any rate.

"I am fine," he said to Two Roads.

"I am glad to hear it," the chief said, but his tone was questioning.

George turned to the group. "I am fine," he announced to them all.

Three Trees Together walked up and took George's hand in his withered own. "That is good," the old man said. "We need all our wits for today's meeting."

George took a deep breath and let it out slowly. He thought of all their plans, all their strategies, and of how he needed to be strong for the day's crucial negotiations. "I am fine," he told Three Trees Together.

The old chief patted George's hand. "Good," he said.

They arrived early at the White House, were ushered within, and were escorted back to the same room they had occupied on the previous day. George took his position behind the chiefs, and Alejandro seated himself in a nearby chair while they awaited the president and his advisers.

They heard the president a good while before he appeared, his angry thunder marching ahead past servants and guards. The echoing tirade brought George back a score of years and made bright the dim memories of his youth. He fought the racing of his heart, the trembling of his hands, and wished for nothing other than the strength to keep his temper in the face of his father's almighty rage.

"Where is he?" Custer bellowed from the doorway, a folded newspaper clutched in his hand. He spotted the ambassador. "You! And just *who* in all *Hell* do you think you are?"

The chiefs stood, but George motioned to them to remain calm. The ambassador rose from his seat.

"Mr. President," Alejandro said. "Is something amiss?"

"You know *damned* well there is." He stalked into the room, trailed by his aide Samuel, and Secretary Fullerton. He waggled the newspaper in the ambassador's face. "I'd have you on the next outbound ship if it wouldn't make matters worse." He whirled on George. "Did *you* know about this?"

George waited a heartbeat before replying. "About what, sir?"

"This," Custer snarled. He snapped open the morning's edition of the *Herald* and slapped the headline. " 'President Prepares to Relinquish Territory,' " he read, and then turned the page over. "Quote, 'This correspondent has learned that President Custer, in a secret, closed-door session with the Cheyenne delegation, has agreed to a fundamental shift in American policy. It was further acknowledged that this shift included the possibility of a retrocession of certain territories' end quote." He turned on the ambassador again. "I said nothing of the kind and

you damned well know it. Hellfire, I had to look up *retrocession* in the dictionary."

Alejandro shrugged. "I am sorry, Mr. President, but I have no knowledge of this."

"Like Hell you don't."

Alejandro's fists went to his hips and he was about to retort when Secretary Fullerton interposed himself between the two men.

"My dear sirs," the secretary said. "Whence the *Herald* received this information is immaterial. If the ambassador says he is not the source of this erroneous account, I suggest we take him at his word. What *is* important for us to agree upon is that the *Herald*'s report is, in fact, erroneous." The secretary spoke in a manner intended to placate, but which only succeeded in annoying. Insofar as he annoyed both men equally, however, he was successful in defusing the situation.

The two men stepped back from each other.

"Agreed," Alejandro said.

"Fine," Custer added.

George quickly informed the chiefs of the gist of the past few minutes, and Stands Tall in Timber, ever practical, asked a question.

"If we all know it is false, why is Long Hair so angry?" George translated.

"Because it puts me in the Devil's own backyard," Custer said. "Because it pits me squarely against my own party and makes me out to be the stooge of Union and Labor. Because now they can paint me as a tyrant, smarting from past failures, willing to do anything to win." He crumpled the newspaper and threw it into the fire. "But let's all be clear on one thing: I am not willing to do anything that is not in the best interests of the United States."

George translated the words, but heard in them a possible opening. When he finished, he asked the chiefs if he might ask a question. Permission was granted.

"Then you are not completely opposed to this idea of retrocession."

Custer frowned and chewed his lip. "Not in and of itself, no."

"Then why," George asked, reiterating the question from a moment before, "does this make you so angry?"

Custer clasped his hands at the small of his back, turned, and began to pace. "Because now I can't control the idea. Your chiefs must understand that. Once the people get hold of an idea, you can't control them, and if you can't control them, you can't govern them."

When Custer's words had been translated, Three Trees Together sat down before the fire. He beckoned to the other chiefs, who joined him on the floor. Stands Tall in Timber handed over the bag that contained the arm-long pipe they had brought, and then the elder chief pulled out the pouch of tobacco that had been the president's gift.

Custer saw the preamble to the smoking ritual and sat down opposite the chiefs. He motioned to Samuel and Fullerton, and after a moment of exaggerated bafflement, they too sat down.

The three chiefs of the People faced the three men of the federal government, and George placed himself at the end, a bridge between the two nations, facing the fire. Alejandro sat nearby, in a chair, a smoldering ire darkening his visage.

Three Trees Together moved deliberately, slowly, removing the pipe from its protective bag, straightening the feathers and decorations. He began to speak as he prepared the pipe, his voice taking on the wandering tone of a prairie breeze.

"For a long time," George translated, "the *vé'hó'e* have been a puzzle to me." The chief took out a small knife and scraped at the bowl of the pipe. "I have tried to understand you, but I am sorry to say that I have not been very good at it. You say that if you let your people know an idea, you cannot govern them." The chief shrugged. "I say that you can't govern them without doing so."

He paused, and the others knew well enough not to interject their opinion. He opened the tobacco pouch and let its sweetness reach around the circle to the others, touching them with its scent of honey, wood, and sunshine. He pulled out a pinch of cut weed.

"I have no control over my people," the old chief said as he filled the bowl. "None of the Grandfathers do. We govern because we are allowed to govern."

George passed the chief's words to the others, and his father waited a proper interval before responding.

"With all respect," Custer said, "the Grandfather of the People does not have to contend with Democrats or union leaders."

"But Father," George said before he remembered his place. Three Trees Together inquired silently after this breach in protocol, and George apologized and translated his father's words.

"Tell him what you want to say," Three Trees Together said.

George took a deep breath and turned to the President of the United States. "Father," he said, "I think you have missed our Grandfather's point. Think of what they call themselves: the People. That is how they think of themselves: as a single entity. A People."

Custer smiled paternally. "And within any people, there is dissent," he explained. "Dissent that must be overcome in order to govern."

"But overcome how? Through competition and dominance, or through consensus and cooperation? This is what *vé'hó'e* do not understand, Father. It is why the United States will never govern the Cheyenne Alliance. *There is no leader.*"

Custer looked at his son askance. "Balderdash. Of course they have leaders."

"No, Father. They don't. I've lived among them. I've seen the differences between us. These men here?" He indicated the chiefs to his left. "They are wisdom, strength, godliness. They are the best of the People, but they are not the leaders. They are simply the focus of our intentions." George struggled for an analogy, something that his father would understand. "If you kill these men" he said, "others will stand to take their place. Kill those, and still others will stand. Just like . . . just like a flock of birds will continue in its migration if you shoot down the birds leading them. So will the People continue. They will continue to govern themselves. They will continue to protect themselves. They need no leader to do this."

Custer, his gaze steady, his face fixed in the expression George knew to be one of deep concentration, said, "It seems to me . . . that I'm looking at one of the leaders of the Cheyenne Alliance."

George realized that his father was speaking of him. "No,

sir. I am only a messenger; an ambassador like Don Silveira, here. I am the voice of the Grandfathers, and the Grandfathers are the voice of the People."

"As you say," Custer said.

"What is it," Three Trees Together asked in the silence that followed, "that you two have been speaking of?"

George flushed with embarrassment. "My apologies, Grandfather. I have just been trying to explain the difference between the *vé'hó'e* and the People."

Three Trees Together chuckled, then laughed, hard. "When you are done, would you tell me?" he said, and then laughed some more.

George did not try to translate it for his father.

They smoked for a time in silence, as befitted the solemnity of the ritual. This was a beginning, and George knew it. All of his long journey to the land of the Iron Shirts, all of the delegation's journey to this place, all of that was preamble. This was where things began, and now was when they began. Three Trees Together passed the pipe around the circle, smiled at Fullerton's errors in smoking courtesy, and smiled again at the President's flawless handling of the long-stemmed pipe. It was the only time George had ever seen his father partake of tobacco; he had heard the stories, of course, some of them from his father's own lips, but he had never really believed them. Now, however, seeing him keep the bowl low, watching him draw the smoke in three grand puffs and let it drift up across his face and into his hair, and then seeing him place the end of the pipe on the rug and pass the stem across to Samuel, it was eerie. George realized that he had never really believed the legends that had surrounded his father. Like stories told to children around a campfire or tales broadened into diversions for comrades and colleagues, they were always too mythic, too imposing to be real.

And yet, here was one such story being played out before him.

How else have I underestimated you? George wondered.

When the smoking was complete, Three Trees Together put a pinch of tobacco on the hearth: an offering of thanks to the spirits. Then he turned to Custer and said, "What shall we talk about?"

Custer shrugged. "Let us say that I am not completely

opposed to the idea of . . . what was the word? Retrocession? What might that look like?"

George's heart pounded as he translated the words. This was what they had discussed and prepared for, back on the prairie, on the deck of the *Maria Argenta*, and late last night at the Spanish Embassy.

Three Trees Together nodded. "Tell him," he said.

"I need a map."

A map of the territories was found and laid out on a table. The majority of the map—the central and western thirds—was blank and bore the unflattering label "Unorganized Territory." Lewis and Clark had headed into that blankness. They followed the Big Greasy up to the Alliance-protected villages of the Earth Lodge Builders but had been allowed no farther. They left, returning to their president with a single line on a map, the Big Greasy, not having guessed at even half of its length.

Today, it was still the only line in the Territory.

George took a pen and dipped it in the inkpot. "This," he said, "is the existing border." He then overdrew the northern and eastern limits of the Unorganized Territory, which ran across the Canadian border and then down along Sheyenne and Lakota rivers past the new state of Yankton.

He glanced at the chiefs who had come to sit with everyone else around the table, and received their approval. He redipped the pen and placed the nib at the confluence of the Big Greasy and the Sudden River. With a sure hand he traced the Big Greasy northwest, following the path of Lewis and Clark until the line ended. He then continued northwest, then west, still along the Big Greasy, then northwest again, along the Trader River, up to the border with Canada.

Returning his pen to its starting point, he drew a second line along the course of the Sudden River—still only a dotted assumption on the map—and when it neared the Sand Hills and the People's burial grounds, he pulled a sharp line south to the Gulf of Narváez.

"And that," he said, "is the new border. All this area"—he shaded in the region south of the Sudden River, and the large area east and northeast of the Big Greasy—"this area is ceded to the United States."

Glancing at the opposing faces he saw the incredulity of

Secretary Fullerton, the interest of Samuel Prendergast, and the narrow-eyed evaluation of his father.

"This area," he said, placing his hand over the region to the west and south of the Big Greasy, "shall remain forever under Alliance control."

Custer looked up at his son's use of the word *control.* George smiled.

"Yes, Father. Control. And here, you and I are talking about the same thing."

Fullerton pushed back his chair and stood as if burned. "My God," he said. "You'd be keeping nearly the entire territory!"

Samuel leaned forward. "Not really," he said, using his fingers as calipers. "They would be turning over something like a third, and keeping two-thirds . . . I mean, two-thirds would remain under Alliance control." He smiled up at George.

Fullerton's displeasure overruled his practiced equanimity. "Two-thirds? Three hundred thousand square miles? And we are just supposed to *hand* this over to them?"

"Mr. Secretary," Samuel said quietly, "one cannot 'hand over' what one does not control."

Custer snorted at his aide's barb. "Still," he said, "you can't expect the United States to simply give up on . . . what?"

"Three hundred thousand square miles," Fullerton provided.

"Three hundred thousand square miles," Custer said. "Control it or not, it's ours. It belongs to the United States."

Now was the moment. George looked to Alejandro, who, remembering the viceroy's promise of ten million dollars, nodded. He looked to the chiefs, who, divining the import of both words and gestures, also gave their silent authorization.

"Naturally," George said, "the Alliance does not expect the United States to retrocede this territory uncompensated. After all, some monies were spent acquiring it." He glanced at his father, trying to gauge his mood, his level of openness. He could not, but decided to proceed anyway.

"In exchange for full retrocession of the lands outlined here, the Alliance is prepared to compensate the United

States of America with the sum of fifty million dollars. In gold."

Alejandro stood.

Custer stood.

"What are you saying?" the ambassador whispered. "Fifty million? Are you insane?"

"What did I hear?" Secretary Fullerton asked. "What did I hear?"

All that anyone heard was Three Trees Together, laughing.

The meeting continued for several hours, during which several more maps were defaced, created, and redrawn. George was kept busy both translating words and providing the chiefs with his interpretation of his father's intentions and stubbornness. But as the hours passed, George noted that the idea of retrocession had traveled from the realm of the ridiculous into the land of possibility. His father and Secretary Fullerton had stopped scoffing at the concept, and while no one was prepared to say that they were willing to back the idea in public, they were both giving it serious thought here in their private meeting.

Alejandro, in contrast, was growing more agitated as the evening approached. During the several breaks they took to rest and stretch muscles made tight by tension and worry, he had tried to approach George, but George's first care was for the three chiefs, and they wanted explanations of the subtleties of *vé'hó'e* behavior.

"One Who Flies," Alejandro said during the latest respite. "We must talk. You are leading us into a perilous situation."

George tried to assuage the ambassador's fears. "All is well."

"But you have based everything upon a false assumption," Alejandro argued. "Lord Serrano will never agree to loan the Alliance such a sum."

"I assure you, Don Silveira, our offer was made in good faith. The People will supplement the viceroy's generosity with their own resources."

Alejandro's eyes twitched and blinked as he worked on what George had said. Finally he put the pieces together. "*¡Dios mio!*" he said in a sudden whisper. "You have discovered gold in Alliance Territory."

"Yes," George admitted. "We did not tell you before, as we feared the knowledge would color our discussions with the viceroy. And if you tell my father now, he will refuse to consider any offer we make. This must be kept between us. Can I count on you?"

The ambassador was not happy. "I do not like surprises," he said. "They tend to upset things. But I agree: telling the president that the Cheyenne have uncovered a wealth of mineral resources would upset things even more."

"Thank you," George said, and returned to the chiefs.

A few hours later, Three Trees Together stood up and faced Custer. "I am grateful," the old man said, "for this meeting, and for the work that we have done here. But I am an old man, and I am tired. I should like to return to the Iron Shirt place, so that I can eat and rest."

Custer pulled out his pocket watch and checked it against the clock on the mantel. "Yes," he agreed. "It has been a long day, and you have given me and my colleagues plenty to think about. We must consider all the things that have been said, and decide how—and if—we might proceed from here."

"Good," the chief said, and the delegation prepared to leave. George began gathering the papers of his notes and drawings to study overnight.

"One thing, though," Custer said.

The chiefs stopped.

"I would like your interpreter to stay here for the evening and join his family for supper."

When George related the request to the chiefs, Three Trees Together beckoned him off to the side near a window.

"Do you wish this?" he asked plainly.

"I think so," George said.

The chief looked outside, and the last light of the short winter's day made his skin seem made of metal. His hand went to the medicine bag he wore around his neck, his fingers touching it gently as if to assure him of its presence.

"You have not been one of the People for very long," he said. "But during that time, you have been of great service to us."

George was surprised by this frank compliment, and more so by the chief's inclusion of him as one of the People. "I . . . I am glad to have been of help," he said.

Three Trees Together looked back at the room in which

they had spent so many hours. "And now you are back among the *vé'hó'e* with all their fine things, their shiny metal, their large buildings, and their rivers-inside-the-lodge. You are back among the people who were once your family. It is easy for a man to become confused among such things. Easy to forget things."

George thought he heard in the chief's words the echo of what Storm Arriving had said the night before. "What are you saying, Grandfather?"

"Just this." The old man touched George's hand. "My heart would be sad if you decided you no longer wished to be one of the People. You are looking for your family here, but there is a family for you with the People, I think, if you seek it."

George smiled, hoping it was true. "If I survive this trip, Grandfather, I plan to go back among the People. I only wish to spend some time with my first family before I return to seek my second. I want to try to reconcile with them, though it may not be possible."

"Peace," Three Trees Together said, "is always a worthy course. Even if it is only a small peace." Then he turned to the others. "One Who Flies will stay here. It is his wish."

And the delegation filed out of the room, leaving George alone in his father's house.

Justine was soft beneath Cesare, pale and pliant, and her beauty only encouraged his thrusts. She moaned and spoke in her native tongue, her words incomprehensible to him but her tone perfectly clear. She grabbed his buttocks, adding her urging to his own. They rocked together in pelvic communion, her eyes closed and her mouth open, his teeth clenched and his gaze intoxicated by her form. He felt the roughness of starched linens, the friendly touch of chenille, and the warmth and wetness of Justine's desire as he pushed into her again and again.

A knock sounded at the door, harsh as a gunshot.

"No," she said, "don't stop," and he obeyed. Her yearning intensified his passion, and with a feral growl he ignored the repeated knock at the door and pressed ahead to his own climactic surge.

He collapsed beside her, spent, his heart pounding and his breath quick in his lungs. Justine cooed and kissed his cheek. "Answer the door," she said, and then, wrapping herself in the chenille bedcover, bounced into their suite's private lavatory—a luxury upon which she always insisted.

At the third knock, Cesare responded. "Yes, yes. Just a moment." He threw on a rumpled shirt and donned his trousers. He was tucking the former into the latter as he opened the door.

Outside stood a young, wide-eyed bellboy, his gaze trying desperately to see past the door, hungry for a sight of Cesare's partner.

"What?" Cesare demanded, and the bellhop started.

"I'm sorry, Mr. Uccido," the boy said. "There is a telephone call for you at the front desk. It's a Mr. Halloran, from New York. He said it was urgent."

Cesare lifted the braces of his trousers up over his shoulders. "I'll be down in a minute," he said.

He had never used a telephone before, and so, when he finished dressing and presented himself at the front desk, the concierge had to show him how to use it.

"Hold it up to your ear, yes, just like that, and speak into this end," he said. "Say something so that he knows you're here."

"What?" Cesare said.

"Yes. Say something."

"Like what?"

"Who's there?" came a tiny voice from the earpiece.

"Hello?" Cesare said.

"Hello?" said the telephone. "Uccido, is that you?"

Cesare recognized the voice, small and metallic though it was. "Mr. Halloran? This is Cesare. Can you hear me?"

"Yes, I can hear you. Now listen, Uccido. We're not happy with the way things went down at the wharf."

"Yes, sir," Cesare said. "I'm sorry, sir. There just wasn't anything I could do. I couldn't get close enough."

"Keep your mouth shut, Uccido. Don't say anything that the clerk or hotel staff might take the wrong way, understand?"

Cesare nodded.

"Understand? Speak up, you idiot."

"Y-yes, Mr. Halloran. I understand."

"All right, then. We're giving you another chance at it.

There's to be a question-and-answer session tomorrow. We're going to get you there, disguised as a newspaperman. You'll be able to get up right next to him. His old man will be talking, and you'll be right next to him. Understand?"

"Yes, Mr. Halloran."

"Good. We'll have people waiting to take you to a safe place. You just get up behind Custer, Junior, and do what needs to be done. We'll take care of getting you out of there. Now I'm going to give you an address. You go there tonight, before eleven. Everything's been arranged. Are you ready?"

"But what about Justine?"

"She stays where she is," Halloran said. "You leave her there. You understand?"

A chill ran the length of Cesare's spine. Since his arrival in Chicago, Justine had traveled with him everywhere, but now she was to stay behind. "I understand, Mr. Halloran," he said calmly, but the bell in his brain had begun to toll.

When Cesare had memorized the address, Halloran reiterated his instructions. "You leave Justine there, now, and get yourself to that address by eleven. And good luck." There was a click, and a buzz, and Halloran was gone.

Cesare handed back the telephone. "Thank you," he muttered to the concierge, and went back up to his room. When he entered, Justine knew something had happened.

"You're to stay here," he told her as he sat down on the divan. He felt the smooth slickness of the striped fabric that covered the seat, then touched the hard satin of the carved wood along the arm.

Will I ever feel such things again, after tomorrow? he wondered as Justine sat down next to him. Will I ever know the pleasure and love of such a beautiful creature as her?

He reached inside his coat, to the inner pocket, and withdrew the folded paper and the treasure it contained. Reverently he opened the folds to reveal the thin silver chain and the sparkling filigree of the holy rood.

"Here," he said, finding the ends of the chain. "I want you to have this."

"Cesare," Justine said, "*mon cher,* no, I cannot."

"Yes," he said. "No argument." He reached forward. Justine bowed her head to accept it, and he clasped the chain around the thinness of her neck. He sat back and admired it as it lay gleaming against the ivory skin of her décolletage.

"What is this?" she asked, picking up the creased and stained paper that had held her gift.

Cesare stood and went to the sideboard. "It is just a piece of paper," he said as he lifted the crystal stopper from a decanter and poured himself a drink. "The men who killed my family had it with them. It's how they knew where to find us, I guess."

"What do you mean?" she asked.

"I told you about it."

"About how you snuck your family out to the territories," she said, "*oui,* but you always said that you were betrayed by the same men who helped you get out there early."

"Yes," Cesare said, his anger at the death of his family rekindled. "A man named Ballard. I had sworn to kill him, but I never had the chance to find him." He gritted his teeth, sure that now he would never have the chance. "The men he sent, they had that with them. It's how they found us."

Justine held the paper, reading it. "But *mon cher,* this is a government order. It has nothing to do with this man named Ballard."

"What?" He sat down next to her on the divan.

"Right here." She pointed to the words; "It says that squatters are to be removed from the Territory, and when they are removed they give up their rights to acquire land. It says that there is a bounty offered for any squatters brought in to the army headquarters at the staging area." She shook her head. "Nothing about a man named Ballard."

The fire of hate blazed up within him, as hot as a foundry. Months of vengeful torment tore at his heart, at his mind, shredding the fabric of his reality. Only one thing kept him from flying apart, one word. "You said it was a government order?"

"*Oui,*" she said, and pointed to the larger letters across the top. " 'By Order of the President of the United States of America.' "

President Custer, he said to himself. Images flared: of his

parents, his siblings, his dearest sister and twin. Memories of their deaths in an alien land. Scars on his soul.

Custer.

The conflagration was tamed, the volcanic fury beaten down. Chaos receded, replaced by a sharp, poignant purpose.

"May I have that paper?" Cesare asked Justine. "I would like to have it with me tomorrow."

George and his father stayed downstairs for a time, while upstairs the family was preparing. Custer sat in front of the fire that the servants had kept going all day. George sat nearby, in a chair now, though he would have felt more comfortable on the floor. His Cheyenne clothing was likely enough of a burr under his father's saddle, and he did not want to seem to be goading the old man. And so he stared into the flames, watched the iron grating glow orange with the heat, and felt the fire bake the skin of his face.

"I have thought often of you," George offered in an attempt to break one of the many silences that had sprouted up between them. "You and Mother. Maria and Lydia. I had a dream about the whole family, in fact, a very powerful dream, last winter."

"'A very powerful dream,'" Custer said. "You sound like them, you know."

George swallowed a sigh. "Yes," he said. "I suppose I do a little. I'm not trying to—"

"I know," his father said. "I know." And another silence was ushered into the room and given a seat near the fire.

More moments passed. George, who had learned well how to enjoy silent companionship among the Cheyenne, felt unable here, with his father, to endure more than a minute's quiet without some word being spoken. His discomfort grew with each successive drought in the conversation. So far, he had mentioned the weather, the coming winter, had asked after the health of everyone at least twice, and was about to ask about the portrait of Jefferson that hung across the room when his father, unexpectedly, spoke.

"Do you like living among them?" he asked.

George was halted by the question, by its probatory nature. His first instinct was to apologize for his feelings, but he stopped himself. Something in his father's tone—a softness, or a gentleness—told him that this was not captiousness, but curiosity.

"I find them to be as human as any people," George said. "Only I find them to be more tolerant of others, and more conscious of their place in the Divine Plan . . . if there is such a thing."

"Oh, there is," Custer said quietly. "I believe that firmly. I understand your attraction to them, you know. I've felt it myself, in fact. But they're not perfect."

"No," George said. "I know they're not. No one is."

Another pause ensued, only this time George did not find it uncomfortable. The pause lengthened into a suspension, and had nearly become a recess when Custer spoke again.

"I do not regret my acts; not a one. I do, however, regret their result."

George, not sure what his father was trying to say, remained silent.

"I mean," Custer continued, "that I do not regret having been a good soldier who followed his orders successfully, but I do sometimes regret the cost others paid for my successes. I fought as hard against the Indians as I did against Jeb Stuart or against Galliardo at El Brazito. I fought as well as I could to achieve my objective and fulfill my duty. I don't regret that. I would not change that. But sometimes . . . sometimes . . ."

"Father, I don't mean to be impertinent. . . ."

"Say it, son."

George swallowed. "It's just that, when Hill was defeated, his country forgave him, and when you routed Galliardo, he went back to Spain. With the Cheyenne, where can they go? It is the reason they fight so fiercely. They are not fighting for a colony or an ideal. They are fighting for their survival."

They both stared at the fire. It snapped and hissed. Flames fluttered and spoke to one another in breathy sighs.

"For a long time, now," Custer said, "I had thought dried, burned up, and blown away like ash the part of me that would take delight in the sight of you, but I swear, by God, that it has not." He stood and George did also. Custer faced his son. "I do not understand you," he said, "and I probably never will. I will never forgive the way you turned your back on your country and your family. But I understand what you think of these people. I do understand why you fight for them." He put a hand on George's shoulder. "Come along."

He led George down the long cross-hall and up a wide flight of stairs. They walked down another corridor, passing a library and several office rooms, to take a second, narrower staircase up to the residences. George heard a piano playing as they walked down a third hallway toward a white door. His father stopped outside.

"It sounds like Lydia has learned a new tune," he said with a smile. "Shall we go in, son?"

George, not sure if he was ready but sure he did not want to wait, took a deep breath.

"Let's."

CHAPTER 20

Tuesday, Christmas Eve, A.D. 1889
The White House
Washington, District of Columbia

Custer stirred to the sound of the wind. It keened through his mind's hypnopompic fog, sketching scenes from blind memory: a harsh horizon, the gloom of a storm, the bleakness of snow.

The wind plowed the drifts with arctic force, gusting them into clouds of stinging ice. Custer raised his arm to shield his eyes. The snow spun, shifted, like white sand on a frozen beach, blasted away by the storm's breath. The drifts ebbed, receded, exposing charred timbers, the stubble of burned grass, and the enemy's fire-blackened bones. A horror flooded him as he stared into the dark orbits of empty skulls. The shadows above became smoke, the snow became white ash on a burned prairie, and winter became the sheer, vile desolation of Kansa Bay after the slaughter of his attack. It was 1876 again, and Custer felt his heart strain.

The wind sang its siren song, haunting his soul, but then came a thump, bringing him awake. Another thump, and he knew it was the shutter, loose once more and slamming against the windowsill. He groaned.

"Autie," his wife said sleepily from beside him. "Is something the matter?"

"All's well," he said. He patted the roundness of her hips. "Go back to sleep."

He rose and went to the window, unlatched the pane, and leaned out to grab the errant shutter. The night's storm had brought new snow, but the wind, unlike in his dream, did not blow it away. Thick, wet flakes stuck to the trunks of trees and to the sides of buildings, covering everything with a plaster of winter white. Custer shivered. He reached for the shutter, caught it, and pulled it closed with a snick of the latch.

The regulator clock on the corner wall told the hour as half-past seven. Late, very late, Custer thought, but then we were up till the early hours. He padded to the door in stockinged feet, opened it, and went into the dressing room. Douglas was there. The old Negro stood as Custer entered.

"I was going to give you another half hour, Mr. President."

"Thank you, Douglas. Let's let Libbie have it for herself."

"Yes, sir."

Custer dressed and went to the sitting room to breakfast. Douglas had brought the morning's papers, but Custer simply held them up, pretending to read them. His mind was elsewhere, drawn by the howling of the wind to the plains of Kansa. After that final battle, he had met with the Alliance leadership, had met Three Trees Together for the first time. Now they were meeting again, but through everything they had said before and through everything that would be said today, Custer still heard the screams of the animals, the wails of people, and the wind from that day long ago.

"They're here, Mr. President."

Custer nodded. He folded the unread paper and put it down next to the untasted coffee. Then, with echoes of agony roiling in his head, he descended the stairs to the final day's meeting.

The chiefs met him with their usual deference, and George—his son once more, it seemed—greeted him with a smile. Only the ambassador seemed out of sorts, but his presence at these conferences had been made moot by the Cheyenne's able negotiation, and Custer empathized: no man liked to be made unnecessary.

They discussed more details, and where yesterday the tables had been covered by maps, today they were covered with calendars. Schedules were drafted, payments outlined, but still nothing was cast in concrete.

"I feel uncomfortable proceeding much further," he said. "Everything must be ratified by Congress. You understand that, don't you?"

"Yes," George translated for the chiefs. "So it is with our People. We must return and talk about this idea with the Great Council. Everyone must have a chance to talk before a decision is made."

Alejandro spoke up from his chair by the fire. "Do you have enough to bring this to your Congress, Mr. President? What I mean to say is, you are scheduled to speak to the press in an hour. Is there any area of the proposal that we should concentrate on before then?"

Custer considered it. He turned to the Secretary of the Interior. "What do you think, Temperance?"

Fullerton riffled through the pages of notations he had made. "I think we have enough to move forward, sir. Congress will require more, to be sure, but this is sufficient for now."

Custer turned to his aide. "Samuel?"

The old man who ran Custer's official life sat back in his chair, a gentle smile on his face. "This is enough, Mr. President. It will be a hard battle, getting them to see the sense of it, but if you're willing to fight, this is enough to make a start. Are you willing, sir? Do you want to make this fight?"

Custer looked over at Three Trees Together, who was listening to the whispered translation of his son. *If I don't,* he said to himself, *the cost will be higher than I care to pay.*

"You're damned right I'm willing," he said, and watched his son smile as he passed his words along.

Cesare's hat was too big, and kept slipping down on his ears. With elbows and a firm hand, he pushed his way through the onlookers until, like a wave reaching shore, he reached the front and the line of men in dark blue uniforms.

"Stop pushin' there, you," said the man in front. He put a hand on Cesare's chest and pressed him back into the crowd.

Cesare's goal was still yards away. Beyond the line of constables, around the last curve of the snow-swept path, were the steps, white as the snow that covered the city: the steps of the White House.

"Back off," the constable said. "I'll not tell you again."

Cesare fumbled in his pockets, felt the pistol in one, then the folded square of the presidential order in another. Finally he found the pad of paper and the large card that would get him to the steps. He pulled out the pad, a pencil, and the card, showing the latter to the constable.

The officer peered at the card and then at Cesare with narrowed eyes. He reached out and took the card, turned it right side up, and inspected it.

"The *Daily Clarion*, eh? That's a new one. You look awfully green to be in on a big story like this."

Cesare shrugged and smiled, hoping his edginess would be misinterpreted as excitement. "My first . . . big story," he said, trying to cover his accent.

The uniform nodded and handed him back the press card. "Go on, then," he said with a smirk. "But watch yourself."

"Thank you, sir," Cesare said, and ducked past the line. He forced himself not to run but to walk, though his heart hammered in his chest and he felt as if his hair might fly off his head if he weren't wearing a hat, ill-fitting though it might be.

Other correspondents milled about in a clump at the base of the stairs. Some wore high-society black, but most were dressed as was Cesare, in the pin-striped brown or gray of the workingman. Several nodded to him in greeting as he stepped in among them, but most—and especially those gray-bearded writers of the upper class—simply showed their shoulder and continued in their private conversations.

But he had made it. He was here, at the steps of the White House. He touched the paper in his pocket and was reassured by its presence. His breath caught in his throat and tears sprang to his eyes. The grace of God was immeasurable! To bring him here, to provide him with the instruments of revenge! He fought to contain his emotions, and wiped his eyes with a hurried hand. One deep breath and he was ready; ready to take from Custer that which Custer had taken from him: his family.

The doors at the top of the steps opened and the newspapermen surged together, jockeying for the best vantage. Cesare found himself at the back of the group, but decided not to worry, not yet. Better to hang back than to force a confrontation that would get him removed.

At the top of the steps came several men in dark overcoats. They stepped to the right side of the stairs while the cold wind played with their lapels and made them hold on to the brims of their hats. Cesare did not know who they were, but neither did he care. They did not matter. His target would be unmistakable. He moved toward the left.

The Indians came next. They faced the wind like weather vanes, feathers and fringe all aflutter. They moved to the left side of the staircase, and he continued toward that side, as well. But still he did not see his target. The men around him began to shout questions. Cesare looked and saw the reason.

At the top of the stairs was the President. Wearing a black suit and a fur-collared overcoat, Custer stood at the center of the scene. Behind him were other men, young and old, and beside him, dressed in the same leathers and furs as the Indians, but with the shiny blond hair of his father, stood George Armstrong Custer, Junior.

The target.

Custer, Junior, moved down the steps and stood next to a man who was the oldest Indian Cesare thought ever to see. He was as dark and wrinkled as last winter's apple, and as the President addressed the crowd, Custer, Junior, whispered into the chief's ear.

"Welcome," the President said. "The weather has turned cold, so I won't keep you here longer than necessary."

A few of the reporters began to shout out questions. The President held up a hand.

"Later, later. Right now, I would like to make a few brief remarks."

The reporters stepped closer, moving up the steps to hear over the whistle of the wind. Some moved around the sides, and Cesare headed up along the left, behind Custer, Junior.

"Today," the President said, "I am pleased to announce a shift in this nation's policy toward the region known as the Unorganized Territory."

The other men were scribbling notes on their paper pads. Cesare opened his own pad and took the pencil from his pocket. The others were writing furiously, transcribing the President's every word, but Cesare, unable to do any more than make his mark on a salary register, feared his ineptitude would be his undoing, and so he only touched the lead to the paper. The wind cut through the cheap fabric of his workman's suit, setting him ashiver. He fought it, clenched his teeth, and moved farther up the steps.

"During these past three days of meetings, we have entertained many new ideas, ideas that we hope will bring forth a new era of peace, a lasting peace, wherein the wanton cruelty and senseless killings so common on the Frontier will become a thing of the past."

Wanton cruelty. Senseless killings. The words hammered a nail into Cesare's heart. He knew of these things, had seen them with his own eyes. The pistol in his pocket grew heavy, tugging on the fabric of his coat, urging him to use it. Wanton cruelty. Senseless killings. Two steps more brought him behind the president's son. He saw the feather in young Custer's hair, saw it twist and flap in the wind.

"And so," the President continued, "we have drafted a document that will serve as a blueprint for this lasting peace. With it, we will accept the Cheyenne and their allies as partners, as neighbors, and as brothers."

One shot to the head, one bullet through that golden hair, and the scales would be even.

Cesare put his hand into his pocket. He felt the gun, cold and heavy, and next to it, the linen-soft edges of the folded paper he had carried for so long.

No, he thought, the scales won't be even. Not nearly even. Not this one young life for six of mine. The price, the price must be higher.

He looked past young George, up the steps, at the President and his bodyguards, and thought:

This is how I even the scales.

As George listened to his father's speech, he noticed that across the steps, Alejandro was watching him. The ambassador's eyes widened as George felt someone lean into him from behind. He turned, saw a man, saw the rictus of hate on his features. The man extended his arm. George saw the pistol.

"Father!"

The gun fired in a raucous flash. Burning powder spat in George's face, and his head rang. He grabbed the man's arm. The gun fired again, and a third time. He heard other shots, from behind. The man pulled out of his grasp, retreated, a hand on his gut, then turned and disappeared into the fleeing crowd. Everyone was running; reporters, dignitaries, guards, police. George turned and saw his father lying on the top stair. Blood, red and angry, sprayed from his throat, drawing filigree arcs on the white stone steps.

"Father!" he shouted and rushed toward him, only to be struck from the side. He cried out as he hit the steps, his head cracking against the treads, the assassin's gun falling from his hand.

He blinked. Spots swam across his vision, then fled. On the top step, his father lay on his back, his head to one side, eyes glaring up at the storm. Men pressed bloody hands on his neck and his chest.

"Father," he cried.

His father's nostrils flared. He breathed through clenched teeth. Red spittle colored his lips, his mustache and beard. His gaze, fierce and defiant, was fixed on the snow-filled sky.

"Hang on, Father," George said as six men lifted his father and carried him into the house.

Then another sound interposed itself: a high wail, a warbled chant. A song.

> *Nothing survives,*
> *Only the earth*
> *And the mountains.*

George looked to where he had so recently stood. Stands Tall in Timber was singing the death song, his head thrown back, his eyes squeezed shut, his words shouted toward the heavens. At his feet knelt Two Roads. The war chief's face was wet with tears, and in his arms lay Three Trees Together. The white shell pectoral on the ancient chief's chest was slick with blood, and though his eyes stared at George, they could see no longer.

"Oh, no," George said as he got to his knees. "Oh, God,

no." He stood to go to them but was pushed back down to the stone steps.

"You're not going anywhere," Campbell said in a gruff voice. The presidential bodyguard twisted George's arm behind his back.

"What are you doing?" George asked.

Alejandro came up. "Sir, leave this man be."

"Like Hell I will," the man said, and George felt a rope being tied around his wrists.

"What the . . . ?"

"Shut your mouth!"

Others ran up, constables, aides, and Samuel.

"Mr. Campbell," Samuel said. "What is the meaning of this?"

George was jerked to his feet. "He shot the President, Mr. Prendergast. I saw it with my own eyes. There's his gun."

Four feet away lay the gun that George had wrested from the assassin's grasp.

"That's not mine," George said. "It was the man behind me." He looked to Alejandro. "You saw it. Tell them what happened."

"Mr. Prendergast," the ambassador said. "One Who Flies is here as a diplomatic chargé of the Spanish Embassy. You have no authority over his person."

"He shot the *President*," Campbell shouted.

"Tell them it wasn't *me*!"

Samuel motioned for silence. "Take him into custody," he said.

"But I didn't—"

"You have no authority—"

"Campbell, take him into custody. We will sort everything out later."

As George was dragged down the steps, he looked back and saw the Cheyenne soldiers and the rest of the delegation gathered around their fallen chief. He spied Storm Arriving. The glower on his friend's face stopped the words in his throat.

"Filthy traitor," Campbell said as he threw George into a waiting carriage. The bodyguard climbed in and sat opposite him, a pistol leveled at George's belly.

"Is that the gun you used to kill my chief?" George asked.

Campbell leaned forward and struck the pistol across George's brow.

"One more word," Campbell said. "Just one more word."

With the crack of a whip, the carriage lurched forward. George, blood dripping down into his right eye, chose not to say anything else.

"This is outrageous!" Alejandro shouted at the Secretary of War.

The Secretary, the president's aide, and the other cabinet members stood near the fireplace in the room that had been the site of such intense negotiations for the past three days. They were, to a man, unmoved by Alejandro's zeal.

"Excellency, I will tell you again," Green said. "The President is gravely wounded; he may die. Under Article Two of our Constitution, his power devolves upon the Vice President. We are calling him to Washington now. Witnesses have stated they saw the president's son perform this act."

"But I say he did not."

"Nevertheless, and without refuting your claim, we have all the cause we need to detain him."

"He is part of a foreign delegation, under a foreign flag!"

"And he is a citizen of the United States, a deserter, who is responsible for other acts of treason, acts that we overlooked in accepting him as part of your delegation. But this act—*this* act we cannot overlook."

Alejandro fumed. It was all falling apart. "Your men *killed* one of the delegates."

"Regrettable," Greene said primly.

"Reckless," Alejandro spat.

"Our men were trying to bring down an assassin."

"They fired into a *crowd*!"

The two men faced each other—Alejandro toe-to-toe with the rotund secretary. Alejandro scanned the faces of the others in attendance and met glowers, scowls, and, in some, unsheathed rage.

"What about them?" Alejandro asked, indicating the

Cheyenne delegates gathered at the opposite end of the room, standing above the body of their slain chief.

Greene looked back at the others for guidance. "We have no legal grounds to detain them," he said. "Though I suggest they leave the country as soon as is practicable."

"Are you deporting them?"

Greene shook his head. "Let us just say that, if President Custer dies, it will not be safe for them."

Alejandro shut his eyes. "Will he die?"

"We do not know. He took three bullets, to throat, chest, and thigh. He has lost a great deal of blood. The next few hours will tell us more."

"And what of our work? Of the agreements we drafted?"

Greene's disgust was palpable. "We don't make agreements with assassins." He turned to a nearby aide, a young man spattered with presidential blood. "Escort the ambassador and the . . . delegates . . . to their carriages. I won't have them in Autie's house."

As armed guards walked them to the carriages outside the south entrance, Storm Arriving came up to Alejandro. "What is happening?" he asked in his heavily accented French.

"We are leaving. You—all of you—will be returning home."

"Where is One Who Flies?"

"Imprisoned," Alejandro told him. "They think he shot his father."

"But he did not."

"There is no convincing them otherwise."

"We won't leave without him."

Alejandro stopped and looked Storm Arriving in the eye, not caring if the Indian took offense. "You *will* leave. If I am to save *anything* of our work here, you must leave, and without One Who Flies. I will work to free him, but not with you here. Your presence here will be a distraction both to me and to those with whom I must negotiate."

Storm Arriving visibly held back his temper at being spoken to in such a manner. He turned his back on Alejandro and went back to his chiefs and soldiers.

"Get moving," said one of the guards.

Alejandro turned on the man. "I'll remind you that I am the Ambassador from New Spain."

"Then get moving, Mr. Ambassador."

They boarded the carriages and headed toward the embassy. Alejandro saw people running in the streets; word of the assault on the President was fleet and spreading quickly. Pointing at the passing carriages, some shouted, others fled. He realized that Secretary Greene, whether he knew it or not, had been correct: It would be very dangerous for the delegation, and very soon. Once they'd reached the embassy, leaving it might soon prove problematic.

Alejandro pounded on the roof. "Drop me here," he said.

He stepped out onto the icy street. "Take them straight to the wharves," he told the driver. "Put them back on the *Maria Argenta*. Have the captain put to sea as soon as he can. Tell him the order comes direct from me."

The carriages rattled onward, and Alejandro hailed an empty hack. There was someone he wanted to see.

Cesare lay on the bed in the dark room. He could feel the bed slats through the thin mattress, and the scratch of the wool blanket on his legs. He was cold. His breath misted the air above him, and steam from his wounds frosted the window next to the bed. Waves of shivers rolled over him like combers on a beach. He felt the warmth from the kerosene lamp on the table near his head, felt the warmth of his own blood as it seeped down his side, felt it cool beneath him as it soaked into the fabric of his shirt, his coat, and the mattress. He felt everything, everything but the pain.

The surgeon worked on the hole in his side, pulling, tugging, swearing. He grunted as he dug for the bullet. The sun broke through the clouds, casting a sudden shower of light through the greasy windowpane. The surgeon smiled.

"Ah," he said. "Got 'im."

There was a meaty, sucking sound, the sensation of being turned inside out, and then the stab of hot, searing pain. Cesare stiffened as the surgeon pulled out the bullet and tossed it into a corner. Cesare growled. The surgeon glared.

"Shut up," the sharp-faced man said as he reached for a curved needle.

"Is he going to live?" asked a voice from the corner of the room. The questioner stepped forward as the sunlight faded, and Cesare recognized him as the man he had met the night before and who had spirited him from the White House grounds back to this hideaway.

The surgeon shook his head. "He won't see morning. I'm just plugging holes."

Cesare smiled. "Save your strength," he said, and delighted in the surgeon's puzzled glance.

A knock at the door brought everyone but Cesare to their feet. The door opened and in walked a tall, slender old man dressed in a black longcoat.

The man in the corner was surprised. "Mr. Ambassa—" His words were cut short by the tall man's hands around his throat.

"What were you thinking?" the tall man said as he throttled the other. "What *could* you and Halloran have been thinking?"

The surgeon swore and went to separate the two men, doing so only after slapping the tall man across the face. "Keep your wits, sir. We have no time for such dramatics."

The tall man stood there, fuming, looking down on them with unclothed revulsion. "Killing Custer?" he accused. "What possessed you? With his son dead, I could have negotiated anything. Unions for you. An army of Cheyenne for me. But now? How am I to deal with such a betrayal?"

"It wasn't me, Mr. Ambassador," said Cesare's handler. "It was him. It was all him."

The ambassador turned on Cesare. He walked up to the side of the bed. "Was it? Was it your idea?" he asked.

Cesare's eyes were heavy and a numbness was spreading from his gut to his chest to his limbs. "Yes," he said dreamily.

"Why?" the ambassador asked.

With his fading strength, Cesare reached into the pocket of his coat. He pulled out the paper, the presidential order, and held it out to the ambassador. The tall man took it, opened it, and read it.

"Custer killed my family," Cesare said. "My parents, my brothers, my sisters. He killed my Fortuna."

The ambassador stared, slack-jawed.

Cesare smiled and closed his eyes. "The scales are balanced."

In the darkness of his mind, he saw a shining length of dark hair, the glint of a dark eye, the glimmer of a cheek.

Fortuna, he called to her. O, Fortuna.

George sat cross-legged on the bed and stared at the stone wall. He did not know where he was, only that he was in a prison cell, one cell in a long line of cells, and had been there for days. He might have been in a federal prison, a state prison, or a military prison. He had not been told.

He could have stared at the iron bars that caged him, but he chose not to. When he looked at the bars, his gaze was drawn to the hinges, the lock, and he was only reminded of the fact that there was a door there amid the bars; a door beyond which he could not go.

And so he stared at the wall. The stones did not taunt him as did the iron bars. The stone was solid, silent, and unforgiving.

Like him.

Footsteps echoed down the long corridor, preceded by the jeers and imprecations of other inmates. As they had many times before, the footsteps halted at his own cell. George did not turn. There was no point. They had not listened to him before. They would not listen to him now.

"Custer," the guard said. "Visitor."

"I told you I didn't want any visitors," George said. He had seen enough reporters masquerading as relatives, and did not care to play their game any longer. "Send them away."

"George," said a woman's voice.

He turned. Beyond the black bars stood his mother. She wore a dress of dark maroon, and not the black of a widow's weeds. George felt his breath catch in his throat.

"He's still alive?" he asked, his voice cracking.

His mother reached through the bars. George stood and stepped into her embrace.

"He is alive," she whispered in his ear as she stroked his hair. "He awoke this morning, but he is very weak. He lost a great deal of blood. He cannot speak because of the wound to his throat, and he cannot move his right arm. The doctors say his recovery will be slow, but he will live."

George breathed in his mother's scent—orange blossoms

and lavender—and felt the gentleness of her enfolding arms.

"Has he told them?" George asked. "Has he told them that I didn't do this?"

"It's all right, dear. They found him."

"Who?"

"The man who shot Aut—your father. They found his body yesterday, in a hotel basement. He had been shot as well, it seems. Both Higgins and Ambassador Silveira have identified him as the man they say shot your father."

George held his mother at arm's length through the bars. "Then why am I still here?" He looked into his mother's eyes and saw her hesitation. "Tell me, Mother."

"Jacob and the generals, they will not let you remain in the country—"

"But what if Father—"

"—and I am in full agreement with them."

He regarded her for a long moment. Her gaze was fixed on him, unwavering despite the distress that pinched the corners of her eyes. "What are you saying, Mother?"

"George, you are my son, and I love you, but I can't imagine who you are, that you have come to this terrible pass. I don't pretend to grasp what startling logic you must have used to justify your actions during these past years, but I have seen the result of it." She released him and paced a step along the prison bars. The heavy cloth of her dress and cloak brushed against the rough metal with a throaty sigh. "You haven't seen what you have done to us: to me, to your father, and even to Lydia and Maria. You haven't seen the looks or heard the snide commentary. You haven't seen Lydia's prospects dwindle, nor heard Maria crying, not understanding why she has become a pariah among her peers. And your father; you have caused him such anguish, such heartache, that I feared at times that he was near madness." She shook her head and looked down at her clasped hands. "We grieved for you, Georgie. You were dead, and then . . . and then you were alive again, but you had become someone else. Seeing you the other night was the hardest thing I ever—"

She stopped, took a breath, and then looked at him with the dark and penetrating gaze that had always paralyzed him in his youth. "You have disgraced us, George. You have disgraced your family, your father, and besmirched his presidency." Tears fell from her eyes and her mouth was a thin line. "They wanted you prosecuted, even hanged for treason, but I convinced Jacob that a trial would only bring more shame upon us, and he agreed to deportation. George, you will leave this country, and never come back."

"But, Mother—"

"I will not hear it, not one word of it," she said sharply, stifling him once more. "You have forced me into a choice that I should never have had to make. You have forced me to choose between my son and my husband and daughters, and that is a choice that is no choice. I must protect my family from the shame you have brought upon us. I will protect them."

She straightened and collected herself. Then she reached out with a gloved hand and touched George's fingers on the prison bars. "You will be released soon and taken to a ship for the trip back to New Spain. The ambassador has arranged it."

"Mother . . ."

She held up her hand to stave off his words, then turned and fled up the corridor, her footsteps swallowed up by the cacophony of the inmates' heckling.

As the cell block settled back into its murmur of echoes, George stood at the bars, devastated. He wondered if she had meant to express it so blatantly.

I must protect my family.

Not *our* family; *my* family.

She had set him outside, apart, severing him from the very thing he had sought.

He returned to his bed and sat down, cross-legged, and stared at the stone wall.

CHAPTER 21

Hoop and Stick Game Moon, Waxing
Fifty-six Years After the Star Fell
Winter Camp of the Closed Windpipe Band
Alliance Territory

Mouse Road walked up the path, a bundle of deadwood on her back. The morning sky was low, and veils of snow drifted downward from the overhanging clouds. The nearby trees were dark in their snowy robes, but grew paler and paler with distance until, at the valley mouth, they were just wraiths in the falling snow.

She wended her way past lodges, shifting her burden from one side to the other when it began to pain her. Her time with the Closed Windpipe band had not been nearly the penance she had thought it would be. Speaks While Leaving and her family had been very kind to her, and their attention made her forget the loneliness she felt, being separated from her band, her mother, her brother, and the man she loved.

At the last bend in the trail she noticed a whistler outside the family lodge. One whistler looked much like the next, but this one had a halter rope made of braided black and white buffalo hair, fox fur trim on the first rope, and a rifle bag that jingled with silver bells every time the whistler moved. Storm Arriving was home!

She dropped her bundle and shouted his name. The doorflap opened as she ran up and threw herself into his arms.

"Oh, Brother, I am so happy that you are home again. You must tell me everything. How did it go? How is One Who Flies? Is he with you?"

She stopped, sensing doom in his rigid stance. She re-

leased him and glanced up at his face. He stared off into
the snowfall.

"What is wrong?" she asked. Through the open doorflap,
she could see Speaks While Leaving and the rest of the
family, all solemn, all grim. "What has happened?"

He took a breath and let it frost the air. "Come inside,"
he said. "There is much to tell you."

The whistler groaned as George urged it onward through
the pelting rain. The stormy sea voyage from Washington
to Havana and on to La Puerta del Norte had been debili-
tating, and riding alone up the Tejano coast had been a
grueling trek. His greatest enemy, though, had been the
dark shadow that had clamped down upon his soul in that
distant prison cell. The events, capped by his mother's sen-
tence of banishment, had stolen his will and wicked away
his remaining vitality. He rode now as he had sat in his
quarters aboard the steamship: uncaring, virtually unseeing,
and more numb than the storm's bitter rain could justify.

As he reached the northernmost extent of the Big Salty,
he halted and tried to decide where he was going, what he
wanted to do. North lay the Sudden River, the White River,
and the sacred heart of the Alliance lands. There, too, were
the winter camps of the Closed Windpipe Band. He tried
to imagine himself there and the greeting he might get from
Storm Arriving or Speaks While Leaving. The coldness he
felt now in his limbs and in his bones, how would it compare to the welcome that awaited him there? And the Tree
People, farther north, how would his neighbors react, now
that Picking Bones Woman was gone and Mouse Road was
living with her brother's band? How might they greet the
man who had brought so much tragedy among them, the
man whom Death seemed to follow as closely as the Thunder Beings?

No, he could not go there. Not yet. Perhaps not ever.
There was another place he wanted to go first.

He turned east and traveled along the coastal cliffs. The
inland sea, with its salty breath, was able to keep the snows
from its craggy shores, but it could not keep back the rain.
George peered through the grayness of the heavy rain and
saw nothing but sodden land, moss-colored grasses, and
muddy rivulets. He could not see down to the seashore or

even to the forests that bordered it. To his right, the world
ended at the cliff's edge, and to his left, it was swallowed
up by the rain and low-hanging clouds. As he prodded his
whistler onward over yet another sedge-covered rise, he
wondered if he would notice the place he sought when he
rode by.

Hours passed, and the rain lessened. The sky lifted up
off the ground and George was finally able to see farther
than a thrown stone. The land of buckled green ended in
broken white cliffs. The wind riffled small puddles of dark
water and pushed the wet grass down on the undulating
slopes. On a nearby bluff, set back from the cliff's edge, he
spied a tall pole sticking up out of the ground. Bare of any
branch and bleached by the elements, it was not the trunk
of some long-dead tree; it was a lodgepole, put there by
grieving hands some years past. As he continued onward,
he began to see other poles, some in singles, some in pairs
or triplets, all leaning in the sandy soil. Other poles lay in
the brush, toppled by wind or other forces. Bits of leather
clung to some, flapping in the wind like trailing pennants.
And finally, as the dark day sped toward evening, he saw
the first bones among the grasses, as pale as driftwood.
Thin armbones. The graceful curve of a pelvic crest. Black
eyesockets beneath an ashen brow.

He pushed his whistler into a jog as the light began to
fail. One mile, two. More. Then he spied it, up on a high
knoll with a commanding view of the sea, the cliffs, and the
land for leagues on either side. Four poles lashed together,
forming a scaffold. He rode up to it and bade his whistler
crouch.

The body was already gone, but George had expected
that. Still, by the finery that remained, he could tell that
the deceased had been a man greatly honored. He looked
at the items that had helped usher this man's spirit into
Séáno. The poles had been trimmed with wolf fur. On each
corner, someone had placed an elk-tooth bracelet, and on
the side toward the sea hung a dream-shield with its deer-
hide covering. On the ground, he saw a pipe sack and a
lance wrapped in otterskin, and on the lattice of woven
leather on which the body had lain was a buffalo robe—
quilled and sewn with shells—and a long bonnet of white
eagle feathers tufted with red yarn.

Feathers and colored strips of cloth fluttered from the cross-braces, and disks of silver, brass, and copper chimed and pinged in the wind. And then, there on one of the posts, George saw a thing that was not fine, but dark and soiled.

From a long thong of leather hung a small fringed bag, smaller than the palm of a man's hand. It was decorated with quills, white ones on the left, dark ones on the right. Black diamond shapes down the middle were the grasshoppers, and crosslike forms on either side were dragonflies. The bottom edge of the bag was fringed, but made dark and irregular through years of use.

George had seen this bag many times. The old man had always worn it around his neck, and his wrinkled, leathery hands toyed with the fringe and rubbed the quills of its design whenever he was listening, which had been most of the time.

He lifted the bag off the post, and felt as if his last breath was pulled from his lungs. His chest burned, and he closed his eyes, wanting only to die on the spot.

He dropped to his knees and sat on the soggy ground, leaning against the pole. His chest jolted in spasm, then heaved as he finally found a breath. It filled his fiery lungs, then turned and fled his body, tearing out of him with a sound that was a scream, a wail, and a shout all at once. He took another breath, smelling the wet air, and cried out again, giving voice to the anger and anguish, the despair and the frustration that he had kept so long within him. He roared; wounded and frightened, he roared. He got to his feet, and roared at the four corners of the world, to New Spain and America, to the Alliance lands and the salty road that led to Séáno. He roared at the ground beneath his feet and then at the thunderous heavens. He took another breath, but it stuck in his throat, and only came out in a choking sob. He fell to the ground once more and lay there as the rain renewed itself, starting as a tentative patter, building up to dark, hissing sheets that pulled a cover across the last of the light.

As George watched the day die above him, he wept. For lost hopes. For lost chances. For the great and fatherly chief whose medicine bag he clutched to his heart. For the sweet woman he loved but could not see.

As the storm built, he wept.

Cheyenne Pronunciation Guide

There are only fourteen letters in the Cheyenne alphabet. They are used to create small words that can be combined to create some very long words. The language is very descriptive, and often combines several smaller words to construct a longer, more complex concept. The following are simplified examples of this subtle and intricate language, but it will give you some idea of how to pronounce the words in the text.

LETTER	PRONUNCIATION OF THE CHEYENNE LETTER
a	"a" as in "water"
e	"i" as in "omit" (short "i," not a long "e")
h	"h" as in "home"
k	"k" as in "skit"
m	"m" as in "mouse"
n	"n" as in "not"
o	"o" as in "hope"
p	"p" as in "poor"
s	"s" as in "said"
š	"sh" as in "shy"
t	"t" as in "stop"
v	"v" as in "value"

LETTER	PRONUCIATION OF THE CHEYENNE LETTER
x	"ch" as in "Bach" (a soft, aspirated "h")
'	glottal stop as in "Uh-oh!"

The three vowels (a, e, o) can be marked for high pitch (á, é, ó) or be voiceless (whispered), as in â, ô, ê.

Glossary

Ame'haooestse Tsétsêhéstâhese for the name One Who Flies

Bands Cheyenne clans or family groups. Bands always travel together, while the tribe as a whole gathers only in the summer months. Bands are familial and matrilineal; men who marry go to live with the woman and her band. The ten Cheyenne bands are:

- The Closed Windpipe Band (also Closed Gullet or Closed Aorta)
- The Scabby Band
- The Hair Rope Band
- The Ridge People
- The Tree People (also Log Men or Southern Eaters)
- The Poor People
- The Broken Jaw People (also Lower Jaw Protruding People or Drifted Away Band)
- The Suhtai
- The Flexed Leg Band (also

Lying on the Side With
Knees Drawn up People,
later absorbed into Dog
Soldier Society)
• The Northern Eaters

The Cloud People — Tsétsêhéstâhese phrase for
the Southern Arapaho

The Cradle People — Tsétsêhéstâhese phrase for
the Assiniboine

The Crow People — Tsétsêhéstâhese phrase for
the Crow

The Cut-Hair People — Tsétsêhéstâhese phrase for
the Osage

Eestseohtse'e — Tsétsêhéstâhese for the name
Speaks While Leaving

Grandmother Land — Tsétsêhéstâhese phrase for
Canada

The Greasy Wood People — Tsétsêhéstâhese phrase for
the Kiowa

Haaahe — A Tsétsêhéstâhese phrase of
greeting, from one man to
another

Hámêstoo'êstse (sng), — Sit!
Hámêstoo'e (pl)

Héehe'e — Yes.

He'kotoo'êstse (sng), — Be quiet!
He'kotoo'e (pl)

Ho'ésta — Shout!

Hohkeekemeona'e — Tsétsêhéstâhese for the name
Mouse Road

Hová'âháne — No.

The Inviters — Tsétsêhéstâhese phrase for
the Lakota

Iron Shirts — Tsétsêhéstâhese phrase for
the Spanish conquistadors

Ke'éehe — Child's word for
grandmother

The Little Star People — Tsétsêhéstâhese phrase for
the Oglala Lakota

Maahótse — The four Sacred Arrows of
the People

Ma'heo'o (sng), — A word that can be loosely

Ma'heono (pl)	translated as "that which is sacred," referring to the basis of Cheyenne spirituality and mystery
Mo'e'haeva'e	Tsétsêhéstâhese for the name Magpie Woman
Néá'eše	Thank you.
Néséne	My friend (said by one man to another)
Nevé-stanevóo'o	The Four Sacred Persons, created by Ma'heo'o, who guard the four corners of the world
Nóheto	Let's go!
Nóxa'e	Wait!
The Sage People	Tsétsêhéstâhese phrase for the Northern Arapaho
Séáno	The happy place for the deceased
The Snake People	Tsétsêhéstâhese phrase for the Comanche
Soldier Societies	The military organizations within the tribe. Membership in a society was voluntary and had no relation to the band in which one lived. The six Cheyenne soldier societies are:

- Kit Foxes (also Fox Soldiers)
- Elkhorn Scrapers (also Crooked Lances)
- Dog Men (or Dog Soldiers)
- Red Shields (or Buffalo Bull Soldiers)
- Crazy Dogs
- Little Bowstrings

Tsêhe'êsta'ehe	Long Hair (General G. A. Custer)
Tosa'e	Where?
Tsétsêhéstâhese	The Cheyenne people's word for themselves

Vá'ôhtáma	The place of honor at the back of the lodge
Vé'ho'e (sng), *Vé'hó'e* (pl)	Lit. spider, from the word for "cocooned," and now the word for whites
Vétsêškévâhonoo'o	Skillet-bread
The Wolf People	Tsétsêhéstâhese phrase for the Pawnee
The Year the Star Fell	In the year 1833, the Leonid meteor shower was especially fierce. The incredible display made such an impression on the Cheyenne of the time that it became a memorable event from which many other events were dated.

About the Author

Kurt R. A. Giambastiani has had short stories published in *Dragon Magazine, Talebones,* and *Marion Zimmer Bradley's Fantasy Magazine,* among others. He is currently a lead analyst in the Seattle area, where he lives with his wife and two cats.

Kurt R.A. Giambastiani

"A RISING STAR."
—William R. Forstchen

The Spirit of Thunder

The story of an American frontier that never was.

Soon after George Custer Jr., President Custer's only son, falls into the hands of the Cheyenne people, he decides to fight side by side with them—against his own father's army.

0-451-45870-2

To order call: 1-800-788-6262

Kurt R.A. Giambastiani

The Year the Cloud Fell

In 1886, the U.S. Army experimental dirigible
A. Lincoln is making a scouting flight above the
Unorganized Territory when a terrific thunder-
storm strikes the craft to earth. Now the mission
commander, the president's only son, is a prisoner
of the Cheyenne Alliance. The Indians have no
reason to love the president, the implacable
enemy they call Long Hair: General George
Armstrong Custer. And only the strange shamanic
vision of one young Cheyenne woman stands
between Captain George Armstrong Custer, Jr.
and death.

**"Impressive...an intriguing mix of historical
speculation and downright invention that is
entertaining and skillfully plotted."
—*Science Fiction Chronicle***

0-451-45821-4

To order call: 1-800-788-6262